First Strike

Douglas Terman

PUBLISHED BY POCKET BOOKS NEW YORK

All of the characters in this book
(who are not normally residents of the CCCP)
are fictitious and any resemblance
to actual persons living or dead
is therefore coincidental.

Lyrics from "Someday Soon" by Ian Tyson are used by permission
of Warner Bros. Music, © 1963 Warner Bros. Inc. All rights reserved.

This book was originally published in substantially different form
under the title *The Three Megaton Gamble*.

**POCKET BOOKS, a Simon & Schuster division of
GULF & WESTERN CORPORATION**
1230 Avenue of the Americas, New York, N.Y. 10020

Copyright © 1978, 1979 by Douglas Terman

Published by arrangement with Charles Scribner's Sons
Library of Congress Catalog Card Number: 79-16759

ISBN: 0-671-83466-5

First Pocket Books printing October, 1980

10 9 8 7 6 5 4 3 2 1

POCKET and colophon are trademarks of Simon & Schuster.

Printed in the U.S.A.

To
R. E. LEAVITT

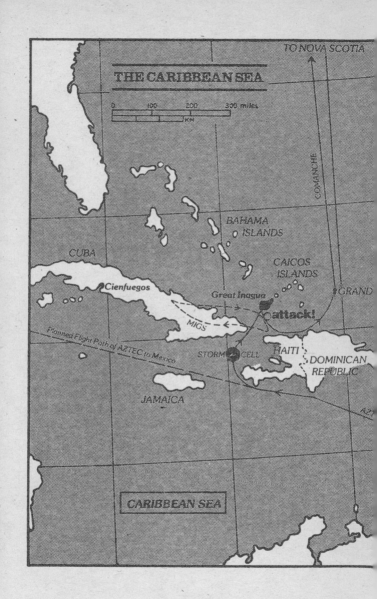

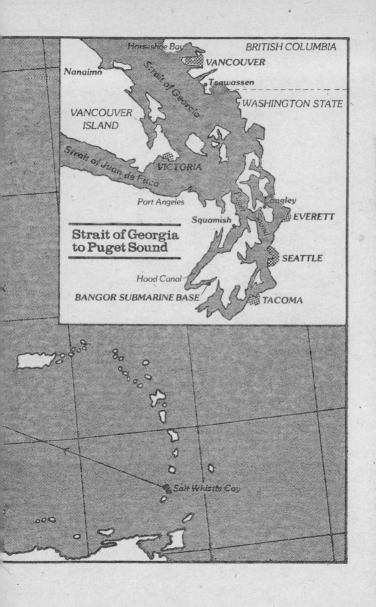

Horseshoe Bay
BRITISH COLUMBIA
VANCOUVER
Nanaimo
Strait of Georgia
Tsawassen
WASHINGTON STATE
VANCOUVER ISLAND
Strait of Juan de Fuca
VICTORIA
Port Angeles
Langley
Squamish
EVERETT

Strait of Georgia to Puget Sound

Hood Canal
BANGOR SUBMARINE BASE
SEATTLE
TACOMA

Salt Whistle Cay

Chapter 1

The nuclear device, measuring .88 meters in length and .063 meters in diameter, rested on its pneumatically cushioned transporter. The only protuberance to mar its cylindrical surface was a flexible, woven wire cable projecting from a quick-disconnect fitting. The cable led to monitoring instruments fitted into a panel that registered internal core temperature, gamma-particle radiation, and status of the arming circuits.

The colonel brushed his hand along the surface of the device, fingernails sensitive to the small imperfections in the machined-metal casing. His hand followed the cable, tracing it down to the panel.

"How safe is it to handle? It has a long way to go."

The scientist, head of the group responsible for the weapon's development, lifted a single folder from his desktop and began to thumb through it. He was an older man, hair white around the temples and curling back into an unruly but artfully cut crop of black. His eyes, hazel, shot through with flecks of green and caged behind yellow-tinted lenses, looked black in the wash of the fluorescent lights. He found the page he was looking for, scanned it to confirm the numbers he knew were there, and dropped the folder back on his desk.

"Short of running over it with a battle tank, quite safe. It will be housed in a reenforced wooden chest as you're aware, and then foamed in place with shock-absorbent isocyanurate. The whole assembly will be

1

waterproof to a depth of two hundred meters. You can remember the incident off the coast of Spain. A SAC B-52 jettisoned four similar weapons in the Mediterranean in 1966. Essentially, nothing happened."

The colonel, without turning to listen, continued to examine the weapon. He regarded the scientist as an adjunct to the weapon, there for information only. Like a clerk in a railway station reciting timetables.

"What's this plaque say?" he asked, stooping down, trying to read the engraved plate fixed to the weapon's belly, unreadable in the shadows.

" 'U.S. Navy, Mark 97-A.' A relatively recent type of warhead used as one of three multiple, independently targeted reentry vehicles in the Trident I-C4 submarine launched ballistic missile. Of course," he added, thumbing the folder's edge, "it lacks the normal altitude-sensitive arming devices and the ablative shield. But the design duplication is exact, right down to the plaque you're reading."

"Even the alloys?" He scratched the underbelly of the weapon.

". . . Even to the alloys. The case is a specific Alcoa composition. It compares closely with what we call T-2887G, except the Americans seem to use about two percent more copper for malleability."

"About two percent?" The colonel stood and turned to face the scientist. "Your directions were to duplicate the weapon exactly. Two men were compromised to get this information and you tell me 'about two percent.' "

The scientist shrugged, sitting back on the edge of his desk, movements slow but economical, like a cat settling down on its favorite cushion. "A manner of speaking," he finally said. "It is 1.79 percent copper if you want a number. Plus similarly exact quantities of manganese, berylium, et cetera." He tapped the report folder. "It's all here if you want to go over it." He nodded toward the weapon. "Even the roughness of the casing which you seem so concerned about—

that's a result of the alloy's heat treatment." He took off his glasses, folded them carefully, and slid the frame into a breast-pocket case. The colonel realized that the gesture was meant to terminate the recital.

"Tea?" the scientist asked. "I have Earl Grey. Or would you prefer coffee?" He stood up and took the report to a safe which stood with its door open. He placed it in an inner compartment, then closed the door and locked it. "My copy. The only other one is at Center."

Colonel Anatoli Antonovich Petrov straightened his tall frame and wiped his hands together. The casing had left a slight residue of oil on his hands. He pulled a handkerchief from the pocket of his green tunic and cleaned each finger carefully. "I'm aware of that. Comrade Rametka's section initiated the project." He stretched, feeling the fatigue of having risen at 3 A.M. for the long flight to Zhignask. Coffee sounded good, but there was still the six-hour return flight to Moscow, followed by the meeting with Yuri Andropov that evening.

"I'll forgo the refreshments," he said, pulling on his leather coat. Nonregulation, but his pride. It had been custom-tailored for him in East Germany—from elk hide, not the plastic things they issued. A gift from his brother-in-law.

"The other two weapons?" he asked, picking up his visored hat from the top of a filing cabinet. "How soon?"

Striganov walked Petrov to the door, hands thrust into the pockets of his white lab jacket. At fifty-five, he was in full command of ninety-three scientists and technicians, leader of Project Group 17, Nuclear Weapons Development and Testing Division, District One. He had a Chaika sedan, special passes to GUM stores, and a wife who wore suits styled in Helsinki. Like the awards he held, they mirrored his value to the state. A colonel in the KGB didn't intimidate him.

"Numbers two and three are in final assembly," he

3

finally answered. "We'll detonate the third one in an underground test at Novaya Zemlya in two weeks." He reached for the doorknob, ushering the colonel before him.

Petrov paused and turned to face the scientist, offering his hand. "You do good work, Doctor. Your name will be mentioned."

Striganov returned a controlled smile. Their hands clasped briefly and then Petrov was gone.

Forty-three meters of reinforced concrete above the nuclear weapons assembly facility at Zhignask, arctic winds scythed across the steppes of Asia.

Yuri Andropov settled back in the overstuffed chair, delicately holding a match between the tips of his thumb and index finger, as if it were a captive butterfly. He drew the flame down into the bowl of his pipe, inhaling deeply in successive draughts until the tobacco caught. The sound reminded Petrov of an old woman kissing a baby.

Andropov shook the match out. "You approve of the plan, Colonel Petrov?" He threw the spent match accurately into the brass ashtray and settled deeper into the chair. Watching Petrov's reactions, his eyebrows knitted together in a scowl.

Andropov was in his late sixties; an elegant dresser but growing bulky. Petrov had met him only twice before but had seen him on reviewing stands with the first secretary and the other Party *vlasti*, moving progressively from the back ranks to the front row as the years passed until 1973, when Andropov was designated chairman of the KGB. There was a minor resemblance, Petrov thought, between Andropov and the first secretary—the eyebrows, of course. Dense and black, forming bat wings between the high forehead and the deeply set eyes. Andropov's hair as well—yellowish-gray along the hairline, sweeping up in a smooth wave, flowing back down along his skull

4

and lapping to a fringe of stubble on the neck. But it was the mouth that was arresting, he thought. There was no upper lip. Just smooth, hard flesh terminating in a slit. For this reason, it was difficult to read his expression; the thin gash rarely moved from the horizontal, as if the muscles in the corner of the mouth were atrophied. Or more likely, Petrov thought, they were held in check by the disciplined brain that had guided Yuri Andropov through a maze of Party intrigues and shifting loyalties for five decades. Andropov's suppression of the Hungarian Revolt in 1956 was a springboard to full Politburo membership and, finally, to undisputed control of the *Komitet Gosudarstvennoy Brzopasnosti*.

"The Rametka plan seems reasonable," Petrov finally replied, as if he had spent the time analyzing each separate element. As he said this, he recognized a qualification in the tone of his voice and added, "As field operative, I can execute my part without problems, Comrade Chairman."

Andropov sucked in on his pipe and blew a blue smoke ring that lifted slowly, penetrating the stratified layer of haze which had formed above his head.

"Relax, Petrov," he said. "This isn't an interrogation. I want opinions and alternatives, how you're going to handle some of the operational details. The first secretary is more than interested in this project. He'll require daily briefings. Most important," he added, "this operation will have a critical impact on our strategic planning—perhaps enough to swing the balance of power."

Andropov's mood had changed, taking some of the tension from the conversation. He bent forward, his pipe turned bowl downward, and knocked the ashes against the tile hearth. He returned the pipe to a rack and settled back, clasping his hands over his stomach.

"An excellent meal, Anatoli. My doctor wants me to run more often. I don't know which is stronger, my

5

love of food or my hatred of exercise. In the mean-while, the fat accumulates." He belched, as if he had forced it.

"The sturgeon was excellent," Petrov replied, "as was the rest of the meal." He picked up his glass and swirled the remaining cognac.

Andropov stood up, a full head shorter than Petrov. "Come," he said, "I have something to show you. Very highly classified." He paused, midstride, turning to Petrov. "Something I don't want discussed outside of this apartment."

He led the way from the library with its preCzarist chandeliers, past shelves filled with books, over patterned Tadzhikistanish rugs in burgundy-and-fawn pile centimeters deep. The chairman's secretary, a man in his twenties and smelling of talc, intercepted them as if by prearrangement and preceded them along the corridor, past a darkened drawing room and the formal dining area where orderlies were now changing the table linen and setting freshly cut flowers in crystal vases.

The corridor terminated in a flush door, in contrast with the ornate panels that marked the architecture of the rest of the rooms. The secretary unlocked the door and then stood aside, letting Andropov and Petrov enter.

The room was an informal workshop and study, furnished in Scandinavian modern with bold-patterned Rya rugs. A small fireplace constructed of white-washed brick held a log fire. The scent of burning birch gave the room a sense of familiarity; a touchstone link for Petrov, who had grown up on the edge of the forests south of Novgorod in White Russia.

"Part of the heritage of a peasant background," Andropov commented, noticing Petrov's reaction. "Reminds one that there is something more than cities." He turned on a high-intensity light over the workbench.

It illuminated an elaborate ship's model, fully rigged.

Petrov examined the work closely. Miniature blocks were attached to yards; chain and running rigging taut, in precise detail. The deck was crowded with miniaturized equipment—bilge pumps and capstans. Bronze cannons on hardwood carriages were run out on block and tackle. The precision and workmanship, Petrov realized, were a mirror of Andropov's mind.

"The French man-of-war *Redoutable*," Andropov said. "From her mizzen-top a French marine shot Lord Nelson, October twenty-first, 1805—the Battle of Trafalgar." He pressed a switch and the far wall of the room was bathed in diffused light.

Petrov counted five shelves, running the length of the wall, each crowded with sailing ship models. The chairman handed Petrov a large magnifying glass.

"If you want to inspect the detail . . ." he said. "They are all exact. Researched to the last fitting." He grunted, the sound of a sort of cynical laugh. "Most of the fittings come by diplomatic pouch from a model specialty firm in New Jersey. They might be surprised to know who one of their best customers is."

Petrov bent down, examining the largest ship. The precision was impeccable. He realized that the models were of the finest museum quality. "These are incredible," he said, turning to Andropov. "This one . . ." he said, moving back to the case. "French?"

The chairman turned away and sat down on an upholstered stool next to the workbench. He fiddled with his pipe, tamping the bowl and then lighting it. "No. That one you're looking at is the H.M.S. *Victory*, Nelson's flagship. The rest are all ships of the combined French and Spanish fleet and the opposing English force. My goal is to finish the entire list of combatants, down to the smallest sloop. Of the total of sixty ships which met off Cadiz that day, I have built thirty-four."

A massive airedale that Petrov had not noticed rose from a mat beneath the workbench, arched its back, and walked stiffly over to the chairman. The dog sat down, head inclined toward Andropov. The man worked his knuckles against the dog's ear and the animal responded, leaning into Andropov's fist, emitting a low growl of pleasure.

"My other weakness, Petrov. The dog's name, of course, is Hardy."

Petrov raised his eyebrows. "It's a name I don't know."

"Hardy was Nelson's flag captain—his friend. Not entirely brilliant. But then again, brilliance should not be a necessary qualification for friendship. However, the keeping of confidential information is." He said this pointedly.

Petrov nodded. "I understand, but why hide this? The work is expert—perhaps the finest I've seen."

Andropov actually smiled. His teeth were yellowed and crooked. One tooth was missing on the lower jaw. "I was told some years ago by my doctor that I couldn't drink. One of those unpronounceable terms for a kidney disorder. So I took this as my addiction. It occupies my mind totally, and yet I do some of my best planning here. And Hardy never disagrees with me." He scuffed at the dog's ear and the animal slowly slid, forelegs extended, into a prone position, his head resting on Andropov's shoes. "I enjoy it," he continued, "for several reasons. It reminds me that wars were once much simpler—that one battle often brought decisive victory or defeat. And it has given me further insight into strategic planning. Nelson was the master. Bold, imaginative, a renegade to established ways of conducting warfare. You see the fascination?" He was animated now, his eyes brilliant, hands moving expressively to emphasize the point.

Petrov returned the smile, drawn by Andropov's magnetism. He looked around the studio and then back at Andropov. "Someone from Center once told me that you spent your evenings locked away, reviewing intelligence reports for the Central Committee—

8

that all of us should model ourselves after you." He didn't add that Andropov was rumored to personally supervise interrogations.

"I'm aware of the rest of it," the chairman shrugged. "The things you didn't say. And that's all to the good. It suits the requirements of leadership to have these fairy tales circulate. This diversion," he gestured toward the ships, "is my own secret. Something to occupy my mind." Andropov snapped off the light. "You know, Anatoli, Nelson would have failed without the services of a spy. He had to keep his fleet well offshore, out of range of coastal batteries and in position so that he could cut off the enemy, regardless of whether they chose to sail north for England or south to Gibraltar. Captain Blackwood of the frigate *Euryalus* lay close to the approaches of Cadiz each night and was able to see the preparations of the combined fleet as they made ready for sea. By signals from Blackwood, Nelson was able to position his ships in an innovative manner—the famous 'crossing of the T,' and each English seaman went into battle that day with a full belly and an unqualified assurance of victory."

The dog had lifted its head, watching Andropov's hands as he moved them in a simulation of the battle.

"And Nelson's instructions to his captains," Andropov continued, "were recorded as being, 'No captain can do very wrong if he places his ship alongside that of an enemy.' Very appropriate to our venture, don't you think?" He stood up, poked the logs, and then leaned back against the mantel.

The studio was stifling, heat radiating in waves from the fireplace. But to Petrov it was an opiate. Combined with the food and cognac, he felt confident and at ease. The magic of Andropov was that he was in no way less a leader than Nelson. "You were a naval officer?" Petrov asked.

The chairman smiled. "Something that the Registry and Archives Department put out. No," he said.

9

"The nearest to the sea that I got was by enrolling in the Technical School of Water Transportation in Rybinsk. I commanded nothing larger than a desk." He turned and looked at Petrov directly, his expression serious. "We have here a parallel," he said. "A crucial engagement, the essential element of espionage, and then the one decisive battle—a battle which decides the balance of power between two great nations."

Petrov realized that Andropov had come to the core of their conversation. The Nelson-Blackwood parallel was an oblique way of underscoring the importance of their relationship.

"The project has been well thought out," Petrov finally said. "Rametka and the first chief directorate have done a thorough job."

Andropov nodded. "So I gather. I've studied the plan, but there are a few things that bother me. You've examined the weapon?"

The question surprised Petrov. He was sure that Andropov had been kept informed of the development reports. "It's excellent from what I can determine," Petrov said carefully. "Striganov and his group are to be commended. He indicated to me this afternoon that they would test in two weeks. The projections are that the fallout signatures will be identical."

"I know all of that. I've talked daily to Striganov. Now tell me why you went to Zhignask."

Petrov massaged the knuckles of his hand. The trip west from Zhignask to Moscow had been a purgatory of cold. The heaters in the *Ilyushin* hadn't worked and the flight had been rough—five interminable hours of buffeting through a winter storm. "No specific reason," he said, moving up to the fire, opening his hands to the heat. "Rametka's report indicated that the device was well made. Better than that: exact."

"Which doesn't answer my question."

"Just that I wanted to see it. To know that the thing had been done properly." He turned to Andropov.

10

"I'm no judge of a technical thing like that, but I understand people. Striganov was very confident, almost to the point of insolence. I think he has done an excellent job."

"You're satisfied?"

"Completely, from what I can see. If the test goes satisfactorily . . ."

"How about the yacht?" Andropov had cut him off, pressing for an assessment.

Petrov took his time, not knowing exactly what Rametka's report had suggested. There had been only seven to select from. Two had seemed adequate, one ideally suited. "The *Hussar*," he said. "It's well known in those waters and the crew is an older couple. The equipment, from what I can determine, is suitable: two diesel engines, radar, and steel construction. Those were prerequisites for reliability. Rametka and I agree on the choice. A charter contract has been forwarded to the owners by the ship's broker."

"I want plans of the yacht," Andropov said. He moved to a telephone on the far side of the room. "You care for another cognac? I generally have a cup of bouillon this time of the evening."

"No, thank you. Not cognac. Coffee if that can be managed."

Andropov spoke into the phone and hung up without waiting for confirmation. "The other part of it—what politician do you feel is suitable?" The dog had followed him, then sat, head down, probing at Andropov's pants leg with its nose.

Petrov was on unsure ground, going against Rametka's proposal. He brushed his hand back through his blond hair, feeling perspiration prickling his scalp. This could evolve into a test of strength between Rametka and himself—a trial that would determine who would be in absolute control. He decided to take the risk.

"Welsh is my first choice. Rametka favors the Virginia congressman, but I think he's too unstable. It's

11

that very factor that Rametka's pinning his hopes on and I've got to concede that the man might be more malleable. He's emotionally unstable—highly religious. But I also feel that this very factor makes him a poor choice when it comes to American voter acceptance."

"And Welsh . . . ?" Andropov said quietly. He settled himself on the stool, fitted a jeweler's loupe into his eye socket and bent down, examining the model's rigging. "Why Welsh?"

"The right background. Liberal but from a wealthy family. Politically ambitious. He's identified with the federal . . ." Petrov searched for a word but it translated badly. ". . . bailout—a projected financial assistance plan for the city of New York."

Andropov nodded. He had used tweezers to fit a minute brass chain to a yardarm, fastening it with a link of black wire. Finally, cutting the excess off with wire snips, he put the tool down. He waited, not moving.

"Welsh," Petrov continued, "has shown a bias toward unilateral disarmament. But it's a realistic rather than an emotional appraisal. An acknowledgment of our power and the cost to the American economy of catching up. We . . ." he hesitated, rephrasing, "*I think* Welsh will buy the proposition. It corresponds with his own philosophy. And he wants power."

"Would you plan to use drugs?" the chairman asked. He turned off the light and then removed the jeweler's loupe. But he remained in front of the darkened workbench, his eyes on the ship, as if in his mind he could see the cannons running out, gunners swabbing the barrels, the gunlayers hunched behind the ports waiting for the roll of the ship to bring the thirty-two-pounders to bear.

"Unnecessary," Petrov said, "and probably unworkable." He drove the idea home. "Welsh is a politician. A survivor. He's too much of a pragmatist to

12

be controlled in the long run by just a few days of drug-induced persuasion. What he does will be from self-interest. Some degree of psychology will be required and several days of intense contact are necessary, but in the end it will be his own greed and ambition that decides the issue."

There was a knock. The secretary opened the door, allowing a sergeant-orderly to enter, bearing a tray. He placed it on a coffee table and then drew himself up to attention. Andropov nodded and the man withdrew. "Tea at six," he called after the sergeant. "And two Jaffá oranges. Peeled!" The last word was emphasized, d the sergeant turned and grinned, as if it were a private joke between them. The door rolled shut.

"What makes you think you can isolate Welsh?" Andropov said. He picked up the cup, stirring the liquid, then drank.

"He vacations every year, generally in the Caribbean. Usually small resorts in the Bahamas or Windward Islands. It's considered fashionable in political circles. Somewhat like going to the Black Sea."

"How would you find out the senator's destination and time of vacation?"

Petrov realized that he was extending an opinion into a commitment. Andropov was drawing him out, looking for an alternative to Rametka's proposal.

"It shouldn't be too difficult," he answered. "Welsh is, like most other American politicians, close-mouthed about taking a winter vacation. It seems that the average politician doesn't want his constituents to know that while they freeze he's lying in some tropical resort. But we have a deep-cover in his locality, someone we can direct to dig out the information."

"Is your coverage a part of an established *aparat?* I want no connections made with any of our established networks in the event something goes wrong. It has to be absolutely clean."

13

Petrov sipped his coffee. It was flat and stale, probably state issue. He put the cup down. "No, the man's Estonian. Emigrated to the U.S. with his wife in the late forties. He's only been used twice for minor intelligence collection. They have two children. There is also his mother who still lives in Estonia. His willingness to cooperate should be no problem."

The chairman stood up and checked his watch. "It's past my bedtime. There are only a few more items. Communications. I want to be continually apprised of progress. Because of the political factors, there is a great deal of coordination required. And forty-eight hours before the weapon is detonated, we'll place the Long Range Rocket Forces on first readiness and move submarines from the Red Banner Fleet into firing position. As Rametka points out, there's the slim possibility that the Americans might react recklessly."

"That part of the plan is satisfactory. We'll utilize *Salyut* satellites. With a schedule of their trajectories, we can operate with very high-frequency transmitters of low power. The propagation is line of sight. The *Salyut* will pick up the message, record it, and then retransmit it over Russia. The maximum delay will be only fifty minutes. It also means that we don't use established networks for message-passing."

Andropov nodded. "I want your outline of the operations plan by tomorrow afternoon. I've already had orders cut placing you in charge." He looked across at Petrov, his head cocked downward but his eyes holding Petrov's. "You realize why I'm doing this? Rametka is an excellent planner. But he's an academic. I don't think that this thing can run like a timetable. The less rigid, the better. There has to be flexibility. I'm appointing you as *Control*."

Petrov extended his hand and shook Andropov's. They moved to the door.

Andropov took Petrov's elbow, squeezing it. "A lot rests on this, Anatoli. A lot. You'll be my Blackwood."

Petrov was picked up in Andropov's entryway by a KGB captain with blue collar tabs. The chairman had called it his "apartment." An understatement, Petrov thought as the two men descended in the private elevator, for Andropov's apartment was one entire floor in the old, nondescript apartment building on 26 Kutuzov Prospekt. Minister for Security Nikolai Shchelokov held the floor just below and the first secretary's town house occupied the one above.

They left the building, first fumbled through two security stations, and went out into the raw dry cold of the Moscow night. It was after 1 A.M. A Volga M-124 was idling at the curb. Gusts of wind picked up the dry snow, driving it in stinging volleys agasint Petrov's face. The captain half bent, saluted, and opened the back door. "To the armed forces officers' club?"

Petrov paused, halfway into the car. He was anxious to be finished with it for the day, to sit down in the club's drawing room, enjoy a double whiskey, and then go to sleep. Except for refining the alterations in the plan, there was little to do until the next afternoon. And it would be purgatory to face Zoya. But it had to be done.

"No. Tell the driver to take the Boulevard Ring Road to Petrovka Street. I'll direct him from there."

The captain smiled, started to say something, and then thought better of it. He closed the door on Petrov after saluting again and rapped on the driver's window. Through the glass plate which separated Petrov from the uniformed KGB driver, he could see the two men talking. The driver argued halfheartedly and then shrugged as the captain made an obscene gesture, the *v karmane* sign, his blunt thumb sticking out between the third- and fourth-fisted fingers. Capitulating to what would probably be an all-night extension of his duty shift, the driver jammed the transmission into gear and pulled out. Petrov saw his eyes flick only once to the rearview mirror to study his passenger.

The streets of Moscow were vacant, only a few figures hurrying out of the icy wind into hallways or toward the stairs of the Metro. Policemen in pairs sheltered in the lee of doorways and shop entrances.

Petrov settled back, fatigued and yet elated. Andropov had clearly ceded him title to the operation. Rametka would remain the planner but still be subordinate. Andropov had guaranteed unlimited funds and authority. Petrov briefly touched the leather-bound sheaf of authorization papers in his breast pocket. It bore both Andropov's and the first secretary's signatures, and guaranteed that all the resources of both the GRU and KGB would be at Petrov's disposal. Satisfying, he thought, for a thirty-nine-year-old colonel. He lit a cigarette, settling back into the cushions. As an afterthought, he closed the velvet curtains on the side windows, leaving the rear window undraped. He arched back his head, working the neck muscles, watching the mercury vapor lights flash by as the car sped through the silent city.

He arrived just as she was putting the boy to bed. She was flustered, not expecting him. At first she pecked his cheek and then, catching her breath, threw her arms around his neck. He rocked her, and felt her hands clutching through the material of his heavy coat. Over her shoulder he saw the boy, standing with his face a mask of indecision, wavering between laughing and crying as a very young child will, mirroring its parent.

Petrov made a face, wanting to amuse, and the boy burst into tears.

"It's all right, Anatoli," she said. She picked up the child, shaking her head against his neck, making humming sounds. "It's all right," she repeated. Whether it was directed to himself or the child, Petrov didn't know.

The boy was no more than two. His hair, like both Petrov's and his mother's, was wispy flax, overly long, so that the child could have been either boy or girl to the casual observer. And he had ice-blue eyes, the shade of Petrov's.

"Say 'goodnight,' " she prompted, taking the boy's limp wrist and flopping it. Prompted, the boy suddenly smiled and waved vigorously. "Night." His smile was all pink gums with only a few teeth. "Night," he repeated, waving erratically, mussing his mother's hair. They disappeared into a bedroom.

The flat had an overused flavor, a scent which combined the odors of meal after meal cooked, of cigarettes left smoldering, of diapers left unwashed. Magazines, some of them from Western Europe, lay in untidy stacks. There was a large burn in the carpeting near the chair. Wearily, Petrov sank down on the sofa, striking a match to a cigarette.

"You look very well," she said, closing the door to the room.

"As you do," he responded, knowing that both of them had thrown out harmless opening lies, skirting the issue.

"The apartment's a mess," she said. "Somehow, I don't give a damn."

"I understand."

"Do you?" She moved to the kitchen, bringing back a half-liter bottle of Stolichnaya and two glasses, setting them down on the littered coffee table. "Do you really, Anatoli?" She poured them both neat portions of vodka and then lifted her glass to his. "To the living." She drank it down in two swallows and refilled the glass.

He looked at her closely. The high cheekbones were an echo of her mother's. A fine nose, perhaps too broad at the nostrils, but she had always tossed her head, teasing him that he had been the cause of it when they had fallen off his bicycle as youngsters. "How can you fly planes when you could not even drive a bicycle properly?" she had said. Her husband, Sergei, two years younger than Petrov, had always

17

roared at Petrov's stumbling explanation. A Ukrainian, Sergei had been dark and explosive, tumbling from heights of good humór to a traditional southerner's remorse, and then soaring back again. He had become Petrov's brother-in-law and then friend and then brother.

Self-consciously, she lifted her hand to her face, tracing the lines around her mouth. "Don't worry, Anatoli. I'm getting better. It just takes time."

"I haven't been back in the country long, Zoya," he started. "I called his wing commander as soon as I heard. Sergei was leading a flight of four aircraft. It was a patrol, the usual thing. North of Finland over the Barents Sea." He picked up the glass and sipped slowly, trying to phrase things easily in his mind.

"Coming back," he continued softly, "one of the planes developed a hydraulic leak. Sergei instructed the rest of the flight to land first, then flew with the disabled aircraft as it burned off fuel. He flew wingtip on the approach, coaching the pilot down. It was a safe landing."

Petrov could visualize Sergei, working down through the ice-fog into the frozen strip on the Kola Peninsula, the weight of his first command a wingspan away. "He didn't have enough fuel for his own approach. He flamed out two kilometers short of the runway." Petrov paused, avoiding her eyes. "There was no fire."

It surprised him that she didn't cry. She leaned over, her face turned from his, resting on his shoulder. Petrov could feel her breath warm on his neck.

"They told me all of that," she said. "Men from his unit sent flowers." There was a catch in her voice.

"These things happen, Zoya."

She lifted her head, facing him. Her eyes were rimmed in red. "They happen to chemists? That's what Sergei was. A fine chemist."

"Like all of us, he had to serve his tour."

"Like my son will," she said, her voice rising. "Is that what the hell I have to look forward to? Will I get

18

a medal for him as well?'' Her voice was a thin shriek.

"It will be over soon," he said. God, that it will, he thought.

Petrov sat into the dawn hours with his sister, holding her hand, not talking, until he heard the cleaning trucks working the streets.

David Fox slumped against the settee in the galley of the ketch *Hussar* watching the unrelenting fog roll in from the Strait of Juan de Fuca. The *Hussar* surged uneasily at her docking lines and he could hear the tiresome slat of a halyard aloft that had not been properly secured. He rose and limped over to the galley stove, poured a fresh cup of coffee, and paused to light his cigarette on the blue flame of the gas burner. He returned to the settee, dropping heavily against the cushions, and listlessly watched the fog bank smother the horizon.

Fox was middle-aged, thin, and balding. A retired merchant ship's captain, he had poured his life's savings, plus his wife's inheritance, into the *Hussar*. In the first year of ownership, he found that there was a great deal of difference between commanding a ship which had a paid crew of twenty-eight and maintaining a large yacht with a crew of one; a woman at that, who had spent her years bowling and giving teas while Fox was at sea. Compounding his labor problems, he found his wife was not the compliant and subservient woman that he had known on leaves from the ship. With more than half-ownership in the *Hussar*, she was pushing him hard to put the vessel on a paying basis. Simply cruising had seemed ideal. But inflation gnawed at his pension, and the prices of paint and equipment had tripled in five years. Fox had come full circle. He was captaining a ship once again, carrying passengers for hire.

Myra, his wife, was in the shower. The pressure water pump cycled in the bilge and, moments later, cycled again. He scowled, noticing that the galley lights had dimmed perceptibly on the last cycle. The batteries were low and he would have to start the generator soon.

He listened for a moment to make sure that she had not left the shower and then withdrew a bottle of rum from a galley locker. Pouring another cup of coffee, he laced it heavily, added sugar, and took two quick swallows. He hated the weakness of the act but knew that it would soften the edges of his nerves. Nothing more until sundown he promised himself, and then leaned against the teak paneling of the companionway and softly stroked the oiled finish as he sipped at the mug. The pump cycled again.

The *Hussar* was a sixty-four-foot, twin-engined motor sailer, built in Germany in the early fifties by Abeking and Rasmussen. Her hull was constructed of six-millimeter steel plating and she had the water and fuel capacity to cross oceans.

Fox had liked her immediately, on finding her on the first yacht-purchasing expedition that he and Myra had made two years previously. The *Hussar* was comfortable and beautifully finished with a lavish galley, four separate staterooms, and a roomy saloon. But it was her big-ship aspects that had attracted him. She had radar, two radio telephones, and massive, modern deck equipment. Better still, the engine room was the full width of the ship, well placed beneath the floor of the saloon. It has nearly standing headroom, steel gratings running around both Mercedes diesels, a 15-kilowatt generator and workshop. Built to Lloyd's specifications, the engine room had collision bulkheads and a steel watertight door. Surprisingly enough, Fox found that he had an aptitude for mechanical repair work. If the rest of the yacht was not maintained in Bristol condition, Fox could justifiably claim that the equipment worked and worked well.

The *Hussar* now lay alongside a floating dock in Sudder's Marina off Horseshoe Bay, British Columbia. In these last days of March the wind roared down out of Howe Sound, churning the bay with whitecaps, approaching Force Seven. And when the wind didn't blow, cold, thick fog smothered the bay.

Reluctant to leave the warmth of the galley, Fox finally finished off his coffee and left the mug upturned in the sink. I'll catch hell for that, he thought. Myra harped about getting the dishes clean and stored once they were used. He reasoned that it was her way of sniping at him. Both their nerves were frayed from the long, wet winter and their shrinking bank account. Summer had better produce some paying charters, he thought, or we'll have to sell this goddamned bucket.

He opened the engine-room door and switched on the blowers, venting any gas fumes that might have settled in the bilge. He timed them, letting them run for a full five minutes and then, satisfied, started the generator. Slamming the engine-room door shut, he dogged it down. The lights were brighter now.

He could hear Myra humming. Thank Christ, he thought, she's in a good mood. They had argued late into the morning hours. She wanted to cut the *Hussar*'s charter rate to get more business and then use the money to get to the Caribbean. "Where the real money is," she had said repeatedly, hammering her fist down on the table. Rate-cutting sounded like a lot more work for a lot less money to Fox. Maybe sell this old bucket and get back into shipping, he thought. It was easy to forget that he had been retired early because of the worldwide economic slump. Hundreds of men, better qualified than Fox, were on the beach.

He set the water kettle on the stove and lit the gas. He would make her coffee, he thought. A peace offering to start a new day.

From behind him he heard a muffled shout. Turning, he wiped the condensation away from the galley porthole and looked out on the dock. Clive Sudder, the owner of the marina, was already climbing aboard through the lifeline gate. He was yelling something but Fox couldn't make it out over the hum of the gener-

21

ator. Limping up the companionway into the saloon, Fox paused to look at the debris of last night's argument with Myra. The coffee table was littered with filled ashtrays and moisture rings from glasses had stained the varnish. He swore under his breath and moved to the hatchway, pulling it open.

The fog was more like a permeable membrane than the fogs Fox had known while growing up on the Maine coast. Here the moisture was so thick that it filtered sound and vision alike, rendering a man senseless. Water dripped from the rigging and Sudder's oilskins were slick with wetness.

"Special delivery for you," Sudder said. Craggy old bastard, Fox thought. More Scot than Canadian. And he could recite your current bill down to the last penny. "You're three weeks overdue in yer dockin' fees, mate." Sudder withheld the thick letter, looking at Fox with the distrust that creditors universally hold for the delinquent payers of the world.

Fox reached for the letter. "Next Monday. It's a bank delay on transferring money."

"Which is what you told me the last time. Best change banks, mate." Sudder handed over the envelope and thumped back down the deck. "Monday," he said loudly over his shoulder. The fog swallowed him up in twenty steps.

Myra had entered the galley from the forward stateroom companionway, flushed from her hot shower and with enough of her housecoat open to reveal the deep cleft between her breasts. She was still stunning in a haphazard sort of way, having reached the age when women either develop a mature grace and beauty or simply fade into some sad and slightly blurred image of their youth.

"What was that all about?" she asked, spooning sugar into her coffee. "Sudder playing Simon Legree?"

Fox ignored her, dropping down onto the settee. He slit the end of the envelope and then tapped out the

22

contents. A cashier's check fluttered to the table, followed by a letter. She picked up the check first, nearly spilling the dregs of his cup.

"Twelve thousand," she said. "My God, Davy—it's twelve thousand dollars!"

He scanned the letter and then reread it carefully, his face making a slow transition from puzzlement to pleasure.

"Davy—what does it say?" She moved out from her side of the dining settee to his, leaning over his shoulder.

"Three frigging whole months of charter," he said in a whisper. "Mid-June to mid-September. Half down and the balance when they board. It's from that queer in New York—the poofy yacht broker. Got a firm contract through some other agent in Hamburg. Two foreign guys want to cruise from the north end of Queen Charlotte Strait to the Hood Canal in Washington." He turned to Myra. "Babe—we'll be in the West Indies by Christmas with this money. The agent says it's a confirmed charter. They paid full rates *plus* the brokerage commission. All in cash!"

Fox suddenly stood up, brushing past Myra, and opened the refrigerator. From a lower shelf, he pulled the bottle of champagne he had been saving for her birthday. He fumbled the cork out, carelessly allowing the wine to foam down his shirt and pants. Pouring the remainder into two glasses, he handed her the smaller one.

Before she drank, she hung one arm around his neck and drew his face down to hers, kissing him.

The cold champagne soaked through his clothing, chilling his skin.

What the hell, he thought. I'll go uptown and buy another bottle. He smiled, looking beyond her head at the fragmented tendrils of fog. Maybe even a case.

In the bay an onshore wind had freshened, pushing the fog inland. Brief snatches of sunlight shone through the ragged mist. A gust, harder than the rest, heeled the *Hussar* slightly and her docking lines creaked heavily with the strain. The flag that flew from the taffrail, edges frayed and red bars faded to pink, snapped in the freshening wind.

Salyut XII swept over the black Atlantic, precisely balanced between the forces that would drag it down into incandescent reentry or would force it farther into deep space. The eight-ton satellite had been launched from Kapustin Yar eighteen days ago, third in its series of reconnaissance satellites, forty-eighth in the Cosmos project. In the first eleven days of flight *Salyut XII* had perversely displayed an almost human reluctance to function reliably. Soviet technicians were forced to fire course-correction thrusters three times to stabilize the orbit, and there was an intermittent problem with backup battery pack number five. But the satellite was now operational, with a projected life of 283 days. At over 19,000 miles per hour, *Salyut XII* arched through the airless void of space, sensors dormant, tracking toward North America.

The New England coast had been coated with a four-inch layer of wet snow early in the late March morning, but by noon the front which had brought the precipitation weakened under the influence of a strengthening high off the Carolinas, and by afternoon the wind had shifted from the northwest to the south. Temperature rose, even in the lengthening afternoon, and by evening the underlying vegetation of spring was fed by patches of melting slush.

At 6:43 P.M., the satellite swept through its trajectory, ninety-three miles above the city of Plattsburg, New York. The sodium-vapor lamps of the streets were switching on section by section, giving the appearance of some gigantic electronic game in progress when viewed from the satellite's altitude. The shape of the city was clearly defined, as well as the shore of Lake Champlain, edged on both the Vermont and New York sides by lightly trafficked freeways. To the north, the mass of light from Montreal flickered and flowed in the refraction of the unstable atmosphere. And to the south, Albany, Syracuse, and a maze of lesser towns framed a loom of light that intensified as the Hudson flowed south to the sea.

Sensors now fully awakened, *Salyut*'s infrared cameras probed for heat patterns on the hardstands of Plattsburg Air Force Base. The information was processed through a converter and fed to magnetic disks for storage. Electromagnetic sensors gathered data that was compared to information obtained in previous passes. Aberrations in the new sweep were updated and stored. Then the orbiting station's solar-paneled wings extended slowly and oriented toward the west, seeking new energy as the satellite overtook the sun in its westward track toward the Pacific.

Far below a man stood by the edge of the still-frozen lake and glanced at his watch as the satellite flared into the sunlight in its westward path. He noted the time on a card and compared it to a hand-printed schedule that he had withdrawn from his topcoat. Satisfied, he carefully pocketed the papers and sighed. For more than an hour into the evening, he trudged along the lake shore, picking stones at random from the semifrozen turf, flinging them out onto the frozen surface. The flattened shale rocks made brittle, ringing sounds as they skipped across the rotten ice.

His wife met him as he was returning, still wandering along the shoreline, hands deeply thrust into the pockets of his topcoat. He barely acknowledged her presence.

"What is it?" she asked. In her late fifties, she still retained the strength of peasant genes, her legs stocky but firm, feet booted in working shoes. She looped her arm through his and they walked together in silence.

He finally paused and turned her toward him. "I got a letter from Orlando, Florida. This morning." He wiped at his nose with a gloved hand. "The postage stamps were all torn on one corner."

25

She was still for a second, at first not realizing the significance, but then she inhaled sharply. "You said it was all over!" she said accusingly.

Mark Sommers nodded. He reached over, pulling her woolen hat carefully over her forehead, brushing back a swatch of graying hair. "I thought so," he said. "It's been five years. I hoped that they were finished with me. Now this." He handed her the pieces of paper.

She squinted at the cards in the darkness and handed them back. "I can't read it." Her voice had an underlying tremor, as if she had already accepted his reactivation. In that instant, she remembered the pressures that the KGB could apply and she knew there was no choice.

"Schedules for one of their satellites," he said. "I'm to purchase an amateur two-meter transceiver. Use certain frequencies which the satellite will pick up."

"And do what?" she whispered. A rumbling sound startled them both.

"It's the lake starting to break up," he said. He started to walk again, holding her gloved hand. He stumbled on the protruding limb of a fallen tree, bruising his shin.

"Whatever it is," she said, "ignore it. As if you hadn't received the letter." But there was no confidence in her voice.

"You know that won't work," he said. The lights of their home reflected on patches of melting snow. They both paused on the knoll, looking down on the small frame house. "There are the children to consider. And my mother in Estonia. If it were just us . . ." He didn't finish the sentence.

"What do they want?" she demanded.

He looked down at his watch, realizing that he had been walking for over three hours. His street shoes were soaked through from the melting snow and his shin throbbed from the fall.

"Information on one man. A senator from New

York by the name of Welsh. Just background information."

She moved toward the house, not waiting for him, and then hesitated. "We both know that there will be more. And more." She turned away and slowly climbed the porch steps, grasping the banister with both hands like an old woman.

Chapter 2

March 23 is a watershed in the annual weather cycle of the Northern Hemisphere, for on that date the sun in its northward migration crosses the equator. The Atlantic High, an elliptical high-pressure system bounded on the west by Bermuda and on the east by the Azores, is by that time fully established. This massive mound of air flows outward and, because of the earth's rotation, begins a fifteen-thousand-mile clockwise journey, touching four continents.

The prevailing winds first flow south along the African coast and then, responding to the clockwise demands of the Coriolis Effect, swing west, spanning the Atlantic, gathering moisture and warming in the sun. On the western shores of the Atlantic this river of air, now known as the trade winds, bends north and brushes the coast of the Americas, bringing warmth to Mexico and the southern states, fog to the coast of the Carolinas, and snow and freezing rain to a winter-battered New England.

Officially designated by astronomers as the vernal equinox, March 23 is more commonly known as the first day of spring. New Englanders, anticipating four more weeks of thaw and freeze, know better.

The middle-aged man circled the day's date, March 23, on his calendar and then turned from his desk and watched the barren trees on the lawn bend under a growing wind. What little remained of the morning snow had melted, but the ground was still matted with the dead vegetation of last autumn. Nothing green, just grays and browns and blacks. Depressed, he turned back to his work.

Although Clifford Welsh was already in his late forties, he retained the firm body of a man ten years his junior. Just over six feet, he weighed 182 pounds and held that weight to within three pounds by habitually working through his normal lunch period, eating only a carton of yogurt. His straight brown hair was still full, and cut weekly by an Italian barber who would use nothing but a razor and patience. What little gray appeared was dyed brown, except around the temples where it was artificially encouraged by peroxide.

Welsh's face complemented the image he affected. His features, plain enough, were offset by an aquiline nose, sharpened and thinned by generations of Welshes living through centuries of bitter New York winters. His soft hazel eyes, widely spaced, had a quality that his supporters called "compassionate" and the opposition termed "vacant." And though his teeth were capped, he rarely smiled, except in public and for the camera.

Welsh picked up the brochure again and thumbed through it. It was one of those slick presentations that cost thousands of dollars and portray remote little resorts in the Caribbean with words which translate into privacy and prestige. The photos showed, of course, buxom blondes and virile young men racing through the surf and smashing tennis balls across an impossibly smooth court. Everyone was young and Caucasian and perfect. And there wasn't a cloud in the sky or a mar in the perfect blue-white beach. All accommodations were in private cottages without telephones. The staff was black and smiled continuously, at least while on duty. And the cost was high enough to maintain some degree of exclusivity. Satisfied, Welsh scrawled a note across the face of the brochure and put it aside in a pile for his secretary to act on in the morning.

For some minutes he toyed with his pen and legal pad, doodling a sequence of sharp arrows and triangles, then overlaying them with graceful swirls and curlicues, subconsciously attempting to minimize the inner conflict. Progressing to ovals, he elongated them, then armed them with barbs, finding no easy resolution in the decision he had yet to make. Welsh tore the sheet from the yellow pad, wadded it, and discarded it in a leather-sheathed wastebasket. In the morning its contents would be committed to the shredder.

Unsettled, he turned back to the window to view the Hudson River and the smog-blurred skyline of Manhattan. More and more boilers were being converted from oil to coal and the emission standards for cars had been lowered twice in the last three years.

"Poor dumb bastards," he thought. The pollution index had long since lost meaning and people were starting to wear surgical masks, like the Japanese. Those who could afford it migrated south to the Sun Belt. In a lead article, *Time* magazine had quipped that "at least in the south, the smog is warmer."

And then he again thought of the fresh clean trade winds that swept the Atlantic, the outpouring of the mid-Atlantic high. His father had told him that sometimes one could smell the cooking fires of Africa on the eastern shores of Barbados. The sun would feel good on his back and shoulders. But it would have to wait and he reluctantly turned back to the reality of his ambitions and the millions who faced him from across the river.

The study had grown dark in the diminishing twilight. Clifford Tannis Welsh II, junior senator from New York, switched on the brass lamp over his desk and drew the curtains behind him. For the next hour he itemized in columns a list of political achievements that he had fought for in the Senate, both for New York State and for the nation.

There was little to fault from the standpoint of a liberal voter. Welsh had introduced and fought through the Senate a series of bills that literally made New York City a ward of the federal government. Indirect loan guarantees had not been enough to salvage the city from its creditors, and even direct federal grants for redevelopment, job training, and make-work projects had done little to stem the outflow of the affluent, the corporate giants, and the disillusioned. But the city still functioned and payrolls were met, with the credit largely due to Welsh. And the voters knew it. Welsh's reelection for a third term was guaranteed by the polls.

Nationally, his record was undistinguished but marketable.

NO on the B-1 and the MX missile.

YES on the Canal treaties, although that was now a disaster. One sixty-millimeter mortar shell had sunk a U.S.-owned freighter, stuffed full of cement, on the Atlantic side of the Pedro Miguel lock. Attempts to clear the wreckage resulted in mortar barrages. The Torrijos government had fallen, replaced by a Cuban-backed army of the revolution. Under article IV of the treaty, U.S. Marines moved in to defend the Canal. Mainly, they shot at shadows and took steady losses.

Welsh leaned back, reflecting. Two-thirds of the Senate had ratified the treaty, even hard-core conservatives. Who would have the balls to single him out? Both parties would sweep that one under the rug. He moved down the list.

YES on withdrawal of aid to Taiwan.

NO on gas rationing. He had, however, deftly covered himself with an amendment proposing that those below the poverty level be given gasoline purchase coupons on the same basis as food stamps, once rationing was mandated. The bill had failed by a narrow margin.

NO, again and again on the Personal Credit Allowance Reduction Act and its five amendments. Bankruptcy was now a national epidemic, but Welsh had argued with a straight face that bankruptcy was a way for the disadvantaged to close the gap with the middle class. The bill failed, and in the last year two major credit-card firms had gone belly-up. It was becoming a cash-and-carry economy.

Welsh scanned the rest of the list. It was a reflection of the downward drift of an industrial society—something that he could do little about except protect his constituents and his own job.

The personal background was there. Moderate wealth but not too blatant, raised in the same stone mansion on the bluffs of the Hudson, and schooled in law at Columbia. His father, a congressman, had groomed him for his first political campaign as state's attorney general with the single guideline of "be visible and vote straight blue-collar issues." The formula, however trite, worked. Welsh kept in touch with the people, spending time in the ghettos, the garment district, and the factories.

With his elbows on the desk, he created a steeple with his hands, resting his chin on the apex. Everything there, he thought. Liberal issues, visibility, and background. Everything except that one missing ingredient: a neck-snapping national issue. One that he must create, and one that would have to be so controversial that it would cut across party lines and split the nation. If he lost, it would be political immolation, but if he won, he would hold the office on Pennsylvania Avenue for four years. Longer, if he had his way.

He leaned back, eyes closed, testing the edges of his teeth with his tongue. The speech in Utica, he thought, would be the litmus paper.

The study door opened without a knock and Judith,

his wife, entered, pushing the door closed with her hip. She carried two glasses.

"It's after six," she said. "How goes the platform?" She set a moisture-hazed glass of whiskey on the desk blotter. It glowed with refracted warmth beneath the solitary lamp.

"Thanks." His eyes rose only enough to take in her form but not her face. Sliding the castored chair back over the rug, he arched his back and stretched his legs far out beneath the desk. With a certain finality, he lobbed the pen like a projectile toward the pad. It clinked against the glass, glowing with 14-karat gold in imitation of the whiskey.

He raised the glass toward her and said, "Cheers."

"Cheers," she echoed, smiling. They both drank in silence.

Random noises filtered down from the floors above as the children and servants made the transition from day into evening. A train whistled in the distance. Welsh removed his wire-framed glasses and laid them carefully over the pad of legal paper, as if in slow motion. Applying his long fingers to the bridge of his nose, he worked at the irritation of wearing glasses for too long, then spanned his forehead, rubbing at the wrinkles which radiated outward from the corners of his eyes.

"It's still garbage," he said dully.

"John Humberstall called and said he would call back about seven and," Judith paused to take a sip of wine, "Hagger from CIA phoned about a meeting of the President's Watchdog Committee on Intelligence. Something about Iraq. It's on for Wednesday. You're supposed to give him a call tomorrow. Nothing immediate."

He rose from the desk and walked stiffly over to the fireplace, fiddled with the gas valve, and then applied a match. The maple logs caught fire rapidly, burning in subtle yellows. He went over to the sofa and sat down next to her, putting his arm around her waist.

"Gets old, doesn't it?"

She shrugged, then rested her head on his shoulder. "Sometimes. But I probably see more of you than if you were out selling steel or bonds or whatever." She drained the little remaining wine in her glass.

They sat together in silence for a time, both watching the growing flames consume the wood, listening to the hiss and crackle of the damp wood burning.

"Seriously," she said, "how is the platform coming? I thought you felt that it was all wrapped up. DeSilva says so."

"The platform?" Welsh got up and went to the concealed cabinet, drawing out a bottle of Bushmill's. He poured himself another glass and then refilled hers with wine.

"The same, I guess," he said, sipping the whiskey more slowly this time. "DeSilva thinks I should push for making city employees federally funded. Maybe a federal pension fund for teachers. I haven't been doing much work on the state election stuff."

She craned her neck, looking down at the legal pad. "What's this then?"

"I'm thinking about not running." The words seemed to reverberate in the silence that followed. Her eyes avoided his, watching the flames.

"What, then?" she said evenly.

"Try to get a Cabinet appointment. Maybe Health, Education and Welfare. Or U.S. delegate to the U.N. Something with national visibility."

She turned on him, her face flushed. *"Why,* for God's sake?"

"Two years of time is *why.* Two years to build an image, a platform, a national identity. For a crack at the presidency."

She carefully set her glass down. "You're sure of this?" she said finally.

Welsh made an exasperated sound in his throat. "Sure? Christ, no, I'm not sure!" He paced across the rug to the fireplace and jabbed a poker into the

33

flames. "DeSilva won't stand for it. I'd lose my power base here. And it ultimately means going against my own party and an incumbent president. I'm unsure as hell."

"Then why do it?"

He dropped the poker back into the rack, turning to face her. "Like DeSilva once said, it's the reaction of a man who finds a fire on the first floor of a building and runs to the roof for safety. New York—for that matter, almost any one of the big cities—is living on borrowed time. We have the aid now, enough to sustain us from month to month. But the tax base is evaporating, going to the Sun Belt or the smaller cities. Each damn tax dollar lost from a corporation gone south requires five dollars in aid to replace it, because with the corporations go the jobs. New York will last another four, five, maybe even six years. But comes the next major economic crunch and the federal aid will dry up. And with it, any politician left in office. I don't want to be the *klutz* left holding the bag. But from a national position, I can capitalize on it, add a vital issue and work from a safe base like HEW. The voters will remember me as the man who made New York work—not the senator who was there when the axe fell."

She stood up, smoothing her dress. Judith Welsh was a *summa cum laude* graduate of Radcliffe. Dark brown hair, falling in a full mass, framed brown eyes and a small, evnly proportioned face. She bore children without a trace, was photographed opening clinics, and held her husband's arm during family interviews. She also had an IQ of 130 which she hid well, even from her husband. She loved him but she knew that he didn't have the conviction, the stamina, and the sheer guts for survival that would win a presidency.

"You need an issue," she said at last. "What is it?"

He picked up a sheaf of notes and laid them beside her. "I want you to read through this. It's the foun-

34

dation of a platform. I need some opinions other than DeSilva's."

She unsnapped her two strands of pearls and laid them on the desk. Picking up the notes, she glanced through them and then laid them back down. "I'll read it later. What's the basic idea?"

"Something I've been thinking about for over a year. I'm trying it out in a speech that I'm going to make up in Utica this weekend. I'm calling it 'The Economics of Peace.' The idea is to reduce the defense budget by twenty percent per year, down to a permanent floor of forty percent of its present level—enough to carry the military pension payments plus a token defense force. The game plan is to convince the voters that we can safely disarm the nation and then use those savings to finance a whole spectrum of social programs."

She tapped the notes with slim fingers. "Defense cuts have been tried before. The bill's sponsor generally gets a bloody nose."

"It hasn't been tried like this. In the past someone generally tried to hack three or four percent off the budget. The savings weren't enough to reduce taxes or make much of a difference to the man in the street." He stood up, animated, beginning to pace. "The beauty of this is that I can tie cuts in defense spending to several different programs—something for everyone. Reduced taxes for the middle class, greater welfare benefits for the poor and subsidies for the farmers. In four years, it would mean that we could free up over three hundred bucks per year for every man, woman, and child."

"What about the country's security?"

Welsh balled up a piece of scratch paper from his desk and threw it into the fire. Almost spontaneously the paper burst into flame. He watched it, as if mesmerized, until the ashes turned black and lifted in the flames; small fragments of his planning.

"Christ—who knows for sure?" he finally answered, irritated. "The Pentagon would have collective apoplexy. But I think we're a damn sight better off completely disarmed than being a poor second best to the Russians as we are now."

"The Administration keeps saying that we have parity," she countered. "The secretary of defense was on 'Face the Nation' just last Sunday. He says that we're even with them. All these graphs with colored lines . . ."

". . . which don't mean a damn thing!" he snapped. "He was comparing twenty-five-year-old American bombers with two-year-old Mach 3 *Foxbats*. And then he trots out a numbers comparison between Minuteman missiles, which are immobile in targeted silos, vulnerable—vulnerable as hell—and the SS-16 ICBM which the Soviets move around on mobile launchers every day like it was a game of musical chairs. And that doesn't even address the problem of the Soviets taking the initiative and launching a first strike." He brushed back the drapes, staring down across the lawn, not seeing, and then finally turned back to his wife. "Do you think you'd be better armed if you had a gun in your purse and some mugger sneaked up and caved in the back of your had with a rock?" He swept the drapes closed again. "Some people in the Department of Defense give us as little as one chance in three of even being able to get off an effective retaliatory strike. Probably barely enough to deter a Russian preemptive war. It's on the thin edge right now."

He poured another whiskey and then sat down at his desk. His voice had a tired quality to it. "If you wanted to write an equation between 'safety' versus 'sanity,' then I'd concede that a strong U.S. military might provide another ten years of relative safety. As much as we've had over the last thirty years. But we can't afford it and if you ask me, disarmament is the only road to sanity. Without strategic weapons we would not only pose no serious threat to the Russians

36

but it would allow us unlimited possibilities for social chang."

They were silent, neither wanting to speak. He waited for her reaction, ready to defend his thesis. Wood snapped in the fireplace.

Agitated, he finally broke the silence. "What do you think of the idea of unilateral disarmament? It's the only sane option we have left. And it would be one hell of an issue in a presidential campaign."

Judith picked up the empty glasses and moved toward the door. "Dinner is just about ready. *Foie de veau sauté.*"

"I want your opinion!" he demanded.

She shrugged, helpless to avoid the issue. "In a world of 'safe' or 'sane,' I would vote for 'safe.' I have two sons and a husband that I love. The rest of it seems academic." She pulled the door closed behind her, easing the latch shut.

For a long time Welsh sat alone, nursing the whiskey, as he watched the flames consume the wood.

The satellite swept west across the plains states, chasing the sun. Fed by sunlight and drawing heavily on the copper-selenide thermoelectric generator, three cameras, the infrared scanner, and magnetometers were running at full output, constantly feeding the data-storage bank. From the near-space of ninety-seven miles up, the continent was dead of color, showing only contrast of earth and snow. The Rockies were still capped in white as were the Sierras, the desert between a contrast in umber.

Over the Mojave, a light sparkled on the desert floor, flickering as it tracked the satellite. Forty-two solar cells of the left-wing panel burned out in the intense blazing heat of the laser, reducing the total power output by 6 percent. Wattage monitors reported this to the memory banks as the Russian reconnaissance satellite slipped past the California coast and sped toward its apogee south of Guam.

In forty-three minutes, with the batteries nearly recharged, the satellite extended microwave antennae, locked on to a ground antenna located in Dobrekinov in the southern Urals, and disgorged eighty-nine minutes' worth of reconnaissance data in a thirty-second high-speed transmission. Data banks empty, *Salyut XII* swept on toward Europe.

The facility at Dobrekinov is still partially unknown to Western intelligence planners. In the conflict that the Soviets still call The Great Patriotic War, thousands of German prisoners were shipped by open coal cars beyond the Volga and the Kirgiz Steppe into the southern range of the Urals. More than two-thirds survived the seven-day journey without food or shelter.

Dobrekinov was originally intended to be a complete underground facility for the production of ball bearings and some aircraft parts. The facility was constructed in a deep valley and blasted out of solid rock to a depth of 123 meters, then built in eight levels with reinforced concrete. Access to the facility was through an S-shaped blast tunnel, protected by eight steel doors sequenced in such a way that only three could be opened at the same time. A compound was built on the surface to house the German prisoners and administrative staff. The winters were so cold that the Germans were forced to stack their dead like cordwood to await burial in the spring thaw.

Following the Soviet victory in 1945, Dobrekinov's future was assessed by many of the same advisers to Stalin who had advocated its use as a ball-bearing production plant. Because of its southern location and remoteness from Moscow, it had little use as a center of Soviet communications, air defense, or even of munitions storage. But in 1951 a committee under the Ministry of Defense decided that its very remoteness and lack of vulnerability to all but a direct hit by a multimegaton warhead would allow Dobrekinov to become a secure record-keeping facility and, ultimately, a center for planning and assessment of strategic intelligence data. A bureaucrat examined a list of available designations and assigned the concrete pit the title AW-4.

The facility at first was staffed by a cadre of eighty members of the Red Army. Records, dating as far back as the beginning of the century, were stored in random stacks among the disused machine tools of the obsolete ball-bearing production plant. Later a primitive microfilming facility was set up at Level Two. Slowly, improvements were made and the illiterate soldiers were supplanted by members of the GRU and by members of the Soviet Academy of Sciences. Four microwave links were established in the mid-fifties, tying AW-4 directly into the Kremlin. Additional hardening was ordered in 1961 so that the facility could take an all but direct hit from an American Mark Five nuclear warhead. Twenty-two-hundred political prisoners were shipped down from the Gulag and bodies were again stacked like cordwood throughout the winter of 1962.

Today the village of Dobrekinov is listed infrequently and casually on the Ministry of Sports' list of athletic facilities as a winter training spa. The only above-ground structures are a speed-skating rink, two wooden barracks, and an unmarked cemetery containing the bodies of over 4,500 Germans, Poles, Czechs, and Russians. This was paved over in 1965 and is now used as a helipad.

But despite this preparation, it was not until a marshal of the Red Army, Gorki Penkovsky, took command and integrated AW-4 into the mainstream of intelligence and strategic analysis that the unit became an essential part of Soviet planning.

Marshal Penkovsky, as a lieutenant of the czar, had been assigned to attend Sandhurst in England in 1910. During this period he learned English and German and polished his French. He blotted up the training, jumping one class, and in the process made the friendship

39

of a military scholar, James Duncan. Duncan was one of the first to evolve the strategic military game. Initial efforts were merely moving lead soldiers in sandboxes. But the concept rapidly expanded to battlefields and then continents.

Penkovsky maintained close touch with political events in Russia, bending when necessary, but never becoming involved. What he planned was for Russia, not for the transient ruling clique. He was granted Order of the Soviet Hero by three separate administrations. His photograph appeared only once in the Western press, poised in the background as an aide to Marshal of the Armies Zukov, who, with his hand flung westward, directed the fire of Soviet artillery along a 2000-kilometer front against the forces of the Third Reich. Penkovsky was a colonel then.

Before his death in 1969 Marshal Penkovsky had assembled a nucleus of staff planners, implemented the Division of Strategic Planning, and filled Dobrekinov with the equipment necessary to accomplish his aims. He died peacefully in his sleep at the age of seventy-seven, an ancient terrier the only one to mourn him. But his ideas survived.

Penkovsky had argued repeatedly in the sixties that the age of planning by generals and admirals was over. Nuclear wars of the future would be fought, as he drolly commented, "during the span of a bowel movement." And the factors necessary for successfully waging war were temperatures over the poles, the depth of the isotherm in the Pacific, the morale of a fighter squadron in Minnesota, and ten thousand other unrelated factors, updated daily and preferably hourly. Computers would compute; men would program. Definite goals would be stated and all effort would be for their attainment.

Penkovsky had one precept for the conduct of both peace and war. "If you are not winning, you are losing. The situation is never static." The cadre of officers beneath him had understood. The most terrifying period was 1958 to 1963 when the American military was at its strongest, with its Atlas and Titan ICBMs, thousands of jet bombers, and nearly forty nuclear submarines. Penkovsky and his cadre cautiously predicted, with the aid of their first vacuum-tube computer, that the U.S. would not strike unless the Americans believed the level of their casualties could be held under 500,000 with no major damage to industry. The period passed, not without tension, but Penkovsky's theory was vindicated. As Soviet strength grew and American strength waned, Penkovsky turned his efforts to appraisal of Soviet chances for winning a war of initiative. He argued that if Russia lost no more than 18 percent of its industry, 12 percent of its population, and could regain its present level of gross national product within five years, a war would be a success, provided, of course, that the U.S. was brought under Soviet control without major loss of industry or agricultural output. This objective would be attained by a one-time, all-out strike on U.S. military installations with a planned overkill factor of five.

From this evolved a multilayer cake of intelligence gathering; each factor was weighed according to its worth. To bring the percentage chance of winning a preemptive war to 100 percent was wasteful, Penkovsky argued. Some risk must be accepted. And it was decided by the Presidium that 89 percent probability of "winning" was acceptable. Penkovsky didn't care. He would have accepted 60 percent with relish. For in the end, he believed determination and initiative, not sheer force, would win. But there could be no vacillation. The first strike must be made based solely on computer projections and not by political consideration. No withdrawal of diplomats, no breaking of ties. Just a clean, surgical strike, based on the printout of a machine.

On this day in March four men and a woman were seated around a situation display table on Level Six discussing factors that would be programmed for the Eighty-nine Percent Level (ENPL), as it was now known. The ENPL situation display was a miniaturization of a much larger display that dominated the walls of a mammoth chamber, which their glassed-in balcony overlooked. By verbal request to attending technicians or by keyboarding the *Zudypo IV* computer directly, raw data could be retrieved, new data inserted, or projections drawn.

The meeting comprised five of the six working members of the Committee for Data Gathering, a rather innocuous title for a group of technocrats that held the power to decide the conditions favorable for war. The chairman was Marshal Georgi Zhivotovskiv, assistant deputy to the chairman, KGB. He stuffed out another cigarette and turned to the woman addressing the group. His voice was cracked and hoarse and he habitually whispered. "Conclusions, Alexandra. Conclusions. The data you have there can be read by the committee at leisure. Get on with it."

She flushed slightly, leafing through the report to the final pages. She was a woman of fifty, features slightly Mongol. Her coarse black hair, drawn back severely and tied in a bun, gleamed under the lights as if it were oiled. Pushing her glasses back on the bridge of her nose, she continued. "The findings of my section indicate that last year the Gross National Product of the United States has risen only 2.43 percent, adjusted annually for inflation, which is presently in excess of eleven percent. Specifically, we do not feel that the U.S. military can sustain its present growth. In the sector of my group's concern, we are projecting a slippage of eight months in the start-up of the production of the Boeing 86 Model C cruise missile. We also think that this, in turn, will result in immediate pressure on spares procurement for the Model B. Overall, we estimate a reduction in mission capability of four percent beginning in April as funds

42

are diverted from operational expenses to research and testing. Any questions?"

A tall, bony man raised one finger. He wore a white lab coat and puffed methodically on a dead pipe.

"Comrade Korkin?" she said, inclining her head toward him.

He rose slowly, unfolding his frame. "Just one question, Alexandra." He hesitated, looking down at his notes. "Why the direct link between spares procurement for the Mod B and the development of the Mod C, which your circulated memorandum indicates is a longer range version of the B?"

She smiled condescendingly. "They are both part of the same program, thus the same funding. If the prime contractor and the Air Force feel that development of the longer-range version will be hindered by lack of funds, they will probably divert money from operational necessities to research and development. Satisfactory?"

He nodded, tapping his pipe into an ashtray. "What is the overall effect on the ENPL?"

She looked into her file again, knowing the percentage to three places, but delaying the answer for greater impact. "Ah, 1.38 percent by April. Perhaps over two percent by July if we get verification of our projections through our U.S. sources."

"Agreed?" The marshal looked at the members of the committee. There was no dissension. He then keyboarded the classification code, subroutine, and percentage points. All eyes of the committee rose to the ENPL display, which flickered briefly and rose from the morning's projected level to a figure of 71.88.

"Bit by bit," he muttered, hardly audible. Lighting another cigarette, he checked his notes and then turned to the short Ukrainian opposite him. "Developments, Dr. Lostnev?"

Lostnev remained seated. He scanned his report and keyboard "zero status change" into the *Zudypo*

IV. "No relevant data at this time, Comrade Marshal. In terms of air defense, we have added eighteen of the MIG-23 interceptors to the bases in the Kola Peninsula. I will suggest a shift of some of these aircraft to the Warsaw Pact areas. We need some additional strength on the Polish border. My report will be complete for tomorrow's meeting." He paused, scratching his chin. "There is one thing. *Salyut XII* reports loss of six percent of her solar panels. The loss was occasioned by a tracking laser device in the western United States. We have been anticipating this."

The marshal raised his dense eyebrows. "In what way?"

Lostnev smiled thinly. "Because we are doing the same. The remedy lies in a selective wavelength transmission coating for the solar panels. We feel that this will allow incident sunlight to penetrate the cells and yet remain a ninety-five percent rejection factor of the laser frequency the Americans are presently using. *Salyut XIII*, which is scheduled to be launched next month from the Tyuratam cosmodrome, will have this coating. I will report further at that time. Otherwise, I have no input for the ENPL."

Marshal Zhivotovskiv nodded slowly, his head hardly moving. "Agreed." His voice was a bare whisper. His eyes swept around the seated members of the committee. He never smiled, only indicating pleasure with the intensity of his look and a slight crinkle around his eyes. He lit another cigarette from the tip of the last one. He spoke carefully, referring to a teleprinter message before him. "Good. All your inputs are acceptable. But the fact of the matter is that the ENPL has risen less than five percentage points in the last year. We are reaching a point of diminishing returns, where major technological advances matter less. We must maintain our lead in weapons and extend it when possible. But as long as the United States has a nuclear strike capability, we will be on a very thin edge." He paused for effect, looking at the faces before him. There was a careful raising of eyebrows.

Zhivotovskiv continued. "You are all aware that," he chose the words carefully, conscious of the tape recorders, "there is some political relaxation by the U.S. with the Chinese, who are growing stronger. Should we wait until we have the military supremacy to accomplish the ENPL, we might well find ourselves vulnerable to an effective Chinese strike force." He paused for effect.

"I have before me a messag from the first secretary. It has been decided that our attentions must be turned toward developing special situations in which it might be possible to effect U.S. disarmament. These are political considerations and quite justly fall under the Department of Political Affairs for this committee. Dr. Vasili Rametka, whom you all know—" the committee turned toward the scientist who had now entered the room and stood before the committee table, "was responsible for our successes in Afghanistan. His most notable achievements to date have been political factors underlying the withdrawal of Italy from NATO. Dr. Rametka has developed a two-pronged scenario for the disarmament of the United States within a period of nine months. I think it deserves our consideration." He turned toward Rametka. "Doctor?"

Chapter 3

The device rested on its pneumatically cushioned transporter in the cool, dehumidified darkness of the bunker. An identical twin to the device was stored in a duplicate vault one-half kilometer away. The third device of this design had been detonated at 10:00 that morning, two thousand meters below the surface of Novaya Zemlya Island, the Soviet nuclear testing facility in the Arctic Ocean.

Test data on the shot were still flowing into the Nuclear Weapons Development Center at Zhignask 2,800 kilometers away by teleprinter, fax transmission, and computer link.

The leader of Project Group 17, Yuri Striganov, munched on a jam-covered bun and examined the teleprinter message which lay before him. He occasionally underscored passages of the text with a pen, grunted, reread passages, and finally pushed the message aside.

"I think, Colonel, that the test data conform exactly with our expectations." Striganov looked up at Petrov, his lips compressed in a smile of self-satisfaction.

Petrov wore the uniform of a colonel in the Long Range Rocket Forces. It had seemed to him that there was no point in advertising a KGB-GRU interest in weapons development. Petrov turned a page, running down a column listing fusion by-products from the test, comparing them with the original projections by Striganov's technicians. Finally finished, he dropped the report into his briefcase and locked the hasp.

"It looks good," he said. "The yield was a little higher than expected—three megatons rather than the expected 2.1 to 2.3. Is that significant?"

Striganov brushed his nose with the back of his index finger. "Nothing to be concerned about. These things are never that precise. Little factors—humidity, outside air temperature, some things we can't even guess at—affect the yield. An American weapon of this type would have the same minor inconsistencies."

Petrov nodded. "Other than that, the signatures match exactly. Generation of manganese fifty-six seems to be within limits and I conclude that you're satisfied?" Petrov stood up and stretched. "I could use some more coffee. The Cuban blend."

"We're satisfied," Striganov answered. "More than satisfied." He paused and pressed a bar on his intercom. "We wish another cup of the Western coffee. A glass of tea for myself and, ah, bring more toast. With currant jam, no butter." A hollow voice distorted by the speaker repeated his order and he released the bar.

"How good is the security on a test shot like this?" Petrov asked. "The Americans—would they be able to monitor and analyze the results?"

The scientist withdrew a folder from the safe and thumbed through it, found the relevant passage and then replaced the folder.

"The security, of course, is excellent. All personnel are politically cleared by your organization. Security clearances are reviewed annually . . ."

"I know all of that."

". . . but we were instructed to make no special attempt to treat the testing in any but a normal manner, so that special security procedures would not call attention to the weapon. As far as American surveillance goes, they'd be able to know we tested, and determine the rough yield in megatons. Seismic detection and satellite reconnaissance. But exact fallout signatures on an underground shot?" He scratched at his lip. "Virtually impossible in my estimation."

47

"How about the Chinese?" Petrov said.

Striganov inhaled slowly and then exhaled, somewhat aggravated. "These things are your province, Colonel Petrov. KGB seldom tells us the results of their intelligence summaries. I suggest that you check with Special Service II, Sixth Department. They handle those things."

"Don't try to be clever, Striganov. I wouldn't be here today if I was some KGB *dezhurnaya*. I've read the reports. I want your own personal assessment."

Striganov raised his eyebrows fractionally. "I don't know," he said. "The Transbaikal region has a great many Orientals. It would be impossible to determine whether there was any infiltration."

"What of Orientals in your group?"

"We have seven. All have been with the group for five years or more."

"Which tells us nothing," Petrov said almost to himself.

A light blinked above the door and an older matron pushed it open as Striganov pressed the release. She served the coffee and tea, deposited a plate of toast, and wheeled her trolley back out through the door.

Petrov poured cream into the dark coffee and stirred it. "I'll have some additional security checks run," he said between sips from the cup. "And I'll reiterate that this project is covered under Security Level Nine Category. I want your files to be forwarded to Center once they're complete. All other records are to be shredded. I don't want one single reference to be retained. Understood?"

Yuri Striganov nodded. "That's agreeable with me. I want orders to that effect in writing, however." He glared at Petrov, challenging him.

"Absolutely brilliant!" Petrov snapped back. "You demand a permanent written record ordering the disposition of records which are not to exist!" He paused, looking at Striganov. "Furthermore," he went on, "weapon number two is to be readied for shipment. You have the specifications for the wooden packing case. Have it readied for shipment by air in two days. Containerize it in a metal shipping canister and ensure that there are no marks except the number two stenciled on the lid. Weapon number three is to remain here."

"I still need written orders, Colonel." Striganov was balking, using his position as a shield. "You think I can simply hand you a nuclear weapon on your verbal orders? We have our procedures . . ."

Petrov withdrew a thin leather case from the inside pocket of his jacket and laid it open on Striganov's desk. "Here are my orders and authorizations. My fingerprints have been scanned by your security people."

Striganov opened and read the orders.

CENTRAL COMMITTEE TO GROPSYNC SECURITY LEVEL NINE STOP BEARER THESE ORDERS COMMA IDENTIFIED COLONEL ANATOLI ANTONOVICH PETROV COMMA TO CONTROL MOVEMENTS OF UNITS TWO AND THREE BUILT ZHIGNASK BY GROUP SEVENTEEN STOP UNQUALIFIED REPEAT UNQUALIFIED COOPERATION REQUIRED BY EVERY AGENCY PRESENTED THESE ORDERS STOP FOR CONFIRMATION OF AUTHORITY TELEPRINT KGB/VICTOR IN TACTICAL CODE DELTA COMMA QUOTE SALMACIS UNQUOTE STOP AUTHENTICATION REPLY IS QUOTE PORT ARTHUR UNQUOTE STOP SIGNATURE FIRST SECRETARY STOP END MESSAGE

Striganov studied the documents carefully, folded them, and returned them to Petrov's side of the desk.

"I begin to understand the importance of your mission, Colonel. Excuse me." He took a deep swallow of the Georgian tea and set the cup to one side. Withdrawing a directory from his desk safe, he thumbed through the pages, finally noting the teleprinter index number of KBG, Section Victor. The room temperature, regulated to 20 degrees Celsius, suddenly seemed very warm. Striganov walked to the telex and awkwardly punched in the coded address and waited. In twenty-two seconds, the answer-back code appeared. He then coded the word *Salmacis* through the enciphering unit and pressed the TRANSMIT GROUP key. The machine chattered softly and then was quiet. He could hear Petrov pacing along the back of the office, impatient.

Approximately one minute elapsed and then the machine came to life, indexing the roll of paper through two lines then printing in clear black type the words PORT ARTHUR.

Chapter 4

The dawn of April 14th brushed the west ridge of the Mad River Valley with grays and reds, which slowly turned to pinks. The first sunlight refracted through the crystals of the last spring snow and illuminated the crest in brilliant white. Rock outcroppings on the ridge were a contrast in gray, their contours softened by the blur of a new snowfall.

Spruces on the valley's walls were overloaded with mounded snow and branches drooped to the point of fracture. With each fresh breath of wind, the snow fell from the branches in muffled thumps.

Lower in the valley, the freshly fallen snow melted,

forming rivulets to feed the roaring waters of the Mad River on the valley floor. Meadows and cornfields showed the first green and cows moved from their barns toward the rocky fields. A tractor fired irregularly and then settled into a steady beat, exhaust rising in the morning light. It would be a day of not-still-winter, not-yet-spring.

On the eastern side of the valley, north of the Common Road and beyond Applewood Farm, a single dirt lane led up into the tree line. Despite the night's snowfall, the road was a mush of rich brown mud. Just at the tree line, an ancient Jaguar XK-120M with mud-spattered sides was parked beneath a grove of young maples. Beyond this, set back into the spruce, was a partially completed A-Frame of indifferent design, still in the shade of the east wall of the valley. The roof was covered only with black tar paper and the spruce siding was unpainted except for dapples of different shades of brown stain, which represented the builder's half-hearted attempts to decide on the shade of finish.

A tan Land Rover with dented fenders was parked close under the overhang of the projecting balcony. Packages of shingles were stacked haphazardly in the vehicle along with partially opened kegs of rusting nails.

A silver-gray Siberian husky loped from around the back of the house, slowed beside a pile of firewood, and sniffed. Rejecting it, he selected a stack of fresh building lumber to urinate on. The husky stood there in the morning shadows, leg lifted, breath steaming, and tongue lolling in obvious satisfaction. Finished, he scrambled up the rock stairs to the front door and nudged against the sill with his nose. No one was there to open it for him and he lay down, whining softly.

The interior of the house was silent, except for the occasional hissing of embers in the carefully banked wood stove. The bedroom still lay in the subdued grays of early morning. Clothes ranging from a blue blazer to muddy Levi's lay about the shag-carpeted floor. A smaller pair of jeans, a t-shirt embossed with a faded profile of Daffy Duck, and a down parka lay folded on the dresser. A leaking faucet from the adjoining bathroom tapped its steady, muffled beat.

The bed was a shapeless lump of twisted comforters and indistinct forms. A swatch of long blond hair flowed across a pillow, face hidden beneath the covers.

"Uhmmmmm," sighed the woman as she stretched her full length. Her hand appeared above the blanket, testing the temperature and withdrew.

The bed underwent a rearrangement of shapes and was still for many minutes. Then another arm, scarred from the elbow to the wrist with burn tissue, projected up from beneath the covers, flexed at the elbow, rotated at the wrist and exposed the dial of a Rolex. The owner's eyes peered out between the comforter and pillow that covered his head.

"Crap," he muttered and withdrew the arm back to warmth.

"Uhmmmmm," she sighed.

The husky waited by the door for another hour, breath rising in small clouds, the morning sun melting snow from his silver fur.

Loss had started building the chalet two years ago. With rudimentary skills and plans torn from a Sunday supplement, he had bought a few materials and started. Using only hand tools, he recognized that the slow, clumsy work was a kind of therapy, but he tried not to analyze it too closely. It took him three weeks to dig the foundation and four to hand mix and pour the foundation. At the end of each day he took the four-wheel drive down to the river and swam, sometimes lying in the shallows, barely covered by the tepid water, and watched the clouds form and dissipate above him. He kept to himself, cooking his meals on a propane stove, and read each night until the light was gone. And he wondered often whether he would see her again.

Like too many of his generation, Brian Loss had *served* in Southeast Asia. *Served* was a word the press had used in the beginning of the war. Three presidents and fifty thousand lives later, the press substituted words such as *fought, survived,* or *died.* A UPI man had once asked Loss's copilot how it felt to *serve* in Vietnam? Lt. Barber, who was a beefy-faced kid from Arkansas with a fully developed taste for girls in the Paradise Bar and a strong desire to survive, replied, "Like on a platter, asshole!"

Barber and Loss flew a twenty-four-year-old gunship. Mostly, they flew over dun-colored tracts of scrubby hills or endlessly canopied jungle. Collins, the cannon gunner, hosed steel into an enemy they rarely saw, whose position was marked only by smoke rockets. For all three of the men, the war was terrifying and boring. A firm bowel movement and a cancelled mission had the same joyful significance.

The gunship was an aging C-47 transport, modified to accept the cannon and painted dull black, carrying patches from three wars. The cockpit stank from the sweat of generations of men, some of whom had humped cargo in India—others who evacuated marines from Inchon.

But their signatures were all there in the logs, faded with time and moisture, the pages spotted with tropic mold. *Kramer, Buckholtz, McClue, Epstein.* Hundreds of names. Barber had once carefully peeled away the paint on the instrument panel with his penknife, counting the layers. He lost track at sixteen.

But Barber was dead now. The gunship was melted scrap and all that Loss had to show for three years of fear and dysentery was scar tissue on one arm, an honorable discharge, and an ingrained distrust of anyone who made speeches.

He mustered out in 1974 with a 10 percent disability;

barely enough to buy a bottle of Scotch every third day. The psychiatrists at the VA hospital in Van Nuys showed him colored cards, talked about his non-existent sex life, and wrote in standard phrases that his adjustment to civilian life was progressing satisfactorily. By 1976 Loss was buying a bottle a day, living on welfare and odd jobs, and pissing in his bed at night when the dream came.

With small variations the dream was always the same. He was in the left seat, Barber in the right. Except that Barber didn't help much but just sat there, groaning, his hands clasped over the bright arterial red that stained his flight suit. Once Barber giggled, pointing to a tube of intestine which projected from the wound. "I got another wang," he yelled over the scream of the wind rushing through the shattered cockpit.

Loss couldn't raise Collins on the intercom. The gooney bird was no more than a loose collection of parts flying in formation, vibrations from the right engine transmitted through the entire airframe. The controls were mush. Loss used full deflection on the yoke to pick up the right wing which periodically would tuck down, buffeting heavily.

The hydraulic fire was out but he knew that he would have no brakes and no flaps. The gear didn't matter. Approach control said that the left main was down and the right main was gone. His left glove had burned through and the flight suit was charred. It had been Barber, good bad-ass Barber, who had snuffed it out with foam. Just before the second rocket had hit them.

He nursed it around into a long final. The radio was now dead but he saw a green flare lift into the twilight and burst into a drooping blossom of emerald.

He had something over ninety knots but there was a sick feeling to the bird—a settling of metal beneath him that he could not correct. He added power on both engines, the right one backfiring. More left rudder. The right engine shrieked to a stop, the prop shaft shearing. Left foot to the floor. He had time to cut the switches and watch the ground rise up and grab him from the sky. In the last second he lost control of his bladder.

Kitzner eventually saved him. At least partially.

Loss had taken to hanging out in a singles bar in Marina Del Rey. Pretzels free on the bar after five and happy hour until seven. He made bland passes at the women who floated by, their hair streaked by the sun, faces tan, California girls from Detroit and Dallas, Wichita and Winston-Salem. Some stopped and talked: about sharing an experience, est, and meaningful relationships. Once or twice they produced keys and asked him home. He tried it once and was impotent. The girl, a psychology major with hard little breasts, cried for him and gave him the card of a shrink in Laurel Canyon. Loss drove his fist through her stained-glass wall hanging, kicked her cat, and changed bars.

He met Kitzner in a little Santa Monica restaurant called The Galley, a cobwebbed collection of rooms with bare floors and walls swamped in photos of the past great. Loss hustled locals on the bumper-pool table and bought steamers with winnings. On really good nights he could buy the twenty-four-ounce steak, which he rationed out over the next three days from a grease-stained doggy bag.

He was just finishing up a man in red Dak slacks, a blue button-down, and nautical-flag belt. Loss leaned against the wall, his cue held like a rifle at port arms and finished the beer. The man missed his shot and flipped a five-dollar bill on the table, not waiting for Loss to sink the final easy ball.

"You on?" The onlooker was in his late forties or early fifties. Solid, compact, porous skin with dark, coarse hair. He laid a quarter on the edge of the table.

Loss nodded and pushed it in the slot, shoving the lever home. The balls dropped from their compartment and rolled noisily within the guts of the table. Loss racked them up and then turned to the man. "Five bucks on the game?"

The man nodded and stuck out a hand. "Kitzner," he said.

Loss, at first, had worn long-sleeved shirts, buttoned at the cuff to hide the scar tissue. But in the last year he found that he didn't care. People avoided looking at the puckered skin, as if it was a California tan gone bad. He gripped Kitzner's hand.

Kitzner broke and then cleaned all but two balls from the table. His arm was like a piston, driving smoothly in the stroke. The deflections and control of the cue ball had a practiced precision. He looked at Loss, his mouth set. "All yours, sport."

Loss caught up, pushing away the bleary well-feeling that four beers had given him. He miscued on the last critical shot and Kitzner closed the game in two quick strokes. Loss passed him the bill that he had colled from Dak slacks.

"Nam?" Kitzner asked, racking his cue. He nodded toward Loss's arm.

"No, cooking weenies at a barbecue."

Kitzner watched him steadily. "Where was the cookout?"

"A place called Quang Tri."

"I've been there."

Loss raised his eyebrows. "Quartermaster Corps?" It was a cheap shot and he knew it, regretting it instantly.

Kitzner made a ducking movement, bending his head down, and then stood upright, his eyes closed. His mouth opened and an eye appeared, moving slowly to the left and then to the right between his lips. He ducked again, spitting the glass eye out, and returned it to the socket. "I do that for smartasses," he said. Moving past Loss, he paused and handed him a card. "I manage a place out in the San Bernardino Valley," he said. "We hire vets only."

He pulled on a windbreaker and then pivoted on one heel, looking back. "Sober vets," he added.

Kitzner's firm made fiberglass trailers. He put Loss on the assembly line, packing layers of fiberglass mat down into a mold and then rollering resin into it, slowly building up laminations. Loss coughed from the irritation of the resin through the day and then lay awake at night itching from the hairs of glass embedded in his skin. But he cut his drinking to three beers a day and then two and then none. Kitzner moved him up into interior assembly and then to supervision.

And as Kitzner had said, they were all vets, most of them Nam dropouts. Kitzner wouldn't hire anyone else. The receptionist was a big, bulky guy by the name of Meeker. It was startling for a plant visitor to find Meeker, a man with the shoulders of a linebacker and arms as thick around as a ship's hawser, delicately tapping away on a typewriter, his white shirt spotless and tie snugged up around his collar. Startling, until Meeker rolled away in his wheelchair, minus both legs.

Within the walls of the plant the men were like children sheltering from a storm, mentally holding hands, gaining strength from each other. Some failed and drifted away but most survived and grew stronger. Among them, Loss.

What little profit Kitzner made went into a large lump of a schooner called *Surprise* which he kept down in the basin. Weekends were open house to any of his employees. Kitzner stocked the galley with thick steaks, salad, and potatoes. He normally served only tomato juice and ginger ale. Drugs allowed on board, by common knowledge, were limited to aspirin and Dramamine.

As with the plant, each man started at the bottom, cleaning bilges, painting the engine, mopping the cabin soles. Those that stuck with it, Kitzner graduated to marlinspike seamanship—a somewhat grand term he used for knot tying and rope splicing. The hard core

that endured became first-rate sail handlers and sea-
men.

They were running back from Catalina with a De-
cember sun hanging, rim down, on the horizon. The
sails, yellowed with age and the pollution of the Los
Angeles basin, had taken on a rose tint. The ship
rolled slightly in the western swell, halyards aloft slatting. Two of the men from Packing were stretched out
on the foredeck, face down, sleeping in the last heat
of the sun. Kitzner sat hunched in the cockpit chewing
on a dead cigar while Loss handled the helm. They
were both burned red from the sun and wind, tired but
content as sailors are, running for home.

"You want some rum, sport?" Kitzner finally said.
Without waiting for a reply, he ducked below and
reappeared with two partially filled glasses, and an
opened coke. "Say when." He started to fill them.

"This the big test, Ed?" Loss said. He flicked his
cigarette away into the wake. "Because if it is, I've
been drinking for the last year."

Kitzner looked up. "How much?"

Loss took the glass from him and sipped. "Swilling
it down," he said, placing the glass in a rack on the
binnacle and putting the helm down a spoke to counter
the swell. "Sometimes a whole bottle of booze in a
month."

Kitzner looked up, smiling. "You win, no one
loses."

"I think you had something to do with it," Loss
said. "I've never said thanks."

Kitzner turned away, avoiding the subject. A large
white tanker was headed southwest toward the sun.
"Outward bound," Kitzner said. They both watched
the ship, trailing a thin finger of smoke, move down
toward the horizon. Reflected sunlight flashed off the
glass of the bridge. They both watched until the curvature of the earth swallowed all but the superstructure.

"With the Canal closed, she'll have to sail eight

thousand miles around the Cape to reach the East Coast. Crude from Alaska. You'd think they could get it there faster by mailing it in milk cartons." Loss rested a leg against the lee coaming of the cockpit, bringing the schooner up a point. "But it has a nice sound to it," he added.

"What does? Crude . . . ?"

"Outward bound." Loss laughed. "Just flop this old gal over on the other tack and head for Tonga."

"You're enough of a sailor now to do it," Kitzner replied. "Give me five more years of stuffing goo in molds and we'll do it together." He sounded dejected. "But you're ready. There's not a bolt on *Surprise* that you don't know. Or for that matter, a job in the plant you can't handle." Kitzner took a swallow and then slopped the rest of his drink into the sea. He lit the remains of the cigar, sucking in heavily and then looked up at Loss. "What would you do next?" he asked. "After this job?"

The lights of Long Beach flickered on. Loss picked up the wink of the outer buoy and altered course slightly. The question had surprised him a little. "Not sure," he said finally. "An aunt in Vermont left me some land there. I guess I'd take a look—maybe build a cabin. It'd be nice to have a place to hang my hat."

"What about a job?"

"Fly maybe. I don't get the dream anymore. I'm beginning to miss beating up the sky."

Kitzner let out a long sigh and looked down, prodding at a seam in the deck with his thumbnail. "Just remember that sail we're going to make to the South Pacific, Loss. In five years." He stood up and stretched, and then walked forward to start getting the jib down.

Loss found a severance notice on his desk on Monday morning, along with a check for two thousand dollars. A small slip of paper with Kitzner's handwriting simply said, *You're ready!* Meeker told Loss that Kitzner was out of town. The door behind him was closed; Kitzner's voice muffled but recognizable, arguing with a resin supplier about pricing.

Meeker stuck his hand out and they shook. "It's Kitzner's way of doing things, Loss. You just graduated."

They lay together in the darkness of predawn, each slowly retreating from sleep, aware of each other but not moving or wanting to wake the other. Finally he murmured and turned toward her, fitting his body to hers, his chin resting on the back of her neck, his knees fitting against her calves. She made a small sound and he felt her pushing back, her buttocks to his groin. Her body was warmer and the cadence of her breathing mismatched his.

He tried to edge back into sleep, wanting those few more minutes. But he was awake now. The window framed grays, growing lighter, and he heard the husky whine.

"Awake?" she asked, voice muffled in the pillow.

The nape of her neck smelled like fresh bread. He pulled her more closely to him.

"No," he answered. "So don't hold me responsible for what's about to happen."

Later, bodies interlocked, they drifted back into sleep.

With a feeling of release unknown to him since he had quit college, Loss packed his things, paid a few remaining bills, and turned his Land Rover north on Route 101 for the Canadian border. What few possessions he owned were stacked in the back of the Rover and the balance of his savings account and Kitzner's two thousand were in his pocket. He drove north through heavy traffic, singing Beethoven's *Ode to Joy*, knowing nothing of the words but bellowing the melody and thumping his fist on the dash in accompaniment.

He drove for eighteen hours the first day, swinging east into the Sierras and then north through the desert. Exhausted, he pulled to the side of the road and wrapped the sleeping bag around himself. Four hours later, with birds pecking on the garbage at the roadside and the dawn washed with orange citrus, he started north again. Tomorrow or the next day was something he didn't want to examine. Not yet, at least. But for the present he ached to see bare silent snowfields and the white reaches of the Canadian Rockies. There was enough money to ski for a month and the future, like the past, had no meaning. When the orchards started to bud in the Fraser Canyon, he would turn east for Vermont.

In two days he had crossed the Nevada desert, spanned the Salmon River country, and climbed up through the Bitterroot Range of Montana. Toward sundown, just south of Anaconda, he saw her and the dog by the side of the road. She wore jeans and a puffy down jacket with a tasseled ski cap pulled low, nearly touching her eyebrows, A backpack on a frame rested in the snow beside her. He hesitated, down-shifting as he passed and then braked. In his rearview mirror, he saw the two of them running toward him.

"Where you headed?" he asked as she and the dog scrambled in. Her pack and the dog divided the back seat into two blurred lumps of darkness.

"Alaska, I think." She pulled off the ski cap, her hair tumbling down over her shoulders. Her forehead was peeling from sunburn and her eyes, too widely spaced for any classical standard of beauty, met his.

He hesitated for a moment before dropping the Rover into gear. Her mouth was a little wide, her nose overly long. Well-formed, her cheekbones accented blue-green eyes. Topaz, he thought. The shade of Indian jewelry. Classical or not, she was stunning.

"OK?" she asked. The corners of her mouth hesitated in an uncertain smile. Her hand was on the door release.

Embarrassed, he smiled and switched off the interior light. "OK," he answered.

They floated along in the gathering darkness, the road a black track of asphalt, walled on each side by aspens and plowed banks of tired snow. She sat there in the glow of the dash lights, humming softly. The dog moved forward and rested his muzzle on the back edge of her seat and panted, his tongue lolling. He was a husky and she called him Total.

"How come the name?" It sounded to him like a brand of breakfast food or something you rolled into your armpits.

"He was hit by a car when he was just a few weeks old." She reached back and gently scruffed the dog's ear. "They thought he was totaled—all blood and broken bones, a real mess. His owner was going to put him down and I just carried him away and took him to a vet student friend. We made it." She turned and buried her face in the dog's fur. The dog responded, growling with pleasure.

They stopped south of Missoula for dinner. They both had enchiladas and split the bill. Finished, he leaned back in the booth and drank the bitter, reheated coffee, watching her chew each bite endlessly.

"Sixteen times," she said without looking up, poking a piece of meat back into the enchilada with her finger. "It's supposed to be good for your digestion. But they taste like cardboard, don't they?"

After dinner they pushed north again. It was beginning to snow heavily and the big flakes flowed smoothly back through the tunnel of light that the headlamps carved out of the darkness. The temperature had fallen and the snow was dry, not sticking to the highway.

"Where I come from, they call snow like this stuff goose feathers," she said. "Premier stuff for powder skiing." Where she came from was Utah. She talked about her life, openly. That she had worked as a night clerk in one of the inns at Snowbird and then skied during the day. But it had worn thin—synthetic architecture and flat-landers on package tours cruising the bars. And the beautiful people. She wanted to see Alaska in the spring. Someone by the name of Donny worked on the crab boats up in Anchorage and she would be with him for a while. "I don't know where I'm going," she finally added. He guessed it was a statement about emotions and not geography.

"What do they call you in Utah?" he asked.

"Holly," she answered.

"Is there a last name that goes with it?"

As if it was her only possession and she was unwilling to give it up, she answered "Utah. Just Holly from Utah."

He smiled, letting it drop.

The three of them drifted up into the mountains of British Columbia for three days and then turned west toward the coast. He told her a little of his past. The war and then Kitzner. Mainly about Kitzner. Talking about it made him relaxed, free; the past gone and almost trivial. But he couldn't bring himself to tell her that he had not been with a woman in four years. Even touched one. A dark part of his mind suggested that he should hope for nothing, ask for less.

The nights were spent in economy motel rooms. She would unpack a few things from her backpack, unselfconsciously strip off her clothing and slide between the sheets. He did the same, feeling both the sharp edges of fear and arousal; an equation that equaled nothing.

As if they were children camping together, she would take hold of his hand, squeezing it tightly, and then turn away, falling into untroubled sleep. Unthreatened, he accepted the situation for what it was: two people traveling together, finding economy in sharing.

Until the third morning, when he awoke with frost glazing the window into an opaque tracery. Her hand held his over her breast. He lay still, feigning sleep, feeling the confident, steady beat of her heart, and felt a stirring within him.

That morning they shared a stack of sourdough pancakes and laughed together when, like conspirators, they asked for more and stuffed the surplus in his jacket pockets for the dog.

In the parking lot, she unexpectedly took his face between her hands and kissed him on the nose. As they pulled out onto the highway, the dog moved up between them, sitting on the driveshaft tunnel, eating bites she tore off from the pancakes. But even after he was finished eating, the dog remained between them, staring at the road ahead, as if he had sensed a subtle shift in alliances.

The sky had cleared after the night's snowfall and was the startling blue of high altitude. Range after range of the Canadian Rockies unfolded to the west, peaks mounded in white. High on the summits, snow streamed off in dazzling banners, backlit by the sun in a halo of color.

She finally told him that her last name was Stone. Holly Stone, just like her great-grandmother who had ridden boundaries until she was seventy. She described Cedar City, Utah, where she was born and still had a father living. And the fragile and yet stark beauty of the high desert and its Mormon people She said that she was twenty-eight or twenty-nine but had forgotten which. "On the low side of the dirty-thirties," she said, laughing.

He asked her how long she had skied at Snowbird.

"About three years." She vaguely waved her hand across the horizon. "And before that, I was a woman architect in an architectural firm run by sixty-year-old men. They let me draw sewer-line layouts and ink in straight lines." Pausing for a few seconds, she glanced to the side, watching cattle huddle against the wind, and then turned back. "There was a marriage that didn't work out. It all piled up and I just had to get away. Snowbird was all right for the time being. But I think it's better now." She pressed a gloved hand over her heart.

The Rover snaked down through the coastal ranges

and into Fraser Canyon, skirting the eastern fringes of Vancouver. He turned north along Howe Sound for Garibaldi Provincial Park.

They rented a single-room cabin behind the grocery store at the base of Whistler Mountain and she said that she would stay as long as she shared in the rent and food. That evening she made spaghetti and they drank two bottles of a Napa Valley red. The dog finished the remains of the spaghetti, eating noisily and rattling the scorched pot across the flagstone floor.

They sat together in front of the hearth and finished the last of the wine. She watched him in the firelight and traced the broken ridge of his nose with her fingertips. "How did that happen?" she asked.

"An airplane stopped and I didn't." He finally told her everything: how it had happened, Barber, and the dream sequence.

"Does it still bother you—the dream?"

He shook his head. "It's gone now. Finished."

She pulled a pillow from the couch and placed it on the floor, then drew him down next to her. They watched the fire dying, embers going to dark orange heat.

Loss lay still for a very long time, his head resting on her breasts, wanting her very badly and yet afraid. And then, thinking of the past, he realized that the events carried in his memory were tragedies that had happened to another man, someone he had outgrown and could now put behind him.

She raised her arms over her head as if surrendering. The fabric of her sweater was stretched taut, the bottom fringe baring her stomach. Her face was turned to one side, eyes closed and skin flushed from the heat of the fire.

Hesitation gone, he gently peeled the sweater over her head and then unsnapped her jeans. Smiling, she took him into her and then, without pain or guilt, he lost himself and then found himself in the soft hills and valleys of Utah.

For three days they skied the face of Whistler

Mountain, dropping down through the powder-snow-filled bowls, falling and laughing and breathless. And each night they went home to the little cottage to eat and fondle the laughing husky and to make love before the bed of dying embers. Once he started to tell her that he loved her and she turned away from him, crying.

In the early afternoon of the fourth day, they sat under an outcropping of rocks in the Western Bowl, eating a lunch of cheese and Canadian wine and sourdough bread and looking out along the curvature of the earth. The visibility was clear and the sky cloudless. Out beyond the Coastal Mountains he thought he could see the Strait of Georgia and a blue haze beyond that—the Pacific.

She cut a slice of cheddar for him. "It's clean up here, isn't it?" she said.

Loss just continued to stare out at the west and slid his arm around her waist. "Clean isn't the word for it. Maybe one of the last great places God made." He turned and grinned at her, his sun-blackened face contrasting with the white band from the sunglasses.

"You look like a raccoon," she said.

He kissed her nose and cheeks. She kissed him back and then rested her face against his.

Then she drew back and took off her sunglasses. She had the small beginning of tears. "You're OK, Loss," she said, standing up and brushing the snow from her jeans. "Be careful."

She kicked into her binding, shuffled off the ledge, and fell away in long sweeping turns through the fresh powder.

He watched her until she disappeared into the tree line, and then he could see her again along the brow of the East Ridge, skiing very fast but carving out turns of perfect symmetry. Her blue parka finally disappeared in the distance.

I'll have to get used to that, he thought, but her changeable moods and independence were part of her whole personality, and it seemed to fit together. He gathered the wine bottle and the bits of lunch, loaded them into his knapsack, and sat back again to light a cigarette.

Looking south toward Vancouver, he caught a long thin contrail of a jet climbing toward the sun. And he thought again of the beauty of high altitude flight and realized that he had missed it. He laughed out loud, remembering how it was at the beginning, when he was first learning to fly. There was no beauty to it then, just the unrelenting terror of failure to pass his flight checks, of the first solo, of the ancient captain who sat in the back seat of the two-place trainer, shouting into the intercom. The first fourteen hours of instruction had been a bath in hell, and Loss's performance had been totally mechanical and unfeeling.

On a July steamer of a morning, Captain Slokum and Loss had done three circuits of the pattern and landed. Slokum was grumbling into the intercom about keeping proper airspeed control on final. He directed Loss to taxi off the active runway. Slokum got out of his cockpit and came forward on the wing. The big Continental ticked over, and Loss could barely hear his instructions.

Slokum blew his nose and then leaned down on the canopy sill and shouted into Loss's ear, "You're so bad I doubt that you will ever make it through this program. Your only hope is to get this *thing* safely into the air and go find some uncluttered sky. Maybe this thing can teach you something about aviating that I surely can't." He thumped Loss on the shoulder, briefly grinned, reminding Loss of a horse baring its teeth. Slokum jumped off the wing and walked away without looking back.

Teeth gritting, Loss spun the T-34 through a 180-degree turn, savagely braking short of the active. He asked for and received takeoff clearance.

The cleaning up of flaps, retraction of gear, the adjustment of power settings and rpm were automatic blurs. Although he knew that Slokum expected him to shoot touch-and-go landings, Loss cleared the control area of the field and headed east. He climbed for the base of the growing cumulus clouds, which grazed like obedient sheep along the edge of the Texas gulf coast. Passing through eight thousand feet, he felt the cockpit cooling to a clean crispness. Leveling off at nine thousand feet, he headed for a towering cumulus that bulged with turrets and ramparts and convoluted towers. He eased in power and banked sharply, scraping the cloud-fabric with his wing; then he reversed direction in a chandelle and tore down in a dive with the engine screaming at redline, smoking through the canyons of the clouds. His mind merely said, "Go there," and the plane obeyed. For two hours he played with the aircraft, alternately bathed in sweat or chilled. He and the T-34 explored the corners of the envelope of flight, from stalls at low power settings to cheek-sagging, high-speed turns. He snap-rolled the trainer, working from his memory and ended up inverted. Shouting at the top of his lungs with the mike button unconsciously depressed, he rolled the aircraft upright. He knew that the sky was his, at least on loan.

Back in the tower, Slokum heard the joyful laughter on the receiver and knew it for what it was.

Loss looked again at the contrail, now dissipating to a blurred chalk mark in the blue horizon. I guess it's time to climb back into a cockpit, he thought.

He reached the cabin by sundown. The fire was lit and a pie sat cooling on the top of the oven. Her things were gone, of course. He read the note she had left on the pine table. It simply read, "We'll come back. Love from Total and me." There was no signature. He smiled and wished her well.

The alarm howled, dragging Loss up from the lower levels of consciousness. He peeled back the top of the down bag and squinted at the face of the clock. Ten of seven. The bedroom was frigid, nearly at freezing. He thought for a moment of shutting the thing off but it was beyond his reach. He pulled the bag over his head, listening to the mechanism run down, willing it to die.

The bedroom door was closed, but he could hear the husky prancing excitedly over the maple floors of the living room, down the passage, sniffing, and then trotting back to the slate kitchen floor. And he could smell coffee brewing.

Consolidating his will, he counted to ten, leaped from the bed, and raced for the bathroom. He flicked on the steam timer and dove back for the bed, shivering uncontrollably before his body heat regenerated some warmth beneath the down-filled cover. Holly's side of the bed was covered with her own bag, opened to its full width and zip-mated to his own. The cold seam of the brass zipper had been covered with tape, which seemed to be the maximum effort that either of them had made toward any permanence in their relationship. Loss sighed and looked at his Rolex, adding ten minutes for steam to fill the bathroom with heat.

Welsh's call had come at five P.M. yesterday, ordering the Aztec to pick up the senator and his wife at Albany the following morning, two days ahead of schedule. Loss had scrambled to get the local aircraft mechanic to finish off the hundred-hour inspection, working with him in the chill April night until 1 A.M. to finish the maintenance. After that he had washed the aircraft, knowing that Welsh would want it spotless for the press who would be bound to cover his departure. He had finally arrived back at the A-Frame by two, soaked through with cold and fatigue.

Loss checked his watch, decided to give the steam five more minutes, and drifted back into lethargic semi-wakefulness.

Her voice carried well, singing something about a cowboy down in Colorado that rides the ro-de-o. A pot crashed to the slate floor and she swore, then resumed singing. He smiled, guessing at the oath. Her favorite obscenity was "bullroar."

She had come back from Alaska in the late spring, six months after they had met in Montana. Donny on the crab boats was not mentioned, and Loss didn't press her for the details. With her help, they finished the framing of the house in less than a week. Her practical knowledge of building was limited, but she was a good architect and she improved the design, fitting in small, attractive details. The greenhouse encasing the kitchen's outer wall had been her idea, and Loss had suffered through a long progression of green, tasteless tubers and bean sprouts for salad. He finally told her that it was diminishing his sex drive and she gave up in disgust, switching to flowers.

During that summer, Loss had answered a blind ad for a corporate pilot and was eventually hired by Welsh, leaving Holly to do much of the finish work. On his return from each trip Loss found something had been changed from the plans. The brick fireplace idea was scrapped and Holly had substituted a Defiant wood stove. A sunken tile tub was sacrificed for a steam bath, and almost overnight stained-glass windows ringed the dining area. Loss saw the bills and winced, feeling that the first house he had ever actually owned was being transformed into a counterculture doll house. She took it calmly, sticking out her lower lip imperceptibly, and called the changes "organic." From there on in, he let her have her way.

They had been more or less together for two years now. The house was still unfinished. She worked in spurts of enthusiasm, interspersed with backpacking trips. Characteristically, she would announce one morning that she would be gone for a while, then kiss him and leave with the dog bounding ahead into the countryside. Once, she had gone to hike along the Maine coast with friends and he didn't see her for two months, receiving only mildly pornographic postcards from Italy to mark her existence. Loss couldn't bring himself to ask who she traveled with.

70

But it was getting better. He thought of it as a consolidation phase. Marriage was a subject closed to discussion, but the ties were becoming more binding. Her trips were less frequent and she used the word *us* more often. She talked of making a trip to Mexico together, and of hiking the length of the Appalachian Long Trail. Loss secretly bought a pair of hiking boots at a slick mountaineering shop in Westchester and began to break them in.

And the job with Welsh was ideal. Loss didn't like or dislike Welsh. It was a paycheck without too much commitment. When the senator wanted him to go somewhere, Loss made the trip regardless of time or day of the week. But when the aircraft wasn't in use, Loss flew back to the valley to be with Holly and drive nails in the incompleted flooring. In Loss's mind, it was an eminently workable arrangement.

But this trip was a little different. Welsh wanted to take a trip to some resort in the lower Caribbean. With the fuel shortage it would have been better for him to go by airline, but Welsh was like that—the fearless politician image. He normally would arrange a few stops so as to be present at some conference and then make voluminous reports on his return. In this way the vacation, if it became public knowledge, was secondary to his information-gathering role as a senator, and much of the expense was written off as necessary travel. This time it was to be a solar energy convention in Florida where he would give an address on the return leg of the trip.

In all, Loss would be gone for two weeks. The thought that she might not be here when he came back bothered him, but he knew he would not press her for a commitment.

Glancing once again at his watch, he sighed and jumped from oeneath the covers. Running to the steaming bathroom, he stubbed his toe, swearing loudly. She must have heard for she appeared a few minutes later, holding a large mug of coffee.

"Looks like you're in the tropics already," she said,

waving the steam from her face and handing him the mug. He stuck out his tongue and she retaliated with a rude finger gesture. Closing the glass door behind her, she called out above the noise of the steam generator that some eggs awaited his pleasure when he was ready.

In ten minutes he sat down beside her. She rose, took eggs from the oven and set the plate down before him on the rough pine table. Pouring another cup of coffee for Loss, she fixed a cup of tea for herself and sat down beside him.

He pointed at the eggs encased in a shell of something which reminded him of roofing gravel and prodded them gingerly with his fork. "What do you call these?"

"Scotch eggs. The shell is soybean sausage. Tons of protein." The husky sat behind her on the slate tiles, drooling. Sunlight poured through the stained glass, giving her hair the tint of tangerine.

The eggs were overcooked but she was irresistible. She had pulled her hair back in a loose bun and tied a red bandanna over her head, peasant style. Her lips showed just a thin gloss of chapstick and, characteristically, she smelled of soap. Washing was almost a fetish with her, he thought, chewing on the yolk. She collected brands of soap the way some women collected figurines. The more exotic and unattainable, the better. I'll miss her like hell if she ever leaves me, he thought.

Loss had swallowed the remains of the two egrs and she stood up and dished out two more, spooning sour cream on them and then sprinkling them with chives.

"My own variation," she said. "I didn't think you'd go for it on the first course. What do you think?"

"Ummm," he answered. Actually, they were better.

"Where is this place you're taking the great senator?"

"Salt Whistle Cay. It's a little hundred-acre rock in the Grenadines. About ninety miles west of Barbados." He finished off the eggs and leaned back, lighting a cigarette.

"How soon do you have to leave?" She looked at a wall clock over the refrigerator.

"By eight-fifteen I guess. That will give me forty-five minutes to file, do the preflight, and get off. I want to be in Albany by ten." He leaned back, stretching. "Do you mind dropping me off at the airport in that junk heap of yours." The Jag was a new acquisition of hers that she had driven back following her last trip. She had found it in a barn in North Carolina. The mice had gnawed through the leather upholstery but she claimed that it would still top 120. Loss doubted her until she showed him the two speeding tickets.

"Yup. I already put all our stuff in the boot. Your flight case is in the mud room. I stuck in the new Jeppesen approach plates that came last Monday. There was some new stuff on the airport in San Juan as well. Extending the runway, I think."

He raised his eyebrows. By some genetic trick, his eyebrows seemed to be linked to his ears and they flattened back, just as his father's had always done. The serious effect was ruined. "I didn't know you knew how to do that. I'll put you on the payroll." He took a final puff on the cigarette and snuffed it out. "I hate filing revisions. It's like taking the same medicine every day and not getting better."

"I'm not just a beautiful face." She laughed. "I read, I write, I do sums on my fingers if it doesn't exceed ten—other things as well."

"Other things especially well," he said, kissing her neck. Her shirt was unbuttoned at the top and her breasts formed soft mounds under the fabric. I've known her for seven hundred days now, he thought, and she can still excite me with just a word or a touch. "We better get going," he finally said.

"Oh," she said, pushing the newspaper toward him. "Did you see what your favorite boss said, supposedly off the record?"

The local paper carried a small clipping about a

73

speech Senator Clifford Welsh had made at Utica College in late March. The article reported that he had been there to dedicate a new wing of the School of Business and had made an oblique reference in his dedication speech to diverting funds from the military into the quest of what he termed "The Economics of Peace." The reporter, in an interview after the ceremony, had asked the senator to elaborate and Welsh had hedged, saying that U.S. withdrawal from the scenes of potential world conflict would be an inducement for other nations to do so as well. "Unilateral disarmament?" the reporter had prompted. But Welsh would only comment that such proposals were always under study and then terminated the interview. Response to the speech had been mixed but generally negative.

Loss pushed the paper away without finishing the article. "Sometimes I think that man has rocks for brains. His father was supposed to be sharp as a whip, but the only thing Welsh inherited seems to be his money. I wouldn't vote for him if he was running for selectman."

"That's not all of it," she replied. "Notice that the speech was over three weeks ago. The article says that the *Washington Post* heard something about it and questioned the reporter who is just a local upstate New York stringer. The reporter finally admitted that he quoted Welsh correctly but that he was asked not to print it. Seems as if Welsh's political manager— some guy named DeSilva—asked the reporter to bury the interview. So the story is just surfacing now."

"Yeah. Well, if Welsh pushes that through, we're going to start building a bomb shelter."

Her face clouded. "I thought you'd be in favor of it. Because of the Vietnam thing."

He stood up and took the dirty plate to the sink and rinsed it. "Nam," he said, "was a political ego trip. It was senseless and a lot of guys paid for political harangues with their lives." He dropped the plate in the drying rack. "But defense is something else. The

Russians want something more than just a few soggy acres in Southeast Asia." He gave her a slack smile. "Not that it matters a hell of a lot. I can't see Welsh pushing something like that through Washington."

He pulled on his sheepskin jacket and stood impatiently by the rolltop desk in the hall while she got ready. Absently, he thumbed through yesterday's mail and messages, noticing a note, scrawled in green felt-tip pen on the back of an advertising circular. The words read "$3,800 for Rover—will call back or see you at airport."

"Hey, Holly. What's this note?" he called toward the bedroom. She came down the hallway, flouncing her hair from beneath the collar of her jacket.

"Oh, Brian. I forgot to tell you. This guy from Plattsburg called last night. Said that he heard you had a Land Rover for sale. Hinted he would pay up to thirty-eight hundred subject to inspection. He was going to call you back this morning or see you up at the airport. Said he had business there anyway."

Total pranced around the door, alternately looking out at the yard and then back at his mistress.

"Funny," Loss said, almost to himself. "I haven't let anyone know that I'd sell it. Thirty-eight hundred is close to a thousand more than it's worth." He paused, looking at her. "You sure you heard him correctly?"

She shrugged and opened the door. "I had him repeat it twice. I guess he's just hot for a Land Rover. Great White Bwana syndrome. Probably wears safari suits."

They walked out into the clean crispness of the April morning, the smell of spruce intense. The earth was greening where the snow had melted.

He glanced toward the Rover, wishing that the salt smears and mud of the winter didn't make it look so shabby. Suits me, he thought. If he wants the Rover he can have it. With that much money, he could make a deposit on a GM van. Something suitable for a long camping trip in Mexico.

In ten minutes she had made the drive to the airport, slewing occasionally in four-wheel slides through the spring mud. Loss directed her to take the Jaguar directly to the hangar so they could load the luggage. The manager, John Malcomb, was just refastening an engine cowl as they swung into the hangar.

"The rest of the birds flew south earlier, Brian," he yelled.

"Wish I could take you along, John. How's the port engine running up now?" Last night they had found a two-hundred-rpm drop on the left magneto. Worrisome, but not critical.

"I replaced the harness and it checks out fine. The insulation was getting old on the high tension leads around number three and four cylinders." Malcomb stood back, rocking on his heels and then absentmindedly wiped his hands on his Levi's. "I'll get your bill ready and call Flight Service." He took a last look at the gold-and-white Piper Aztec and started for the office, then turned back. "By the way, there's some guy named Sommers waiting for you in the office. Been here since eight o'clock."

"Tell him I'll be down," Loss called after him. He turned to help Holly loading the luggage. Her blue nylon seabag lay on the asphalt among his flight bags.

"What's your bag doing here?" He smiled, puzzled.

"Going to visit a friend. Can you give me a ride as far as Albany? I'll catch a commercial flight from there."

It took him by surprise. She hadn't mentioned anything about being gone. "What about Total?"

She set a tight smile on her face, as she usually did when confronted. "Do I have to stick out my thumb to get a ride? John Malcomb and his wife are taking care of Total. What's the answer?"

He shrugged. "Yes—no, I mean sure you can come down to Albany with me. It was just a surprise."

She nodded, turning back to load the remaining luggage.

He walked to the operations building through the remains of corn snow, avoiding the muddy areas and patches of fragile new grass. He felt pleased about her coming down with him. This was the first time they had ever flown together. And with the arrangements for the dog, he knew that she would be back. The day seemed to be sunnier, despite the low stratus that hung in scattered patches over fhe valley. It would be clean on top.

A tall thin man in his late fifties smiled at Loss as he pushed open the office door. He wore a lumberman's jacket and his hair was speckled with gray.

"Good morning, Captain Loss. I'm Mark Sommers of Sommers Electronics over in Plattsburg." The man extended a blue-veined hand.

Loss shook the hand with his own left because of the flight bag he carried. "Yes, good morning. I'm sorry but I really am in a rush. I have to leave for Albany."

Malcomb peered out from his cubbyhole and waved a paper. "I'll have your bill in a second. Flight Service reports that you'll have three thousand scattered all the way to Albany. Winds two ninety at fifteen knots. Nice weather." He ducked down behind the partition and Loss could hear an old mechanical adding machine ratcheting.

"Yes, Captain Loss," Sommers interjected. "I'm sorry that I couldn't get here sooner. It's not easy to get over here with the fuel shortage and the demands of business. But I'm glad I caught you. I wanted to buy a Land Rover. I understand yours is for sale."

Loss cringed at the title "Captain." It was like calling a guy who drives a sixteen-foot boat "Skipper." He felt uneasy with the man.

"Look, Mr. Sommers. The Rover really isn't worth that much. Maybe to me, but not on the blue book price. The engine's good but the body's in need of some work."

Sommers nodded. "I'm aware of the retail value.

77

But Rovers aren't easy to find. It's for my son and me. We hunt a great deal. His heart's set on having a Rover." Sommers lifted his shoulders as if to comment that his son was crazy. "I'd like to take a look at it. If it runs well, I'll make you a more-than-generous offer. Better than you could get elsewhere."

Loss nodded. "Fair enough. When I get back in two weeks I'll drive it over. Let your son see it as well. Maybe we can come to an arrangement."

A look of indecision crossed Sommers's face. "I don't know whether that would be satisfactory, Captain. There's a Rover advertised up in Montreal. It's difficult—all the paperwork with importing a car. But we want to make up our minds soon." He hesitated, looking out across the field. "Perhaps . . ."

"Perhaps what?"

Sommers shuffled his feet and then looked directly at Loss. "Perhaps you could leave the keys with me. I can check it out today while I'm here. If I like it, I'll cable you an offer immediately. If you accept, I'll give Mr. Malcomb here the agreed upon price and drive it home. We can settle the paperwork when you return."

"I can't give you a forwarding address, Mr. Sommers. I fly the plane for my boss. He doesn't like to give the information out."

Sommers looked genuinely disappointed. "Surely that doesn't matter. I'm quite serious about purchasing your Rover. I assure you that . . ." His voice trailed off and he shrugged.

It was ten after nine. Loss had to get going. He thought for a second. "OK. It's not that important. I'll be there by tomorrow afternoon. If you want it, make a firm offer by cable. I'll reply and the cable will be your authority to take possession. John here will take your check and verify it with the bank." He scrawled a cable address in Sommers's notebook and extended his hand. "It's a deal," he said.

Sommers smiled and nodded his agreement. "It's

a pleasure, Captain Loss." The two men shook hands.

The twin-engined turbosupercharged Aztec F fired on the left engine, missed and caught again, throwing blue exhaust as it picked up revs, and then settled down into the smooth, assured idle of a well-maintained engine. Sparrows pecking at the newly seeded grass beside the hangar took to startled flight. Patches of corn snow exposed to the prop blast scattered at buckshot velocity downwind of the aircraft. The right engine turned stubbornly at first, then fired and held evenly. Loss taxied from the parking spot on the ramp toward the taxiway. The pucks on the disc brakes squealed lightly as the aircraft turned downwind on the runway and taxied to the takeoff position.

The first traces of April buds hazed the maples near the end of the runway in a suggestion of green. Where there wasn't snow, there was new grass. And the birds were returning.

The Aztec pivoted on the end of the runway and turned through 180 degrees in the narrow space of the runup pad and aligned on the centerline. The flaps were lowered to their limits and returned to the tailing position. The props were cycled between the fine pitch of takeoff and the coarse pitch they would assume for efficient cruising speeds. There was a small frame of time when the aircraft sat, seeming reluctant to commit itself to the air. The wind was quiet; the shadows of clouds moved across the fields.

Then both engines rose in pitch and the aircraft, pinioned by the brakes, crouched down on its nose gear, waiting to leap. The turbos spooled up, and with brakes released, the Aztec rolled. From the cockpit, the movement of the centerline stripes progressed from individual movement of each stripe to a blur, to a solid line, and then with liftoff, the line fell away.

The landing gear hesitated and then tucked up into the aircraft belly, and the Aztec climbed through the thin stratus and into the raw spring sun of early-morning New England.

Loss settled the airspeed into best rate of climb, trimmed out the control pressures, and slowly eased back the rpm. The not-white, not-green valley fell away to the ragged ridge of the Green Mountains. And then the ridges melted into the snowscape and the horizon spanned the White Mountains to the east and the Adirondacks to the west; the blur of Montreal to the north and the haze of the Hudson Valley to the south.

He leveled the aircraft at 10,500 feet, slowly eased back the power and rpms, retrimmed and cut in the autopilot.

"Now I understand why you do this." Holly sat relaxed in the right seat, scanning out over the nose and alternately pressing her face against the right seat window, looking down.

The pentagonal starform of Fort Ticonderoga lay in the neck of Lake Champlain to her right, two miles below. And to the immediate south, the valleys of Vermont and New York spilled out onto the plains of Schenectady.

Holly reached into the aft seat and retrieved a thermos of coffee. From her purse she withdrew a plastic glass and filled it. "Why don't you ever talk about this? It's beautiful." She looked down suddenly, stretching over the instrument panel to watch a flight of Canadian geese vectoring north less than a thousand feet below them.

"It's not always like this," he replied. "Sometimes it's boring and sometimes it's just hard work. But you're right. It's times like this that make it worthwhile." He turned and smiled at her and raised the coffee cup in salute.

"Will you teach me then, Brian?" She hesitated. "I mean, in a little airplane. Not this. It's too big." She stumbled for words and smiled helplessly.

"Yes. OK. I will but you have to start in sailplanes. That's where it all started and probably that's where it will probably come back to. Difficult to explain so we'll save it for when we get back. But it's a promise. For when we both return."

She digested his words in silence, sipping coffee and pouring him more from the flask.

"Where do you go from Albany?" he asked, keeping his voice level and disinterested. He pulled back the power slightly and retrimmed.

He thought that he had spoken too softly or that she hadn't heard but eventually she answered. "It's a place called Carriacou. It's not too developed, but it's nice."

To Brian, the name sounded almost familiar. Venezuela or maybe in Scotland. He thought and couldn't place it.

She slid her left hand up behind his neck and rubbed his muscles. "I have a friend who is staying near there and I want to see him."

Loss called Albany Approach Control and was fitted into the sequence of aircraft approaching from the north. The farmlands slipped beneath the wings, much greener and more cultivated than those to the north. They flashed over a river and both could see the smudged outlines of Albany.

"Brian, you're a stubborn bastard. Damned if you're going to ask me where Carriacou is." She looked straight ahead and leaned over the instrument panel, watching the countryside slide beneath the Aztec, her face set, cheek muscles hard.

He sighed. "Look, Holly. We don't have much time left. Things are going to get busy in about two minutes and when we land, I've got to let you off and get the aircraft ready for Welsh. But, yes, if it pleases you, I *am* interested in where this place is. You live your life the way you want to and I have to accept that as part of being with you." He paused and pulled back the power, adjusted the revs, and spoke to Albany Approach Control. Then he turned briefly toward her and then looked forward against the glare of the sun.

"Try to understand this," he said. "I asked Welsh

if I could take you along and he flatly said no. I wish I could have, but I can't. All I can say is that I wish you could be with me. OK, so where is this Carriacou?"

He eased down flaps and switched to tower frequency. She turned in her seat and watched him manipulate the controls, delicately feeding in power, adjusting pitch, willing the aircraft to follow some perfect path.

"Carriacou," she said, "is just as far as you want to make it." Then she faced forward to watch the runway grow larger in the windshield.

Chapter 5

Mark Sommers stood in the cloud-dappled sunshine, staring south long after the Aztec evaporated into the distance. Without wanting to analyze it too closely, he felt uneasy about knowing Welsh's destination. By itself, it had no meaning. A scrap of information. But placed in the mosaic of some larger pattern, it would have context, take on significance . . . He turned his mind away from speculation.

The sound of the engines was gone and Sommers could only hear the hum of a light wind moving through bare branches, flexing them occasionally in an irregular tattoo. Snow melting formed shallow pools of water, the wind teasing the surface into irregular patterns. Sommers felt very old and somehow fragile.

Malcomb thumped out of the building, banging the door, whistling something from a pop opera, hands in the pockets of his denim jacket.

"Sounds like you've bought yourself a Rover, Mr. Sommers." Malcomb passed him and walked over to the aviation gas pump, noted the gallonage and printed a figure on his palm with a ballpoint pen.

Sommers stamped absently at the granular snow beneath his boot. "Perhaps. I've got to inspect it first."

Malcomb nodded. "I know the bus. Loss keeps the engine in first-class condition. Helped him do a valve job on it last fall. A little work and the body would be like new." He looked again at the gas pump and booted it without enthusiasm. "Hardly get fuel anymore. The Aztec has an allocation card and some of the rest of these owners do as well," he said, waving toward the few aircraft tied down, "because they have class-two business authorizations. But the rest of these bastards get enough to fly about three hours a month. Great for business."

"Captain Loss told you about the arrangement? If I find the Rover suitable, I'll make an offer by cable."

Malcomb pushed his cap back on his head and then grinned, his teeth perfect. "He cables back an acceptance and I take your check." He extended a gloved hand. "Just drop back and let me know. My wife's in the back office. She'll tell you how to find Loss's place." Malcomb turned and walked toward the hangar, stopping occasionally to stomp down mounded frost heaves. The wind carried the tune he whistled very clearly and Sommers watched him until he was gone from sight.

Sommers was finished inspecting the Land Rover in twenty minutes. It was a sham, now that he knew Welsh's destination, but he went through the motions convincingly, tracking up the snow around the Rover, inspecting the underside of the chassis and running the engine. He drove it out to the road and then back, playing with the four-wheel drive. And his final act was to slam the door in a simulated disgust as if he had found some fatal flaw.

He dropped the keys by the airport office. Malcomb wasn't there, which Sommers was grateful for. He left a note with Malcomb's wife saying that there was a whine in the power train, and then left for Plattsburg in his VW. Turning west onto the interstate, he took two pills from his breast pocket and placed them under his tongue. This part, at least, was over, he thought.

The trip to the ferry crossing of Lake Champlain took more than an hour. Traffic was thin but Sommers held the VW to just over forty. His chest felt constricted and, despite the rawness of the April morning, he kept the window rolled down. Two state police cars passed him slowly and his heart beat with labored agony each time.

The ferry was late, forcing him to wait in line. His fingers felt numb but his neck and arms were soaked with perspiration. He tried to subvert the anxiety of delay but it was difficult. *Salyut XII* was due in eighty-three minutes.

By 5:39 Eastern Standard Time, Sommers had tuned up the VHF transceiver in the basement of his home. He had translated the location of Salt Whistle Cay into latitude and longitude and then enciphered it into four-digit groups. Rechecking his watch and the schedule, he waited nervously, listening to the receiver.

At 5:44 *Salyut XII* crossed from darkness to sunlight over the Canadian Maritime Provinces, streaking west-southwest. Within the eight-ton satellite, sensors and cameras were already probing the North American defenses, translating images and infrared data through analog computers, storing the information on magnetic disks for later transmission.

At 5:47 incoming telemetry data were received from a fleet of twenty-eight Soviet-bloc fishing vessels in the Atlantic, giving temperatures of the water over the Continental Shelf, surface wind direction and velocity, locations and levels of thermoclines beyond the hundred-fathom line, and placement of U.S. naval units along the Atlantic seaboard.

The inertial navigation accelerometers computed the path of the *Salyut* 480 times per second, programing frequency schedules for transmission, reception, and data correlation. Like a globe turning beneath the hand of a schoolmaster, a continent flowed by.

Magdalen Island, Prince Edward Island, New Brunswick.

At 5:49 the satellite transmitted coded messages on 17.155 kilohertz, directing Red Banner Fleet Submarine Z-689 to return to Severodvisk near Archangel for retrofit of SS-N-8 missiles and to Soviet Attack Submarine RZ-122, congratulating the navigation officer on the birth of a 3.9 kilo son.

Maine, New Hampshire, Vermont, New York.

At 5:53:30 *Salyut XII* oriented a parabolic antenna toward northern New York State and transmitted a seven-dot grouping on 144:217 megahertz. And then waited.

Sommers heard the identifier and quickly transmitted his code groups three separate times within the span of forty seconds and then listened carefully. The seven-dot groups came back clearly, followed by a retransmission of his own groups. As he listened, the frequency shifted and faded as the satellite orbited southwest into Pennsylvania and beyond.

He shut down the transmitter, disconnected it, and replaced the unit on the top shelf of his workbench.

His heartbeat was shallow and rapid but the pain in his chest had subsided. From the floor above him he could hear his wife's footsteps in the kitchen, moving about, preparing dinner.

I will do no more for them, he thought, and then burned the schedules and enciphering sheets, spreading the ashes beneath the workbench. Turning off the desk lamp, he sat in the cellar's darkness for another half hour, listening to his weakened heart pulse against the cage of his chest.

Salyut XII spanned the North American continent in eleven minutes and eighteen seconds, dipped into the Pacific, and then recurved to the north over the

South China Sea. By 6:38 a multichannel microwave link was established between AW-4 and the satellite. Minutes later, the processed and decoded message from Sommers was torn from the teleprinter in the office of the first chief director, Specialized Operations, Western World.

"I read this to be 12 degrees 34.2 minutes North, 61 degrees 19.7 minutes West." The older man pushed his trifocals up over his forehead and looked down at the colonel of the Soviet Long Range Rocket Forces. Petrov was stretched out on the tan leather couch, his tie loosened and eyes fixed on the ceiling. He lifted one boot and used the heel to scratch absently along his other shin.

"Look it up. Central Data will have something on it. I would guess that it's somewhere near the north coast of South America; po sibly Trinidad or in the lower Caribbean." Petrov withdrew a cigarette from his shirt pocket and lit it, propping his head up on the armrest of the couch.

Vasili Rametka, deputy director, Specialized Operations, lowered his eyeglasses again and reread the coordinates. He depressed a bar on the intercom and spoke softly to someone in Central Data whom he called Iosif. Satisfied, Rametka released the bar and sat back in his chair, thoughtfully chewing on the end of his pen. "You consider the devices produced by Striganov and his group to be adequate, Colonel?"

Petrov nodded. "You've seen the reports. I've submitted a recommendation to Chairman Andropov that Striganov be considered for the Order of Lenin. The job was creditable."

Rametka gritted his teeth and slammed the pen to the desk. "Petrov, I want you to understand one thing. My directorate has conceived this operation. The KGB has been assigned to carry out the operational phases but I am directing it. I have personally asked for you to head up the teams based on the merit of your work in Ethiopia and Belgium. You come well recommended, Colonel. I would like to work in harmony, but let us have no doubts about chain of command." Rametka was small, taken to wearing pinstriped suits cut in the fashion of the prewar years. His face had an unhealthy pasty color, the texture of unbaked dough, except for the mouth which resembled a reopened wound. He bent forward over his desk, palms downward, supporting his torso. "Is that *clear?*"

"Very clear," Petrov responded. He sat up, stretching his arms. "Except that we are at the crossover point. Where planning merges into operations. Chairman Andropov has appointed me as *Control*. There's an order to that effect being forwarded to you. Signed by the first secretary." He gave Rametka a conciliatory smile. "Let's say it this way, Doctor. You and your staff are in charge of planning and evaluation. I am in charge of operations. Once I am in the field, you will have only a supportive function." He ground out the cigarette in an ashtray with overly meticulous care—a gesture meant to convey Petrov's own authority to Rametka. He looked up and smiled again. "Let's not resort to resolving this question by taking it to our superiors. It wouldn't look good for your directorate and we don't have the time to squander."

The older man was caught between indecision and anger. He started to speak and then thought better of it, realizing that the plan was well conceived. If it went wrong in the field with Petrov in control, his directorate would bear little responsibility. He returned Petrov's smile, the pouches beneath his eyes gathering into a network of wrinkles.

"Agreed," he said evenly, giving no hint of his reason for capitulation,

The teleprinter bell chimed, and the machine started printing. Line after line of material fed out of the machine on a tongue of pulp paper. Finished printing, the unit indexed through three more lines and fell silent. Both men rose to read the information. Petrov noted

Rametka's breath was sour and his armpits smelled. There would be no future conflict of power, he thought absently.

The file was spare but adequate. It read:

12/580P CENDAT TO SPECOPS AW-4 STOP LOCATION SALT WHISTLE CAY IN CARIBBEAN SEA COMMA WINDWARD ISLANDS GROUP STOP RESORT ISLAND APPROXIMATELY ONE KILOMETER SQUARE COMMA VOLCANIC AND CORAL GEOLOGICAL STOP FORMERLY BRITISH COLONIAL TERRITORY NOW ALIGNED BARBADOS/TRINIDAD BLOC COMMA PRO WESTERN DASH NEUTRAL STOP ISLAND USED SOLELY AS LUXURY RESORT COMMA SEE FILE TAPE 2958889ARG STOP TOPOGRAPHICAL PROFILE AND COSMOS SATELLITE NINE SCANS FOLLOW SOONEST BY FACSIMILE TRANSMISSION STOP COMMUNICATIONS TELEPHONE AND MARINE RADIO TRANSMITTER STOP TRANSPORTATION TO ISLAND ONLY BY SEA WITH LIGHT AIRCRAFT LANDING STRIP ON NEIGHBORING UNION ISLAND STOP STAFF POPULATION APPROXIMATELY FORTY STOP ADDITIONAL DATA BEING FORWARDED BY RESIDENZ COMMA BARBADOS COMMA ON REQUEST FOR SPECIFIC DETAILS STOP SECURITY CLASSIFICATION NONE COMMA CENTRAL DATA TAPE 2203795ARG STOP END MESSAGE

Petrov smiled. "A Caribbean resort island vacation for Senator Welsh. Perfect, I think?" He phrased it as a question.

Vasili Rametka ran his hand over his balding head

and reread the message. Pulling three folders from his safe, he seated himself at his desk and leafed through the separate binders. Finally he pushed them aside.

"Welsh is not ideal, Colonel. Of the three politicians under consideration, he would be my second choice. The most promising subject is still our Ohio congressman. Welsh shows strong psychological profile identity, and a pragmatist at that. He might be very difficult to handle."

Petrov scraped his tongue across the edges of his front teeth. "We've been through that, Rametka. The only way I can work with any of these men is to approach them during their vacation period. I think that it will take a minimum of five intensive days of work with any of them to achieve reasonable control. The Ohio congressman spends his vacation in a religious retreat. It would be an impossible situation." He snorted, making a face. "Can you really picture me as a priest?" Petrov paced across the room and back, rapping his knuckles against Rametka's desk.

"No, Vasili, Welsh will have to do. The area is isolated and it will be simple to meet him as a fellow vacationer. From there on it will be a question of slowly feeding him with visions of power. Doctor Lunt of the Šebsky Institute has prepared an outline as to how I should proceed. He's studied Welsh's entire background and anticipates no significant problems."

Rametka nodded. "True. The situation lends itself to establishing a relationship. But I caution you now that you must proceed slowly. If Welsh seems in the least hostile, it will be necessary for you to withdraw. He must feel that he is making his own decisions." Rametka reamed out the bowl of a clay pipe and loaded it with coarse tobacco. Lighting it, he leaned back and rested his head against the wall. Neither man said anything for many minutes. Rametka decided that he would enter his views in the project folder in case Petrov failed to achieve control. It would absolve his own directorate of responsibility. Finally, he leaned forward and handed the Welsh dossier to Petrov. "Welsh it will be, Colonel Petrov. It's your decision, as you have so clearly pointed out." He puffed on the pipe, letting the smoke rise, only to be fragmented by the air conditioning. "How do you intend to handle it?"

Anatoli Petrov gave the barest trace of a smile. Rametka's transfer of power was complete. He took the folder and dropped it in his briefcase. "Handle it?" he reported. "Quickly, I should think. Welsh has pushed his schedule ahead by two days. It would appear that Sommers nearly didn't get the information on Welsh's destination. I'll fly to Zurich tonight to finalize the financial end of things and then onward tomorrow morning. I'll be using the German woman as a 'wife'; the one I used in The Hague last summer. She's very well trained in psychology. For the rest of it, I will use Heiss for documentation and camera work. Both he and Sommers will be terminated after the Welsh contact is completed."

Rametka raised his eyebrows. "I thought that there was to be no *mokrei dela*." He had used the expression which originated in the Stalin era—a typical Beria saying.

Petrov made a sound of disgust in his throat. This is what comes of dealing with old men who have been around for too long, he thought. "Wet affairs, as you term it, Doctor, belong to the past. The expression sounds messy. Termination means just that. Clean and attributable to accidental causes. Both Heiss and Sommers are links and those links must be broken. It is simply an operational necessity." He paused, picking up a framed photograph from Rametka's desk. It showed a woman sitting with two young children. A disinterested dog lay in the foreground. "Yours?" he questioned.

Vasili nodded. "My wife and children. She's dead now—nine years ago of a tumor."

Petrov nodded, the thought reenforced that old men

were chattels of their past. He thought briefly of Sergei and put the thought firmly aside. He resumed pacing, laying down the final tiles of the mosaic.

"Another thing," he said. "I want the psychological profile and background on Welsh's wife. Her likes and dislikes. Also any information on his pilot—this Brian Loss."

Rametka nodded and spoke into the intercom. There was a short delay and then a muffled reply. "They will have the information in half an hour. Let's go up on the surface. I haven't been out of this place in three days. I've forgotten what the sky looks like."

Both men donned coats, Rametka pulling on a tweed with the enameled pin of the Order of Lenin on its lapel. Petrov shrugged into a dark sage military coat and they left, walking along the carpeted corridors of Level Seven. Signing out through the security station, they rose by elevator to Level Four. Petrov excused himself for a minute and entered the office of KGB Liaison, firmly shutting the door behind him, leaving Rametka in the corridor. Irritated, the Soviet planner waited.

After twenty minutes, Petrov reemerged and took Rametka's elbow, guiding him down to the main bank of elevators. Petrov seemed animated now, relaxed. He spoke to Rametka about small things, the record of the Dynamo soccer team. They rose to Level Two and passed through the final security station. Petrov called the guard by his first name, commenting on his promotion to sergeant. Smiling, the guard snapped to attention as they left.

The two men passed through the sequence of blast doors, slowly climbing the shallow concrete ramp, finally seeing blue sky beyond the last door. Both of them surrendered their interior identification passes to the control desk at the entrance to AW-4, substituting green outside-area passes. They walked into sunlight.

The Urals rose on each side of the valley. There was still snow on the higher elevations. Rametka put

91

on his fur-trimmed hat, the black mink contrasting with his pallid face. He guided Petrov along a wooden walkway to the edge of the ice rink. Three off-duty technicians were skating. One of them, a red-cheeked woman with Kazakhstanian features, was very good, gracefully pivoting in midair and then landing on one skate, back arched, arms spread in icy flight.

"I have always wanted to do that, Anatoli," Rametka said, watching the skaters. "I have two children, both young. It will be good to retire and spend my time with them. It seems an insane thing, but I often sit at my desk, imagining the three of us skating together in Gorki Park, hands together, listening to the music. We have chocolate later and then go to the theater."

Petrov watched the face of the older man, the tributaries of wrinkles forming in the corners of his eyes, running to the rivers of his sagging cheeks. Only the eyes were strong. "I understand, Vasili. There must be a time in all our lives when we get tired of this. Perhaps in a few years we will have won." He stooped and picked up a handful of snow, compressing it tightly in his bare hand, squeezing the moisture from the white granules.

Rametka removed his hat and turned to face the sun, closing his eyes. "It feels good, doesn't it?" he said unnecessarily. "The device. How soon will you ship it?"

"I already have. It's being positioned in Vladivostok in Weapons Depot Number Three, awaiting *my* further orders." Petrov accentuated the word. He dropped the wasted ball of snow to the ground and kicked it with his boot.

Rametka nodded, accepting without protest the implication of command. "And after Welsh? I want final confirmation with our group of psychologists as to their analysis of the recordings between you and Welsh before we finally commit ourselves."

Petrov barely raised the corners of his mouth in a

smile. "Yes, I have thought of that too. I will not have enough time to bring the material back here. I will probably fly from the resort to Mexico and then on to Cuba. I will meet you there with your team. If our timing is satisfactory, I will have time to return to the resort while Welsh is still there, should it be necessary." He patted Rametka carefully on the back as you would do with a fragile grandfather. "It will work out well, Vasili. Your retirement pension and Order of the Soviet Hero are well assured." Petrov said it with a touch of contempt which Rametka failed to notice.

The two men looked south from the valley toward the plains of the Kirgiz Steppe where they would be planting wheat now. Petrov was smiling.

Chapter 6

There is some question about the creation of the Blue Antilles. Geologists have assumed that the chain of islands, arranged like a handful of emeralds strewn on blue velvet, are merely the tips of extinct volcanos thrusting up from the seabed.

But Carib Indian legend relates that God placed his hands side by side on the ocean floor and, thrusting down, formed ridges between his fingers. The eternal sea and timeless trade winds eroded these ridges, leaving gaps as wide as the land remaining.

The Blue Antilles range from Hispaniola and Cuba in the north of the Caribbean Sea to Trinidad in the south and are divided by size into the Greater and Lesser Antilles. Cuba, sweating in the sunlight, Puerto

Rico, cowering beneath eternal clouds, and Hispaniola just wishing to be left alone, are the Greater Antilles.

The Lesser Antilles really start with the Virgins, leap the Anegada Passage to Saint Maarten, and arch south and east to Trinidad. The southern half of this chain is called The Windwards, and the seven islands that grace it are named for saints and sinners, navigators and thieves, all long dead.

At the very bottom of this chain are the two islands of Grenada and St. Vincent and between them, an archipelago of tiny islands, wave-swept reefs, and still lagoons called the Grenadines. One such island, for a reason long forgotten, is named Salt Whistle Cay.

The Aztec eased over into level flight from its climb, leaving St. John's International, Antigua, forty-one miles behind and 12,000 feet below. Loss adjusted manifold pressure, rpms, and mixture, settling the aircraft down into cruise power. Number one VOR receiver was indicating solidly on Guadeloupe and number two was just coming to life on Lamentin in Martinique, 170 miles to the southeast.

Welsh sat beside him in the copilot's position, playing with the time and distance computer. He fidgeted with the ADF radio, trying to pick up a local station and finally snapped off the switch with impatience. Clifford Welsh was never at ease in an aircraft. Loss hated to fly with him, for his presence was one long succession of tapping instrument dials, questions about fuel remaining, times of arrival, and imagined engine noises. And yet, in the media, Clifford Welsh was known as the Flying Senator. He knew the terms, had taken a few lessons, and affected the manner and dress of a pilot. The deep-gray sunglasses, languorous movements, clipped sentences. Someone had forgotten to tell him that that stuff went out at the end of World War II with the fifty-mission crush. But the press gobbled it up.

"How long now?" Welsh asked, adjusting his sunglasses. He looked down at the white-flecked sea below.

Loss retrimmed the aircraft slightly and punched numbers into the computer. "I make it to be about forty-eight minutes to Martinique and one hour forty-six to Union Island. I called Salt Whistle Cay from Antigua with our estimated time of arrival. They should be able to meet us there on time. We're running about five minutes ahead of schedule."

Welsh visibly relaxed. He looked out ahead toward the string of islands lying before them. "What do you think of this, Brian?" he said, waving his hand across the front of the canopy.

Loss leaned against the Plexiglass and looked down at the sea before him. The ocean out to the east was the indigo of deep water, burnished to brass by the western sun and flecked with white by the wind. Before him spread a chain of islands, perpendicular to the steady flow of the trade winds and sea, each island ringed with white surf and mounding up in humps and folds of olive green. From the summit of each mountainous island a stream of cumulus clouds trailed downwind to the west. It was spectacular. "It's very nice, Senator," Loss said, wishing he was over this quiet sea alone, with only the sound of the engines and the rush of wind past the cockpit.

Welsh settled back in his seat, adjusting the sunglasses. "You can forget the Senator, Brian. I appreciate it but we've got two weeks of unwinding. Just make it 'Cliff.'" He adjusted the ribbed polo shirt beneath the camel's hair jacket. "I'd just as soon not have the hotel guests know that I'm a senator. We just want to relax."

Loss nodded, knowing that Welsh would smoothly let the senator-thing drop within the first two hours, probably first to the manager. "Fine, Cliff." Loss turned on the boost pumps and switched from the mains to the auxiliary tanks, watching the fuel pressure gauges for fluctuation.

Welsh had turned in his seat and was looking aft.

95

His wife lay curled sideways across the aft seats, a blanket pulled over her body. Her mouth was slightly agape and she was asleep. Welsh adjusted her blanket and turned back. "Judith's really tuckered out," Welsh said. "Actually, so am I. The reelection thing is coming up in a few more months. Between that and the normal workload, I'll be ready for the zoo by November." He laughed, more of a grunt.

Loss eased in an increment more cabin heat and glanced sideways at his employer. "It looks like you've got the election sewn up. Will you have to do all that much campaigning?" In his peripheral vision, Brian saw Welsh make a small shrugging movement.

"It depends, I guess," Welsh said quietly.

Guadeloupe was passing below the left wing tip. They both watched the verdant, convoluted coastline unfold beneath them into shallow bays and bold peninsulas, spotted with small fishing villages. A large schooner was running free, with sheets eased, down the coast, white wake contrasting with the blue coastal waters.

"Picture-book stuff," Welsh remarked, pointing downward toward the city of Basse-Terre. Then he pointed off to the left, toward the mountains on the southern part of the island.

"La Soufrière. The volcano that erupted in seventy-six." The crater was plainly visible, the center filled with a small yellow lake. Mud-colored mist trailed off downwind from the crater.

Loss nodded and eased the aircraft into a shallow bank to the left, leveling on a more southeasterly heading. Before them now was a broad channel spotted with islands and beyond that, Dominica shrouded in cloud. And beyond that, Martinique and St. Lucia and St. Vincent. Loss was happy that Welsh was relatively relaxed and quiet. The islands were unbelievably beautiful: one long chain of poetry flowing south. He whistled softly between his teeth.

"You like flying, don't you, Brian?" Welsh asked.

"It gets me there. The pay's good. No complaints,"

Loss said, irritated with Welsh. It was like asking a kid with a sweet tooth whether he liked candy.

Welsh nodded wisely, settling back into the seat. "It must be nice to have a profession where you don't have to deal with a bunch of idiots. Between the party bosses, political managers, the goddamn voters—it begins to get to you." Welsh was quiet for several minutes, thinking. "You know, Brian, I checked you out pretty carefully. That is, when you first applied for the job of flying me around."

Loss raised his eyebrows in surprise. "How so?"

"Well, beside the flying part of it, the licenses and total flying hours, I had the FBI check your security clearance, political affiliations, air force records—that sort of thing. The only thing that seemed a little fuzzy was the period that you spent in California. Working on some assembly line producing, ah—what was it?"

"Recreational vehicles," Loss said softly, supplying the answer. The aircraft droned on, Loss sliding back in time. His only letter to Kitzner had come back unopened, stamped with the post office smeared-ink epitaph, "Addressee deceased." He wondered what had become of the vets, the small cinder-block factory, and the *Surprise*. Like the films it made, California had the ability to dissolve from one scene to another, the past neatly faded out. Kitzner's factory probably now made skateboards. Loss realized that Welsh was still talking and he snapped back into the present.

". . . and at first glance the crash you had in Vietnam seemed to rule you out." Welsh laughed, embarrassed. "Of course, you realize that I didn't want someone flying me around who was pranging airplanes into the ground. But we got hold of the accident report and realized that you were pretty well shot up." Welsh smoothed his hair back into place, lifting a few stray strands carefully over his ears. "But how is it that you spent all that time working in a factory. I would have thought the airlines . . ." He let the sentence trail off.

"Rehabilitation," Loss said. "It happened to a lot

97

of guys I knew." He thought again of Kitzner and Meeker, Damian and Kosolick. "It takes some time to readjust."

The Aztec swam through the crystal sea alone. Below, the mountains of Dominica were cast in shade under the building afternoon cumulus. Loss watched the great long swells which rolled in from the Atlantic, patterning the sea into liquid corrugations. The surface was dappled in shadows: elongated silhouettes of the clouds above, all moving steadily to the west as if linked.

Welsh had been dozing, head thrown back and mouth open. Loss could see the parting line of the capped teeth. Welsh's face had an unhealthy texture, accentuated in the harsh afternoon light. Loss suddenly felt a touch of compassion. Welsh looked old, used, strung out, as if he had lost a race not even run. Loss turned away, embarrassed, and switched frequencies on the channel selector. It was just a paycheck, he reminded himself.

The noise must have awakened Welsh. Groggy, he shook his head and yawned. "What time?" he asked, stretching.

"Quarter to four. Another thirty-five minutes."

Welsh rubbed his finger over an imaginary blemish on the cowling. "These things start to fall apart from the day you buy them." Loss grunted general agreement, silently reminding himself that much of the purchase and operating costs were subsidized through tax write-offs. "It's better than swimming," he finally commented, trying to lift Welsh out of his dull mood. "At least nobody shoots at you."

Welsh nodded, giving a reasonable imitation of a smile. "That ever bother you much?" he asked. "Being shot at?"

Loss shook his head. "No—only when they didn't miss."

The senator laughed. "I'll tell my manager that. DeSilva's a realist." Welsh scratched his growth of beard, musing. "You know, I could use that in an after-dinner joke. Something about having eggs thrown at a political speaker." He laughed to himself. "Only when they didn't miss," he repeated.

"How goes the reelection?" Loss regretted asking that question almost immediately; it really wasn't an issue he wanted to get involved with.

"So-so," Welsh replied. "DeSilva thinks I should stick to improving garbage collection schedules for the Big Apple. I'm getting sick of it. The same thing, over and over." He looked sideways at Loss. "You ever think of the arms race, Brian?"

Loss realized it was a loaded question. He tried to sidestep the issue. "Only that I'm glad I'm not a part of it."

"You are," Welsh stated flatly. "You vote for the people that continue it. Your taxes pay for it. Do you ever think what would happen if there was no U.S. military—no NATO?"

In the reflection of the mirror, Loss could see Welsh facing straight ahead but watching him out of the corner of his eye.

"You're talking about disarmament?"

Welsh nodded. "One-way, initially. Unilateral disarmament."

"I think they'd run over us with a steamroller, as quickly as possible. We'd be flattened."

Welsh leaned back and sighed, removing his glasses and then rubbing the bridge of his nose. He fitted the glasses back on and then scowled against the molten afternoon sun. "I don't know, Brian. We can't go on with this idiotic race forever. An accident, some trigger-happy bomber pilot, some psychotic ICBM commander and the whole thing goes up in smoke. Someone has to take the first initiative in disarmament and it should be us."

Loss leaned down and retrieved the newspaper from his flight bag. "And you're planning to do the initiating?"

Welsh read the article and handed it back. "Just

feelers," he said. "DeSilva jumped in and tried to kill it." Welsh paused and tapped one of the fuel gauges, frowning. "He doesn't think the voters will buy that kind of a program." He paused, then said almost wistfully, "But if we could disarm, Brian, it would free up over 300 billion a year for social programs. Think about the changes that could bring about."

Loss thought about it. About New York and make-work programs and federally guaranteed life-styles. "That really would be something," he said, looking at the far southern horizon. "That really would be something."

Welsh laughed, the nervous exclamation of a man who has just learned that the pain in his throat isn't cancer. "Well, we'll see, Brian. I think it could work. The people will want it if it's explained properly."

Which people, Loss wondered.

Twenty-five minutes later, the Aztec squeaked down on the asphalt airstrip at Union Island. They were waved through the small custom's office by a smiling brown-skinned officer and then boarded the diesel fishing boat that was to take them the final four miles.

Loss watched Welsh, his head fitted with an up-turned straw hat, his face thrown back to catch the dying sun, smiling.

Carl Heiss thoughtfully read the coded telegram from Zurich for a third time, and then shredded the paper into vertical strips and flushed them down the toilet in two separate flushes. One small strip remained in the bowl and he disdainfully flushed the bowl for the third time.

He reentered the living room of his small flat and spread the gray lace curtains, looking out over the Straits of Dover at the white-capped sea. He sighed, thrust his hands in the pockets of his terrycloth bath-robe, and smiled. Some days bring unexpected pleasure, he mused.

Scratching absently at a pimple over his right cheek, he dialed a Surrey number.

A female answered. "Mulgraves Film Processing."

"Yes, love, this is Carl Heiss. Is Martin there?"

She answered in a slur of words and the receiver was mute except for a distant conversation. Heiss could hear the background noise of BBC-1 rock music. He waited, without impatience, picking at the pimple and rubbing the back of an ancient cat, which brushed ingratiatingly against his bare leg.

"Martin here," the receiver said, the "A" squashed and the "R" strung out. Heiss kicked the cat absently, its tail and genitals presenting an end view in retreat.

"Martin? Carl speaking." The breath at the other end sucked gently for air. Heiss continued. "Look, Martin, old bag. I've been called away on assignment, some damned travel thing. You know, a layout thing on Caribbean travel. Can you take care of my work while I'm gone?" Heiss paused and listened to the breathing. He thought that some day soon Martin would have a heart attack.

The receiver made protesting noises although no coherent sentence emerged.

Heiss overrode the conversation. "Look, Martin, it can't be helped. This is a good assignment and I'm afraid that you'll just have to bear up. I'll be back in about three weeks." He hung up.

Carl Heiss walked to the full-length mirror inset on the wardrobe door and looked at the lean figure standing in a slouch before him. The blond hair was straight and overly long, even for an Englishman, which he was not. Tufts curled forward over his ears, and he thoughtfully twisted at each in turn, curling them with his fingers. The long, narrow face was bland and without bone structure to diminish the monotony of shallow planes. He pursed his lips and parted them, revealing synthetically perfect teeth, straight and even like rows of dice. His pale-blue eyes were pieces of stained glass.

The cat watched his master from the bedroom doorway sill, swishing his tail in agitated strokes.

Heiss opened his robe to reveal his body to the mirror. The face, which was ordinary, seemed at odds with the strong, graceful frame. A thin hairline scar traversed the right hip to the groin. Heiss was almost hairless. His legs were stark white in contrast to the rest of his tanned body and well roped with muscle.

Above, in the upstairs apartment, he could hear the muffled laughter of a canned TV audience. You could almost pick out the words of the announcer.

With annoyance, Heiss pondered the cat, which now stood rubbing its face and whiskers against the divan leg. He had not time to arrange for its care, and he couldn't leave it to fend for itself in the alleys of Ramsgate. And inevitably it would return to his doorstep.

He reached down and grasped the cat by the scruff of the neck.

"I'm afraid you'll have to go, Peter," he said, brushing the moist pink tissue of the tom's nose with his lips. Peter responded by splaying his feet, frightened. Heiss adjusted his grip on the cat's fur to encompass the neck and squeezed abruptly. The cat's eyes widened to an impossible angle and it convulsed in spasms. Heiss made a snapping motion with his wrist, and the cat hung limp in his hand. He placed it in a paper sack, dropped it in the plastic garbage pail, and washed his hands.

Forty-three hours later, Carl Heiss finished the last of a Beefeater's and tonic and placed his forehead against the cool pane of the double-layered perspex window to watch the sea below. Through a scattered cloud deck more than 30,000 feet below, he saw areas of empty indigo sea and nothing more. The low-humidity, high-altitude flight made the aftertaste of the gin-and-tonic slightly metallic.

"Boring trips, these." The statement, without the

inflection of a question, came from the passenger to his left. Since they had left Heathrow, England, the elderly man next to him had dozed, eaten only a small portion of the in-flight dinner, and consumed two copies of the *Economist*. His accent was public school.

"I suppose," Heiss replied, discouraging a conversation. He made an attempt at a smile and turned toward the window again, touching his forehead to the cool pane.

"Camera boffin, eh?" The voice of the pudgy man inquired, pointing down at the aluminum case between them on the middle seat. "Good hobby. Remember years ago my wife used to play with these things. Had quite a mess of lenses. You know, the usual thing. Cost a fortune. Dead now." The speaker waved his clutched *Economist* for emphasis. He was short, florid with a hawkish face. The thin gray hair was swept straight back covering a bald spot and continued over the back of his head to curl along the nape of his neck. His tie was Royal Thames Y.C. and slightly askew.

Heiss sighed inwardly, wanting to be alone with his thoughts, and he replied unenthusiastically, "Yes. I do enjoy cameras. I sometimes do photojournalism assignments. Nothing much. Just for my enjoyment. Tax thing, you understand."

A stewardess came down the central aisle toward them, giving passengers a cool, synthetic smile. She picked up the plastic glasses with accustomed grace and continued aft toward the economy-class section.

The pudgy man lit a Dunhill, sucking the smoke down and then hacking lightly. "Cigarette?" he inquired, thrusting the pack toward Heiss. "Damned habit. But I can't quit now. About the only thing I enjoy." Heiss lifted his hand in a negative gesture and sat back into the seat, irritated but his face an expressionless mask. The pudgy man leaned back in imitation.

Sunlight and shadows wheeled slowly across the

cabin of the Boeing 747, picking up motes of dust, pinpointed in suspension. The engines, barely noticeable in their constant tone, dropped an octave.

The background tinkle of music stopped and a confident voice said, "Good afternoon, ladies and gentlemen. This is Captain Goodwin speaking. We are presently descending from 34,000 feet and expect to be in Barbados in twenty-three minutes. Surface temperature is 22 degrees Celsius under mostly sunny skies."

The smooth baritone continued, "Please fasten your seat belts and observe the *No Smoking* signs. We hope that you have enjoyed your flight with Euro-Caribbean Airways as much as we have enjoyed having you with us." The Muzak resumed and the seat belt sign winked on.

"Good weather, eh?" the pudgy man intoned. Heiss nodded, uncaring whether the passenger to his right understood or saw his acknowledgment.

They touched down on runway 08 at Grantley Adams International Airport, Barbados, twenty-six minutes later.

Heiss was one of the first of the passengers to Immigration. He passed through without question, giving Barbados as only his overnight stop before traveling onward. The customs officer displayed no interest in his two-suiter but pondered the aluminum case. The dark face searched Heiss's, looking for telltale unease or too cool an expression. He found only flatness and impatience in Heiss's eyes.

"Open this case, please."

Heiss rammed his hand in his pants pocket, searching for the key, his face expressionless. The locks were opened and the lid lifted. The interior was lined with sponge rubber and fitted depressions. A Hasselblad camera wih three lenses, a Minox, and a pocket tape recorder were nested in the recessions.

"These are expensive cameras, suh." The black customs official lowered his hand to a lens but watched Heiss's hands which held the case on either side. He saw no contraction of the muscles in the white tourist's hands.

"These are all personal possessions, Officer. I don't intend to sell them." Heiss paused, looking directly into the dark pupils of the customs officer's eyes. "And be careful with that lens. It cost three hundred quid."

Their eyes met for a second. The dislike was mutual. The sergeant turned from him and beckoned the next in line. Heiss found his armpits wet beneath the cord jacket. He brushed aside a baggage porter and walked out into the incandescent sunlight of Barbados.

The pudgy Englishman turned from the second-floor window of Barbados Airport Security and smiled at the black lieutenant of the Barbados Home Defense Force who sat behind the desk. The lieutenant adjusted his Sam Browne belt and eased back into the chair.

"What do you think?" queried the Englishman, stabbing his cigarette at the set of photographic prints. To no one, he muttered, "Damn bastard, filthy bugger," and paced the office puffing jerkily at the cigarette, finishing it and lighting another from the tip.

The black lieutenant calmly ignored his visitor and listed each item shown in the photograph, cross-indexing to a manual for the weight of each specific object. He applied the results to a pocket calculator. "Well, I make 9.22 kilos. That's according to the manual, yet our Mr. Heiss has a case that weighs 2.3 kilos more. Our telephoto shows only the Hasselblad, three lenses, and the recorder. The case is a common one. It is conceivable that he could have filters under some section of the foam rubber, but not over 100 grams worth. However, Mr. Campbell, it is not the policy of our government to, ah, insert ourselves in your Foreign Office affairs. We are anxious to cooperate if there is an infringement of our laws. Otherwise, it is your affair."

The Englishman thrust a packet of cigarettes at the

black lieutenant. The lieutenant declined. "No, I sometimes think that I'm the only one left in the world foolish enough to smoke these filthy things," he commented, and stood before a portrait of the Queen, looking at the familiar face as if to draw some guidance from it. "No, lieutenant. It is strictly our affair. You're right, of course. I don't think Heiss is up to anything here. We shall find out who he contacts, if anyone. But Heiss showed onward reservations to Aruba. We'll check his flight, you can be sure. But for your own knowledge, there goes," he pointed toward the draped window with his cigarette, "a Section V KGB German who is absolutely top drawer in surveillance, photography, and on two known occasions, political assassination."

The lieutenant looked again at the photographs, two taken from directly overhead the customs counter by a camera with a 600-mm lens. The others were full face and profile, again, taken by telephoto lens. The surface was still damp from processing. He looked up at Campbell, tapping the photos with polished fingernails.

"I suppose that you are something less of a menace to our security, Mr. Campbell?" The question could be taken as a statement. They looked at each other and Campbell shrugged.

The telephone rang once and the lieutenant answered. Campbell paced to the window again and looked out over the flat plains hatched by canebrakes and palm-lined highways. The horizon shimmered in the heat.

The lieutenant hung up and spoke hesitantly. "Heiss left our first cab, took another going in the opposite direction, and left that one on a corner in Bridgetown. We've lost him."

Campbell felt his eyes aching in the glare of sunlight, and the portrait of the Queen offered no inspiration.

Heiss pushed his way past a lottery-ticket seller on Church Street and went down the stone-paved alley.

He glanced back fleetingly and could see no one following. The smells of cooking and urine smothered him. He looked up between buildings and saw the face of a black woman office worker raised toward the open sky. She didn't look down. He pressed into a brick-arched doorway and tried the handle of the door. It was locked and possibly barred. Deeper into the alley, Heiss could see an open garage door. Waiting for several minutes, he stood in the arched doorway, watching the mouth of the alley. No one entered. His watch read 4:23.

Finally, he slowly walked down the alley to the garage and glanced in. It was empty. There were the remains of a washing machine in one corner with the motor assembly exposed and wires splayed from a terminal box. It was rusting badly. The rest of the garage was barren. The rafters overhead were partially covered with plywood and a small stack of scrap lumber.

He looked out of the garage again. There was a small boy at the head of the alley, walking toward the garage, perhaps a hundred meters away. Heiss quickly made a decision. He tossed the bags up onto the rafters and, scrambling on the washing machine, drew himself up in a swinging backhanded vault with the ease of a gymnast. He quickly walked across the rafters to the floored portion and drew his bags onto the platform. He had over forty seconds to spare before the boy scuffed by, kicking a stone.

It was unbelievably hot in the attic of the garage. The platform was partially occupied by three bald tires, thick with dust. The near corner of the door to the garage contained stacks of the *Barbados Advocate, Town and Country,* and journals on rock collecting.

Heiss opened his photographic case and extracted the Hasselblad and a telephoto lens. He disassembled both with a small screwdriver he carried in the case. The Hasselblad yielded the aluminum frame and cartridge clip of a Polish Laskoy seven-millimeter automatic. The telephoto lens offered two choices of slides and barrels. He selected the longer nine-centimeter barrel and fitted it to the frame. From a close-up lens, which he disassembled, he withdrew a baffled silencer. He assembled the weapon in less than ten seconds. Working the action, he chambered one cartridge and eased on the safety. He would wait now.

Heiss was agitated. After fourteeen years now, he was reasonably sure that British Intelligence had no knowledge of his existence. On only two occasions in those fourteen years had he made contact with his control and the result was the simple act of waiting in the parking lot until his designated target had approached a car. Heiss had called to the person in each occasion, asking change for fifty pence and then had fired two hollowpoint bullets at close range with his silenced Laskoy automatic. Always the same. Always effective.

During his residence in England he worked as a free-lance photojournalist for trade magazines and in particular for labor unions. A lot of the material on union leaders, their weaknesses and indiscretions, found its way to the diplomatic pouches of foreign embassies representing countries east of the Oder River. But it was all very discreet.

No, he thought, it had to be pure chance or perhaps imagination or mistaken identity. He reasoned that had there been doubt of his identity or the contents of his camera case, he would have been stopped at customs at Adams International. From a matter of routine, he had switched cabs and only at the last moment had the Austin Princess behind him tried to execute a U turn. He caught the faces of three men, one Asian and two blacks, in the Austin staring at him. One was pounding the back of the seat with his fist in frustration. He had lost them. But the doubt remained.

Heiss dozed most of the afternoon, lying in the stupefying heat, his clothes saturated with grime and sweat. At 6:42 a small truck or car entered the garage, and moments later the overhead door was drawn down and locked from the outside. Heiss listened to the footsteps receding up the alley.

He decided that it would not be safe to move around in the garage until 11:00 P.M. The meeting with Control was not until 9:00 A.M. tomorrow. The wait would be a pain in the ass.

Heiss removed his suit coat and shirt and used them to wipe the dust and grime from the platform underneath him. He stifled sneezing repeatedly until finally he fashioned his undershirt into a crude mask against the dust. After this he discarded his remaining clothes and lay back to rest and let the sweat on his body evaporate.

The evening had lowered the outside temperature and the roof overhead was growing cool to the touch. Heiss lay there, feeling his body with strong fingers, relaxing and slowly regaining confidence. Turning aside, he opened the two-suiter and withdrew a flask of vodka, which he used to cleanse his body, using the undershirt as a washcloth. Cooler now, he lay back and waited until his body dried.

He heard a truck or auto drive slowly down the alley and tensed, but it drove by without apparent decrease in speed and did not return. His watch read 7:55. Three hours to wait.

The one small windowpane in the peak of the garage, long ago broken, admitted only the dankness of the tropic night and distant street noises. Heiss sighed, and groped for the thin plastic tube that rested in the false telephoto lens. Carefully, he unscrewed the cap in the dark and tapped the tube gently into his cupped palm, using his lighter to determine the amount. He recapped the tube and replaced it in the lens and extinguished the lighter. Raising his palm to his nostrils, he inhaled sharply and felt the warm rush of cocaine. Lying back, he waited for release.

Chapter 7

Carl Heiss awoke, chilled and stiff. His watch read 4:18. Hunger gnawed at his stomach and he was reluctant to get up. But for 10,000 quid one could endure all kinds of things, he thought.

He crawled to the edge of the platform and looked down into the darkness. He could sense, rather than see, the vehicle parked below. Flicking his lighter, Heiss saw the outlines of a small blue van one meter directly beneath him. He dropped lightly down to the roof of the van and then vaulted to the floor. Listening now, he could hear no sound, even from the distant street. The front seats of the van were empty except for the sports section of the *Barbados Advocate* and an empty cigarette pack. With the weak interior light on, he found an assortment of tools, canisters of freon, and an elaborate set of pressure gauges in the rear of the van. The owner was obviously in refrigeration repair. Heiss's eye caught the glint of a bottle, partially wrapped in an oil-stained towel, and he withdrew it to find the remains of a fifth of white run. Smelling it carefully first, he took a swallow. The raw liquor blossomed in his throat and hit his stomach with the impact of acid. He gagged and spit out the remainder, but he was fully awake now. Laughing to himself, he returned to the rear of the van. He could imagine the headlines. *Master Spy Caught Nude in Barbados Garage* . . . then in smaller print . . . *Denies Spying Whilst Intoxicated*. Heiss felt good now, vital.

Leaving the dim interior light on, he retrieved his

two-suiter and camera case from the loft and returned to the interior of the van. Using shaving cream and cologne to lubricate his skin, he shaved carefully, nicking his chin lightly. Then, using cotton, he packed his lower jaw gum line, giving his bland face the appearance of fullness and age. From a plastic container he removed tinted contact lenses and slipped them in changing the cold blue to hazel. The hair would have to wait.

He dressed in a fresh pair of hopsack trousers and a lightweight blue blazer, leaving the nylon shirt open at the neck. From the camera case, he removed the bottom padding of foam and peeled it open along an almost invisible seam. He withdrew a Dutch passport, identity cards, credit cards, and odd bills, which he exchanged for the contents of his wallet. On the most recent entry in the counterfeit passport was stamped an entry for Barbados. With careful practice he entered a date of two weeks ago and the signature of the immigration officer, which he copied from his Carl Heiss passport.

He appraised his mirror's image with the passport photo of one Pieter Bolken. Except for his real blond hair not matching the gray of the Bolken identity, he was ready to face any casual inspection. The image was one of a middle-aged Dutch businessman, not wealthy, not poor. For the time being he would wear a faded tan cap to cover his hair. It didn't match the tone of his outfit, but it might be the exact thing a man, unaccustomed to a tropic sun, would wear to protect a balding head.

At first, Heiss was reluctant to leave the luggage behind in the loft, but he reasoned that carrying luggage would make him too identifiable. With reluctance, he returned the cases to the loft but retained the weapon, which he stuffed in his inside blazer pocket. It created no more bulge than a heavy wallet.

By now it was almost six and the owner of the van would soon pick up the truck for his day's work. Heiss

111

carefully examined the floor around him and the truck for any trace of his night's presence. Satisfied, he returned to the loft.

At 6:48 the owner opened the garage door, started the van, and left. And at 8:00 A.M. Heiss, now Pieter Bolken, dropped gracefully to the floor of the garage and strode with complete assurance out into the deserted alley and headed for the central taxi stand on Bridge Street.

One hour and ten minutes later Heiss slowly walked along a palm-shaded avenue, holding a large bag of groceries, for all appearances a white resident of Barbados on his way home after a morning's shopping. The luxurious apartment building across the street had only four units set back discreetly from the street. The upper unit displayed a Red Cross sticker in the left-hand window; the meeting was now confirmed. Heiss looked both ways down the residential lane and crossed over, then walked down the hibiscus-edged path and climbed the stairs to Apartment 2. He pressed the bell for seven seconds by his sweep second hand, waited three seconds, and repeated the seven-second ring.

The door opened inward almost immediately, held from behind. Heiss entered. He made no sudden movements but placed the groceries on a low, ceramic-topped table to his right. Carefully removing his jacket but without turning to view his host he said, "I am Carl Heiss."

The Laskoy was gently removed from behind his waistband where he had transferred it prior to obtaining the groceries. A woman's voice behind said, "Yes, we have been expecting you. Please take a seat. I will serve you coffee. The bathroom is directly back at the end of the hallway to the right."

Heiss walked to the sofa and sat down and looked back at the woman. She was a medium-tall blonde in her early thirties, thin and with fine bone structure. Her long straight nose spoiled prettiness but added character and complemented the high cheekbones.

112

"You will call me Lousje. He will be with you in a minute." She turned away, Heiss watching her economical movements as she walked to the kitchen.

He sat for a few minutes, absorbing the atmosphere of the room—a large space, appointed in cane furniture and batik wall hangings. The terrazzo floor was carpeted in handwoven grass mats. Beyond the sliding glass doors on the ocean side of the room Heiss could see blue stretches of the Caribbean Sea, hard and bright in the reflected sunlight. In all, it was luxurious, expensive, and totally lacking any hint of the owner's character. As if it had been designed by a color-coordinated computer.

Lousje returned with a tray. Setting it down on the coffee table, she poured him a cup of coffee, and then set a small pitcher of milk and a bowl of sugar next to it. "Local sugar," she said, indicating the grainy brown texture. "It's amusing that nations once fought for it, as they do now for oil." She formed a polite smile, like something you would give a sales clerk.

"Hello, Heiss."

Heiss rose to shake hands. "You're Petrov?"

The two men touched hands. Heiss noticed that his own was damp. They sat back down on opposite sides of the table, Petrov unfolding comfortably, Heiss feeling awkward in comparison. Petrov was wearing a light cord suit and a knitted cotton shirt. The usual alligator appeared to have been swallowed by a pelican.

Petrov appeared to have already acquired some trace of a tan but Heiss noticed that there were dark smudges under his eyes.

"Call me Robert Klist from here on in," Petrov said. He carefully examined Heiss, as if he was memorizing each pore. "How is London?"

"Ramsgate," Heiss corrected. "I don't get up to London often."

Petrov nodded as if he had known. "Let's see your passport."

Heiss handed it over, then watched as Petrov held

113

it up to the light, felt the texture of the cover and leafed through the pages, examining visa entries. "Very good," he finally commented. "Pieter Bolken . . ." He looked at Heiss and then at the passport photograph and then back again, comparing the man and his image. "Very good. You'll take care of the hair, of course, before leaving." Petrov swung one leg up over the arm of the woven cane chair. "Bringing the automatic in was stupid."

"I thought it might be useful."

"I thought *you* might be useful," Petrov said carefully. "I'm beginning to doubt it." He withdrew a photo from his jacket pocket and skidded it across the table to Heiss. "Was this the man?"

A grainy, overexposed photograph of the Englishman had caught his profile, casting him in bas-relief against a darker surface in the background. The blur of what looked like a face obscured the bottom right-hand corner.

"Shot from a car in Portillo Road. Not very good," Petrov added.

"That was the man," Heiss admitted.

Petrov nodded and retrieved the photo. "Your Martin Hughs-Scott of—what's the firm . . . ?" He snapped his fingers softly.

"Mulgraves Film Processing."

"Correct—has taken to selling M15 little bits of information. Exactly what, we don't know, but as this bears out . . ." he fluttered the photograph between his fingers, "he's told them that you were on the move. How much more did he know?" Petrov had turned to watch Heiss face on. Heiss felt uncomfortable and tried to hold eye contact.

"Nothing. I told him I was off on a photojournalistic assignment to the West Indies. Nothing beyond that."

"How about your onward ticketing?"

"I held tickets to Aruba and then return to London via Caracas, all in the name of Heiss. Who is he?" Heiss gestured toward the film.

"Ian Campbell. Political Division, M15. Hughs-Scott must have known about some of your previous activities and they put a tracer on you." He pocketed the photo. "Campbell is a relatively low-scale field-man. It's bothersome, but I doubt critical. If they had anything, you would have been held instead of followed. Besides," he added, "Barbados is independent, as is the rest of the Caribbean. So Campbell will have to work alone."

"How did you get the information on Campbell so quickly?"

"We have a friendly consulate here. One with communications facilities. That part of it is not your business. This man is." Petrov tossed Heiss another photograph. It was a glossy blowup of a newspaper clipping, showing a handsome man standing before a battery of microphones, his hands clasped together in a self-congratulatory victory gesture.

The three of them ate a late breakfast. Unobtrusively, Heiss attempted to watch the woman as she economically forked food into her mouth. She wore a print sundress with the bodice lapped in a V. Hard points stressed the material on either side where her nipples thrust against the material. Heiss couldn't take his eyes off of her. He tried to imagine the color and shape of the auroras. Wide, he guessed, in a dark, bruised purple. Occasionally a strand of hair would fall over her forehead as she leaned over. She looked Scandinavian he decided.

Heiss carefully moved the toe of his shoe to touch hers. She turned to him, a smile forming on her lips. And then brought her spiked heel down, putting an effort into it that distorted her face. "You're a pig, Heiss," she said, adding that he was regularly capable of suckling from his own appendage, all hissed in low-German *zunftsprache*.

"Charming," Petrov said, finishing off a last slice of mango. He patted his mouth with a napkin and regarded both of them for a moment. Her face was

115

flushed; Heiss's set in a dangerous smile, his eyes bright. "I can do this without either one of you," Petrov finally commented. "Except that I don't think either of you would enjoy the consequences."

"She started . . ." Heiss objected.

"NOTHING." Petrov saluted, swinging the flat of his hand across Heiss's face, using the heel of the palm to snap the jawbone. In the last instant, he flattened the fingers, softening the impact. Heiss staggered backwards, tripping over the rug, then falling.

Petrov stood over him, flexing his hand and then inspecting the fingers. He looked down and then placed his shoe carefully on Heiss's genitals. "Say the word, Heiss. In view of your background, a little squashing might improve your disposition." Petrov gradually applied pressure.

Heiss frantically groped at Petrov's foot, trying to dislodge it. The Russian rocked forward, transferring weight from his left foot to his right. Heiss's eyes bugged out, a scream starting in the back of his throat.

Withdrawing the pressure, Petrov stood back. "No more mistakes, Heiss," he said calmly. "Do you understand?" He turned away, unconcerned, as if he had almost crushed an insect and then thought better of it, not wanting to soil his shoe. "Give Mr. Bolken a half glass of rum, Lousje," Petrov called from the living room. "I'm ready to discuss his duties when he's decided to put aside his bad habits."

Fifteen minutes later, Heiss sat down opposite Petrov. He restrained an inner compulsion to take Petrov by the throat and kill him. He felt quite capable of it. More than the pain, he had been humiliated. But the obverse side of it was that, somehow, he had felt a sexual arousal with Petrov hovering over him, and from it, a desire to please. The conflicting emotions worked at him but he kept his face blank. It was the woman's fault, he decided. Without her, there would have been no conflict. Reconstructing the scene, he decided that it had been the woman who moved her foot to touch his. Petrov was dominant, the woman in his shadow. "I'm ready," he acknowledged.

Petrov inhaled, then exhaled very slowly. He quartered Heiss's face with his eyes, mistrusting an easy surrender. He was looking for signs of an armed truce.

"You understand that this is important, Heiss?"

Heiss nodded, breaking eye contact. "I was tense from the thing yesterday," he explained. "Unexpected." He lifted a hand in a conciliatory gesture.

"Ten thousand pounds for five days of work. One-third deposited to your account in Zurich, the balance on finishing the job. It's straight surveillance. Photographs of Welsh and myself. Shaking hands, walking together. I want the impression of a close relationship. You have the lenses for this kind of work?"

Nodding, Heiss answered, "Five-hundred millimeter and fast film. I have the Minox for close work."

"This is the recorder you'll be using." Petrov handed him a black anodized case. "A Czech R-121. It's voice actuated so that it will only run when sound is above a certain level. Check the tapes and batteries once a day. You'll have ample opportunity. The doors to the cottages are not locked and the maids' schedule should be evident if you're observant."

Heiss let some rebellion surface. "I know my business."

Petrov ignored the defense. "Nothing you've done thus far indicates that. If I could replace you, I would, but it's too late. Just do the job as I've outlined it. Lousje will be your only contact on the island. Don't avoid me, but remember that you're just another guest. Shoot a lot of film so that you establish yourself as having photography as a hobby. Clear?"

Heiss sipped at the rum, nodding. "How do I leave Barbados?"

"By chartered aircraft. You'll make arrangements this afternoon in the name of Bolken for a flight to Guadeloupe, and then tomorrow you'll hire a plane to fly you down to Union Island where the hotel's yacht will pick you up. I'll make arrangements to have your luggage picked up."

"What if I'm spotted at the airport tonight?"

The muscles of Petrov's jaw contracted. "If you are, and I doubt that you are of that much concern to them, keep quiet and get a lawyer. We'll have a man from the consulate covering your departure." He leaned back against the sofa's cushions, the briefing terminated. "But," he added, "we would consider that your final mistake."

He stood in the earliest dawn, when the flat black of the sea is crazed by the first streaks of light. Then the sun came up as a distended bubble, erupting from beneath the sea's eastern horizon. In a few short moments the illusion was gone; men had started their clocks for the day.

Clifford Welsh watched the sun with the intensity of a man who has forgotten what it looks like, just as he had done for the last two mornings. The particular quality of early-morning light tinted the small world of the island in cotton-candy pinks. He breathed a deep sigh of contentment and sipped the pungent coffee.

He wondered whether he should wake Judith and looked automatically at his wrist for the watch that still rested in the drawer of his dressing table. The white left by the band had disappeared into the tan of his skin. He looked at his arms and body, pleased that his skin was browning.

The Welshes' cottage was poised on the edge of a high bluff, overlooking the eastern beach of the small island. Century plants, reputed to bloom only once in a hundred years, dotted the area in front of the veranda. The bluff fell away to a sugar-sand beach two hundred feet below. Beyond that, the sea was contained by reefs that encircled the eastern approaches to the island and beyond that stretched the Atlantic.

Welsh looked down the beach to the south and saw

a solitary man running along the hard, surf-packed sand. The man neither avoided the waves nor the softer berm, but ran in a straight line, his legs lifting high, directly toward some imaginary goal. One moment, Welsh could see the showers of soft sand spraying from beneath his feet and the next, splashes his legs made in the foaming surf. The man neither asked for nor accepted favor from his environment. Welsh speculated that the man would live his life like that, directly, avoiding no obstacle. Perhaps a difficult man to deal with.

Her arms enclosed him from behind. He turned to his wife and they watched the solitary man driving down the beach until he was lost from sight. The gulls and frigate birds were climbing in the wind that swelled upwards and over the bluffs. Soaring on the rising current of wind, one frigate hung stationary before them, its eyes fixed on the sea below, motionless in flight.

"It's really a marvelous place." Judith hugged him enthusiastically.

He brushed her hair with is hand. "I thought you might like it." He sipped at the coffee and offered her the remains. "I'm sorry that it's cold. But there's more in the thermos. They make up a batch for me every night."

She smiled and accepted the cup, drinking the remainder. Setting the cup down, she sat on the stone wall that edged the veranda, overlooking the sea. Her white terrycloth robe fluttered in the wind like something alive. But she remained motionless, a statue cast in bronze, forever looking out over a copper sea. They remained on the terrace for many minutes, not speaking, watching the sun grow.

Far out beyond the reef, a native sloop beat its way up to windward, only the sail visible. Up to the east, a pinnacle of rock stood out from the blank horizon, its top white with bird guano. Sail Rock, Welsh had heard it called. And he understood how a man aloft in a sailing vessel could mistake it for a man-of-war, hull down on the horizon.

Judith Welsh unfolded her legs and stood up. She turned to her husband, brushing her long hair from around her eyes. She walked into his arms, drawing the knot that held her robe. He bent down to kiss her, noting that her face was warm with the heat of the sun.

Much later, they sat together on the terrace, eating breakfast. Welsh had finished off two halves of papaya, a rasher of bacon, and was still eating a two-egg omelet. While he finished, she sat there watching him, amused.

"Not your usual boiled egg and tea," she laughed.

He nodded several times, his mouth full. "Getting old," he said and forked in another bite of omelet. "Need the protein."

She stretched and leaned back, sun hot on her face. "Never know it, Mr. Welsh. Never know it. You get a B for technique and an A for effort." She punctuated it with a laugh.

"You sound like my secretary," he said straight-faced, and she kicked him hard in the shin. "Uncouth sod," she said, and the frigate birds squawked at his shout of surprise and dove toward the lagoon.

He finally finished and wiped his mouth, smiling. "I've put on two pounds already. Got to stop eating or get out and do some exercise."

"Swim?" She poured both of them another cup of coffee.

"We could go snorkeling if you'd like." He pointed to a section of the reef to the southeast near a small rock just awash in the seas. "That's where the manager's wife says to go. Take a dinghy and anchor it over the coral. Work from there into the current."

She thought for a moment. "Is it difficult? And what about big fish and things that go bump in the night?" Taking a strand of hair, she drew it across her upper lip.

He took one step and stood behind her chair, massaging her neck, finally kissing the golden down at her hairline. "Only *we* go bump in the night," he whispered, and as he said it, he felt young and foolish and alive. Like it had been when they both were fifteen years younger. He straightened, trying to be serious. "No, Mrs. W. It's a piece of cake. Easier than swimming. The mask over your face is full of air and that gives you buoyancy. You just breathe in slowly and snort out. It clears the tube of water. And kick your flippers slowly to keep moving." He stepped into the cottage and rummaged for the hotel literature.

"All explained here in fine print," he said, laying the folder down before her. He stood back, legs spread and hande in his bathrobe pockets. She thought he looked younger. Much.

"You like it here, don't you?" she said, looking up at him, shading her eyes. "How's the sunburn?"

He rubbed the tops of his shoulders and swore. "God, that was stupid lying in the sun yesterday. But I'll use some blocking cream today. If it doesn't peel, I'll be beautiful. The darling of the working class."

He had tainted their private amusement, and they thought in silence for some minutes, and then she reached up to hold his arm. "It's a long way from New York, isn't it, Cliff? You know, I listened to some of your conversation with Brian when we were coming down—I mean about disarmament. You sounded less sure of it. Have you changed your mind?"

He rubbed his unshaven face, enjoying the day, not wanting to be dragged back into the reality of his political life. "Changed my mind? No, not really. DeSilva's dead against it. But I think mainly because it means that he loses the security of running a two-time winner into a third term. He's pushing me to run for senator again. Like he wants to keep me locked into New York. But he did say that he'd run some polls on voter reaction to unilateral disarmament. He should have it finished by the time we get back."

She sighed, leaning back in the chair and fluffing

her hair from around the collar of her bathrobe. "But you're still having second thoughts, aren't you? And Loss seemed to be against it, didn't he?"

Welsh snorted derisively. "Loss is a conservative. Can't reframe his thinking. What he and everyone else like him don't understand is that we *have* to rethink our military commitments, both in terms of what our economy can support and what the Russians are going to do if we don't back off on this damned rearmament thing."

He paused, looking out over the sea, aggravated. "Judy, you know that I'm on the President's Intelligence Watchdog Committee. What goes on in there can be hair-raising. But basically it boils down to what most intelligent people already know. That we're behind the Russians in just about every category. The B-52 bomber force is just about junk and the cruise missile program won't be up to full strength for six more years; longer if Congress can have its say. The Trident sub program is just starting to replace the old Polaris class and some of the Minutemen ICBMs are over twelve years old. People keep talking about us as a first-class power. Goddamnit, we're not! Every freeborn son of a bitch in this country thinks that it's our collective God-given right to be Number One in the world. If the Administration goes along with this rearmament thing, it's going to shove up the inflation rate even higher and ruin the economy. And more important, it's going to destroy every program that we have now or in the future for rebuilding the cities and for all the social programs that we need."

She got to her feet and held his arm. "Calm down, Clifford," she said, smiling. "I've read your platform. You can convince the voters. It's just going to take time."

"And lots of money," he added. "But more important than that, Judy, it's going to take something special to get me nationally known."

She led him toward the bathroom by the hand.

"Maybe you could help me take a shower and explain your position a bit better. Any position will do," she said laughingly. "Come on, big shot."

He followed her, swatting at her rump with his free hand. "You're on," he said.

Chapter 8

Loss pulled the light coverlet over his head and pushed deeper into the pillows. He lay like this for some minutes, slowly coming awake, picking up the sounds of the new day. A lawn mower had started up and he heard the sound coming in slow waves as if the operator was making long passes in overlapping patterns. Loss could almost submerge the sound into the background, drifting off into sleep, and then the groundsman would gun the throttle, as if he had encountered a patch of weeds longer and more stubborn than the rest.

An expression that Barber had used came to him. Barber, with no taste for variety once he was on to a good thing, had spent what R&R he had in Saigon. "Fuckin' 'Paris of the East,' " he called it. If Saigon was that, then the Paradise Bar was nothing less than Barber's Louvre-Montmartre-Left Bank wrapped up in one steamy package. Hungover, red eyed, and broke, Barber had stumbled into the hooch, exclaimed that his mouth tasted "like sour owl shit," and crashed onto his bunk like a fallen Atlas.

In half-consciousness of waking, Loss pushed Barber's memory away, as if it were a tangible mass, a dark wobbling thing that he couldn't penetrate, cir-

123

cumvent, or remove from his life. "Like sour owl shit," Loss said to the pillow, now fully awake. There had been one rum and ginger too many, a last cigarette. He could visualize Kitzner mocking him and resolved to bake it out in the smoking heat of the sun.

Loss looked at his watch. Ten straight up. Pushing back the covers, he sat up, yawned, and scratched his scalp. His feet, dangling over the bed, touched the cool tiled floor. He kicked into leather clogs and ambled over to the balcony, looking down at the anchorage.

The hotel's yacht, *Striker,* lay stern-to at the dock, engines warming up for the morning trip over to Union Island. More guests leaving or arriving, he thought. Hendrick, the skipper, was on the foredeck, swabbing down the aluminum surface.

Gulls wheeled in the anchorage, the blue of the shallow water reflected from their bellies and wings, tinting them in shades to match the sky. Small cumulus, already formed, sailed in close formation down to the west. Loss estimated the wind was probably east-southeast at roughly ten knots, a few white-flecked waves forming in the channel. The day was brochure-perfect, as if God had turned the handle and cranked it out of a machine, letter perfect.

Loss belched and turned, scuffing toward the bathroom. Standing under the shower, intentionally leaving the hot-water tap untouched, he sang off key, stumbling over the words. Shaving afterward, he nicked himself and found the razor shook a little in his hand. Wiping moisture from the mirror, he said to his blurred image, "Boozers is losers." His image stared back, unimpressed. Two drinks maximum tonight, he promised.

Gradually, and in spite of himself, he began to feel good. Welsh was paying the ticket and there was nothing to do for six more days. Loss thought briefly of Holly and cursed Welsh for not allowing her to come. He missed her and imagined her sitting on the end of

124

the bed, brushing her hair, unaware of the beauty of her nakedness. He thought of how they could have passed the days together: swimming out beyond the reef, sailing the sloop out to the smaller islands to the north, picnicking on cheese and wine and love. As it was, she was loose somewhere, perhaps with someone else.

So much for that, he thought. There were always beautiful women around the hotel and the stunning girls who came ashore from the charter yachts looked friendly enough. God, he thought, in just the last evening there had been a Rhodesian, an Australian, and two English girls, all from the same yacht crew. The skipper had never showed up—probably resting. He grinned now at the thought of a man of thirty, burned out by the birds in paradise. Barber would have loved it—and then Loss locked the memory out of his mind. The dream was gone. It was only before sleeping and on waking that he thought of Barber and the rest of them, their features now blurred but events sharp in pinpoint clarity.

He put on white cotton slacks, a striped crew neck that Holly had given him, and sunglasses. Breakfast sounded like getting stuffed with food that would be barely digested in time for the luncheon buffet. Tennis maybe in the cool of evening. And then he decided that he would hitch a ride over to Union Island with the *Striker*, top up the fuel tanks, and wash the Aztec down. And if there was time, see a bit of the island while the crew of the launch picked up supplies and met the next contingent of guests.

He started down the shallow lawn toward the dock, Two departing guests were being helped aboard and the twin diesels rapped, the yacht backing down as the docking lines were cast off. Loss gave a piercing whistle, waved, and ran the length of the dock. He leaped aboard, out of breath, already sweating, as the crew cast off the bow mooring and threaded out through the anchorage.

125

The departing guests, an older couple, had settled down in deck chairs in the cockpit. They looked up and gave him the polite smile that the already-tanned reserve for the sunburned. He exchanged greetings with them and then went forward to the bridge where Hendrick was at the controls.

"Morning, Hendrick," he said, settling down in the upholstered chair next to the helmsman's seat.

"Good morning, sir." Hendrick flashed a smile, teeth brilliant white against the tanned frame of his face. He wore a lumpy yachting cap, dark curls of hair sprouting out from beneath the stained band. "You finish off that backgammon game last night?"

"That one and three more. Richardson took me for sixteen bucks." And four drinks, he almost added.

Hendrick shook his head. "You playing with fire, man. He has luck like he got a contract with an obeah-man." He eased both throttles forward, bringing the yacht up onto a plane as they passed the western edge of the island, skirting a reef.

Loss ducked under the deck house and went aft to the tuna tower. He climbed it until he was well above the deck. The smell of diesel fumes had vanished in the sweep of the fresh trades. Union was dead ahead on the bow, about three miles distant, rising up out of the sea like a miniature edition of Morea: volcanic peaks and dull olive forests. To the north lay numerous small islands with the outline of the main island, St. Vincent, barely distinguishable in the haze beyond. To the south an island larger than Union, with a razorback ridge and palm-lined shores, spanned the horizon, breaking the flow of the trades. He could see a cluster of white buildings set on the ridge. The view would be spectacular, he thought, for within the sweep of the eye were islands and sea. Great swells, rolling in from the Atlantic, humped up as they met the shoaling of reefs, hesitated, and then broke in a cascade of white water, leaving a halo of prismatic color in their death. He wished she were here to share it with him.

126

He climbed back down and settled himself in the seat once more, offering a cigarette to Hendrick and lighting one for himself. There was the moisture of salt on his lips and it tasted fine.

"A beautiful part of the world," he finally said.

Hendrick nodded. "So the tourist board tells us." He turned to Loss, grinning. "But how long could you take it? June like September, man. I know August from February only 'cause I don't catch as many fish." He took a quick puff on the cigarette, blowing out the smoke without inhaling it. He shrugged, throwing the stub away into the sea. "I never seen snow, Mr. Loss. You think you'd like that?"

Loss smiled, knowing that he was probably right. Ice cream for dessert was a treat. With every meal, it would cause decay and fat.

He dropped the subject. "How long will you be at Union?"

Hendrick was pulling back on the revs as the *Striker* passed the outer buoy and edged along the reef which skirted Clifton Harbor. The deck boys were laying out fenders and preparing the docking lines.

"An hour or more. We pick up ground provisions, drop mail and some other things. These guests are staying one night here and flying out tomorrow morning on LIAT. But we got to wait for some guest coming in by charter flight. Give it maybe two hours. I'll see you at the airport."

After they docked, Loss went ashore, passing children who sold black coral and older men who sat, expressionless, just dreaming in the sun. A small black boy approached him at the end of the concrete pier, holding a limp snapper, offering it in a repeated demand for "jus' one shilling, man." Loss declined, smiling, and the boy smiled back, serious face splitting into a dazzling grin.

The two of them followed a dirt lane, past rum shops and dusty, pastel-painted shacks, the boy running ahead, then sitting in the shade, impatient for Loss to catch up. And then as if he were leading a parade of two, the boy would skip ahead, the fish occasionally dragging in the dust, leading the way. Loss forgot the lethargy of the morning, absorbing enthusiasm from the boy and the day.

By 11:30 he had filled the tanks, aired out the cockpit, and hired the boy to wash the landing gear of the Aztec. When the boy finished, Loss gave him two dollars and got the fish as a bonus. Satisfied, he locked the aircraft and wandered over to a small restaurant bordering the airstrip. He had an excellent meal of quiche Lorraine and a light Chablis, musing at the great diversity of foods which the islands had integrated into their culture. French, English, Spanish, Dutch, Chinese, and Black. Like their nationalities, it seemed as if their foods had been haphazardly thrown into a kettle, stirred once, and then served. There was a certain intermingling of flavors; enough to enhance the finished product, but not enough to blur the essence.

Pushing back his chair, Loss refelected that he felt as if he was a traveler, waiting on a bench between two segments of his journey. The past was past; the future indefinite. But there was a certain peace between, one that he was enjoying.

He picked up the faint drone of aircraft engines, aware of the sound, like any pilot, long before those that bind their lives to the ground. The blue and white Cessna 310 came down the valley between the mountains, far faster than it should have for the approach. It pulled up into a sloppy chandelle, dropping gear and partial flap. Loss winced as the twin-engined aircraft turned on short final, pitching up as it lowered full flap. It touched down, well over one-third down the runway, slamming the gear onto the asphalt. The pilot stood on the brakes and the plane hunched forward over smoking tires. The Cessna stopped just short of the seawall, swung through 180 degrees and taxied clear of the runway.

"Our new guests might need a rum punch." Loss

turned to find Hendrick standing against a post, relaxed and smiling.

They walked together down the flagstone steps and across the tarmac to the aircraft. The pilot was heaving theluggage out of the cargo compartment, sometimes pausing to chat with the customs officer who had driven out from town to meet the plane. The lone passenger paused in the doorway, blinking at the brightness, and then fitted a pair of mirrored sunglasses across his eyes. Ignoring Hendrick, who had walked toward him with hand extended, the man walked toward Loss, KLM flight bag slung over one shoulder, an aluminum camera case held in his left hand. He stopped, sticking his hand out. Loss could smell the taint of mint on his breath.

"I'm Pieter Bolken," the man said. "I'll need help with my bags."

The three of them had dinner on the veranda, beyond the dining room of the pavilion. The wind had dropped and the stars were out. They spoke little during the meal, requiring nothing more than gestures. The dinner was elegantly simple: green turtle soup followed by tanya cakes, glazed carrots, and fresh dolphin.

There was no flamboyance, flaming sauces, or obsequiousness. Just quiet, discreet service. They finished the dinner with cognac and Martinique coffee.

"I wonder why there are so few places like this in the world," Judith Welsh said. She leaned back in the canvas officer's chair, more handsome than Loss had ever remembered her. The three-day tan on her face and arms was a deep cocoa and she wore no other makeup.

"Do we have a moon tonight, Brian?" Welsh asked, swishing his cognac around in the snifter.

Loss nodded. "Later on. It's a gibbous moon. Nearly full." He paused and smiled. "That was an excellent meal. Many thanks."

Clifford Welsh showed his excellent teeth in a quick

flash. "It's our pleasure, Brian. We're enjoying our-selves." Loss wondered whether Welsh's cordiality was an invitation to leave. Welsh had mentioned that they were meeting another couple for after-dinner drinks.

Neither of the Welshes offered any more conver-sation and Loss felt awkward. He raised his glass to both of them and finished the cognac. "A wonderful evening. Again, thanks," and he rose from the table. "I'll have to leave you both to hold up the stars. I've got a tennis date at six in the A.M.," he lied.

"Good night then, Brian," Welsh said, making no effort to rise, but toasting Loss with his near-empty snifter.

Brian left them sitting in the dark shadows, holding hands beneath the table, touching each other like young people in love, or whatever it was that young people felt. He passed through the bar, pausing to watch Richardson and Hendrick working out the end phase of a backgammon match. The man named Bolken sat on a barstool alone, watching, saying noth-ing. They exchanged glances without greeting.

He stopped briefly to say good evening to a Cana-dian couple who lived in the cottage fifty yards down the leeward beach. They were from the Maritime Provinces and retained the languid ease of colonial English inflection; they drank tea in the afternoon. In their vocabulary, whiskey meant Scotch, and not blended, please. And he liked them for saying what they felt, perhaps their only Canadian characteristic.

She tossed her short-cropped, curled gray hair and said, "Do sit down, Mr. Loss. I have been watching all evening and the young crew of ladies from that lovely yacht has not yet come ashore." She inflected each adjective with an upward lilt. But her fixed smile was more conspiratorial than admonishing.

"Thanks, Mrs. Kent," he replied, easing down into the camp chair. "I'm just on my way down the path. May I offer you something?" Brian motioned for the waiter.

130

"No thanks, Brian," Edwin Kent replied, "but take care of yourself. Sam," he motioned to the waiter, "please place this on my account. A whiskey for Mr. Loss." He turned to Brian, immediately at ease and old school. "Damned fine aircraft you have there, Brian. Margaret and I had a look at it yesterday over at Union. Beautiful thing." He was silvered and touching on sixty, but Loss saw the fine muscle structure, good reflexes, and most of all, the decisive use of his hands in everything Kent did.

Loss answered, pausing to raise his newly arrived glass. "Thank you. The Aztec's not mine. I am what you would call a company pilot. Mr. Welsh, who I think you have met, is the owner. But yes, the Aztec is great for what it is."

She touched his arm lightly, which he thought was a singularly English thing to do. "Edwin flew for the RCAF. He always drools over airplanes. Scruffy little things, big aluminum things; if it flies, he drools. Like some old dog, without teeth, over a bone." She had no malice to her voice.

"I still shamble around," Kent offered. "I've got an old Piper Super Cruiser. Had it since fifty-one. I put floats on it in the summer and skis on it in the winter, just to get away from the old girl." Edwin Kent chuckled gently. "No, Margaret is right. I flew first in the RAF, no Battle of Britain thing. Just Lancasters. Then later I came back to Canada and we did air defense for a while. CF-100s and the usual lot."

Loss suddenly remembered who Edwin Kent was. Kent, a vice-air marshal of Canadian forces in NATO, had pulled two flaming, fuel-saturated men from the fuselage of a burning Canberra bomber that had crashed on a fog-shrouded runway in France. Because of that, Kent had left his left leg buried in in a field of France. But he had demanded and received permission to still fly first-line interceptors. Kent was still legend in Canada.

Loss looked again at Edwin Kent. "I think I've heard of you."

131

Kent laughed. "Shouldn't believe it all, Brian. They're likely to say some good things about me when I kick off. Damn liars all." He raised his glass.

"Good evening." The voice passed behind Brian's head and he turned to watch the attractive couple take a table near the Welshes on the patio.

"Nice couple," Margaret Kent said without conviction. She lifted her hand in recognition, but they had not looked back.

"Klist, I believe their name is," remarked Kent, watching them settle at their table. "I believe the journalist chap over there," indicating Bolken, "says he's some sort of industrialist in Holland. Transistors and things."

"It's a fairly international group," Loss commented. "I like to see people other than Americans abroad. This couple, Klist I think you said their name was? He's the one who pounds up and down the beach every morning, isn't he?"

"So Margaret tells me," said Kent. "I'm still tucked in at that hour. But I'll vouch that he's not originally Dutch. I spent three years in Germany during the last go-around. I'd swear he's not Dutch." He paused and smiled. "Margaret is telling me with her foot that I should be more discreet, but then again, here we are, good Canadians with a closet queen. Keep a Union Jack hidden under the mattress. That sort of thing," and he snorted with laughter at the illusion.

"What nationality do you think he is?" Loss questioned.

Kent rattled the cubes of ice in his drink in a circular motion, thinking.

"I can't say exactly, Brian. German or Polish, perhaps. European traits have tended to merge over the last thirty years. But it's partly the bearing, the assurance, the devotion to a strong body. Just strikes me that way. Can't exactly pinpoint it. But he's not Dutch." Kent looked toward the couple and noted

132

that they had joined the Welshes. Kent nodded discreetly in their direction.

"Looks like they have joined your employer and his wife. Incidentally, it's Senator Welsh, not just Mr., isn't it?"

Loss hesitated just long enough to confirm the statement. He shrugged, answering, "I guess he wanted to keep it quiet. Something of a vacation. But I would ask that you not make that information public."

"Edwin's such a snoop," Kent's wife remarked to Brian. "No, of course we won't say anything. But you know, Canada is not such a long way from New York. Senator Welsh has gotten wide coverage in some of our newspapers. He seems to be trying to pull New York up by its scruffy bootstraps, and that's just the same thing that is going to have to happen in Montreal." She paused and put her hand beside her mouth and said in a stage whisper to Loss, "Don't talk to Edwin about French Canadians. He goes livid."

Kent laughed and pushed back his chair. "Pay no attention to her. Just as long as I don't have to learn to speak French in my lifetime, I can put up with them. Incidentally, why don't you take a sail with us tomorrow? Margaret and I have chartered the hotel's sloop. Plenty of room for you as well."

Brian thought briefly, knowing that there was no likelihood of the Aztec's being used. "It sounds like a great idea," he answered. "Where are you going?"

Kent dug around in his jacket pockets and came up with a small printed brochure. He read through it, holding it almost at arm's length. "Eyes don't accommodate well anymore. Ah, yes. It says that we go down to Tyrell Bay on Carriacou."

"Where was that?" Loss suddenly injected, his hand held his glass halfway to his mouth, motion arrested.

"Tyrell Bay," Kent repeated, drawing a pair of glasses from his breast pocket and putting them on. "It says it's about a two-hour sail from here to the

133

west coast of Carriacou. Nice hotel there. We have lunch on the boat, drive around a bit, and then sail back in the late afternoon.''

"Two hours . . ." Kent's wife said. "How far would that be?"

Loss set the glass down, smiling. "Someone once told me that it was about as far as you want to make it.''

Chapter 9

Carl Heiss sat uncomfortably on the bar stool, bored and restless. The backgammon game continued at the far end of the bar, now drawing a group of dining-room staff who had finished up for the evening.

The Canadian couple sitting with Welsh's pilot had left, and the pilot himself left moments later after signing for his bar bill. Two other couples, whom Heiss didn't recognize, still were in the game-room annex, playing darts. He finally realized that they were off one of the yachts. The younger woman in their group obviously wore nothing beneath the thin shift.

The bartender broke off from watching the backgammon game and started to mix another round of drinks. Heiss waited patiently and watched the waiter carry the tray to the patio. One round of drinks would give Heiss a clear twenty minutes. He left a five-dollar bill on the bar top and left through the now darkened dining room. Four figures sat at the Welsh table, their faces indistinct in the single candle flame. They were raising glasses to each other.

Heiss stood beyond the stone wall of the dining-room patio, waiting for his eyes to adjust to the darkness. Except for pathway lights leading to the pavilion and muted stateroom lights in the yachts riding at anchor, the island was dark. He picked out the sound of an outboard motor running in the anchorage and strained to watch if someone were coming ashore. Spreader lights on the schooner anchored farthest out in the bay flooded the deck briefly and went off. Just crew from one yacht visiting their friends.

As his eyes accommodated, the forms of trees emerged from the blackness, and then he could see the outlines of the dirt path the staff used to walk to their quarters. Heiss followed the path, pausing every fifty steps to listen. The path steepened as he climbed the hillside and became coarser with spalls of chipped rock. Unexpectedly, he stumbled and fell heavily, pain from one hand forcing a rush of breath from his lips. Lying for a minute in the pathway, Heiss drew the injured hand to his lips and licked at the wound. The blood was warm and salty, like melted butter. He got slowly to his feet and could feel the pain throb steadily with each pulse of his heart. A cool draft blew through a vent in the knee of his pants. Heiss cursed inwardly. The pants were new and had cost twenty pounds on Bond Street. "Fucking sod," he muttered.

In ten minutes the path leveled again, and over the rise of the hill he saw the indefinite shapes of the two large staff buildings. The area before him was open, and he altered his course to the left, avoiding the buildings and moving down through the high lemon grass toward the road that led to the four cottages on the eastern bluff.

A spent cigarette arched into the blackness and died in a shower of sparks not more than twenty feet to his right. Heiss froze and slowly lowered to the ground. The grass pressed up into his face, and he thought that he could hear the sound of insects scattering beneath his body's weight.

The West Indian accents were indistinct, thick monosyllables. One of the two voices was a woman's. She

135

giggled and then very distinctly said, "Keep your hand still." But she laughed again. The man's voice was blurred by his deeper tone: short, insistent words. Heiss looked at his watch, alarmed by the high luminosity of the dial. He had consumed twelve minutes already, and he painfully began to inch his way down to the left, relying on the sounds of the wind in the grass to mask his movements. In four minutes he gained the protection of a clump of scrubby trees and rose to a crouch, pausing to listen. The voices were nothing now, and he could hear more distinctly the numbed roar of seas breaking on the windward reef.

The Welsh cottage, Number Four, stood alone on its individual bluff. The access road was dark, but a few lights illuminated the path leading to the front doorway.

Heiss listened for two minutes more, straining to hear or see anyone approaching on the path. Satisfied, he calmly walked across the road and strode up the bluff, keeping clear of any illumination from the lighted path. He listened at the door and scanned the road again before entering the cottage.

The three rooms were vacant. Switching on a penlight, he examined his wounded hand and torn pants. He gritted his teeth in anger, cursing his stupidity. Obviously, he should have walked from the pavilion to his own cottage and then simply approached the Welsh cottage from the beach side of the bluff. "Twenty fucking quid," he mumbled again, squeezing the open wound in his hand and watching the dark blood flow thickly. He licked it again, holding the taste in his mouth like a bubble of sour wine.

He removed his shoes, noting carefully that no dust or mud had been tracked upon the tiled floor, and then stood on the backboard of the bed and scanned the ledge of the stone wall with the flashlight. The recorder was undisturbed. He carefully changed the tape, substituting a fresh reel from his inside coat pocket. The battery indicator showed that the cells were still fresh.

Tapping the contact microphone with his thumbnail, he watched as the reels moved a fraction of a revolution and stopped again. It was unavoidable that the sounds of the shower, toilet, and human movement sometimes actuated the mechanism, but the tape had a capacity of four hours, easily spanning a normal day of conversation.

Heiss serviced two more recorders, one on a beam in the patio and one hidden under dirt in the frangipani bushes bordering the patio. It was a chance that Welsh would look for surveillance devices, but unlikely. A microphone had also been attached to an FM transmitter under Welsh's dining table, but the range to Heiss's receiver-tape recorder in his cottage had been too great for actual use. There was a great deal of fading so hat only one-third of the recorded conversation was usable. Heiss had considered moving the unit closer to the pavilion but knew that Lousje would have a recorder in her purse for any important meetings.

A sound startled him as he finished changing the tape in the third recorder. Flattening himself behind a lounge chair on the patio, he heard the voice of Judith Welsh. The bedroom was suddenly bathed in light and shadows from forms passing in front of the bedroom lamps spanned the patio in rapidly shifting shapes: oblique characterizations.

Knowing that any movement would probably be seen, Heiss lay still, heart pounding. Raising his head minutely to clear the cushions, he saw Welsh and his wife changing to bathrobes. He noticed that her stomach had traces of flab but the rest of her body was firm and tanned; her breasts were small but satisfactory. They both moved into the bathroom, and Heiss counted to ten slowly, planning to vault over the stone retaining wall. He tensed, carefully planning his movements, and then Judith Welsh walked back into the bedroom and spent several minutes stirring around the contents of her cosmetic case. Welsh reentered the room and sat down on the bed, examining his sunburnt shoulders before the mirror as his wife walked back into the bathroom area, pausing long enough to pass her hand across her husband's neck.

It seemed too risky to move, thought Heiss. It would be better to wait for an hour or so and then move off after they were asleep.

A toilet flushed and Heiss imagined three tape recorders faithfully committing to permanent magnetic memory the sound of waste being passed down a pipe.

His wound was oozing again and Heiss sucked on it.

The lights were extinguished first in the bedroom, and then as Judith Welsh reentered the bedroom, the last bathroom light flicked out. He could hear them talking in low tones at first and then silence and then the sound of love making. He timed them, counting off thirty-one minutes. Fucking sod, thought Heiss, growing stiff in the night wind.

The two men jogged along the beach in the early morning sunlight. They passed the southern tip of the island breathing heavily, pounding through the loose dry sand, then gained the broad sweep of tide-washed flats that ran north beneath the windward bluff. Browsing land crabs scuttled to their holes, sensing the vibrations of the running men.

The younger of the two forced his breath to a faster rate, and faltered in his pace. He would try not to embarrass.

Welsh looked over at the young European and staggered to a halt. The Dutchman was breathing heavily as well, but there was no visible triphammer pounding beneath his rib cage. Welsh felt his own heart thudding, the sound reverberating in his mind. They both sank to the still-cool sand and silently watched the lagoon rising to feathered whitecaps in the fresh wind.

Welsh spoke, surprised at the harshness in his throat. "I should be doing that every morning, Robert." He exhaled heavily, thinking that at least he had matched the younger man.

"I find it difficult to do every morning," replied Petrov, pouring sand through his hand, allowing it to engulf two ants struggling with some particle of food. The ants reappeared from the sand in seconds and Petrov showered them again with a fresh avalanche. They did not reappear.

They had talked briefly last night of their backgrounds. The Russian asked him directly, within the first five minutes of conversation, whether he was not the senator from New York. Welsh acknowledged this, pleased that a European would know his name and recognize him.

Petrov spoke, so softly that Welsh had to lean toward him to hear. "I follow American politics closely, Clifford. It seems much more of an honest . . ." he groped for the word, "game than in Europe. What are your aspirations?"

The question was so direct and blunt that Welsh answered without much consideration.

"Robert, I really don't know. I guess that every politician wants a shot at the presidency. I've thought about it, but I'm young. Perhaps in several years, perhaps sooner, I'll make a try at it."

"So was Kennedy young," replied Petrov with a shrug, as if it were nothing. He turned and looked at Welsh directly, again speaking softly. "Many people in Europe are worried about the drift of American political thought. Others, including myself, find some hope."

Welsh tensed slightly. The subject seemed directed, but he discounted this after thinking for a minute. The Dutchman was obviously no reporter. He remembered that the opinions of others concerning politics were difficult, no, impossible to obtain, just because of his political position. He decided to milk this Dutchman of as much European bias as possible and resolved to give nothing in return.

Petrov sensed the change in the man's mood and discussed his admiration for Welsh's handling of the New York City financial crisis. They talked for another twenty minutes, the sun warming them now, the heat easing cramped muscles.

They drifted in discussion of European money matters and the return to gold as a monetary standard among the fractured IMF countries.

"Yes, I grant you that it was a major mistake for Burns to continue the policy of demonetization of gold," Welsh said. "We forced France into this corner repeatedly." He made a throwaway gesture with his hand. "I'm glad that it's resolved."

"It's not really over, Clifford," replied Petrov. "The boom in Europe is stabilized, but those who hold gold are worth great fortunes." Petrov said this evenly, with no inflection in his voice.

Welsh erupted in laughter. He started to speak and then stopped again to laugh. "I wish to God that I had a few kilos tucked away, Robert, but the closest relationship that I have to gold is a batch of fillings in my teeth."

Petrov turned toward Clifford Welsh, shading his eyes with a hand. He looked awkward, about to salute.

"Didn't your father, a congressman, I believe, favor the policy of backing currency with gold reserves?"

Welsh didn't stop to analyze the depth of this question. "Of course," he replied. "My father fought Roosevelt tooth and nail on the subject. Thought it was irresponsible to allow the amount of paper currency in circulation to be tied to the whims of politicians. I personally think he was right. But I don't recall that my father ever personally invested in gold."

Petrov stood up abruptly and brushed the sand from his warmup suit.

"We must talk some more, Clifford. I think that Lousje will be ready for breakfast soon. Will you join us for cocktails this evening at our cottage?"

Welsh staggered to his feet, one leg numb from restricted circulation. "Yes, of course, we'll join you. What about five?"

And the Russian nodded without looking back, striding easily north along the tide line.

They met again as agreed, on the patio of the Klist cottage, high on the road edging Telescope Hill. Welsh noticed that Klist was wearing perfectly tailored slacks and a shirt of raw silk. The shoes were probably Gucci and by comparison, Welsh felt shabby. Klist's wife, Lousje, served catered canapes, swimming around the room like a graceful, exotic fish, her full-length dress strangely not out of place. Welsh and his wife both sensed that the meeting had been carefully planned, in the manner that good hosts plan perfect things.

"Your hospitality is nothing less than overwhelming," Welsh commented, raising his glass in salute to the women. Neither host commented but merely returned the toast, smiling evenly.

They all sat for some minutes, watching the anchorage. *Mintar*, the hotel's chartered sloop, could be seen, hard on the port tack, close-reaching up the bay. The shadows had lengthened with the last of the sun pinking the mountain tops of the islands to the south and west. And as always, the wind seemed to abate as nightfall approached.

There were seven yachts in the anchorage now, ranging from a traditional staysail schooner far out in the roadstead to a small fiberglass cruising ketch, moored stern-to to coconut trees lining the beach. An hibachi flared at the stern of an English-rigged cutter farther down the bay. Welsh swallowed appreciatively at the vodka and tonic, letting his mind slide.

The sun was just touching the western horizon, a globule of orange fire, flattened by refraction.

"We will have a green flash, yes?" Lousje said, more statement than question. "There are no clouds on the horizon." She stood behind her husband, an obedient servant waiting his command.

Welsh felt ill at ease. The Klist woman was too perfect a sort of showpiece. He doubted that Klist and this woman were married. He never saw the small touches of either dislike or love that pass between all married people. The Dutch couple were more like actors, playing some role, unrelated and only artificially adept at small gestures. He was about to say something, vaguely supportive, when the Dutch woman turned and said, "Judith, I wish to go down to the boutique to pick up a shift. You know these prices, I think. Can you come with me?" It was a line from a script.

Petrov nodded as if he had excused her, and Welsh, caught unexpectedly in a situation he did not understand, nodded as well, not quite knowing what was agreed to. The men rose, and as the women departed, Lousje said something in Dutch, repeating in English for Welsh that they would meet them in the pavilion for dinner in one hour's time. She blew a kiss and they were gone.

Petrov first spoke, indicating the sun as it was swallowed by the western sea.

"If you look carefully, there will be the lightest blink of green. It is rare to see it, only when the horizon is free of clouds." And as if on cue, the sun poised on the horizon, the top arch flattened by distortion, and disappeared, leaving behind a divided second's flick of emerald. The sun was gone now, but radiating from its invisible point below the horizon were graduated blues and tones of gold across the sky, like sun rays on Sunday School posters.

Petrov got to his feet and took the partially empty glass from the table in front of Welsh. He refilled the glass and his as well, and eased back down into his chair. He looked intently at Welsh for a long period of time, his face open and relaxed. Finally, with a measure of reluctance, he said, "You know, Clifford, I have not been honest with you. But I think you know that."

Welsh looked at him, with a gaze as steady as he could manage. Klist's eyes, blue by daylight, were points of black in the gathering darkness of the tropical evening.

"In what way?"

Klist picked up a cigarette from a flat gold case and lighted it, relaxing with his exhalation as if the alchemy of the nicotine brought some inner peace and decision. He started slowly building the explanation.

"First of all, Clifford, I am not Dutch. Let us say that I am European. Perhaps all of us there may someday feel that way. Also, I am not what I appear to be. I am wealthy, yes." Klist paused to inhale the cigarette and then continued, exhaling as he lay the words down in neat, precise bundles.

"I represent, along with myself, a select number of European industrialists who are, surprisingly enough, not specifically interested in profit. But," he continued, "we are interested in stability."

Welsh held up his hand in a gesture of denial, starting to speak, but Klist interrupted. "No, let me finish, Clifford. It is not what you think. I am approaching you for my group *because*," he paused for emphasis, "because we think we can support you in an early bid for your presidency without attempting to dictate to you any terms. Simply put, we want to help you."

Welsh was staggered. He sat in silence, his mind trying to reach ahead, probing through his experience with Klist for some recognizable point of contact.

"Continue," Welsh said flatly, letting no emotion alter his voice.

As if the roles were reversed now, Klist became sincere, open, sometimes faltering for words.

"To allay your obvious opinion of me, Clifford, I must say that had we been seeking a candidate who would grant trade concessions or other sorts of favoritism, you know as well as I that there are men who stand much closer to the presidency whom we could buy. Politicians the world over are open to bribes. No, that is exactly what we do not seek.

"We do seek a man who can take command of your country with the full will of the people and bring a halt to a new race for armaments. This is what we fear in Europe."

They sat together in the darkness, the sea wind bringing coolness. Welsh slowly digested the words, repeating in his mind their implication, feeling already caught up in something. "Put it straight to me, Klist," Welsh said, pleased with the note of firmness in his voice. "You are saying that you and other people in Europe will support me financially in a campaign for the presidency without attempting to dictate policy. Is that it?"

"Yes," the Russian answered, "within the limitations of what we know you stand for. The major position that we are concerned with is disarmament. We are not concerned with your internal policies. We feel that we have no legitimate say in such things."

"Keep talking," Welsh said, feeling detached.

Klist finished the cigarette, the ash glowing, subtly lighting his high cheekbones. "NATO, as you know, Clifford, is a hollow shell. As long as America retained the balance of power, the weaker nations felt obliged to contribute to the common European defense. We wish it were otherwise, but your country has greatly reduced her commitment both in Asia and in Europe. The Eastern bloc, conversely, has made sizable gains in power. Although your intelligence organizations may feel otherwise, we feel in Europe that there is no danger of war, *as long as you do not challenge the Russians*."

There. It was out, thought Welsh. How did they know his feelings on this? Perhaps it was just self-evident that some United States politician would make this opinion felt. They had done their homework. "Where did you pick up any indication that I was inclined toward unilateral disarmament?" he asked, trying to seek out some truth in the face opposite him, now cast in shadows.

"It may surprise you, Clifford, but we know of eight such men who we feel are within range of the presidency. It is not an uncommon thought now, but as you would say in America, the idea has not been mar-

144

ket-tested. No, we follow the lives of men we feel are important on a global basis. Your speech in Utica . . ." Klist trailed off in his explanation.

Welsh sat in the darkness, carefully rethreading words, testing them against his own beliefs. It would be unthinkable to allow Europeans to interfere with American policy or, for that matter, politics. But if the goal were common—"Peace in our time" crossed his mind, and he angrily rejected the quotation. But he could listen to their proposal. He already thought in terms of "their" rather than "his"; Klist was nothing more than a messenger. "If I were to agree in principle with your concept of disarmament, what would your friends be able to do in assisting my campaign?" Welsh asked, relaxed now. Smooth.

Klist replied, almost eager. "A great deal, but all of it indirect. For example, you know that Europe has expanded its trade boundaries to include much of the Middle East, the Far East, and South America. Consequently, we can bring economic pressure to bear that will be beneficial. For example, if you were to propose a bill in the Senate, ceding *all* U.S. rights to bases in the Canal, plus the U.S. right of intervention in the Republic of Panama's territory, that new leftist government would respond by ceasing all hostilities, allow presently positioned U.S. troops to withdraw, and would make every attempt to praise your initiative. You would be invited to Panama on a 'fact-finding commission.' You would return home with a draft for a treaty of peace and friendship and for passage without charge for all U.S. ships in perpetuity. Thus, such a move on your part toward conciliation would gain you national prominence. I don't think that I have to mention that a similar proposal by any other member of your government would be met with indifference. Similar situations could arise by your introduction of a bill to allow Cuba to take back ownership of Guantánamo Bay over a three-year transition period. I think that you would find Cuba would take imme-

145

diate and effective steps to remove her military force from Africa. There would be extensive praise in the foreign press citing your vision of a new détente.''

Klist seemed confident, and the two scenarios had been carefully presented, as if there were no doubt as to the outcome. "Who do you represent, Klist?" Welsh said. "This is unbelievable. What you're saying is that your group controls the top echelons of major governments. Is that correct?"

Welsh has bitten, thought Klist, and he smiled in the darkness. It will work now, if I feed him bit by bit. "No, Clifford. Don't forget that the United States has always been dictatorial in its demands. Concessions are rarely made by your country unless under duress. There is strong sentiment for governments to respond to an open-ended gesture. We merely supply enough influential opinion in the halls of power to effect the results desired. And in regard to your question concerning our members, you could probably name ten of the top industrialists or second-level leaders of government in Europe and have a fair idea of our membership. But it was decided that your knowledge of those names might influence you unduly in future years. We want no favoritism, nor any possibility that you might feel obligated to us. Our influence will only be beneficial to your rise to higher office. You will have no past to shed.''

"Then all this, ah, assistance hinges on my stand on disarmament," Welsh said.

Klist stood up and walked slowly back and forth across the patio, his head bent, his hands clasped behind his back. He made several attempts to start speaking and each time stopped, reforming his words. Finally he said, "It is difficult for you, as an American, to appreciate the European mind. No, I know. You have spent many months in Europe and speak two languages. But you must remember that Europe has been a battleground too often for there to be any firm national commitments, even from the West Germans, to fight in a nuclear war that will basically be between the United States and Russia. And it is a commitment that your country can ill afford to bear alone.

"On the other hand, we have the Russian leadership, still stupefied by losses of twenty million people during the Second World War. It is a reflexive action on their part to overarm. If they see one of your tanks in Europe, they will build three to counter it with. But they cannot maintain this insane pace of weapons manufacture. There is too much demand from below for housing, consumer goods, food, and better transportation to sustain this effort.

"The crucial point has arrived. The world now views yours as a second-rate power, but there is much discussion now within the United States for massive and rapid upgrading of weapons within the limitations of the SALT II agreement. If this were to happen, we greatly fear that the Russians would launch a preemptive strike before you could accomplish your goals."

Klist paused. "I'm sorry, Clifford," he said. "You know these things as well as I. I don't mean to sound so academic." He picked up the glasses and started to refill them.

"I don't care for another," said Welsh.

"I think you will," Klist said, placing a filled glass before his guest. "There is yet more to what I have to say. It is the most important part."

Klist settled in his chair, pausing to drink from his glass. He lit a cigarette and paused, trying to compose the words. The effort was discernible, even in the darkness. "Clifford. What I am about to tell you now cannot be proved. I have no . . . as you would call it, documentation. Let me tell you the way this came about.

"One of our members was in Prague last spring to discuss building a rolling mill for high-tensile steel. While he was there, he was invited to the estate of one of the party members whom he had been dealing

147

with. After the dinner was over, the host detained our associate until the guests had left, asking that he remain behind for a meeting. At eleven or shortly thereafter, a man entered the study of the host. This man was, and still is, third-ranking man in the Soviet Presidium. He discussed with our associate just what we have been speaking about. This Russian claimed that it is impossible for them to initiate major concessions in disarmament due to their somewhat dogmatic approach as leader of world communism. Any relaxation at present, if initiated by the Soviets, would destabilize control of their satellites.

"On the other hand, they view rearmament by the United States as a warlike act, and militant members of the Presidium would demand what he termed 'surgical removal of United States military capacity.'

"However, he feels that if the United States were to make moves toward unilateral disarmament, the Soviet Union could respond in kind on a gradual basis, finally falling to a level sufficient only to achieve a balance of power with the Chinese."

"I find this difficult to believe," said Welsh, wanting to believe.

"No," replied Klist. "I assure you that it is true. I would not have come to meet with you if we thought otherwise. The obvious question is why this Russian should approach us rather than meeting with U.S. policy makers directly. The answer is simple. The Russian claimed that such an approach has been made within the last two years directly to your secretary of state. He refused even private discussions at working levels. The Russians feel that the present U.S. Administration is closed to the subject. These men who govern your country are brittle pragmatists. And their pride is dangerous.

"Consequently, the Russians felt that if a U.S. presidential candidate took a positive stance on unilateral disarmament, and if he were supported by an organization such as ours, he might be able to win in the coming election. This would leave the Russians latitude to gradually reduce their armament in a spirit of cooperation without absolute constraints such as SALT II or III might impose. Remember, they still must match the Chinese, a reality that the SALT talks have not encompassed.''

"How do I know that the Russians will keep their word?'' Welsh asked, mentally making the quantum leap from desire to decision.

"There is no assurance, Clifford. There does not have to be. Should you gain the presidency and initiate disarmament, you *must* do so on a token basis. If the Russians respond, you will know that you can safely, but cautiously, proceed. If they do not keep their word, you would be under no pressure or obligation to continue the disarmament. But think for a minute. Can you visualize the impact that it would have on world opinion if you, as a future president, were able to accomplish a nuclear-weapon-free world. Think of the great good that could be done in a society that was free from fear!''

Welsh nodded in the starlight.

Chapter 10

Loss joined the Kents the following morning. The three of them stood on the jetty, waiting for the sloop *Mintar* to come alongside. The sun was still low in the east, hammering the sea into silver. Loss inhaled deeply, smelling damp earth scents mixed with the tang of salt. Down to the west, where they would sail, the mountains of Carriacou jutted up in hills of rock and green—somehow calm and yet dynamic. He exhaled, quite content.

"It looks like a fair day, " Kent said. "I look forward to getting slightly drunk and disorderly. What say, Margaret?" He leaned over and ruffled his wife's hair.

"Keep your sticky hands to yourself," she replied, frost on her voice but winking at Loss. "I will be very cross with you, Edwin, if you're not coherent when Mr. Loss introduces us to his lady."

Loss raised his eyebrows in surprise. "You've met Holly?"

Margaret Kent nodded, smiling. "Two days ago. She came up on the lumpy little boat that they deliver eggs and produce on, just for the afternoon. She asked for you, and Edwin did his usual intelligence-gathering routine and dragged the story out of her. To my knowledge, you were off poking around some reef."

Kent smiled at Brian, slowly dropping one eyelid. "Believe that she bought two bottles of champagne to take back with her. From experience, I think it might be something of a peace offering."

His wife made disgusted sounds in her throat and punched her husband lightly in the chest. "Edwin, you're so *crude* at times. Really!"

Loss laughed lightly. "I should have guessed she'd do something like this. By the way, where is she staying?"

"A place called the Mermaid Tavern," Margaret replied. "But take care, Brian. I take it that she spends quite a bit of time with a young English biologist who works down at the marine laboratory. Flies his own plane as well—private income and some sort of a very generous grant."

The thought made Loss uncomfortable. He was pleased, however, that she had made her own way down here, despite Welsh's unwillingness to share the use of his aircraft. Perhaps Welsh would relent for the return trip. But that he might have competition rankled his ego. Perhaps jealousy, as the saying predicted, was the best aphrodisiac.

The charter sloop came alongside the jetty just before nine and they boarded, Kent swinging easily aboard despite his artificial leg. Giles Tobin, the skipper, led them to the cockpit where he had hot coffee waiting. They drank together from enameled mugs while Giles outlined the day.

In his late twenties, Tobin had an owlish face and a lean body with long, ropy muscles. Aviator glasses spanned his eyes and covered his cheekbones, emphasizing the blank-wise look. Tanned to the shade of walnut, he wore only cut-off jeans which had faded nearly white. His hair was long and sun-bleached, but tied neatly in a queue, like some seventeenth-century foretopman who had sailed before the mast.

Giles finished the briefing, tracing his finger along the marine chart. "We'll come back up through these off-lying islands, harden up for Gunn Point and tack back up to Salt Whistle Cay. Should be in by eight-thirty—nine at the latest."

A Mini-Moke thumped down the dock, the rear seat loaded with blocks of ice and a case of beer. Giles flicked his eyes to Kent and then to Loss. "Mind giving me a hand, Mr. Loss?"

Loss helped Giles shift the ice from the dock to the deck of the *Mintar,* then down through the foredeck hatch. Loss followed Giles down, taking one corner of the block with Giles moving aft to the galley.

They heaved the block into the ice chest and Giles attacked it with a pick, breaking it down into manageable lumps.

"A Hilyard, isn't it?" Loss leaned back against a bulkhead, his hands looped over the skylight beam. The little ship smelled of the amalgam of all small boats—diesel fuel, cooking fat, and varnish. It didn't have the elaborate joinerwork of Kitzner's *Surprise,* nor the spaciousness, but the small sloop had the feel of a tight, sea-kindly boat.

Giles paused in the chopping, turning to look at Loss. "Not many people would know that. She was built at Littlehampton in 1949. Pitchpine on oak frames." He paused, lifting the sunglasses to his forehead. "Pardon for saying so, but Americans think that sailboats always come out of a mold. Hardly anyone on your side of the Atlantic makes wood boats anymore."

Loss nodded. "I wouldn't have known except there was a Hilyard moored next to a schooner I used to sail on. Knew the guy that owned her." He told Giles about Kitzner and the *Surprise*.

Giles almost vibrated with excitement, asking Loss about fine details—how did Kitzner run the topping lifts on the gaff, whether she had a fisherman staysail and how it was tacked. Confident, Loss answered, detailing the *Surprise*, as Kitzner had said, down to the last bolt head.

"Sounds like a fine ship!" Giles said. His eyes were unfocused, dreaming as sailors do of the perfect ship.

Margaret Kent broke the silence. Arching her head over, she looked down the companionway. "Have you more coffee, Giles?"

"Coming up," he shouted back. Pumping on a handle, he trickled alcohol into the burner and then lit it, waiting for the heat exchanger to begin to vaporize the fluid.

"Why not use propane?" Loss asked.

Giles stared back at him. "Damned dangerous stuff," he said. "Had a mate in Gibraltar who blew up his boat that way. The stuff sinks to the bottom of the bilge. Start a pump or some other kind of electrical gear and the whole thing can go sky high."

While the water was heating for coffee, Tobin showed Loss the rest of the *Mintar*. Forecastle for sail stowage, a small forward head with a Baby Blake marine toilet that Loss estimated would fetch a fortune in an antique store. Moving aft, Giles swung open a panel and showed Loss the miniscule engine room.

"Stuart-Turner diesel, two electric bilge pumps and batteries," Giles commented. "About enough power to get four knots out of her in a calm sea." He dropped the panel, latching it. "Hate engine rooms, Mate," he said and smiled.

Loss carried the fresh coffee up the companionway and joined the Kents, anxious to be under way. Below, they could hear Tobin moving around, stowing things, singing under his breath about the sea, the men on and under it, and the women left behind.

While the Kents shared the coffee, talking in clipped sentences which seemed to be their own private shorthand, Loss moved around the deck, inspecting the rigging and running gear. He paused for a second near the anchor winch, looking toward the shore. The grounds' staff were spaced out across the open lawns, trimming hedges, spading in flower beds. One man pushed a mower along the edge of the lawn where weed met grass. By noon, Loss thought, the men would be one step removed from the shade of the sea grape trees and a cold bottle of beer.

Along the beach to the south, two men jogged, keeping a hard pace in the morning sun. He knew they would be Klist and Welsh. Welsh and his wife were with the Klists almost constantly, eating meals in each other's cottage and only coming down to the pavilion for an evening drink. The men kept to themselves, talking intently, and when Loss had approached Welsh yesterday afternoon, Welsh had dismissed him as curtly as he would have a servant.

Welsh is an odd one, Loss thought. The public image of the lean-tough-incorruptible politician was one thing. But the real man was different. Neither the emulsion of a photograph or the phosphor of a TV tube conveyed the vacillation, the need to be constantly reassured, or the hunger for justification. The man seemed to be driven by some inner, inflexible image of himself. For his dead father or perhaps his wife. Maybe for the people of New York or DeSilva.

But regardless, what Welsh did was not for its own reward. There had to be a prompter in the wings and applause down front.

The Klist relationship was probably some business deal but it had all the hallmarks of an elaborate setup. Too controlled, too perfect, and now growing far too intense. Loss made a mental note to check with the manager to find out when the Klists had made their reservations. If it had been prior to Welsh making his, then there was probably nothing to worry about.

Giles finally came up from below, wiping his hands on his cut-offs. He moved forward, his frame awkward and stringy, but the placement of hands and feet oddly precise, without waste of energy. Probably a good man on windy nights, Loss thought.

Tobin spoke, detailing the procedure of getting underway. "We'll be off now, right? Mr. Loss—cast off the docking lines, bow first and then the stern. Mr. Kent can stand by the main halyard to take in the slack as I get it up." He gave the tiller to Mrs. Kent. "Just keep her down to the west once I get off the dock." They nodded, pleased to be part of the crew.

By 9:30 the *Mintar* was underway; Tobin content in his familiar world and the Kents relaxed and easy, just flowing with the day. Loss was expectant now, feeling the sloop moving easily under his feet in the following sea, thinking of Holly.

Heiss watched them leave. His 7 x 50 binoculars could pick out the small details of the yacht and the individual faces. He cased the glasses finally and walked down the road which bordered the seafront, watching as the yacht ran off before the wind. Near the southern end of the island the sloop gibed over onto port tack and raised a small staysail, making good time now in the fresh breeze.

He lingered, watching the *Mintar* until it was just a small triangle of white, hull down before the trades. Heiss fantasized, seeing himself as the master of a yacht, churning along the Côte d'Azur, touching at the harbors where the very rich played. Not a sailing boat, he thought. Something with two engines and a crew in whites. He thought of the women that he would meet in places such as Cannes, Nice, and San Remo.

Heiss slung the case from his shoulder and climbed the path to the beach which Loss occupied, stopping occasionally to examine the flowers and gaze out over the anchorage. He passed two West Indian house-keepers pushing a linen cart before them, giggling to each other, carefully hiding their mouths to suppress their shared laughter. He drew opposite them and they both became quiet, smiling, polite, playing the auto-matic role of blacks near whites. He heard them laugh again when he was past them, thinking that they were laughing at him. Bitches, he thought.

He entered Loss's cottage after knocking first. The room was clean, the bed freshly made, and pillow plumped. Fresh hibiscus had been placed in a vase.

He checked the only recorder, finding no more than five inches of tape on the takeup reel. The batteries were now a bit low, the charge indicator showing in the caution zone. He changed them, replacing each cell with a gloved hand so as to leave no print.

This was the first time that Loss had been absent from the island. Heiss methodically inspected the con-tents of drawers, the pilot's flight case, and a worn B-4 suitcase that still had the faded stencil indicating the owner was Captain Loss, USAF.

The closet yielded a leather briefcase, scarred and discolored, but firmly locked. Heiss carefully noted the position of the case as it rested on the floor and then inspected he entire case with his penlight before moving it, looking for the strand of hair, the bit of paper that would tell its owner of tampering. He then worked with the locks, probing with a small tungsten-bladed tool until they yielded.

He carefully opened the case and found that its contents were mainly the ordinary things a traveler would carry: a passport, several books of traveler's checks, and a stack of oil company credit cards bound by a rubber band. But the item of most interest to Heiss was a nine-millimeter Luger, carefully holstered. Heiss eased the weapon from its case. It gleamed in the morning sunlight, dull black with age and oil. He smelled the barrel and then handled the gun, feeling the compact power it gave his extended arm as the ramp sights came together in perfect union.

Interesting, thought Heiss. It was not the type of weapon an agent or bodyguard would carry. Too dangerous to carry with a round in the chamber and subject to misfires. He guessed that Loss would carry the weapon out of habit formed in the service. Interesting, nevertheless. It was helpful to know of the weapon's existence. But he would not report this to Klist. This was a bit of private knowledge that he would save against an uncertain future.

Heiss replaced the weapon in its holster and returned it to the briefcase. After locking it, he replaced the briefcase exactly as it had been, with the handle on the correct side and a tennis sock resting against the edge.

Leaving the cottage after a careful survey of the path and the hill above, Carl Heiss walked slowly toward his own cottage, pausing along the road to poke at flowers as any normal guest would do. All part of the job, he thought sardonically. The sun was higher in the east now, the pathway hot beneath his sandaled feet. Sweat soaked the armpits of his shirt and his scalp prickled with the heat. And his eyes ached with the brightness.

Heiss looked up toward his own cottage and saw a flash of white clothing retreat from the open door of his patio into the dark interior. He paused in the shade of a manchineel tree, breathing heavily from the exertion of the grade, waiting for long minutes to catch some variation in the dark patterns. Cursing himself, he remembered the binoculars he carried. Withdrawing them from the case, he focused the glasses on the interior and picked up the shape of a person moving around; a woman surely, but clothed in a bikini or banded-patterned dress. But not a black.

He strode normally to the cottage pathway, sure that he was highly visible from the darkness of the interior.

Lousje lay in the chaise longue, drinking from a chilled glass. Her long legs were crossed in composed grace, the darkness of her tanned skin in strong contrast to the white of the bikini. The sweat on her body gave a dull sheen to her skin, as if she had oiled it. Dark stains marked her body's outline on the chaise's cotton mat.

"Sit down and listen, Heiss," she said. "I don't have much time." She gestured toward the caneback chair.

He ignored her, walking to the bar and pouring himself a beer. He drank half of it down, wiped his mouth, and then turned to her. "You're a dumb slut. With you up here the maids will know. It'll be all over the bar in an hour, discussed in the kitchen by supper, and Welsh will know about it before seven."

"I'm here at Senator Welsh's suggestion. I told him that I needed advice on what type of filter to use for my Pentax." She indicated the camera case lying on the tiles near the doorway. "He suggests that you might know since you're always carrying a camera." She made a motion with her head, nodding toward the chair. "Sit down and shut up. We're wasting time."

Heiss finished off the beer and drew another from the cooler. She had a very good body, he realized. Not thin as he had first imagined but full-blown and firm. She saw the look; saw his eyes move down her body.

"As I said before, Heiss, you're a pig." She said it conversationally, as if she were commenting on the state of the weather. "Neither Petrov nor I are people

157

to be fooled with. Just do your job and collect your money. Save your little games for some other woman." She paused, swirling the cubes around in her glass. "Or are you keen on little boys, Heiss?"

He started to come at her, but she lay there, unconcerned. "Try me, Heiss. I'll break your balls." She sipped at her drink, looking at him noncommittally over the rim of the glass, then lowered it, licking her upper lip.

There was something lethal in the way she said it, he realized. She had no fear of him. He pivoted away, looking out across the lawn.

"As you say," he finally muttered. "There are little boys that you couldn't hold a candle to. Twenty deutsch-marks would be about the right price." He took a sip of the beer. "So tell me what you're here for?"

She set the empty glass on the tiles. "Petrov," she said, "wants to know whether you have sufficient recordings. Also, the number and quality of the photographs."

"I have two or three full reels of tapes between Welsh and his wife. Over eight between Welsh and Petrov. I haven't had time to go over them for the quality but they're bound to be readable."

"Photographs?"

"Two or three hundred. I've shot ten rolls of film. Good groupings, full face, profile, running on the beach together. And several more of Welsh and his wife. High ASA. They should be good but until I can get them developed. I can only guess."

She stood up, pulling up the bra of her bikini, looking out beyond the patio, taunting him at some lower level of consciousness. It was a movement as natural as brushing her hair from her eyes, yet designed to provoke. She picked up the camera and hung it over her shoulders and moved to the door.

"Petrov wanted me to remind you that you're not to rewind the tapes and listen to them. There's a mark

158

on them which will betray any snooping, and we both know that sort of thing is hazardous to your health.

"Be prepared to leave tomorrow morning. You'll be flown directly to Mexico. From there, you can convert some money into pesos and find lots of little *mestizas* to buy. Your job will be finished."

"How am I going? There's no flight for—"

"By private plane, Heiss. It's being arranged." She walked out, the bag swinging against her hip. He watched her as she walked down the concrete path toward the Welsh cottage.

Chapter 11

Welsh leaned back in the camp chair, teetering on the rear legs, his eyes closed. Despite the shade cast by the table's umbrella, he could feel the sun burning through the fabric, through his shirt, his skin, down through his very bone marrow, thickening his blood, burdening his heart, slowing his brain.

He was working on his third rum and tonic and it was not yet noon, but he was buttressing his resolve to tell Klist that the thing was finished, kaput. Eyes still closed, he clasped the glass more tightly, swirling the drink, listening to the ice clink against the walls of the glass. Besides being slightly drunk, he was goddamned tired. Judith and he had argued over the decision well into the dawn hours. Finally he had reluctantly conceded that she was probably right.

"It won't work," he finally said.

Petrov glanced up from writing, laying his pen aside. "What won't?" He stretched, leaning back in

159

imitation of Welsh, yawning. It was late morning, the sun at its strongest, baking the ground to rocklike consistency. The wind had fallen and thus brought no relief from the heat. "What won't work?" he repeated, mildly irritated.

"The whole goddamned thing, Klist. The whole half-assed scheme. I'm backing out."

Petrov rocked forward, torso falling into the shadow of the umbrella. His face tensed, his eyes carefully examining Welsh's expression. He took a long breath, exaggerating the inhalation and slowly expelling it. "I'll ignore what you've just said. You've had too much to drink. We're both committed too deeply to reverse the process."

"You don't hear very well," Welsh replied, gaining confidence, sure now that there would be no crisis. "I've thought the thing through. It's too chancy, too iffy, to stake my whole political future on. And I don't like the idea of being controlled." He opened his eyes, watching Petrov's face for a sign of acceptance. "Look, Robert, I don't doubt the intentions of you and your group. I'm flattered that you've chosen me as a likely candidate for the presidency. But the whole thing is too bizarre. It won't work."

Petrov stood up abruptly and walked into the living room of the cottage and opened his briefcase, withdrawing a sheaf of papers. He paused at the bar, poured himself a glass of orange juice, and returned to the patio. For a long time, gently slapping the papers against his thigh, he stared out over the anchorage, sipping the juice, his back turned to Welsh.

"Suppose you give me your reasons," he said finally.

Welsh noticed an almost disinterested quality in the European's voice, as if the discussion were academic. "I can't take the chance," Welsh countered. "It's too slick, too pat. You're proposing that I stand up in the Senate and introduce a bill ceding the Canal to a Marxist revolutionary government. We both know that will go down badly; even liberals will have problems swallowing it. And if your influence peddling in Panama doesn't work, I'll be left as the sponsor of a resolution that will be defeated by probably a ten-to-one margin. With that kind of political egg on my face, I couldn't even hope to get elected dogcatcher." He set his glass down on the table and pushed it away, smearing the rings of condensation. "I can't chance it," he continued. "On top of that, if the content of our discussions were ever to become public knowledge, I could be tried for God knows what violations of Senate ethics codes, perhaps even federal law."

"You've discussed this with your wife." It was a flat statement. "And she feels that you're selling out." Petrov drained his glass.

"Something to that effect." Welsh felt the hairs on the back of his neck lifting, as if he had seen a vision of his own funeral.

"Not something like that, Clifford—her words exactly. Am I correct?"

At first Welsh had lied to his wife, telling her nothing more of the discussions other than the fact that Klist had a good grasp of the European view of disarmament. But she saw through Welsh's awkward explanations, and after two days of intensive discussions with Klist, Welsh had spilled out the truth to her.

"You're after this presidency thing simply so that you can spit on your father's grave, aren't you?" she asked. She had rolled over in bed and he felt her breath on his shoulder.

"Not necessarily," he lied. Welsh dimly perceived that his long drive for political power was an attempt to meet the impossible standards that his father had relentlessly set. Stroke oar, achiever on campus, and then New York State's youngest attorney general. His father was dead now, but the legacy of striving for and never quite meeting impossible standards still ruled his life.

She kneaded his neck muscles in silence for a few minutes, and said, "Then ask yourself whether Klist's methods would have been acceptable to your father. You're selling out—at least your integrity."

"And beyond that?" he snapped back.

"What you used to refer to as your country," she had answered, very softly, almost hesitantly.

Early this morning he had given in to her argument, half-frustrated because he knew that Klist's proposal had a chance of working, yet relieved that he would not bear the responsibility of guilt if he failed.

Welsh looked up at Petrov. "How did you know what she had said? I mean, said exactly?" But he knew, expected the answer: every word they had uttered was on tape.

Instead of replying, Petrov spread the papers across the table. He picked the first one, glanced at it, and skidded it across the table toward the senator. "Your Swiss account, inherited from your father. All properly registered, Swiss taxes paid, transfers ready for your signature." He leaned back, his fingers laced across his chest, watching Welsh's reaction. Again, Welsh had the disconcerting impression of being looked through, as if the outcome of the discussion were a foregone conclusion.

The paper was stiff bond paper with an embossed letterhead: *Crédit Suisse Commercial, S.A.,* addressed to a lawyer in the Cayman Islands. The first two paragraphs were obsequious phrases, the type of thing almost mandatory in European business correspondence. The third paragraph was the meat of the letter:

The present value of the holdings, including the value of the estate in the Algarve of Portugal (appraised valuation enclosed but subject to prevailing market fluctuations) is now $3,872,221 in U.S. currency. We will be pleased to act as agent in both trading matters and in transfers of funds should Senator Welsh desire the services of our firm.

The signature, in precise strokes but unreadable as the Dead Sea Scrolls, was followed by the title *Trust Manager, M. Darrelline*.

Welsh felt his armpits leaking moisture, as if a tap had been turned on. "I know nothing about this. My father died nine years ago. There was nothing in Switzerland."

Petrov retrieved the paper and glanced at it. "This says differently," he commented. "Very differently. I know little of U.S. tax codes, but isn't it a violaion of IRS statutes to draw on dividends of foreign investments and not report them? Your tax returns from the past eight years show no indication of such income."

Welsh sat upright, his heart pounding. "No one would believe such a goddamned . . ."

Petrov lifted his eyebrows. "Believe what? That an American citizen, finding that he had a secret inheritance overseas, failed to report it?" He lifted another sheet from the stack of documents, a stiff manila ledger with accounting entries covering both sides. As if quoting chapter and verse, he droned, "Cable transfer to the Bahamas in 1971 of twelve thousand some-odd dollars. Another to Denmark in 1973 of nearly twenty thousand kroners. Three more—each approximately eight thousand in the years 1974 to 1977. And each transfer coinciding in time and place with your foreign travels." He dropped the card onto the stack of paper. "You asked who would believe. Perhaps it would be better to ask who would *not* believe? Isn't that the temper of your political climate these days?"

Welsh's mouth hung slack, his eyes riveted on the European. "You've set me up, Klist! For some kind of blackmail operation!" He stumbled to his feet, almost tipping the table over. Some of the documents slid on the inclined surface of the Formica and spilled to the patio floor.

Petrov gave no reaction other than to lift his hand. "Sit down, Clifford," he said evenly. "These documents need never be made public. The situation is not at all what you think."

"What I THINK . . ." Welsh screamed at him, "is what I can read with my own damn eyes." He snatched up the letter and hurled it in Petrov's face.

Petrov retrieved the paper, flattening it under his palm on the surface of the table. He leaned over and carefully picked up the other documents, then inserted them in order. "Sit down, Clifford. Give me three minutes to explain. Then you can act as you wish."

Welsh was halfway to the door but paused. What Petrov had in his hands was disastrous, inexplicable even if untrue. It had to be resolved. Welsh changed direction and, going to the bar, poured himself a stiff measure of rum. He came back onto the patio and sat down. "Three minutes is exactly what you've got, Klist. Make it good."

Petrov's manner changed, became a mirror of what it had been over the last few days: open, warm, confident. "Listen, Clifford. In many respects, this situation is my own fault. I told you there were several candidates. What I didn't tell you is that you were the second choice as far as my associates were concerned. When I first arrived, I was prepared to talk to you, test your reactions, and probably concede that the first-choice candidate was the best selection. But I found you had much more depth than any dossier would convey. Two days ago you convinced me that your strengths as a decision maker would benefit both the United States and Europe, and that your policy on arms reduction was well considered and meshed exactly with the realities of the world political situation. Remember, at that point you gave me your assurance that the plan as I had presented it met your complete approval. In short, I called my associates and told them that under no circumstances should any other potential candidate be contacted, and that this account in Zurich should be activated and an emissary be sent immediately to Panama. These things are in motion now. They can't be stopped."

Some of the tension had gone out of Welsh. He sat quietly, analyzing, working his fingers along the bridge of his nose. "I'm listening," he said.

"You have to understand one thing," Petrov continued. "You made a commitment. Now we have made a commitment—the depth of which is measured in tens of millions of dollars. But what is even more critical is the short time we have to project you into a credible attempt at the presidency. If this attempt fails, we believe a continuation of your country's present policy toward rearmament will precipitate a war in Europe. To wait another four years for the next presidential election would be intolerable."

"That hardly explains blackmail."

Petrov hunched his shoulders forward fractionally. "I think what you term 'blackmail' is more correctly defined as *realpolitik*—the application of real political power in a real world. As much as I didn't want to threaten you with these documents, you must realize that we could not merely pin our hopes on simple faith in one man—a single, fallible man, open to the capriciousness that we all suffer from as human beings." Petrov made a helpless gesture with his hands, the palms turned upward. "It would have been the same with any candidate we selected. Once we felt you had accepted our proposal—and remember, Clifford, you did that two full days ago of your own free will and without threats or offers of reward—we had to be sure that you would carry through. As I've said, the stakes are too high for us to merely gamble on your cooperation. We have made tape recordings of all our meetings, photographs of us together, recordings even of discussions between you and your wife. And, of course, these documents. As I've said, they will never be used—only as a last resort should you suddenly alter the commitment you have already pledged yourself to."

Welsh had tightened his lips, the anger evident. He started to object, but Petrov raised his hand. "Damn you, Clifford. I've laid my life literally on the line because I felt you were the right man. Give me the courtesy of a few minutes and then you can do as you desire." Petrov turned away slightly, his face averted, his voice softer. "I know from the recordings between you and your wife that she doesn't trust me or the proposal I've put forward. I've known for months before this meeting that much of what you've attained in your political career has been the result of your attempt to meet the standards your father set. In a way, we're all captives of the people we love—and I include myself as well. I can tell you without shame that what I am doing here is a direct result of my brother-in-law's death. He died because of the insanity of war—a war that is almost surely going to be fought unless you and I can help stop it. I loved him deeply. His death was, perhaps, a sacrifice made to impress upon me the vital necessity of what you and I are doing, Clifford. And in those terms, I cannot apologize for what you call 'blackmail.' We have to succeed." He turned back, a hard edge to his voice, clenching his fist. "You understan—we *have* to."

"What do you plan to do with these things—the recordings and this trash from the bank?" Welsh was leaning forward, intent.

"Nothing, Clifford. Absolutely nothing. And nothing has changed between us. You will shortly be informed by another letter from this bank that your father left you his investments on the condition that you were not to be informed until ten years after his death—perhaps enough time for the investments to grow in a booming business climate, and perhaps also because he wanted you to achieve something on your own first, without the weight of money behind you.

166

His reasons are given in a will that will accompany the letter. You must then simply declare his assets to your Internal Revenue Service and pay the appropriate taxes. The remainder of the funds will serve for your initial campaign expenses. These other letters and the recordings would not ever become public."

Welsh leaned back in his chair, eyes closed. "And if I don't follow our scenario . . . ?"

"You would leave my associates no choice. Your career would be ruined, as would mine. The stakes are so high, Clifford, that I could easily lose more than my reputation. I am the one who has gne against the majority in selecting you. We would have both lost everything and gained nothing, not even honor." Petrov dropped his hands to the table, palms down, as if to signify that he had presented his case and awaited judgment. "Do you understand now, Clifford?"

Welsh heaved a long sigh. He looked closely at Petrov. "You know how goddamned lonely and tough it is, trying to lead, trying to achieve something decent, making hard choices; bargaining a dam in Utah or a logrolling, pork-barrel project in Texas for teacher-pension support in New York. The whole system is one big trade-off." He clasped his hands together, looking down at the veins. "All right," he finally said, looking up. "This is another fucking trade-off. I want the presidency because I think I can do a decent job. And I want this disarmament thing to go ahead. I believe in it. But I want your assurance of one principle and I want it right now—I'll use the situations you've outlined—the Panama and Cuban operations—and you can be damned sure I'll fight for disarmament. But you can expect nothing else from me. No favoritism, no special deals, nothing. You read me, Klist?"

"Agreed," Petrov said quietly. "Except there is one final situation I had planned to discuss today. Perhaps the critical one for success."

"What situation?" Welsh asked wearily.

"Let's review the scenario," Petrov answered.

"We have two events that will propel you into national prominence—the Panamanian and Cuban accords. These will prove your ability as a bold, imaginative, yet just maker of foreign policy. With these two victories alone, our computer projections give you a forty-percent chance of winning the election."

"Which is good enough," Welsh interjected.

"Which is nowhere *near* good enough," Petrov retorted. "Not when that figure can be raised to over ninety percent by one short speech you could make on national television."

"Speech about what?"

"Unilateral disarmament, and the hidden and undiscussed danger of nuclear weapons storage in the United States."

"I think your computer blew a transistor."

"I'm not finished," Petrov snapped. "Consider your position at that point: a dark-horse candidate, nationally known but without any real bloc of convention delegates. You'd stand a good chance as a vice-presidential candidate—a dead-end street in politics. Suppose, however, that in this speech you emphasized not only the economic benefits of converting guns to butter but also cautioned the American public of the dangers in nuclear weapons storage: the possibility of an accident in handling, the leakage of radioactivity from warheads, a bomber's crashing, or inadvertent detonation in training exercises. That, in fact, there are over six thousand nuclear warheads—six thousand potential nuclear accidents—stored within the continental limits of the United States."

Welsh scoffed. "Fifty-eight long-haired freaks from the Clamshell Alliance would stand up and cheer. The rest of the voters would yawn."

"But let's say," Petrov continued, "that two weeks later, eighty sheep grazing three miles downwind of a Minuteman missile silo in Wyoming die of radioactive poisoning."

Welsh stared at him.

"Sometime prior to your speech, the watering troughs of these sheep will be contaminated with radioactive materials—iodine 131 and barium 140. These are typical fission-weapon by-products. Ingestion by the sheep will cause lesions, diarrhea, and ultimately death. The process on test animals indicates about a two-week waiting period."

"NO!" Welsh rasped.

"The material decays rapidly," Petrov continued calmly. "About an eight- to twelve-day half-life. There will be no possibility of harm to humans. But the sheep will die from a massive overdose of radioactivity, and the Air Force will be powerless to prove that it wasn't some sort of catastrophic leakage from a Minuteman warhead."

Welsh started to rise, shaking his head. His skin had an unhealthy cast, and perspiration was soaking his armpits.

"It's been planned carefully, Clifford. These isotopes are being brought in from a nuclear powerplant in France and the man handling them is a trained nuclear technician. I can assure you that all of the contingencies have been evaluated and provided for. No connection can possibly be made to you."

"I said *No!*" Welsh was on his feet, moving backward toward the patio door.

"I want you to take some time to think about this," Petrov said. "But I want your decision by this evening. If we're to go ahead, your pilot will have to be informed about taking Bolken and me to Mexico tomorrow morning. And I have some cables to send." He paused and walked toward Welsh, relaxed. "Eighty sheep sacrificed for our project, Clifford. A minimal risk for the potential rewards. And besides," he added, "it's part of the package. Non-negotiable, you might say."

Chapter 12

Sunlight spilled in splashes of gold across the weathered floor, the dark curtains breathing heavily in the wind. The century palms in the courtyard rustled in accompaniment, flicking fronts against the outer walls of their room. There was the sound of bare feet treading down the hallway outside their room and of ice clinking in a pitcher, and then the sound retreated toward the far end of the hall and down the stairs.

"Welcome home," she said, her fingers kneading the small of his back, pulling him into her. "Be still. Just lie like that. I want to be able to feel you for a long time."

He could look down into her eyes, vision blurred at this closeness. Just the tan and darkness of her face, her eyes closed, lashes impossibly long. The white and floral patterns of the pillow beneath her head gave an impressionistic background—abstract Gauguin.

An involuntary surge of desire traversed his frame, but he stilled it, thinking hard about not thinking. Her breasts were points against his chest. He bent his neck to find a hollow against her shoulder, lips against her ear. "This is Carriacou," he said, and she made a marginal nod, breathing more deeply, her exhalations coming in small shudders.

His back was wet with perspiration and felt alternately cool and warm from random gusts of wind and stillness. She moved her hands more strongly, holding his waist, pulling him against her. Tightly, not easing the pressure.

He started to move against her, unconscious of his own thrusts.

"Slowly," she said. Neither statement nor command. Just Holly, warm and full, tasting of salt crystals. "Slowly," and her breath was growing more shallow. She started to move under him, no clear direction. More pressure than movement.

He thought of himself suspended in the sea, motionless, the hollow sound of breathing from tanks, the bubbles making bright patterns in the sunlight above. Green world. The vestiges of a deep Pacific swell reaching him at this depth and lifting him in rhythm. Kelp fanning in haze yellows against the invisible waves. Out beyond the ring of sunlight, darkness.

The rafters creaked in the heat, an outboard humming in the bay. Small sounds without continuity reached his ears. Sounds she made, deep breathing, shallower breathing, sounds of moisture between their skin. Coarse sounds. He realized it was his own lungs drawing for air.

Her body convulsed in small shudders, her breath catching. Seas breaking at the crest, but the longer Pacific swells keeping their measure of time, lifting and receding.

She convulsed again, her mouth pressed against his shoulder, kissing the skin, saying little monosyllables, her closed eyes spilling tears, fingers tighter now against his back, probing.

"Now," she said. "Please now." And she closed her thighs, forcing her legs up between his, arching her back, cupping his buttocks and drawing him into her.

He came to her, holding her head in his hands, kissing her salty cheeks, saying things stored in the far corners of his mind.

The sun moved west along the sixth parallel, the barometer fell three millibars, and the tide checked to the east. During this time they slept and then awoke and made love to each other and slept again.

He awoke at 5:18 P.M., arose from the mahogany four-poster, and went to the window overlooking the courtyard. Two blacks sat beneath the almond tree. They were playing checkers and drinking beer from dark green bottles, slamming the wooden men down hard, because that is the way a man shows his confidence in winning. He could hear the rattle of their board, their talk in low tones, and their laughter. The *Mintar* still lay anchored offshore, rolling languorously in the beam swell from Hillsborough Bay. Puffy afternoon cumulus were trooping along in the northern quadrant of the afternoon sky.

"Do you have to go?"

He turned to her. She lay stretched out, arching her feet, hands behind her head.

"Yes, soon," he replied. "Will you come with me?"

"You look funny standing there, speaking to me so seriously, your thing flapping around in the breeze." She brushed her hair from her eyes, laughing. "Men should go into battle naked. They'd be so terrified of having it cut off they'd never fight. But give them a pair of pants . . ."

"Will you go with me?" he asked again, annoyed, pleased, a little embarrassed.

"Yes. Don't you remember that I came to Carriacou to see a friend?"

They met the Kents in the bar below and ordered rum punch after signaling Giles to bring the dinghy ashore. Margaret looked at their faces and smiled, knowing, and then to relieve their embarrassment, poured out her purchased treasures of hawksbill turtle bracelets and bric-a-brac. Kent filled in the gaps by telling them of the trip to the hospital up in the hills with the cannon on the front lawn overlooking the bay. Throughout the story, his eyes were laughing.

Giles came and they all had a second punch and then left for the yacht, taking turns rowing the inflatable dinghy. By six they were under way, beating back up the lee coast in light northerly winds.

172

The sun was setting as it does in the tropics, early and rapidly, leaving no twilight. The vaulted dome above them was streaked with cirrus, which splayed out from the north.

"Windy weather coming, Giles?" Kent asked, sweeping his hand across the sky.

Giles threw his cigarette to leeward and watched the sky thoughtfully, chewing on the corner of his lip. "I don't know," he answered. "We see so much high cloud down here in the winter. Usually means heavy weather farther north. If I were in the English Channel, I'd be runnin' for a port." He looked again at the sky in the dying light. "Mare's tails, they're called. Usually what you see a coupla hundred miles in front of a cold front. North of that they'll be thunderstorms and low scud and plenty of rain." He ducked down the companionway, giving the helm to Kent. Five minutes later, he reappeared with a thermos of cocoa and some mugs. "Barometer's down over six millibars. Sure to be a front up north and likely to blow like hell tomorrow. Good day for workin' below."

Holly leaned against Loss, edging back against the cockpit coaming. He felt the warmth of her body through the thin material of her windbreaker. Shoving her fingertip into his ribs, she whispered, "If it rains tomorrow, we'll have to stay in bed all day."

He protested, groaning, but thinking of the two bottles of champagne still untouched in her duffel bag. "We could do crossword puzzles," he said, smiling, and she shoved her elbow into his stomach. He looked up to find Kent laughing behind the hand his wife had cupped over his mouth. Margaret was looking noncommittally astern. Good people to share good days with, Loss thought.

The twilight faded and merged into the blackness of the sea. Giles turned on the running lights and binnacle, casting his face in soft red shadows. The stars

173

wheeled west in the dome above them, and they drank their cocoa in silence, listening to the wind and the chuckle of water under the bow, each of them content with the small moment of suspended time.

The *Mintar* tacked up through the reefs to the east of Carriacou, Giles taking bearings over the top of the compass on shore lights from Petit Martinique and Salt Whistle Cay. The yacht was making good time now, eating its way up to windward, chewing bites out of the northerly swell and spitting them out to leeward. They sailed into the anchorage with sheets started, the wind now going light and further into the north.

By 8:40 Giles had laid the sloop alongside the jetty and they wished him good night. He watched them disappear into the darkness beyond the jetty light and powered back to his mooring, taking time to lay out a second storm anchor and place additional gaskets on the sails. Work done on deck, he sat in the companionway, enjoying a final cigarette, and watched the stars in the northern quadrant of the sky become obscured, one by one, with the advancing storm.

The wind had backed into the north and he could feel a surge working its way into the protected anchorage. With the sensitivity of most men who sail alone, he noted the difference in the sound of the seas breaking on the windward reef. They now broke with muffled hollowness, like the seas off Corsica before a winter storm.

The wind was coming now in puffs, with short lulls in between. Much drier now, he thought, noting that no dew had formed. And colder. He slipped below and lit the oil lamp which swung from its gimbaled brackets above the salon table. The barometer had paused in its downward race just before sunset, but it was falling again rapidly. The old receiver could barely pick up Miami's marine forecast for the Caribbean, and, at the most, he could only hear a garbled voice between crashes of static.

Sighing, he laid out his oilskins on the starboard

berth and undressed, setting his alarm for midnight. He would check the anchors then and try to get the Trinidad forecast.

"Bloody fucked-up business, this," he muttered to himself. He snuffed out the flame and eased his body into the narrow bunk.

Loss had seen the message tacked to his cottage door when they returned from Carriacou. On the following morning he stood in Welsh's cottage, beads of water dripping from his foul-weather gear.

Welsh didn't turn to greet him but instead stood by the plate glass windows, watching the channel to the south. The sea was flecked with white and the sky was overcast with black scud racing in from the northeast. Most of the yachts that had been anchored in the lee of the island had left for more protected anchorages, except for the *Mintar*, which was rolling heavily at her mooring.

Welsh sighed and turned to Loss. "Did you get the Barbados forecast?"

Loss pursed his lips and exhaled heavily. He wondered whether Welsh realized that forecasting on the western fringes of the Atlantic was largely dependent on aircraft and ship reports and that in this part of the world, such reports were relatively scarce. "Barbados says there's an extensive low pressure area to the north, coupled with a strong cold front. *Tiros* weather satellite shows extensive cloud cover from Trinidad to the Straits of Florida. Their barometer is down to nine nine two millibars, which is about the bottom of the barrel. They have no reading on winds aloft, and several of the commercial flights have been canceled. In short, the weather's marginal."

Welsh got up and paced the glass-enclosed veranda, looking out to the east. It was the type of day that travel agents don't talk about. He wished fitfully that he was away from this goddamn son-of-a-bitching place. Back up in his home on the Hudson, in the

175

study working on something that he could grasp and control. "Brian, I have to put it this way. Klist is important to me. He has to get to Mexico today. I'm under a good deal of pressure to help him out. Can you make the trip?"

Loss watched the channel for some minutes. The surface wind looked at least thirty knots, and it would be a lot stronger aloft. There was bound to be some icing over the 15,000-foot level, and it would be rough as a cob. "Yes, I can make it," he said. "If not, I'll go into Puerto Rico and wait it out. They've got good instrument approaches into San Juan. But I'm telling you right now, the trip is going to be a real bastard."

Welsh poured himself another cup of coffee and sat down heavily in the chaise longue, spilling some of the liquid on his shirt. He didn't seem to notice. He drank the contents and set the cup down on the tile floor. "Brian, Puerto Rico's out. So is the Dominican Republic. Klist wants—I want you to make the flight direct. You've got plenty of fuel, and I know that we've made much longer trips together, even in bad weather. This trip is politically sensitive. I'm committed, and this trip to Mexico is crucial to the . . ." He paused, groping for words.

"Crucial to what, for Christ's sake?" Loss interjected, angrily. He was immediately sorry for the verbal punch. Welsh looked ten years older. Dark rings sagged in pouches beneath his eyes, and his tan was a sickly yellow. The perfectly cut hair was unkempt and dull.

Welsh wheeled on him, his mouth gasping for words, his face flushing. "Loss, you stupid bastard. This is one of the most important things in my life. I pay your salary. I don't have to explain everything I do to you. This is tough enough for me without your kicking comments around."

"Look, *Mister* Welsh, the distance involved is roughly 1,300 miles. Even with the long-range tanks, it's going to be tight. And if I go direct, I've got no means of radio navigation. I could hit the coast of Mexico one hundred miles either side of Cozumel. I'll go, but I'm going to first head for Santo Domingo and get a radio fix there and check the fuel remaining before I start tooling off over seven hundred miles of open sea. It's either that or I don't go."

Welsh pulled his hand through his hair and slumped back. "You're probably right, Brian. I talked to Klist, and he said that would probably be your reaction. He'll go along with that as long as you keep off the airways and maintain radio silence. If you have to refuel, he's got a place about eighty miles north of Haiti where you can land to get fuel. It's the southernmost of the Bahamas, a place called Great Inagua. The airstrip is unattended, but there's fuel available and he says that if necessary, you can make an instrument approach on the radio beacon. It's not much, but the island's dead flat. You're not going to run into any hillsides."

Loss stared at his employer. "You mean to say that you want me to make this flight without filing a flight plan? And how about Mexico? If I fly into there without clearance, they're going to confiscate the aircraft and put the whole lot of us in one of their fucking jails."

"Why don't you just shut up and listen," Welsh shouted. "Klist says that he has powerful friends down there. He's cabled them this morning and they're making arrangements. He'll use the long-range single-sideband radio to contact them once you're airborne and get confirmation on the clearance before you enter Mexican airspace. The Great Inagua alternative is also being taken care of. He apparently has strings that he can pull in Nassau. So just do like I say, Loss, or start looking for another job."

The anger was starting to rise in Loss's mind. Subconsciously, he tried to restrain it, thinking of the job, but somehow he knew that it was over. He walked over to Welsh and hunched down so that his face was inches away from Welsh's. "What's going on, Welsh?" he said in a hoarse whisper. "Are you running drugs or what? I can lose my license, not to mention spending a good ten years of my life in a Mexican clink."

Welsh started to say something and then closed his eyes, the strain on his face showing. He leaned back again and said, tonelessly, "Just do it, Brian. There's nothing immoral about the flight into Mexico. But this way Klist can't be linked directly to me. That's why the secrecy. I'm willing to give you a one-time bonus of five thousand for the trip." He paused, thinking, and then said, "And this person Bolken will be going along. He's some sort of bodyguard or courier for Klist. God, I don't know what he is, but Klist wants it that way. Just get them there and come back the following day. I'll be ready to leave as soon as you return. This whole thing has been too much for me, and I want to get back to New York as soon as possible."

Loss stood up and looked down on the wasted man lying in the chair before him. He ground his teeth together, still angry, and then came to a decision. "OK, Welsh, I'll take them. If anything goes wrong, you're the asshole that's going to bail me out. And once we get back to New York, you can start looking for a new pilot to haul you around." He hadn't intended to go this far, but the words lay like rotting fruit in the damp atmosphere of the room, leaving an unpleasant scent. Something you couldn't ignore.

Welsh stood up and looked at him with the contempt of an adult for a rude urchin. "Just fly the airplane, Loss. Klist will take care of the rest of it. And your resignation is gratefully accepted." He turned away from Loss toward the window and looked blindly out to sea, past the raindrops and smears of salt upon the glass.

Chapter 13

The trip from Salt Whistle Cay over to Union Island had been bad. The four-mile stretch of channel, normally docile, was now a gigantic washing machine— waves slopping up at acute angles and seas breaking at random, without pattern. The helmsman yelled at Loss that it was because the tide was running against the direction of the wind and that there was no real problem. Klist had sat below in the cabin, smoking and reading an ancient *Newsweek* while Bolken hung over the rail, spewing out the remains of his breakfast. Some trip this is going to be, Loss thought.

Rather than going to the main dock in Clifton Harbor, Loss directed the helmsman to steer for the small jetty in the north end of the harbor that was next to the single-strip runway. He didn't want to pass the police station, which would house the customs and immigration officer as well.

By the time they landed, the rain was hosing down, visibility less than a quarter of a mile. Loss told the boatman not to wait. Mr. Klist was meeting friends here in Union, and he would be taking Mr. Bolken up to Martinique to catch an Air France flight. The black man smiled, cocooned in yellow foul-weather gear, and swung away from the dock with a bark of the diesels that was almost smothered in the roar of rain.

The strip was deserted except for a flock of grounded seagulls that preened and pecked at the remains of a broken bag of garbage lying on the grass beside the runway. Loss could barely see the end of the half-mile strip, which terminated at the water's edge. Beyond that was the reef-protected harbor and he could hardly make out the indefinite forms of local trading schooners lurching uneasily at anchor and heeling heavily in the harder gusts.

He herded Klist and Bolken into the aircraft, stuffing most of the luggage in the aft compartment, along with their saturated foul-weather gear.

Bolken took the back seat, now silent and highly nervous. Despite the sopping condition of his clothes, Loss could smell the stink of fear on Bolken's person. This cabin is going to smell like an overripe mango, he thought, watching Bolken store the camera case. "Strap that thing down with the spare seat belt," Loss said snappishly

"It's going to be rough?" Bolken said, his eyes worried.

Loss didn't answer, only giving Bolken a wolfish grin and nodding.

Loss eased the seat forward and ran through the checklist. Klist sat in the right front seat, quietly uninterested and yet familiar with the cockpit environment and procedures. He had insisted on taking this position, saying that he had the frequencies and procedures for entering Mexican airspace and would need access to the single-sideband radio. Loss agreed, glad that this part of it would be off his back. He gave Klist a briefing on the radio's operation. Klist indicated that he had operated equipment similar to this and that it would be no problem. Loss shrugged and started the engines.

Minutes later, the Aztec lifted off the runway and accelerated, the gear sucking up into the fuselage. The aircraft flashed out over the harbor, the stubby masts of a schooner disappearing beneath the nose as Loss banked toward the north. He reduced power and rpms for best rate of climb and eased the nose of the aircraft up. Slowly he milked up the flaps and completed post-takeoff checklist. Below, Loss caught one last glimpse

180

of an offlying reef, smothered in waves from the heavy, rolling sea, and then the aircraft was swallowed by the ragged scud.

On instruments now, Loss carefully trimmed out the aircraft and turned up the panel lights. Heavy rain was rattling against the canopy and the air was turbulent.

Klist leaned over and spoke into Loss's ear. "Pitot heat on?" More angry with himself than Klist, he flicked on the heating element for the air-speed probe, an item he had missed in the checklist. With the probe iced over, he would lose all indications of air speed, and there was bound to be ice once they had climbed through the freezing level.

Loss looked over at Klist who sat in relaxed composure, watching the instruments. He knew before he asked the question. "Do you fly, Mr. Klist?"

Klist didn't answer, but there was the barest trace of a smile on his lips.

They climbed for half an hour through alternate layers of cloud and rain showers. The turbulence was wild at times, slamming the aircraft with hammer blows. Loss donned oxygen at 12,000 feet and instructed them to do the same. At 18,000 they broke out into a blue valley tucked between towering cumulo-nimbus. He flew the aircraft up through the valley, topping most of the cloud structure at 22,000 feet, their ice-crystalled anvils trailing away in the upper levels of the jet stream.

Loss set the autopilot on a heading of northwest and retrimmed the aircraft for level flight, easing back power and mixture settings for maximum range. The indicated air speed settled on 145 knots, and fuel flow was running a little higher than he had expected. This would be cutting it very fine. He switched to outboard wing tanks and started timing the fuel flow, determined to squeeze every last drop of fuel from the cells.

"It would seem to me as if you're rather far north of course, Captain Loss," Klist said, holding the oxygen mask back from his lips. He gave an innocent smile and tapped the directional gyro with his fingertips.

"Look, Klist. *Mister* Klist. This trip sucks, and I'm not a fucking airline captain. I'm keeping north of course in case we have to go in somewhere to refuel. Until I can get some reliable radio reception off the Dominican Republic or Haiti, I don't have a clue as to our drift or ground speed. Without that, I'm not turning this pile of junk west toward Mexico. We're pushing the range as it is."

Klist sat slumped in his seat with half a smile before answering. He took a deep breath from the mask and then said, "Yes, I understand, ah, *Mister* Loss. I think that might be wise. As you probably have guessed, I fly as well. Several thousand hours of multi-engine time. But hold your proper heading. I want to stay well south of Puerto Rico's approach control radar. A fix off the Dominican Republic will be quite sufficient." Klist clamped the mask back over his face, sucking on the oxygen, as serene as if he were on a flight between Boston and Washington. The period of time off oxygen seemed to have no effect on him, even at this altitude, Loss observed. The perfect Aryan type, he thought; Klist sat there composed, hair still damp but neatly combed, his nose straight and perfectly formed. And his ice-blue eyes were never still.

Loss swung in his seat to look at Bolken, to make sure the man was using his oxygen mask properly. Bolken returned the look, without apparent emotion, his mask concealing his lips, the muscles of his cheeks taut. Congenial couple this pair, Loss thought sourly.

Loss adjusted number one VOR to Ponce, Puerto Rico. The needle deflected erratically and then recentered, the warning flag exposed to show the reception unreliable. He tried Santo Domingo, and this time raised some indication. He plotted and found, surprisingly enough, that the bearing matched the flight plan with some degree of accuracy. Klist looked sideways at him, his eyes gently reproachful, smiling under his mask. Loss shrugged and noted the time of the bearing, planning to check it again in ten minutes for a rough running fix.

"Do you mind?" Klist asked, pointing to the HF single-sideband radio. Easing his mask into a more comfortable position, Loss shrugged.

"I think that it would be wise if I alerted my people in Mexico," Klist said. "They'll be listening for us and can set up our entry into Mexican airspace."

"It's all right by me, Klist. You seem to know a lot more about this flight than I do. If you have such great contacts, how about getting a weather briefing for Cozumel and a check on their radio beacon. I've found that Mexican navaids are about as reliable as their tap water. But bear in mind that we're not committed as yet. I still want that fix."

Klist nodded, listening to Loss as if he were an anxious child, nodding but not caring. Consulting a notebook, Klist carefully dialed in 6.2893 megahertz and tuned the set carefully. He called briefly in German and waited. A reply came back in English almost immediately.

"Go ahead, Zulu Four, over."

"Shifting, over," Klist replied, and reached down, readjusting the synthesizer for a frequency 10 kilohertz down and switching to lower sideband.

There was a pause of three or four seconds and a different voice came back, slightly stronger, warped slightly by a slight frequency drift. "Situation and position, Zulu Four. Fox Alpha listening."

Klist shifted frequency again, changing to upper sideband and spoke rapidly in German. The speaker rasped again, this time in yet another voice, replying in German. Klist shifted frequency and sideband again and on all subsequent transmissions, finally terminating the communication with three clicks of the mike key.

As if such procedure were entirely normal, he shut down the set and replaced the mike. He scanned his notes and relaxed back into his seat, now with his mask replaced, breathing deeply on 100 percent oxygen.

Loss sat for some moments, feeling the first prickles of the fear that is bred of uncertainty. A feeling he had last in the gunship flying north over the DMZ years ago. Klist was no businessman. It was doubtful that he was anything approaching legitimate. Certainly Welsh was implicated in something well over hs gullible head. The job was blown at any rate, and it would be better to get this mess on the ground and sort it out from there. He glanced sideways at Klist and found him relaxed with eyes closed. Loss edged into the gentlest of turns, the instruments hardly reflecting the bank, only the sun shifting slowly across the canopy. The Dominican Republic was somewhere on the right wing, moving slowly under the nose.

"Why are you changing course, Loss?" Klist said as he lifted the mask from his mouth. "You will destroy the running fix on Santo Domingo. Get back on your heading, ah, three-four-three degrees, I believe. I have a full weather briefing. We will be getting more of a tailwind as we get further west. Our terminal forecast is three thousand scattered over Cozumel, wind 30 degrees at 18 knots. The fix will give us some idea of our fuel remaining, and *we* can make the decision then. I would like to point out that we are flying into improving weather with a favorable tailwind and a good terminal forecast. What are you frightened of?" Klist then turned to Bolken and spoke to him in muted tones, clearly to keep Loss from understanding. Loss slowly turned back to his heading and noted his watch. Three minutes to run before he could get the other leg of his fix. With that information, he could plot a heading for Santo Domingo. The weather did seem to be slightly improved to the west but the indefinable suggestion of danger still rankled at is subconscious.

The suggestion of Klist's, hinting at fear, was real, but it is only those men who have no fear who fly into mountains on dark nights.

At the end of three minutes, Loss centered the VOR needle and read off the bearing and carefully plotted it. Klist leaned over his seat, watching carefully. The legs of the two bearings fell 110 miles south-southwest of Isla Alto Velo, a small island on the southwestern tip of the Dominican Republic. Loss spent several minutes with the hand calculator, working out fuel consumption and fuel remaining. He finally turned to Klist, showing him the results.

"It's marginal. I estimate that this gives us no more than twenty-five minutes of reserve fuel over Cozumel at our present ground speed. Before you say it, I'm not buying your forecast. I know how poor forecasts can be, even in the U.S. We're going to get fuel in the Dominican Republic. I want to call Welsh and ask him a few questions as well. This whole thing is illegal, and although I'm not concerned about your affair with Welsh, I'm not going to jeopardize either my license or your lives. If Welsh doesn't like it, he can go to hell. I've already told him that I'm dropping this job when we get back to the U.S."

Klist sat looking at his notes. He then took the folded Enroute Low Altitude Chart and scanned it casually, then replaced it neatly in the clipboard. "Perhaps, Brian, this can be settled without either of us getting upset. Santo Domingo is now behind us. Head for Haiti but let's delay in calling their approach control radio. I think I can convince you of a better alternative."

"It better be damn good," Loss said and selected the frequency of the VOR station in Port-au-Prince, Haiti. Klist had turned and was speaking to Bolken in guarded tones. The consultation was one-sided; Klist in clipped sentences dictating, Bolken grunting acceptance.

Port-au-Prince VOR was starting to show some indications of life on the indicator head and Brian corrected slightly to the north. He waited for Klist to make his pitch, sure that he would push for the Great Inagua alternative.

Klist pulled the mask back from his lips and spoke. "Look here, Loss. You are correct in probably assuming that I'm not a Dutch businessman. But I do represent a group of people who are interested in assisting Senator Welsh in his forthcoming campaign. How we do this is immaterial, but I assure you that it will be in the best interests of both Senator Welsh and your country. But by virtue of the fact that we are European, this assistance must be kept secret. Do you understand what I am saying?"

Loss nodded, believing nothing but listening.

"For this reason," Klist continued, "this flight must be kept quiet. I can assure you that we are not smuggling anything or engaging in any deceptive practice. The Mexican authorities are fully aware of our flight. I cabled my friends in Mexico last night, and as you can see," Klist said, indicating the longe range radio, "we are in radio contact with them.

"I anticipated the possibility of a refueling stop, and I have selected Great Inagua Island. This is just seventy miles north of Port-au-Prince. It has a 5,000-foot paved runway and a radio beacon you can home on. There is plenty of fuel there and the problems with authorities will be minimal."

"Where is this place?" Loss said.

Klist picked up the enroute chart for the Caribbean and pointed to a speck north of Haiti. The island had only one settlement, Matthew Town, and the airport was four miles farther north along the coast.

Loss expelled his breath. His throat was dry from the oxygen, and he had the start of a headache. He turned to Klist and said, "OK, I'll go along with it. But I want a couple of things understood. First of all, if there are any problems with the local authorities, you're responsible. Secondly, I want you to get on

186

that damned radio and call your friends. By the time we get within a hundred miles of Mexico, I want an official clearance from the Mexican Air Traffic Control people to enter their airspace. Understand?''

Klist lifted his hands and dropped them again into his lap in a gesture of decision. "Agreed. I'm going to use your radio again." Without further discussion, Klist switched on the single sideband and called on the last used frequency, again in German.

The reply was almost immediate. The frequency change procedure went into effect again, and Loss realized that with this routine, the chance of anyone monitoring the transmissions would be greatly minimized by the continual alterations of frequency; an effective, makeshift form of scrambling.

This time, Klist's tone was more urgent. There was a delay of several minutes in answer to one of Klist's questions. He finally signed off and finished writing in his black leather notebook. "My friends say that it is all arranged. You need only contact Cozumel Tower on one-one-eight-point-one when we are a hundred miles out, and they will clear you for the approach. You may remain there overnight and return tomorrow. As far as Great Inagua is concerned, I will deal with the local authorities." He patted the wallet in the breast pocket of his jacket and smiled.

"You must have some organization," Loss said, gritting his teeth. "What are you, Klist? German?"

The Russian shrugged. "Does it make any difference, Mr. Loss? It's all in a good cause." He placed the oxygen mask back over his face and breathed deeply.

Loss switched back to the main tanks and prepared for the descent. The weather had altered little in appearance. There was still an unbroken cloud deck beneath them with high towers of black storm cells probing up through the lesser battlements. He wondered how low the ceiling would be over the sea. Since Great Inagua had no control tower, he would have no way of knowing at what altitude the Aztec would break out of the overcast. If it was anything like this morning, it would be less than three hundred feet, but still time enough to get everything squared away for an approach.

He removed the mask and turned to Klist. "I'm going to call Port-au-Prince Approach Control for an altimeter setting and local weather. It should give us some idea of the Matthew Town weather."

Klist sucked the oxygen mask, shaking his head. He removed it and said, "I can well understand where you got your last name, Brian. I keep telling you that we have to minimize our contact with normal air traffic control. If you called them, they would want your registration number, position, and destination." He tapped the VOR indicator with his pencil. "We're almost into Haitian airspace now. It's best that we avoid their radar. Start your descent out to the west and then turn toward Matthew Town. You can home in on their radio. In this way, we'll stay well out of radar contact with Port-au-Prince, and you'll be letting down over the open sea without any mountains to worry about. However, it wouldn't be a bad idea to monitor the Haitian Approach Control frequency. You might pick up their weather if they're in contact with other aircraft."

Loss nodded. You're just too cute for words, he thought and eased into a turn to the west.

They descended, power back to the stops, the aircraft sinking at over two thousand feet per minute; Port-au-Prince Approach Control frequency silent. Loss tried to estimate the probable altimeter error. If the ceilings in this area were down to about three hundred feet over the sea, he would have enough time to level off after breaking out of the overcast. Goddamned fool, he thought.

The Aztec plunged into the murk of a rain shower, the turbulence shaking the aircraft. Loss eased in nose-down trim, trying to keep the air speed near the top of the air speed indicator's green arc, retaining control against a stall and yet keeping a safe margin against excessive speed. He adjusted the panel lights to full bright and sank his seat to its lowest position, sweeping the instruments and ignoring the black shroud of sky beyond the windshield.

He could hear retching from the back seat. The stench of vomit would be unbearable when they removed their oxygen masks.

The radio spattered suddenly with an unreadable voice.

The reply was fragmented by heavy static: "——showers, ——derstorm to the west. Current alt——niner —— five. Wind north at forty gusting fif——"

Loss could feel the shirt soaking on his back, his armpits saturated. A small rivulet of sweat trickled down the edge of his rib cage. The weather could be solid crap right down to the deck, he thought. Wind very strong in the north, and the altimeter setting could be anyone's guess.

He estimated that they were well to the west of Port-au-Prince now, descending rapidly. No time to tune in the ILS for Port-au-Prince now, but the presence of another aircraft to the west, setting up for an instrument approach was a terrifying thought. The odds were enormous against a midair collision, but the nightmare persisted.

Passing through eight thousand now. He richened the mixture and eased in slightly more power, checking the rate of descent to 1,500 feet per minute.

"Set in the frequency for Great Inagua," he shouted into Klist's ear, the rain hammering against the windshield in a continuous staccato of gunfire. Loss didn't bother to look at Klist, using his eyes to scan the instrument panel. But a hand reached for the ADF radio, set in a frequency, and selected a switch on the audio mixer panel. The faint beat of a frequency punctuated the precipitation hash and coughing static of his speaker; the code identification was unreadable.

Through five thousand now and the rain, if possible, was worse, tricklets of water now forcing through the weather seals of the windows.

The Aztec was suddenly slammed upwards in a bowel-wrenching blow, the G-forces sagging their cheeks, their arms leaden with the sudden weight. The altimeter, which had been unwinding in their descent, shuddered and started to climb like some clockworks gone berserk. The instruments, once stable, shuddered and blurred with vibration.

Loss pulled back the power to idle-cutoff and still they rose in the core of the storm cell, the rain now mixed with rattles of hail, the aircraft porpoising and rolling erratically. No control movement seemed to dampen the wild tumbling of the Aztec.

Someone or something was shouting in the back seat, a fist beating against his seat.

Fly attitude, he thought. Forget everything else but the attitude indicator. The mask was suffocating, not supplying enough oxygen, and Loss flung it from his face. The control yoke tore from his grip, slamming his knuckles. He grabbed it again, this time with both hands, trying to cushion the shocks, concentrating all his energy and mind on the translation of a simple white bar in a glass-covered cage into some semblance of order for his universe.

The hail intensified, becoming a torrent of sound. Loss thought briefly of damage to the wings, of hail impacting against the thin-skinned aluminum, pounding it into aerodynamic mush. The altimeter blurred through 16,000 feet.

At least we are going up, he thought, and then they went down. The Aztec didn't falter in its climb. It was squashed like a bug with a flyswatter, and then it fell in a waterfall of wind, tumbling over cataracts, smashing against invisible cliffs of air.

The stall warning horn was shrieking in Loss's ears, and the alternator failure light illuminated. His mind registered this, but it seemed trivial. The negative G-forces had scattered map cases, pencils, sunglasses, and trash throughout the cockpit. Klist had lost his Prussian-like composure and was screaming things at Loss in some language, not German, not English.

The vertical velocity indicator was bottomed out at six-thousand-feet-per-minute down, the needle hard against its peg. Trying twice to reach the throttle quadrant and both times nearly losing control of the aircraft, Loss yelled at Klist, the sound puny in the bedlam of noise. "Give me full power. I can't take my hands off the controls."

Klist stared at him wildly, both hands gripping the central windshield support, trying to dampen the shocks against his body.

Loss screamed at him again. "Klist! The fucking throttles!"

Klist started to react, reaching down to the mixture controls, pulling them back, shutting off the flow of fuel to the engines. The right engine quite immediately, windmilling. The left engine was beginning to stammer.

"Oh, Christ," Loss screamed, smashing his right elbow against Klist's face, forcing him to release his grip on the engine mixture controls. He caught a strobe image of Klist in a lightning flash, blood streaming from his nose and mouth. Klist was howling, his hands pressed against the cabin ceiling, trying to stabilize himself against the buffeting.

The Aztec was yawing heavily to the right, nose high. The right wing dropped, and the plane started to spin. In desperation, Loss let go of the yoke with his right hand and slammed the throttle, prop, and mixture controls to full forward position in one sweep of his hand. The Aztec heaved up on her right wing tip, one engine howling to redline and the other backfiring explosively. He rammed the yoke full forward and stood on the left rudder, praying.

The air speed was beginning to build up rapidly, the altimeter a blur. A lot of hail was impacting against

191

the aircraft now, the sound incredible. Like a truck-load of pots falling down an elevator shaft. The turn and bank indicator centered and he eased off the rudder control and pulled back on the power. The spin was broken, but air speed was building up to maximum allowable—the *never exceed* velocity. Loss started to pull back on the controls, easing the aircraft out of its terminal dive. Still a lot of lightning but the hail was gone, replaced by rain sluicing over the windshield with the pressure of a firehose.

He could feel the G-forces pressing down on him, his face and body tissue sagging under the excessive load. Turbulence less now, he thought, straining to keep his sagging eyelids open, looking for a brief flash of open ocean that he would see a microsecond before impact. Something cracked behind him, and then with an explosive roar, the left rear passenger side window blew out, sucking papers and dust through the opening. Loss was conscious of the sound, but it meant nothing. His eyes flicked down to the altimeter now and watched it unwind through a thousand feet. We're far beyond structural limits, he thought abstractly, but the air speed was bleeding off. It's worth a try, he thought, and hit the flap switch.

The flaps partially extended, slowing the air speed further and creating lift at a speed forty knots beyond safe extension speed. The flap motor jammed against the pressure and the circuit breaker blew. But it saved Loss two hundred feet of altitude that he would have otherwise lost.

The aircraft slowly eased up into nearly level flight, air speed rapidly decaying. He felt the buffeting of an accelerated stall. Although he added more power, the aircraft was still sinking.

They broke through the overcast and then were immersed in low stratus again. He glanced down at the altimeter, knowing that it would be in error. It showed something over four hundred feet, still unwinding. He had full power in now, and still they were sinking.

The Aztec flew out from beneath the overcast again and Loss looked down, horrified to see the wavetops cresting less than fifty feet beneath him. The controls were heavy and he retrimmed, checking to insure that he was pulling full power. The right engine was running four hundred rpm low and he couldn't get anything more out of it. The left was a sweet, steady roar.

Most of the circuit breakers were blown, and he shoved them in with the heel of his hand. Two popped immediately but the alternator warning light extinguished and the radio was coming to life.

He tried to get the flaps up, but the breaker kept blowing. The aircraft was just holding its own now, shuddering on the edge of a stall, but still flying. He chanced a look down at the black sea, each crest frothy and breaking off into spray driven by the storm's wind. The troughs were rippled silk, slick and green between the breaking seas.

He could hear retching from the back seat over the roar of the wind. Klist was upright now, looking over the cowling at the sea below. The blood was a dark stain against his face, the perfect complexion flawed. He stabbed his finger at the side window, indicating the wing. Loss looked and saw the top surface and leading edges coated in rough, irregular ice. That's why she won't fly, he thought. Beside the sheer weight of the ice, the irregular surface was destroying the lift. He checked the de-icing equipment and found the circuit breaker blown. He reset it and this time it held.

"Get this thing to land, Loss." Klist's voice was cracked, hoarse from screaming.

Loss scanned the instrument panel and searched the horizon again, a small gray bowl of breaking sea and rain. "I can keep this flying, Klist, but you've got to do some of the work. Get me Port-au-Prince VOR and retune the ADF for Great Inagua. Trim in some left rudder, but, dammit, do it slowly. This thing is hanging right on the edge."

There was a tearing sound from the right wing, and

the Aztec yawed suddenly left, Loss automatically compensating with rudder.

Klist shouted something, gesturing toward the wing on his side. A large patch of clear ice had broken away in the warmer air, leaving the wing stripped of paint. The leading edge was a mass of hammered metal unrecognizable from the indentations caused by hail.

"The radios, Klist," Loss shouted. "Just get the radios."

Despite Klist's repeated attempts, the VOR remained dead, the circuit breaker unwilling to reset. The ADF needle showed life, hunting in the general direction of the left wing tip. The code identification was faint but now readable. "That's Matthew Town," Klist said, more composed. "Turn now." The imperial imperative.

"We wait until some of the ice breaks off the left wing, you stupid bastard," Loss said, not looking away from the sea's horizon. "If we turn now, we could dig in a wing tip. Look, the air speed is up five knots. Just relax and do what I tell you to. The engine exhaust-gas analyzer is on your side of the panel. Give me the temperatures for each cylinder of the right engine. It's running ragged as hell."

Klist slowly selected each position, giving the temperature. All but two of the cylinders were overheating, but not badly. Oil pressure low, oil temperature high but in the green. The Aztec flew, just barely, hugging the waves, searching for the cushion of ground effect that would reduce the drag on its tattered airframe. Loss tried to turn toward the direction of Great Inagua and found he could, using just the smallest increment of bank. The turn took over four minutes.

Ice was beginning to shed off the wings now, and Loss was able to gain over one hundred feet of altitude. Life was looking better, he thought. If only the damn right engine would hold together.

They flew on toward the island, slowly gaining altitude. The wave pattern beneath them was changing, becoming more confused but less dangerous looking. Loss realized that his body was aching from the strain of searching ahead for land.

Two bosunbirds flashed by beneath the left wing tip, and the sea took on a yellow cast. Bits of weed from the storm indicated nearby land.

The ice was gone now from the aircraft, the load lighter, but the battered wings were barely providing lift. Loss had maintained power and slowly climbed to two hundred feet, just brushing the base of the scud above them.

Out of a rain shower, the shore suddenly appeared: a ragged beach bursting with spray; a single street with frame buildings lining it. They swept by the single radio tower and altered course to the northwest. Brown flats beneath them now. One lone donkey bowed in the rain, rump toward the wind. To the south now, along the coast, the dish antennas of Cable and Wireless appeared and then the runway swept beneath them.

"Tuck in now. Belts on tight." Loss adjusted the power and cycled the flap motor circuit breaker. Useless. He swept out to sea in a wide, flat turn, the aircraft shuddering.

The runway straightened in front of them, two miles away. They had only fifty feet of altitude.

"There's a tremendous crosswind and I can't get this thing any slower. When I drop the gear, it's going to produce one hell of a lot of drag. So it's a one-time shot. Klist, when I say 'gear' you drop it and keep your finger on the circuit breaker. If it doesn't extend, we belly it on. Get out as soon as we stop moving."

The Aztec bored down final approach, bucking gusts of fifty knots. Crabbing into the wind to offset drift, the aircraft approached the runway, which was pooled with water and slick black in the failing light. Full power now and the engines shrieked with pain, badly overboosted. The shore was under the wing and Loss called, "Gear!"

The wheels swung outward on their undercarriage,

195

locking seconds before they met the pavement. He chopped the throttles and slammed the nose gear to the asphalt, braking and steering, forcing the aircraft to hold to the centerline. But with diminishing air speed, the rudder and steering became less effective, and the Aztec entered a series of skidding turns o the left, into the slamming crosswind.

No runway remained now, and Loss savagely applied full left brake. The aircraft drifted into a ground-loop, shredding tires; the magnesium rims ignited in a curving trail of flame. Screams now and then silence.

Chapter 14

Colonel Anatoli Antonovich Petrov, KGB, Section V, wiped the cold rain from his eyes and watched the Aztec burn. Except for the black smoke from the burning aircraft, the airstrip was devoid of life or movement.

He picked up the two suitcases, one his own and the other containing Heiss's tapes and photographic film, and jogged easily into the tall lemon grass that edged the field. Twice he looked back over his shoulder at the aircraft, now burning with a dense black smoke in the area of the undercarriage.

The rain was harder now, saturating his thin cord suit and plastering his hair flat against his skull. The edges of his jacket flapped violently in the wind and he paused to button it, turning the collar up for some protection against the chill.

He estimated that the small settlement of Matthew

Town could not be more than four miles from the airstrip. The aircraft as it approached from the sea would have been seen, and he doubted that more than a few minutes would elapse before someone arrived at the field.

He saw the remains of a fifty-five-gallon oil drum resting in the grass, scrofulous with rust and nearly overgrown. He lay down on the leeward side of the drum, protected slightly from the waves of rain that swept in from the north. The aircraft was burning heavily now. Orange fingers of flame were probing the roots of the wing and the cockpit. He decided to wait, to be sure that the entire aircraft was consumed.

The decision had been easy and automatic as he recalled the final minutes in the Aztec.

Loss had done a superb job landing the aircraft. Petrov doubted that he, himself, could have kept the aircraft from flipping over in the slamming crosswind, which he now estimated at close to forty knots. The groundloop was unavoidable, and as the aircraft had begun to skid, Petrov had thrown his hands up in front of his face and braced himself against the padded cowling over the instrument panel. Both tires had blown almost simultaneously—muffled reports punctuating the sounds of the shrieking metal, and then the aircraft was still. Petrov had raised his head from the protected position to find the aircraft upright and intact, the nose of the plane resting against an embankment four or five yards off the asphalt strip. Loss lay slumped over the controls, his head gashed and bleeding from impact with the corner post of the windshield.

Petrov reached down and shut off the master switch and the magnetos, immediately fearful of the possibility of fire. He turned to find Heiss lying huddled in the back seat, his face and the seat it rested against pooled in vomit. The stench was unbelievable and Petrov's stomach convulsed, making him retch.

Frantically, Petrov opened the passenger door. The impact of driving rain and the cold wind clarified his mind. First, he must destroy the Aztec and Loss. Heiss too. He had accomplished the tape surveillance, and the evidence rested in Heiss's aluminum camera case.

Petrov got out onto the wing and looked down the runway toward the approach end. No vehicle or person in sight. Crawling back into the right front seat, he leaned over and grabbed Loss by the hair and raised him to a sitting position. Loss was groaning now, on the edge of consciousness. Petrov, using Loss's hair as a grip, slammed Loss's head into the instrument panel with all his strength. Three times he did this, the instruments fragmenting under the impact, blood spattering the panel.

Petrov left Loss slumped over the controls, sure that he was dying. He turned to find Heiss sitting upright, staring with terror at Loss.

"We're getting out of this thing, Heiss. Quickly. Pass me your camera case."

Heiss's eyes were dilated with shock, his face ashen. His thin lips hung slack, exposing the even teeth of his lower jaw.

Petrov swept his knuckles across Heiss's face, the impact flinging the partially dried vomit from Heiss's chin.

"Move, you idiot," Petrov screamed into the face that gazed at him, uncomprehending. "The case. Give me the case."

Heiss's hands groped on the floor of the aircraft, raising the aluminum container hesitantly, questioning the eyes of the man before him, almost pleading.

"Yes, yes. Good," Petrov said, taking the case gently from Heiss's grasp.

"Yes, good." Petrov pushed open the aircraft door and backed out onto the wing. Heiss was starting to regain coherence, unstrapping his lap belt and following Petrov onto the wing. Petrov allowed Heiss to move the seat forward and start to step over the door's ledge onto the wing. As his head emerged through the door, Petrov slammed the door in his face. Heiss cried out in pain, almost an animal wail. His hands pushed open the door, almost unbalancing Petrov on the rain-slick wing. Carl Heiss pressed his hands to his face, fully conscious but in shock.

Petrov made another lunge at the man tottering before him, thrusting his stiffened right fingers into the man's solar plexus. Heiss collapsed like a sack of wheat, falling back into the aircraft, sprawled across the right front passenger seat, head lolling back against Loss's slumped form.

It had been less than a minute since the crash. Petrov stood on the wing, his mind now clean and methodical. He bent down and shoved Heiss's feet into the cockpit, fastened his lap belt with some difficulty, and brought him erect in the seat. Grasping his hair as he had done with Loss, he brought Heiss's head forward in a smashing arc into the control column.

Closing the cabin door, he jumped lightly to the ground, careful to land in the scarred tracks of the undercarriage. He quickly retrieved his own suitcase from the luggage compartment and carried both items of luggage into the adjacent grass.

Fifty feet back from the aircraft he rested, his breath coming in great gulps, the rain tasting like champagne on his tongue.

There was just a flicker of orange from the right main gear. The tire had blown and the magnesium wheel had caught fire from the friction of the final skid across the runway. Brake fluid dripped down from ruptured lines and was feeding the flame, causing a spluttering sound. The fire was growing in intensity.

I have to make sure, he thought, running back to the aircraft, trying to stay within the torn earth tracks. He bent briefly under the wing, shielding his face from the fire and opened the left main fuel drain. The clear blue fluid drained in a gush over his hands and, panic stricken, Petrov sprinted for the grass. But there was no explosion and even now, as he lay in the tall lemon grass, he was surprised that the aircraft had not gone up in a sheet of flames.

But even as he watched, there was a white-hot pinpoint of light that blossomed into a black-orange rose, sheet metal singing high into the air as a fuel tank exploded. A cloud of black smoke rose, obscuring the aircraft.

Petrov relaxed now, the thing finished. He watched anxiously as the ball of smoke was whipped away in the wind, expecting to see only flame. Instead, the aircraft, minus most of the right wing, had settled in the mud, the landing gear collapsed. Flame still fluttered sporadically around the engine cowlings of the left wing, but it too died in the torrential rain. The remains of the exploded wing were thirty or more feet from the aircraft, engulfed in fire but too far to cause the aircraft to reignite.

A movement far down the runway caught Petrov's eye. He flattened himself into the grass, thinking of the obvious tracks he must have left in the mud around the aircraft. The movement was blanked from sight by the grass, but he could hear the sound of a blaring car horn. Cautiously, he parted the grass, enough to see two black men in foul-weather jackets splashing through the mud and over the debris toward the smoking aircraft. Their movements were shielded from his view as they gained the far side of the aircraft. Petrov could hear muffled shouts, carried by the wind. The two men reemerged from behind the aircraft, dragging two bodies through the mud.

That will obliterate my footmarks, he thought with satisfaction. He could see the vehicle now, parked much too close to the smoldering aircraft. These men were obviously civilians. The car was a mid-fifties Chevrolet, rusted and paintflaked. A front fender was missing, and the word "taxi" was crudely painted in white across the door. A second vehicle was coming up the runway now, and then a third. Both Land Rovers, dull gray with the black stencils of government service across their hoods.

Petrov flattened himself into the sodden earth, wearied now, his adrenaline level falling. He mentally retraced his steps since the aircraft had crashed and was content that he could have handled the situation in no better manner. It was just bad luck that the explosion had snuffed out the fire. Now Heiss and possibly Loss might live. But if he could reach a telephone or radio, that situation could be rectified.

Petrov's body shook uncontrollably now from the cold torrent of wind and water that swept Great Inagua. But he had known cold before: day after day of walking through mud and freezing rain when he and his mother had resettled their farm after the Nazi retreat. And he had known the brilliant, polished cold of Manchurian winters, instructing the Chinese to fly MIG 21s. Cold so intense that metal broke like kindling. And where it was a crime, punishable by death, to stop the engine of a vehicle, for it was certain that the engine would never start again until the spring. Compared to that, this was no more than an inconvenience and he disciplined his body, separating it from his mind.

A vehicle started up, the sound carried clearly by the wind. It was raining less now, but it was colder. Another vehicle started, and headlights swept the grass as they turned on the runway and sped off in the direction of the town. One Land Rover remained, the windows fogged with condensation; obviously the man or men left to guard the remains of the demolished Aztec.

Petrov watched the lone sentry vehicle for over half an hour. The motor would start and run for short periods; probably an attempt to keep the cab of the vehicle warm. This served to further fog the windows. Not once did anyone emerge into the gusting rain that swept the bleak landscape in waves.

Satisfied, Petrov slowly retreated through the grass, crawling backwards, dragging the two pieces of luggage behind him. He encountered a line of scrubby trees that hid him from any possible observation, and rose to a running crouch. Knowing the wind was from the north, he headed south toward the coast.

Twice he met rough asphalt roads, only one lane in width, the roadside strewn with broken glass and empty beer bottles. Crossing these, he kept to the scrub and stunted trees. He topped a rise and, although there was no habitation as yet in sight, the ridge of a hill farther to the south was transfixed by the monolithic dish antennas of the Cable and Wireless installation that he had seen through the rain-spattered windows of the Aztec on final approach.

This would be the site of the remote transmitter, probably largely unattended. He wished desperately for a cigarette or something warm to drink. The late tropical afternoon, already washed in the gray of the storm, was growing dark. He moved on, resolute, his mind disconnected from his body.

The next rise gave him a clearer view of the transmitter site, and more important, he could see the sea. The southwest coast would probably be the most protected coast and, consequently, there would be some type of anchorage for small craft. Cuba lay only eighty kilometers to the west. And Cuba meant the Russian installation at Cienfuegos.

Petrov turned east along the coast, paralleling the beach but staying close to the scrub that bordered the wide berm, keeping to the depressions in the grass-covered hillocks. He stopped twice, once to check the contents of Heiss's bag and to extract a sweater from his own bag, which he used as a muffler around his neck. The other stop was unplanned as a small rusted coaster swept down the coast only two hundred meters offshore. He watched it as it passed, flattening himself against the sand and weed thrown up by the storm. The coaster carried no flag, and he estimated it to be no longer than fifteen meters, a single thudding diesel washing the wake with roiled white in the following sea. Beyond the small pilot house the decks were clean of superstructure. It was what it appeared to be, a fishing coaster, and he sighed heavily with relief, doubtful that his presence on the shore would be noticed.

The antenna installation was a disappointment. Although uninhabited, a triple strand of barbed wire protected the top of a four-meter cyclone fence around the perimeter.

He kept to an easterly direction, avoiding the few fishing shacks that dotted the foreshore. Lights glowed within one of them, the dull yellow of kerosene.

The rain had quit now, and the wind was diminishing, the low ceiling having lifted to a more uniform overcast. And the light was failing. Checking his watch, he found it was almost six. He found a dense place in the scrub and settled himself on the two handbags, waiting for darkness, planning ahead to Cuba and beyond. There must be, would be, a boat moored along this coast he could steal.

By 6:30 the light was completely gone. His eyes had adjusted to the darkness and he carefully picked his way east again to intersect the road he was sure would lead toward the small settlement of Matthew Town. The lights of the town were not visible, but they were reflected in the low cloud ceiling. He picked up the road again and turned east along it, walking slowly and carefully on the shoulder, stopping frequently to listen for any approaching vehicle. He noted that the overcast was starting to break up, an occasional glint of a star visible in the ragged patches.

Now civilization was becoming more apparent. He passed two construction sheds, both heavily padlocked, and then the rusted shell of a Volkswagen and a cinderblock house that was set back in from the road by a small lane. A dog barked once and he froze. He heard the slam of a door and an indistinct voice. The door sound again, then quiet. He waited patiently for five minutes and then resumed his progress to the east.

The road now ran parallel to the coast, separated from the broad beach by the stunted scrub pines. The smell of the sea gave him fresh energy, its impact tangy and pungent. The breakers were gentle here, less frantic in their beat upon the shore than those to the north. The asphalt track wandered inland again and rose toward the low crest of a hill. To the seaward side of the road on the crest was a two-story building, dimly visible against the light from Matthew Town. The building was dark, and he climbed the hill toward it, finding a pathway lined with conch shells.

He circled the building and found it was built on a low bluff overlooking the sea. A roofed veranda circled the building, providing cover for him for the first time in three hours. He walked along the porch after first removing his shoes and leaving the bags stored near the base of the steps. From here he could clarly see the main street of Matthew Town, probably less than a kilometer distant. There seemed to be little more than two streets fronting the shore with sparsely placed streetlights blinking through foliage.

More important, he found a sign fixed to the wall near the main door. The sign, faded and dim, read "Great Inagua Aquatic Club, Members Only." So there would be some sort of anchorage or boat basin near here, he thought. In confirmation of this, he found two aluminum masts for small sailboats stacked against the side of the building, sails still bent on and laced with gaskets.

At the back of the building steps led down to another pathway, this time leading down the bluff toward the sea. Retrieving the bags and his shoes, he followed the path down through arbors of frangipani and bougainvillea. The path branched once and he followed the right-hand deviation only to find it a dead end with a small group of sheds for storage. All were stoutly locked.

He retraced his steps and continued downward, finally breaking out of the arbor onto a rough concrete ramp. Before him was a small basin with mooring space for a small fleet of yachts and commercial craft.

Beyond that was the dim outline of a seawall with the opening marked by a single red light.

The basin wasn't much larger than one hundred meters square, a literal hole in the wall. There were no lights on the landing, but Petrov could see the outlines of small sailing boats rafted together on a short trot line. Beyond, there were indistinct shapes of one or two powerboats. On the western edge of the basin, darker against the cliff wall looming over it, was the indistinct spear of a mast and rigging, a vessel larger than the rest.

He walked carefully along the concrete ramp that led to the west side of the basin. The ramp was slick with moss. Things scuttled beneath his feet; the air was fetid with dead marine growth.

A sloop materialized out of the blackness, surprisingly small for the size of her mast and complex rigging. She was painted in some dark color, possibly green. Beyond that the details were too indistinct for Petrov to determine.

He set the bags down on the edge of the ramp and stood in the darkness, his next movement as yet undecided.

Beyond the breakwater, the remains of the storm's swell made a muffled rumble along the rip-rap, almost the sound of a distant train moving slowly over a trestle. The sky was clearer now, batches of stars burning in the blackness above the ragged cumulus.

The small sloop before him moved easily against the restraint of her mooring lines, her mast tracing arcs against the sky. Closer now, he could pick out details of the superstructure and rigging. The lifelines, three strands, circled the deck and were held secure by robust stanchions. And on the stern were two life rings attached to marker buoys. Even in the darkness, the name of the ship stood out in black-painted letters— *Ulla, Göteborg*.

Without warning, the deck of the yacht was suddenly flooded with light from the two spreaders high

205

in the rigging. Petrov, startled, stood poised to run.

"Yes?" a male voice called from the companionway hatch, more in question than in challenge.

"I'm sorry," Petrov said, his voice strained. "I thought that—well, I—I was looking for the yacht of a friend of mine. Due to arrive today."

"No one in today or even yesterday," the voice replied, young and with a Scandinavian lilt. The spreader lights went out, and a man came up into the cockpit, pausing to turn on a small electric lamp.

He was young and tall, fully bearded. He wore just a large bath towel. The small table lamp illuminated his heavily tanned body and sunburned face.

Petrov, confident now, walked to the edge of the ramp and looked down into the cockpit. The Scandinavian opened a package of cigarettes and took one, offering the opened pack to Petrov.

"Good Swedish cigarettes," he said, smiling. "They taste like cabbage."

Petrov, unsure whether the offer included boarding, took one and then searched his pockets in the universal gesture of looking for a match.

"Oh, come on board," the Swede said. "I have a light."

"I think that I have interrupted you," Petrov said apologetically, swinging easily down to the deck, using the rigging as support.

"Anders is my name," the Swede said, extending a huge hand. "No, you weren't taking me away from anything. I was just sitting there in the dark listening to the radio with the headphones. Trying to get some kind of report on this fuckin' weather." He pointed haphazardly toward the clearing sky. "I think maybe we got what we see tomorrow. Good weather again."

Petrov bent down to accept a light for his cigarette, inhaling the bitter, strange smoke from the cigarette, feeling almost giddy as the smoke filled his lungs. He coughed and looked at the brand name, unable to see it in the dim light.

"I said they were like cabbage," the Swede said, laughing a little. "I only got wine. Would you like some?" he said, moving into the companionway.

"Yes, Anders, I'd like that very much," Petrov replied. "My name is Robert Kline. The yacht belongs to a friend of mine. We were meeting here for some diving in the Bahamas. I guess that the storm's held him up."

Anders appeared in the companionway again, handing up a fruit jar of dark wine to Petrov and then coming back up the companionway ladder, a similar jar in his other hand.

"Yes, yes. I know. We been here for three days, waiting for this fuckin' storm to get over with. Skoal!"

They lifted the wine in toast and drank for some minutes in silence, each smoking and sipping at the rough wine.

"This seems like a fine yacht," Petrov said finally, noting the obviously well-cared-for condition of the sloop.

"Yes, yes. Thank you. Ulla and me have been sailing her for three years now. We been all over the Med and across the Atlantic. I think maybe now we take her to the Panama Canal and into the Pacific. Before things get much worse there. These guerrillas blow up one U.S. ship. Maybe Swedes next. Pretty soon maybe they blow up the whole fuckin' ditch."

Petrov shrugged. "I doubt it," he said. "The new government will probably make peace with the Americans. Soon, I think."

Anders thought about it and then lifted his jar of wine toward the shore's direction. "All these places are good," he said, "but maybe they don't like white people so much. I think maybe Ulla and me will like it better in the Pacific."

"Ulla is your wife?" Petrov asked, motioning toward the companionway.

"Yes. Well, almost like my wife," the Swede replied, laughing. "Maybe some day we do that. She help me out rebuilding this boat, and she owns half. We sail together. I even cook sometimes. Terrible cooking!'' and he laughed again.

Petrov traced his fingers across a sheet winch. ''You have good equipment. Barrient winches, I'm told, are the best.''

Anders nodded. ''Good gear,'' he agreed. ''Sometimes too much of it.''

''What do you have in the way of radios?''

The Swede snorted, shaking his head. ''Radios. That's the last fuckin' thing we need. Ulla and me, we got no time for radios. They just take up space, and they're no damn good half the time.''

Petrov suddenly realized that the Swede was drunk. ''You have no radios, then,'' he asked evenly, swirling the wine in his glass.

''Just the opposite,'' Anders said, hocking over the rail. ''My fuckin' government won't let a small boat go out to sea without all them goddamn radios. The little men in their business suits come down and tell you that you can't go here or there without all these radios. We got VHF and low frequency single side-band. They take up space, add weight. I hate the fuckin' things.'' He deftly dropped down the hatch and reemerged with a four-liter jerry can of wine. Refilling Petrov's jar and then his own, he sloshed the burgundy onto the clean teak of the cockpit floor.

''You excuse me. I just got a little drunk tonight. Sitting here in this harbor for four days is no good. My father,'' he paused, drinking nearly half his freshly refilled jar in one long swallow, ''my father, we work salvage tugs together, and he always used to say that when in port, ships rot and men go to the devil. He's goddamn right. Me, I never drink at sea. Just here.'' He speared his thumb toward the shore again.

''You'll leave tomorrow, then?'' Petrov asked.

The Swede nodded, picking at the skin of his sun-burned nose. His face, splotched by the peeling skin, was nevertheless handsome, both hair and beard bleached white by the sun. His eyes were dull with drink, but his teeth white and even. And he smiled a lot.

"Well, maybe I'll see you again," Petrov said, rising slightly as if to leave. "My friend and I want to do some diving." And then, almost as an afterthought he said, "But I worry about sharks. My friend always has a crew member stand watch with a rifle."

The Swede laughed, shaking his head and lighting another cigarette from the glowing tip of Petrov's. "No, that's stupid." He looked up quickly, his forehead pinched in concern. "Not you, I mean. Just that Ulla and I thought so too, before we came sailing. We thought sharks were like all those films. Attacking people. But we never seen one that bother us. They just nose around. We got this old Husqvarna shotgun, and we used to bathe in the sea, even in the middle of the Atlantic when the wind was calm, with one of us standing guard. But it doesn't matter. And I think if a shark ever decides to get you, you never know about it."

The Swede made a motion with his hand, indicating the slashing attack of a fin. He spilled the wine jar, the small amount left staining his bath towel.

Petrov relaxed, sitting back against the cushions. "Husqvarna," he said. "Fine weapon. My grandfather owned several of them over the years. Would you mind if I looked at yours? I do a lot of shooting."

The Swede looked up smiling and nodded.

Chapter 15

Loss opened his eyes and closed them again quickly, the intensity of the white-hot sun too great to bear. He ached in some indefinite sort of way, pain overlapping consciousness. Nerve endings dull, no report from the outer periphery. Someone-thing pressing down on his head. Sinking down into the green depths again, bubbles from his mouth drifting upward. He felt the surge of Pacific rollers fanning the sea grass. Like her golden hair. Like fields of wheat in the wind. The wind hot, though. Very dry. The sun, illuminating the waters overhead, just gave brightness to the green depths. He pushed the throttles forward to go higher into the sunlight, but they didn't respond. Very sluggish. Green again. Darker.

His eyes opened again, the sun very small and then a dark shadow. A smell like vodka. An insect stung him as he walked through the field of wheat and he lay down to smell the earth and sleep. And sleep.

A long time of darkness and light and pain. The gunship smelled of carbonic acid. Barber was sitting beside him coughing up blood. The gooney bird was barely flying, and his muscles ached with the effort of holding the controls. Right main gear not down. Someone on the interphone calling him.

"Loss?" The voice female. "Mr. Loss?"

He wanted to tell them to shut up. Too much effort. They're dead back there anyway. The whole airplane dead, dying. Burning. Ice on the wings. Have Klist get the gear down.

"Gear down now," he said with great effort, all in slow motion. The sound of his own voice hollow in the interphone, very distant.

His arm hurt again. A burning pain and he heard a door close. The instruments blurred into blackness.

"He come around again," the nurse said, dropping the hypodermic into an autoclave.

The matron nodded and made a notation in the ward book.

"Just three cc's and tetracycline now every twelve hours. Dr. Detrick will prescribe oral medication for the pain. Did he speak, Nurse Wylie?" the matron said, looking up from the desk, tapping the pen against her logbook.

"Yes, mum. Something about gear." The nurse stood there awkwardly, wanting to be dismissed. The white uniform framed and accentuated the blackness of her skin. It was past 2:00 A.M. There would be tea for her in the nurses' pantry.

The matron tapped the pen impatiently again, a small tattoo of sound in the silent corridor. The night was sultry, dampness on everything. Insects beat against the screened window, flinging themselves at the single dim light within. The matron sighed, wishing she were in Nassau again, cool and efficient within the air-conditioned sanctum of Princess Margaret Hospital. Not here in the Out Islands with these ignorant people.

She lifted her 190 pounds of bulk in the wicker chair, feeling betrayed by the same black skin that linked her to the girl standing before her, fidgeting like some nervous child.

"Stand properly," the matron said sharply.

"Yes, mum."

"I will tell you for the last time, Nurse Wylie. You are to address me as Matron. You are not my domestic." She sighed, a blend of impatience and resignation, mentally promising herself to apply for transfer back to Nassau—the eighth attempt.

She looked up at the young girl and spoke, her voice mechanical, precise. "Before you go off duty, see to it that the night porter wakes up Dr. Detrick promptly at seven and that he is informed of the white patient's condition. See to it also that Mr. Campbell is informed. He is staying in the government guest house. Dismissed."

The young girl nodded quickly and stepped backward into the darkness of the corridor, away from the dim pool of light that highlighted the tapping pen of the matron.

Then she turned and walked quickly down the scrubbed wooden floor of the hospital, anxious for the night to be through.

Fat black bitch, she thought and grimaced.

"I take it that you shouldn't be smoking, Loss." The speaker lifted nonexistent creases with thumb and forefinger and sat heavily in the chair by the window. "Therefore I shan't offer you one. Rotten things anyway. Do you mind if I do? No, of course not. Probably smells good. Back with the living, I mean."

The short man tapped a filtered Dunhill against his wrist and placed it between his pursed lips. His hawk-like nose, florid complexion, and the cigarette between his lips gave the illusion of a bird eating a worm. He lit it and inhaled, holding the smoke in his lungs with obvious relish.

Brian Loss lay back against the pillows, not caring who or what this man was. Pain still pulsed through his body, even though the drugs muted it. Twenty-two stitches, the nurse had said, from the bridge of his nose to his right ear. His head was pounding and he felt nauseated. His forearm was burning and oozing beneath the dressings.

"Can't we do this later?"

"I'm sorry, Mr. Loss. I should go away and I will do so as quickly as possible. But I must talk with you before the police do. In your best interest, of course." The florid-faced man tapped the cigarette onto the windowsill, spilling ash across his shirt.

Loss tried to place the stout Englishman and failed. The man had the face of a drinker, burst capillaries beneath the skin, the eyes pouchy, eyelids flickering nervously. Well-trimmed hair, though, and long in a way that the English had always favored.

Brian shaded his eyes against the early-morning glare. His right arm hurt like hell.

"Pull the blind, please. The brightness hurts my eyes," he said.

"Yes, of course." And with surprising grace, the visitor leaned over the arm of the chair and drew the blind. The armpits of his white shirt were already dark with perspiration.

"Yes, Mr. Loss," he said, easing back into the chair, "we haven't met. My name is Campbell. Ian Campbell. Of Her Majesty's Government. Rather unofficial, of course. The Bahamas is no longer a colony, and I am here on their sufferance."

Loss sighed, tired beyond anything he could recall. He closed his eyes and said, "What branch of the government, Mr. Campbell. Civil aviation, police, what?"

"No, not that at all, Mr. Loss. I expect that I should bring you up to date, all right?" Loss nodded, listening, eyes partially open. His chest was hurting now. The drug's effects probably subsiding.

Campbell resumed. "You crashed off the end of the runway here six days ago. Here, of course, being Matthew Town."

Loss started opening his eyes wide. He attempted to sit up and nearly passed out with the pain.

Campbell made a restraining gesture, his palm flat and down, fingers dark with nicotine. "No, no, Mr. Loss. Please relax. No one has died. You're the primary casualty and you'll live. But the authorities are quite cross with you." He held up his left hand and ticked off his fingers. "One, possession of a firearm, two stealing an aircraft, and three, prohibited narcotics, although I think they'll drop that charge, which, in truth, should be lodged against your friend, Bolken."

Loss groaned, "What in Christ's sake are you talking about? Yes, I carry a firearm in my briefcase. I always have. But I don't carry drugs, and I was directed to make this flight by my employer. I was carrying Bolken and Klist to . . ." He paused, almost said "Mexico" and thought better of it.

"Who is Klist?" Campbell said carefully, withdrawing a pen from his shirt pocket, rummaging in the pants for a notebook which he withdrew. "Spell the name."

"Klist," Loss replied, impatiently. "K-L-I-S-T. What does he call himself now? And where's Bolken?"

Campbell was silent for a minute, carefully lighting another cigarette from the glowing tip of the first one. He inhaled and coughed, the deep, liquid cough of a man courting emphysema.

"No, Mr. Loss," Campbell said carefully. "There were no passengers other than Bolken. They found you both still in the aircraft, your face smashed into the panel. You took a severe concussion plus a nasty gash across your forehead. One broken rib as well. Broken was in the right seat, face badly cut. The aircraft had caught fire but apparently an explosion in one of the fuel cells blew the fire out. The rain did the rest. No one got to the airport for probably ten minutes after the crash. It's unattended, as you know."

The window blind rattled in the wind, and Loss could hear the low-frequency throb of what was probably a large diesel generator. Footsteps came and went in the hallway, muffled voices in the next room.

"What is your position in this, Mr. Campbell?" he asked, laying his head back into the cleft of the pillow, eyes closed.

Campbell pulled the chair closer to the bed, the feet

214

of the chair grating over the rough floor. He replied in a lowered voice, so close that Brian could smell the staleness of his breath. "Loss. We may not have a lot of time. The local surgeon should be here any minute. Basically, I am with a division of Her Majesty's Service concerned with the movement of aliens of undesirable political habits within the United Kingdom and even within the Commonwealth. I followed the man you call Bolken from England to Barbados and lost him there. Three, no four days ago it was, the Bahamian authorities contacted Interpol with Bolken's prints. Incidentally, he claims to be Dutch. My department surveys these messages as a routine since political activities sometimes parallel criminal activities. One of the brighter chaps in our section caught it and contacted me. I had traced Bolken only as far as Guadeloupe." He paused, picking at his collar, loosening the tie

"We have vetted your background and I believe that you are what you say you are. Your employer," he paused to consult his notes, "Senator Welsh, claims that you were instructed to drop Mr. Bolken in Martinique so that he might catch a flight. No mention of this person Klist. The senator states that your absence was not alarming due to the poor weather. Thought you were grounded in Fort de France, enjoying the dollies, et cetera."

"That's insane," Loss replied, propping himself up, not caring at the pain. "Welsh directed that flight and Bolken and Klist were the reason for it. I was to fly them to Mexico. We got beaten up badly in a storm cell west of Haiti. You must have seen the hail damage on the wings."

"Gently, gently," Campbell said. "Don't shout. I believe you. Let me continue. The local authorities have, of course, removed the aircraft from the runway. There are just two constables, you see. I doubt that a print remains intact. Officially, they view it as simple theft. The plan seems to transfer you to Nassau

215

and charge you with possession of a firearm and stealing an aircraft. Possibly, there will be further charges from the Civil Aviation Department. Bolken is slightly cut up about the face and has a great egg of a lump on his forehead but is staying at the hotel. There was a small quantity of cocaine in his valise, which normally the Bahamian authorities would be most alarmed about. But two days ago, a German lawyer, resident in the Bahamas, arrived from Nassau by chartered flight, and it would appear that the charges have been overlooked for a considerable sum of sterling. Bolken is simply being deported to Haiti by the next flight, which I believe is in two days. Bolken, of course, has made no official statement, but it would seem that he and his lawyer are not entirely friendly. In other words, someone else seems to have arranged for the lawyer, not Bolken himself."

"It looks like I've been screwed, doesn't it?" Loss said numbly.

"It could have been much worse, Mr. Loss," Campbell said. "I examined your aircraft very carefully. I doubt that it is your habit to fly around with the fuel drain cocks open. It would seem now that there was a third party who got out of the aircraft intact and then opened the fuel drains to ensure that the fire consumed the aircraft. Very naughty, wasn't it?"

Loss opened his eyes and stared at the man who sat beside him.

"Yes, Mr. Loss. And I don't think it was Bolken. His goose egg and cuts are real enough. And there is dried vomit in the back seat from what I can determine. Rather thought at first it was chipped beef. Is that where Bolken was actually seated, in the back seat, I mean?"

Loss nodded.

"Yes, then. I'm beginning to see," Campbell said, almost to himself. "It would appear that you've been made the sacrificial goose. Let me check with my people in London about this person Klist plus a few other things. I will need to talk to you again, oh, perhaps this afternoon or tomorrow. In the meanwhile, I would advise you not to make any statement. Say you want a barrister to represent you. Don't muddy up the water. And I'll try to get Bolken detained in some manner as well."

He heaved himself up out of the seat. "Take care," he said and was gone, the latch clicking shut behind him. Loss sighed and drifted back into sleep.

She came much later in the afternoon, across the lawn where children rolled the rims of discarded bicycle wheels over the burned grass. She walked down the cool corridors of the small hospital past empty rooms. Then she stood in the doorway, hesitant to wake him. As he slept, the muscles in his cheek twitched; his face was sallow and unshaven. He had lost a lot of weight. His forehead was bandaged, and his hair was tangled and wild. He stirred and rolled over, burying his face in the crook of his arm, grunting as he moved.

Twenty-two stitches, she thought. The scar would be brutal. The hospital matron said that he had taken six pints of blood in the first day of admission, and she could believe it, having seen the dried brown mess that had been the instrument panel of the Aztec.

"It smells like you're wearing *Caress*," he said, his head still buried in the hollow of his elbow, eyes partly open.

She was slightly startled, his voice unexpected and coarse in texture, as if he had been yelling too much. Sitting down on the edge of the bed, she bent over and kissed him on the nape of the neck. "You're a mess, Loss. But you look like you'll make it. That's the official news, anyway."

He turned over, saying nothing but wincing, bunching the muscles in his cheeks. He grinned at her, his lips dried and cracked, two top teeth badly chipped. "I'm one hell of a mess. Think I ought to give up driving airplanes and associating with politicians." He reached for her hand. "Thanks for coming. How did you get here?"

"Long story." She dug into a straw shopping bag and withdrew a variety of things. "I brought you a doggie bag. Some cheese, a couple of candy bars. Just stuff that I picked up at the local market. These too." She placed two miniatures of cognac on the night stand. "At your discretion. But definitely not for now."

He peeled back the paper on a candy bar and bit into it, wincing occasionally with pain but obviously relishing it. "I had some sort of mush laced with fish bones for lunch. And mashed bananas for breakfast with tea. You don't know how good this tastes."

She watched him eating, feeling like a mother who has had her son come home from a schoolyard fight. Battered but with the spirit left in him. She sat down on the bed, taking his head between her hands and kissed him. "You'll do," she said. He kissed her back, tasting of chocolate.

"You understand what's happened?" he said, wiping his lips on a corner of the sheet.

She was silent, watching his eyes.

"Klist is gone," he said. "Bolken was the only other person in the plane when they got to the crash. The police say that I've stolen the plane. Grand theft. I'm to go up to Nassau to face charges in a couple of days."

She nodded. "There's more," she said. "I can only tell you what I know and what I've been able to piece together. A call came in from the Bahamas the afternoon you left. From the police in Nassau. Welsh took the call. He then disappeared for about an hour and as far as I can tell, he and Mrs. Klist had a long talk. Then he called back here through the operator in Nassau. I don't know what the call was specifically about, but apparently he got confirmation that the only occupants of the aircraft were you and Bolken. Then he

218

declared that you weren't authorized to take the aircraft. Something about dropping Bolken off at Martinique. He filed charges against you over the phone."

Loss struggled upright. "Christ," he swore. "Certainly there were some people down at the resort that knew Klist left with us."

"No, Brian," she replied, lighting a cigarette. "Most people knew that all of you went to the Union Island airstrip but no mention was made of the flight. You took off in the rain and I doubt that more than one or two local people were around when you boarded the aircraft. Customs and Immigration on Union Island claim you didn't clear with them and that no flight plan was filed. And on top of that, Mrs. Klist said that her husband went over to Union Island to meet some friend of his on a yacht. She said that she was joining them in Grenada in a few days. Then she flew out the next morning by chartered aircraft. Completely unconcerned."

"What about Welsh and his wife?" he said, unconsciously scratching at the growth of beard.

"They're gone too. Back to Barbados and then by commercial flight to the States. He's filed an affidavit with the local police in Union Island, and they've forwarded it to Nassau. He made a big show of putting you down before he left. Talked about you being a heavy drinker and how he had already fired you, effective after they returned to the States from this trip."

He sat there on the bed, feeling tired and broken and trapped. He would lose his license for openers. And forget about being hired for anything other than a pea-patch flying school. But the rest he could fight. Get an attorney and somehow get Bolken detained to serve as a witness. Some witness, he thought.

"Listen," he said gently, "don't worry. You've done everything and more. But there's one thing. You've got to get on the phone to Nassau and dig up a lawyer; I guess they call them barristers here. Start to get my defense together. There are plenty of traveler's checks in the briefcase. The local police must have it in their possession, and then—"

She cut him off, violently shaking her head. "No, Brian," she said, looking down at the bare, scrubbed floors. "No. I've already tried. I've called fourteen different law offices in Nassau and Freeport. No one will take the case. They know all about it. They just listen to me for five minutes and then tell me that their case load is just too great and politely turn me down. It's fixed. Someone has applied really heavy pressure."

He lay back against the pillow, eyes closed. "I can't believe that Welsh could do this to me," he said, almost a whisper.

She sat down next to him. "There's more," she said, her voice low. "Welsh talked to me before he left. Said he was sorry but that it was beyond his control. He's beside himself. The man looks eighty years old. But he told me that if you plead guilty, you'll only get three years. And you'll receive three thousand dollars per month for every month you're in jail, paid into any account you designate. And also that if you fought it, he couldn't personally guarantee your safety. Either way, he said, you'll be found guilty."

"The filthy bastard," he whispered, looking beyond her, as if his stare would penetrate the wooden boarded walls. "The filthy, miserable bastard." He paused and looked at his hands, rubbing them nervously together. "Klist and Welsh have this whole thing wired. And I'm the one chosen to take the fall." He hunched forward, grasping his knees. "The only option left to me is to get the hell out."

She got up and went to the door, opening it and looking down the hallway. Satisfied, she closed it softly, lifting the latch and dropping it quietly in place. She sat down on the bed again and took his hand. "You remember Stroud?"

"The biologist guy you met in Carriacou?"

She nodded. "He was the only one I could turn to. To fly up here commercially would have meant going all the way to Miami and then back down on the feeder airline. He offered to bring me here directly. He's got a little single-engine airplane."

He opened his eyes, listening more carefully. "And?"

"Brian, there's nothing between Stroud and me. It's just that he, well, he loves me in some sort of funny way. Not physical. He understands the situation—that there's no other option. He's willing to let you take the aircraft. Because of me, because I asked him to."

Loss breathed slowly out, eyes closed, listening to the sound of children playing in the distant field.

Chapter 16

Campbell sat opposite Loss in a disintegrating wicker chair, endlessly flicking his butane lighter. The wind had fallen, and the air was stale and oppressive, even under the shade of the almond tree where they sat. Beyond them, across the baked grounds of the lawn, the small hospital building was aching white in the sunlight.

A black constable, young and filled with self-importance, paced back and forth at a discreet distance from the two men. He watched Loss closely. The white man was bandaged heavily about the forehead, and his arm showed a cuff of white dressings beneath the bathrobe. He had walked with the older man to the chairs beneath the almond tree with a pronounced limp. No, it was doubtful that he would attempt escape.

Elias Wilson switched his baton to the left hand and turned in a wheeling march to the right, back toward the two men. He strained to catch some of their conversation, but it was useless; the afternoon's quiet was overlaid with the cries of the children playing on the cricket pitch across the street.

His superior, Chief Constable Edwards, had been in a foul mood this morning, and Constable Wilson had taken the brunt of it for no good reason. Nassau had called early in the morning and informed them that details for the transfer of the prisoner were complete. Two plainclothesmen would be down on tomorrow morning's flight to retrieve Loss. Edwards had wanted to go personally, and now his moment of glory was forfeit. Coupled with this irritation was the annoyance of the Swedish yacht's illegal departure seven days ago. Edwards had really laid into Wilson for that.

With only two men on the force, it was normally Constable Wilson's duty to act as immigration and customs officer. The Swedish yacht had simply left in the night without proper authority, and Elias had taken the brunt of the blame.

Wilson was not overly concerned about the dressing down. He had stood rigidly at attention before his chief, taking notes where appropriate and had finally departed with a bone-snapping salute. The old man was near retirement, and therefore not important to his career. The reports were filed and queries made to neighboring islands to locate the yacht. He had covered himself well.

His shirt was beginning to prickle against his skin in the blasted heat. We've been self-governing for over ten years now, and we still wear the standard British woolen shirts, he thought. And this *red-leg* honky, Campbell. Some connection with the British Foreign Office. What right does he have to interfere with our affairs. He looked like a parody of the nineteenth-century colonial servant.

Wilson completed another leg of his circuit and, transferring the baton to his right hand, he wheeled his dusty brogans through a left turn. He smiled inwardly. In five months, he would be made chief constable and then there would be some changes. He watched the two white men carefully.

"It's a complete zero," Campbell said, his eyes averted. "The officials in Nassau are quite adamant that Bolken is being deported on the first flight to Haiti and that you are to be transported to Nassau on tomorrow morning's flight. Very simply, Bolken's lawyer has paid a fine and the matter's closed."

"What did you say Bolken's real name is?" Loss said, flicking his cigarette butt into the dust at his feet.

"Heiss. Carl Heiss. Born in Grossenhain, Germany, 1931. Immigrated with his guardian to England in 1938. Short stint in the British army in the late forties but discharged for what is termed here as 'maladjustment.' That's a polite name for sexual deviation, according to his records." Campbell consulted his notes, flicking through the pages with his thumb as a teller would count bank notes. "Heiss is a photographer by trade; mostly union journals. Four trips back to Germany during the late fifties."

"Why the phony name?"

Campbell wiped the sweat from his florid face and tucked the handkerchief back under his shirt collar. "Some things I can't tell you, Brian. Except that Heiss has done some very nasty jobs for the Russians. More than that I can't say."

Loss came erect in his chair. He bent forward toward Campbell, seeking his eyes. "Are you telling me that Klist also works for the Russians?"

Campbell scratched at his eyebrow, avoiding Loss's stare. "Can't say, Brian. We have no prints, no photos, nothing. He could be anyone. All we know is that the passport was a fake. There's no Klist of this description in Dutch passport files. We know that he entered Barbados, flew by charter flight to Union Island, and stayed at Salt Whistle Cay. Then poof. His wife claimed that he has gone sailing, and now she has conveniently returned to Europe via Venezuela. No forwarding address.''

Loss leaned back in his chair and watched the constable pass them. I feel as if I'm in the slammer already, he thought. He turned back to Campbell and said, "I know damn well that Klist must still be on this island. There haven't been any commercial flights in or out in the last seven days. No boat traffic from what Holly has been able to find out. So where is he? Why don't the police try to find him?''

Campbell lifted his hands fractionally. "Because he isn't here. Your lady is not entirely correct, Brian. There was a Swedish yacht moored in the basin the day you arrived. It left sometime that night without proper customs or immigration clearance. I doubt that it will be heard of again.''

"Where would he go? He's bound to make port somewhere.''

Campbell chuckled. "Yes. At least that's the theory. The Bahamian authorities have requested the other neighboring islands to be on the alert. But I would imagine that our resourceful Mr. Klist headed due west to Cuba, assuming of course that he is linked in some way with the Russians. It's a pleasant little sail of about ten hours, directly downwind. Piece of cake, really.''

"What about Heiss?'' Brian asked. "Can't he be detained? He's the only one who could verify my story.''

Campbell frowned and shook his head. "Heiss is being deported with a minor fine for possession of narcotics. This decision comes straight fron Nassau. I've made all the noises that I can to the British high commissioner and have been told, very politely, mind you, that this is not our jurisdiction any more. In fact, I am to return to London on the first transportation available. Very touchy, politically speaking.''

Loss stared at the ground. A column of ants were

224

fighting over his cigarette butt. He looked back up at Campbell. "So what defense do I have? What help can you give me?"

Campbell looked embarrassed. He dropped his notebook into the old-fashioned briefcase and started to rise to his feet and said, "None, Mr. Loss. Absolutely none, I'm afraid. As they would say in an American film, 'You've been had.' Someone in a very high place has been paid handsomely. Your employer, Senator Welsh, claims that you have stolen the aircraft. Heiss denies any knowledge of wrongdoing and is essentially being set free. You *did* have a firearm in your briefcase, which, in the Bahamas, is punishable by at least one year's confinement." Campbell paused and looked across the lawn to the cricket pitch where the children were playing. "No. I'm afraid that I can do nothing more for you." He extended his hand toward Loss. "I must be on my way."

Loss shook hands with him, finding the grasp firm and surprisingly cool. Campbell turned to go and then, almost as an afterthought, said, "Oh, incidentally, Mr. Loss. Your personal possessions, which will, of course, be forwarded to Nassau, are locked in a rather flimsy filing cabinet in the chief constable's office next to the Cable and Wireless building. I have heard it said that the key to the office is generally over the door sill. But then again, these are just rumors. The security is rather lax down here in these islands, as you might well expect it to be. Last murder in 1923, I believe. Very law abiding, really. Well, take care," and he picked up his briefcase.

Loss rose to shake his hand again. Campbell smiled. "You know, Mr. Loss, you really have a lovely young lady. Very resourceful. Asked me to get the weather forecast for tonight and tomorrow, which, I am pleased to report, will be excellent. Something about winds, easterly at fifteen knots at the 12,000-foot level. Perfectly clear all the way to Miami except for a few isolated afternoon thundershowers. But as you know, weathermen are eternal optimists. Well, cheers." He turned and without looking back, trudged across the burned grass toward the Government Guest House.

Peter Bates Stroud transferred the last of the five-gallon jerry can's contents into the outboard tank of his aircraft and fastened the tank lid with a firm twist. He checked his watch and, noting that it was 5:18, calculated that he had approximately forty-five minutes remaining before dark. He carefully drained the residue of gasoline from the metal can and placed it on the tarmac, opened neck toward the wind to purge it of fumes.

Next, he checked the oil and, although the dipstick showed eight quarts, he carefully transferred another quart of Shell aviation oil into the filler neck and secured it. With the cowling of the engine compartment still open, he traced each high tension lead and inspected each critical fitting, and only then, satisfied with his preflight inspection, did he close and lock the snap fittings that secured the sheet aluminum cowl.

Stroud continued to work methodically through the late-afternoon twilight, examining each part of the aircraft, pausing occasionally to survey the length of the asphalt road that led from Matthew Town to the airport.

The aircraft was a single-engine Piper Comanche, a smaller and older relative to the Aztec that now lay burned and gutted in the grass half a mile down the runway. It was the type of aircraft that a man would buy for himself if he wished to travel a great deal with a large quantity of baggage. Normally, the aircraft could seat four with a moderate amount of luggage, but Stroud had done extensive modifications to the interior so that now the aircraft could carry only two people in comfort. The rest of the space was given over to fuel tanks and storage for his equipment.

Stroud had bought the aircraft in Canada four years previously, and although the blue and white paint was badly faded, the aircraft was mechanical perfection. Contrary to the regulations of the Department of Transport, Stroud did all his own maintenance, allowing certified mechanics only to inspect and sign off the work in his logbooks. He strongly believed that reliability was a direct function of meticulous and constant care, particularly the reliability of an aircraft that regularly flew over vast stretches of wilderness and, most particularly, if he was the man who was flying the aircraft.

Stroud, now thirty-four years old, had been born to middle-class English parents, nurtured on the pablum of the welfare system, force-fed with leftist liberalism in the London School of Economics, and, finally, had passed it all out of his system, counting the mutilated bodies of his army comrades in the rain misted streets of Belfast.

After being mustered out of his national service stint in the British army, he switched majors, becoming a biologist. From there on in, Stroud spent as much time removed from human habitation as his work and an annual grant would allow.

Having firmly rejected one society, he began to formulate his own by observing the patterns of intelligent mammals, living and playing with complex but logical systems of coexistence. Animals, supposedly lacking the powers of free will, appeared freer than humans, for they seldom subjected themselves to the constraints of a highly structured society, choosing instead a life of freedom and self-determination within loosely defined limits of peaceful cooperation, food gathering, and territorial rights.

In comparison, Stroud observed that man had elected to give up self-determination and, in turn, his own free will, for shallow benefits and the marginal security of a society that progressively extracted more and returned less. It was that simple. He saw no cure for man's dilemma and, with this conclusion, strove only for his own salvation. Using his savings and occasional grants, Stroud wandered the wilderness areas of the American continents, studying the infrastructure of select animal societies, totally at peace with himself and as far removed from man as generally possible.

The plane had been a gift to himself. He reasoned that by flying directly to his study site, he would save a great deal of money, frustration, and time. More important, he would retain the twin virtues of flexibility and independence.

With money from a grant for the study of hair seals above the Arctic Circle, Stroud set about first learning to fly and then purchasing an aircraft. Because he would operate in the wilderness areas, he bypassed the chrome-plated pilot factories and instead chose a shaggy Scotsman who flew the Canadian bush, spotting elk migrations. With equal doses of Calvinism and aeronautical instruction, Stroud learned the practical realities of staying alive in a hostile environment.

The choice of an aircraft was more difficult. Since Stroud had 15,000 Canadian dollars to play with, the Scot recommended a high-winged Cessna 180: something that you could put skis or floats on, a plane for all seasons. The Scotsman described it as a "bonny bit of tin."

Stroud, operating in the far Canadian north only during summers and the southern latitudes of Argentina for the balance of the year, chose range, cargo-carrying capacity, and speed instead. With dire warnings and great reluctance, the Scot helped him find and convert such an aircraft. And the Comanche had been a success. In this, his fourth year of ownership, he had never had a failure while accumulating close to six hundred hours on the aircraft.

Stroud had been working his way north from Argentina, leaving the South American fall behind, flying into the North American springtime. He wanted to be at his seal-observation camp north of Hudson Bay by the time the snows melted. While he waited for the spring thaw in the Canadian Northwest Passage, he worked at the marine biology station in Carriacou, studying dolphins and the passing pods of humpback whales.

Stroud had met Hollister Stone at a depth of seven fathoms along the reef that protects the windward shore of Carriacou. He happened upon her quite by chance, being primarily intent on following a group of three bottle-nosed dolphins *(Tursiops truncatus)*, which were playing along the ten-fathom line. She emerged out of the blue depths, swimming opposite to his direction, wearing nothing more than diving tanks and a mask. She waved casually at him, as one might do seeing an acquaintance across a busy street. And then she was gone.

He found her again, two days later, lying on the shingled beach off of Gunn Point, reading Darwin's *On the Origin of Species*. In thirty minutes' conversation, Stroud was completely charmed by the only other person he had ever met whom he considered to have a completely free will.

He did not consider himself to be even remotely handsome, and he was right. Stroud's gawky frame of over six feet was topped by a painfully thin face and a brown mop of already thinning hair. His hands, unfulfilled except when working with specimens or flying, were overly large and ill at ease. But in her presence, he felt eloquent and graceful.

He spent two unadulterated days of joy with her, talking of things he had kept within himself for five years. Not once had he touched her hand or smelled her hair, but he was surely in love as any man can ever be.

That she had left Carriacou with Loss worried him not in the least, for he was content simply to treasure the thought of knowing a free soul. And perhaps this kind of love was better for its distance. Stroud would willingly have given a great deal for her admiration, and the loss of an aircraft now seemed little enough.

229

The sun was at last swallowed by the horizon, and Stroud adjusted his thick prescription glasses as he watched its ingestion into the western sea. He felt pleased with himself, having foreseen those possibilities that might arise. The aircraft was now parked on the cracked concrete hardstand, awaiting flight. All the tanks had been filled to maximum capacity, and the ten metal jerry cans of fuel were carefully strapped down in the back seat and luggage compartment, allowing a total range of over two thousand miles.

It is considered a very unhealthy practice for one to carry metal containers of one-hundred octane fuel within the cabin of any aircraft. Fumes from the fuel provide an explosive mixture that can cause catastrophic results with only one small arc of current across a switch contact. Compounding this is the problem of expansion and contraction as the cans are subjected to the pressures of changing altitude. Even such strongly constructed structures as thermos flasks may burst at high altitude if not properly vented.

But Stroud had found it necessary to carry extra fuel on his pilgrimages into the far recesses of the continent in pursuit of his studies. Good fuel was generally unobtainable, and consequently he had devised a system to carry his own reserves. Each individual can was fitted with its own plastic vent tube, which was connected to a brass manifold and vented to the outside air. A separate system allowed the unorthodox accomplishment of in-flight refueling. With the aircraft on autopilot, Stroud would lean into the back seat of the aircraft and individually connect each can of gas to a squeeze-bulb siphon pump, similar to those that are used to connect gasoline tanks to outboard motors. The process was time-consuming but relatively safe; there was only manual energy involved in the transfer of fuel to the main inboard tanks. That such a procedure violated every published standard of safety was all the more reason to use it, for it demonstrated that each man can define his own system and come to live with it. Stroud had developed his own set of rules for safe transfer, and he had committed these to a small index card that was secured to the sun visor over the pilot's seat.

For Loss's benefit, he had also left detailed written instructions as to the final disposition of the aircraft, whatever its destination, for in order for Stroud to collect the insurance if the aircraft were damaged, there must be evidence of forced entry. This pricked his conscience, but he dismissed it as a necessary measure, even if Lloyd's of London were the ultimate aggrieved party.

He looked at the aircraft once more as he got into the rented Ford. It seemed larger, more vital than he had ever remembered, and he wished that it was he who would make this flight with that woman. But it was his gift to her and that was sufficient.

He drove carefully back into Matthew Town, finding the road completely deserted except for scuttling land crabs, which he cautiously avoided. He passed the hospital and the droning shell of the power station and parked in front of Cable and Wireless Ltd. He entered and queried the night switchboard operator for any overseas calls. She replied in a sleepy negative, returning to her magazine without even looking at his face. Stroud thanked her, somewhat embarrassed, and returned into the cool night. He stood in the blackness for some minutes, watching the street that was vacant except for one passing Land Rover going in the direction of the eastern end of town. A small shop farther down the street, perhaps two hundred yards distant, throbbed with the reggae beat of a hard-pressed juke box, and there would be men drinking rum and arguing the merits of cricket players. But beyond that, the town had ground to an end of the day.

Stroud adjusted his glasses and nervously glanced through the window of Cable and Wireless. The operator sat slouched behind the counter, absorbed in the magazine. Her hand occasionally strayed beneath the counter to pluck some sweet from a hidden package and convey it to her mouth. But that was all.

He moved softly to the door of the constable's office and felt along the sill for a key. His fingertips touched a cool metal shape and he retrieved it and inserted it in the lock. He entered the office quickly and closed the door behind him. From his poplin jacket, he withdrew a pair of soiled leather gloves he habitually used for flying. The leather was soft and close fitting, and the scent of the glove gave him momentary assurance, like a friend met in a strange place.

Within three minutes he had located the filing cabinet and forced it with nothing more than a screwdriver. The briefcase that Holly had described was on the bottom shelf, and he opened it and examined the contents with a penlight. Aside from the books of traveler's checks, passport, and aircraft manuals, the light reflected from the oiled metal of an automatic pistol. He pondered the advisability of leaving the weapon, for this man, Loss, might be the vindictive sort. But in the end, he left the weapon in the briefcase, feeling that it was Loss's decision.

He stood by the curtained window for another two minutes, attempting to scan the street in both directions. It was as silent and deserted as before, and he finally left the office, carefully locking it and replacing the key. He placed the briefcase in the trunk of the Ford along with the gloves and walked off with a light step, almost a bounce, in the direction of the hospital. He was enjoying himself immensely.

Loss was making a nuisance of himself. He briefly checked his watch and noted that it was 5:18. Holly had left roughly ten minutes ago. He rolled on his side and thumbed the buzzer. Far down the corridor, he heard it rasping, like an insistent insect. He waited for another twenty seconds and thumbed the buzzer again, repeatedly. He could hear steps in the hallway, echoing along the bare floors. He smiled and relaxed back into the deep pillows.

The door opened abruptly.

"Yes?"

He looked up at the day nurse and scowled.

"I'd like some water."

"There some on your night table." The nurse was plainly impatient with him; her dark face was devoid of expression, the thick nostrils flaring slightly.

"Yes, I know. But it's warm."

"Matron tell me she replace your water four times today. That's enough." Nurse Wylie looked at the white man with distaste and shut the door on his objection. Composing herself, she walked briskly down the corridor, the sound of his voice muffled but demanding, following after her.

She paused to stop at the desk and made an entry in her log. She hesitated and counted his calls in the log. Water, codeine, requests that his shirt be washed for the trip to Nassau. And on and on. Fourteen calls since the noon hour. That the man was white didn't bother her. She regarded herself above all that, unlike her brother. But this man was a torment, and she wished him ill. There were only three other patients on the ward and this one asked for, no, demanded, more than any patient she had yet experienced in her two years of service.

Loss smiled and settled back in his bed. The woman did have patience, though. If he had been her, he would have long ago ignored the repeated requests. Even though she was inexperienced, she had tended him with care and skill for the first days of consciousness. And she had displayed that most alarming, total smile that rent the professional mask into honest pleasure as he complimented her for care he honestly felt was superior to any that he had ever seen in any hospital. He regretted doing this to her.

After 5:30 now. He withdrew the Comanche flight manual from beneath the covers and read on. The air-

233

craft held no problem for him, but he wanted no fumbling in a darkened cockpit in what might be a tense situation. With the aircraft overgross at 2,950 pounds and the center of gravity well aft, he would want seventy-four knots for liftoff. Visualizing the air-speed indicator, he branded the number in his mind, eyes closed with concentration. Maximum range would be the name of the exercise, and he carefully calculated climb speeds and power settings. Best range would be 40 percent power at 15,000 feet. No oxygen, but that was acceptable.

No one here would know of Stroud's jerry-rigged fuel supply, nor would they definitely know that the aircraft came equipped from the factory with optional long-range tanks. Stroud would lie to cover this fact. Also, it was logical to assume that any attempt to escape would be at high speed and consequently at high fuel consumption. But Stroud had reasoned differently and had formulated the outline of a workable plan, which Holly had relayed. Stroud would be left tied up at the airport, the infuriated owner of a stolen aircraft. His estimates of range would be initially accepted and later checked, only to confirm that the probable range under average fuel management would be little more than eight hundred miles. But with careful leaning of the mixture and low-power settings plus the fuel provided by both the long-range factory tanks and the Mickey Mouse fuel reserve, Loss calculated a range in excess of 2,100 miles.

It was useless to turn south into the Caribbean. Most of these countries would have firm diplomatic links with the Bahamas. Mexico was out of the question. Initially, flight into the United States seemed worth consideration—to confront Welsh on his home ground. But in the end, Loss remembered the Kents from Nova Scotia and knew that the dirt airstrip on the Kent farm would be a method of entering the North American continent with minimal chance of detection. From there, he would have time and facilities to deal with Welsh. And be well beyond any accusations voiced in the Caribbean.

There was also the question of what Heiss might know, but the question was how to extract that information.

Loss gritted his teeth and slammed his fist into the pillow. The frustration of being made the scapegoat for something obviously illegal grated continually at the corners of his mind. The fact that Welsh could turn and accuse him of theft, willingly condemning Loss to complete loss of professional reputation and three years of life in a foreign prison seemed unbelievable. What Loss had accepted as fate initially had now become the realization that he was simply a minor character in some play, and readily expendable. For once in his life, Loss was beginning to know the literal meaning of the word *hate*.

There was a knock at his door, and it opened without his response. Nurse Wylie entered, carrying a food tray. She placed it on the night table without comment and started to leave.

"Take it away."

"I'm sorry, Mr. Loss," she enunciated carefully. "This is the food that all patients get. This is what we eat. Perhaps they feed you better in Nassau." She immediately felt regret at lowering herself to conversation with this honky. Her brother was right, in his own way.

Loss softened his tone, leaning back against the pillows and closing his eyes. She could hardly hear his slightly slurred speech.

"Miss Wylie, Nurse Wylie. I'm sorry. I can't eat. Just remove the tray, please, and give me two or three sleeping tablets. No visitors. Nothing. My head really hurts."

She regarded the white man and then understood his irritability. The stitches would be pulling now, and probably the worry of tomorrow bothered him.

"Yes," she said, hesitantly. "Yes, I'll be right

235

back." She removed the tray and left the room, pausing to adjust the blanket that had almost slid off the bed.

She left the room and walked down the corridor, relieved that her professional attitude had not been corrupted by the irritant of Loss's behavior. And now she understood. And with medication for his pain and sleeping tablets, he would be no more trouble for the evening. Tomorrow he would be gone.

She returned in under five minutes, two separate paper cups containing pills and a fresh glass of cold water balanced on her tray.

He took them without comment and sank back into the pillows.

"Thanks. I still think you're the best nurse I ever saw."

She smiled at him now, relieved.

"I'll be in to see you at eleven. To check your temperature." She watched him with professional pride, the thing now back into a controlled patient-nurse relationship.

"Can't we just skip that this evening? I haven't had a temperature in three days and I want to get a solid night's sleep."

He said it quietly, reasonably. She knew the matron would require it, but she would forget it for this night.

"It will be all right, Mr. Loss. Just this once. Sleep well." She smiled as she left the room and closed the door softly.

Loss listened to her steps retreating down the corridor, hollow echoes and then quiet. It was a small risk that his absence would be discovered. But the woman would catch hell in the morning, which he felt genuinely sorry about.

He spit the four capsules into his hand, and washed out his mouth with the water. He discarded the two sleeping tablets in the wastebasket but retained the partially dissolved pain capsules for future use, pocketing them in the robe.

His Rolex showed sixteen minutes after six. He moved to the window and watched the dark hospital grounds and the street beyond. No sign of Stroud's Ford. The power generation station emitted its hollow thrumming, which he could just fa...tly hear against the prevalent sounds of the trade winds. The Cable and Wireless offices were lighted as they would be until midnight. All the other shops were dark as far as he could see along the sea front with the exception of the rum shop much farther along Bay Street toward the eastern edge of town.

He turned reluctantly from the window. Now nineteen past. Rolling a blanket into a tube, he stuffed it beneath the covers. Crude. Maybe enough to pass for a man in the dim light from the corridor. He wanted to shave, to have a shower. But it was an impossibility. He regretted that he had not asked for his billfold and sunglasses. Perhaps even his blood-stained clothing. But there was only the hospital robe. It had to be enough.

The sound of an insect rasping against the screen. He turned and watched a hand draw a fingertip down across the window screen.

"Stroud?"

"Yes." A face appeared, lean, serious, almost comical. His glasses, thick as glass biscuits, reflected doubled pinpoints of light. The face smiled. "Let's get going."

Loss turned the bed lamp off and walked to the window. He watched as Stroud cut a flap in the screening, neatly and without haste, as if he were dissecting a specimen.

Loss's rib hurt as he dropped to the ground and the two men grasped hands. Loss felt vaguely embarrassed, as if this were a meeting of two child conspirators, about to recite a secret oath and then swab the farmer's cows with white paint.

"I'm Stroud." He stood there in the blackness, only the reflection of his glasses and the white teeth visible.

"Yes. You lead. My eyes aren't adapted to night vision yet."

They kept to the dark shadow of the building, trampling the carefully tended flowers; the crushed leaves released a pungent smell. Loss thought of his first date and the scent of lilac. Forever ago.

"The car's over there," Stroud said.

"Did you get the briefcase?"

"Yes. Your weapon too."

Loss paused, seeking the right words. "Stroud, I don't have time to thank you properly for this. Perhaps some day."

Stroud smiled, his teeth bright in the darkness. "It's quite all right. I'm sure you'd do the same. The aircraft is all refueled and preflighted. Use up the main tanks first and then refill them from the reserve cans while you run on the auxiliary tanks. The procedure is on an index card on the left-seat sun visor. I think that you can stretch it to twenty-two hundred some odd miles. There's some tables of actual petrol consumption at various power settings in the dash compartment. You probably will find them helpful."

"OK, Peter, I understand," Loss said. "Look, I don't want to tell you where exactly, but I'm going to try to make Canada. I'll leave the aircraft there in one piece if possible. I'll cover all the expenses and time on the aircraft and leave the money in cash with some friends who will take care of the aircraft. But until then, you just have to convince everyone that it was stolen and, if possible, that the range was short of eight hundred miles on the fuel available. We'll remove the backseat tanks in Canada and store them so that there won't be any embarrassing questions. Agreed?"

Stroud nodded. "It's fine, Brian. Do whatever you have to do with the aircraft. It's insured. Just don't implicate me on your end, and it will work out. Incidentally, I've overfilled the oil by one quart, but she burns a bit. That should still give you at least minimum

238

oil required by the end of your flight. Just keep the power settings low if you can."

"Thanks. Good to know. Let's move."

The two men watched the street for a few more minutes. The sparsely placed street lamps swung in the wind. Beyond that, there was no movement. They crossed the hospital lawn and then the street, moving carefully and without haste. Loss moved into the back seat of the Ford, allowing Stroud to drive.

"Airport?"

"No," Loss replied. "We've got one other stop to—"

"Get down," Stroud hissed. The door of the Cable and Wireless opened, and the night operator moved into the doorway, looking down the street to the east, chewing slowly on some object. Stroud got out of the car immediately, not turning to look at Loss, who hunched down behind the seat.

"Oh, you've received it?" Stroud asked, politely standing just on the edge of the shaded lamp's rim of brightness.

"Received what?" The girl turned to him, scowling, still chewing methodically.

"My cable. I've been waiting for it all day. A cable from Barbados. For me. Peter Stroud." He stood somewhat humbly before her, now moving into the light. He smiled, hesitantly.

"No cable," she said, turning and shutting the door.

Stroud returned to the car and started it, allowing the engine to warm up, not moving yet as if undecided. Finally he pulled away from the dirt parking area onto the asphalt land and drove slowly away. "Where now," he said.

Loss laughed from the recesses of the back seat. "Very cool." He rose from the back-seat floor and said, "OK, Peter. Here comes the harder part. Take the second left down here and go up two blocks. You know the place they call Mary's Beach Cottages? They're not exactly on the beach, but I guess in a town of four or five hundred, you can get away with that." He pointed to the turn. "Here."

They swung left from the bay front and onto a dirt road. The street lights disappeared behind them and only a few scattered houses lined the street—the more prosperous section of town.

"From here on out, Peter, you have to play the captured aircraft owner. I'll have to tie you up with nylon fishing line and gag you. I'll be leaving you in the front seat. Next, I get Heiss out of his cottage and his lawyer as well, if they're rooming together."

Stroud nodded; his face was just faintly illuminated in the glow of the dashboard lights.

"The important thing is that you must listen to everything Heiss tells me and report this to the police. When we get to the airfield, I'll question him. It may be a little rough. Both of you will be tied up but well separated. Watch out for him, Peter. Don't trust him an inch. Campbell says that Heiss is violent."

"And then?" Stroud asked, shifting gears smoothly.

"After we find out what we can, Holly and I will take off, leaving you both behind. Your bonds will be loose enough for you to work out of them after a decent period of time. Don't make it seem too quick. Heiss will be really well secured, so don't worry. We'll climb out to the south and then eventually turn north after we're out of sight and hearing. You leave Heiss where he is and trot smartly into town. Give the stolen-aircraft story routine and tell them we departed to the south. Tell them what Heiss has said. From there, just wait until you hear the aircraft has been recovered. Submit an insurance claim as well, I guess. All of this clear?"

"Sounds like good fun," Stroud replied. "Here you are."

Stroud slowed the car and pulled off to the side, extinguishing the lights as he did. A complex of cottages and a central guest house were set back into the grove of white cedar and sea grape trees. The grounds were neatly fenced by low shrubs. The guest house had several lights burning, and movement from within could be seen just as blurred shapes. The sound of a Jim Reeves recording was faint on the humid night wind.

They sat in the darkness for several minutes watching the complex of buildings and the grounds. No real movement except in the main guest house.

"Cottage Four is the unit Heiss and his lawyer have rented," Loss said, indicating a building set deep into a grove of sea grape trees, far to the left. A light shone dimly behind the drapes.

Stroud rubbed his chin, almost bored. "What's on the program now?"

"That depends. Have you brought the gear that Holly briefed you on?"

"It's in the boot—trunk—whatever you call it. Two-hundred-foot coil of eighty-pound-test monofilament line. Some adhesive tape. Box of plastic garbage bags and sweets. Chocolate, if you don't mind?"

Loss eased out of the Ford and crouched in its shadow, listening. Satisfied, he opened the trunk and extracted the equipment. He opened his briefcase and groped for his Luger. He released the clip and counted the rounds, snicking his thumbnail down the loading slot. Eight. Loss reinserted the clip and chambered a round. He felt himself slipping past that point of return, where rules made sense.

Loss extracted the monofilament fishing line from the small heap and returned to the driver's side. Stroud obediently turned and crossed his wrists, which Loss bound. Next, the ankles. Finally a tape across the mouth. Loss gently placed Stroud in the right front seat, the Englishman faintly complaining through the gag. Loss squeezed his shoulder and said in a whisper, "Sorry about this. But if I'm caught, just tell them that you were forced. I'm going in to get Heiss now. Stay low on the seat," and he was gone, the Luger cool in his dry hand.

Loss stayed low, running in a crouch along the line of sea grapes that bordered the property. Heiss's cottage was the furthest one, and he gained the wall of the unit without exposure.

His head was pounding now, and he felt weak and lightheaded. The thin bathrobe was a sieve to the night wind, and he rested briefly against the wall of the cottage.

The curtains to the cottage were drawn, but he could hear the sound of a toilet flushing and moments later a door closing.

Loss felt his way along the edge of the wall to the back of the cottage. One window of a bedroom was opened, the drapes parted, but Loss could not see the full extent of the living room beyond. There were no voices, only the faint strains of the country-and-western ballad from the main house.

I can't delay this damn thing forever, he thought, and retraced his steps along the wall of the cottage to the front door. There was a doorway light recessed in a globe over the sill, and he unscrewed the unlit bulb and cast it aside on the lawn. Tapping lightly with his fingertips on the door, he murmured "Cable, Mistah Bolken" and leaned against the door, Luger leveled at chest height.

The door opened and Loss pushed in, ramming the barrel into Heiss's stomach. Heiss stumbled backward, tripping and falling heavily to the floor. Loss had the door closed before he had recovered.

"Roll over on your stomach, Heiss, and put your hands behind your back. Where's your so-called lawyer?"

Heiss complied, looking over his shoulder at the man standing over him. Loss stood above him wearing a light-blue bathrobe, shod only in tennis shoes. His head was bandaged about the forehead, eyes haggard. The Luger was a black hole, boresighted on his head. He didn't doubt that it was loaded.

242

"What do you want, Loss? I can't help you. They're deporting me."

"Where's your lawyer, Heiss?"

Heiss started to sit up and Loss stepped back, crouched and raised the weapon to a two-handed combat stance, sighting over the barrel.

Heiss sighed and lay down, rolling over, hands crossed behind his back. "You're a fucking lunatic," Heiss said. "You're only going to get three years and that's at three thousand dollars a month. Any trouble from you and Klist will simply snuff your lights.'

"Your lawyer, Heiss. Where is he?" The words came in a hiss.

"He moved to Cottage One."

"Do you expect him to come over here?"

Heiss shook his head. "No, he's got some sort of radio schedule to meet."

Loss had fashioned a loop with a slip knot from the fishing line. He rammed the Luger's barrel into the cleft in Heiss's buttocks and stood hunched over him, feet straddling the prone form.

"Heiss. Listen carefully. I'm going to tie your hands. Don't move or I'll blow your balls off." A Ranger in Nam had told Loss about this approach. A man can roll with a gun in his back, but the thought of losing his testicles puts a prisoner into paralysis. He quickly slipped the loop over Heiss's wrists and pulled it tight, taking subsequent turns to secure the bond.

"Keep still, Heiss. I'm going to do your ankles now. If you twitch, you'll only be fit to sing in church choirs." Heiss felt the long probe of the Luger, hard and alien. He wanted to urinate badly.

"Look, you asshole," Heiss whispered. "If you snuff me, you'll be up for murder. I can't give you any information. Klist is gone. He made it to Cuba; that's why this lawyer is down here. Klist arranged it."

"Why were you with Klist?"

243

"Just simple stuff. I was recording conversations. Taking pictures. That's the extent of what I know. I don't have any idea what your boss and Klist were up to. Christ, Loss, can't you see? You're getting in way over your head."

"Listen carefully, Heiss. I'm not going to jail for ten minutes, let alone three years. I want sufficient evidence to clear me. I'm also beginning to think that Welsh is into something that might be very unhealthy, and I want to know more about that. If I have to squeeze your balls in a nutcracker to find out, I will. You and I are going for a little drive, so let me explain the ground rules very carefully."

Heiss lay perfectly still now, his eyes wild.

"This is a garbage bag," Loss said, unfolding the green plastic square. "I am going to place this over your head and shoulders and secure it around your neck with your belt. I will then undo your ankles. We will walk very calmly to a car I have outside. If you run, I don't want to shoot you. I will just clobber you over the head, and since I am not experienced in these matters, I may break something. You have sufficient air in that bag to last for over a minute if, and I emphasize this strongly, if you keep calm. If you run, you either get a broken head, or you suffocate. Understood?"

Heiss closed his eyes and nodded.

Edging back the curtain, Loss looked across the lawn at the complex. No way of knowing which was Cottage One. But he could see no movement.

Stripping the belt from Heiss's pants, he got an idea. Keeping the weapon trained on Heiss, he backed into the bedroom and swept the closet of clothes hanging there. He brought them into the living room and selected a pair of gray flannel trousers and a pullover sweater of light wool. Exchanging these for the robe, he checked the complex again and then knelt beside Heiss and helped him up. Heiss stood up, tottering slightly. Loss slipped the plastic bag over his head and torso and secured it at the neck with Heiss's belt, taking two turns and tying it loosely. Next, he cut the fishing-line bond at the ankles. The bag was expanding and contracting with Heiss's breath now, the appearance almost comical.

"Easy, Heiss. Just conserve your energy and you'll make it." Loss guided him through the doorway and across the yard, keeping to open ground to avoid wasting time.

Opening the back door of the Ford, Loss pushed him in across the seat and paused long enough to retie his ankles before ripping open the bag. Heiss lay gasping, his face bathed in sweat.

Loss closed the door and entered the driver's side. Starting the Ford was an agony, the engine catching and then dying. He tried again, careful not to flood the carburetor. It caught finally, at first firing on just a few cylinders before smoothing out to a steady rhythm.

Loss cursed his own stupidity. He would have to go more carefully. He left the headlights extinguished and backed the car in reverse over one hundred yards before switching on the headlights and turning around.

Stroud lay silent in the seat beside him, Heiss still panting loudly in the back.

The town was relatively deserted as Loss drove through. Near the rum shop two men stood on the dirt pathway that bordered the street, apparently arguing, arms gesturing. No lights in the hospital in his room's wing of the building. His headlights swept across the benches of the park on the western edge of town as he turned onto the coast road. Two people, both black, sat there apparently just enjoying an evening together. The man was smoking a pipe.

They were beyond the outskirts now, only an occasional house now along the road. He drove past the turnoff to the yacht basin; the club building was dark. For another half a mile, the coastal road ran straight between stunted scrubs, wisps of sand drifting across

245

the asphalt, driven by the wind. To his left, he could catch occasional glimpses of the sea, flecked with light from a slipper moon. At the turnoff to the airport road, he stopped the car and extinguished the headlights. Almost immediately, a cigarette lighter flicked in the blackness ahead and then was extinguished. He relaxed and waited.

She moved along the driver's side, keeping away from the car.

"It's all together," he said. "Use the back seat. Watch out for Heiss. He's tied up. Just push him onto the floor."

She entered the car and leaned over to kiss him. She smelled of lemon grass and sweat.

"Thanks for coming," he said. "Anyone on the road?"

She leaned back into the seat and breathed out heavily. "No, I've been here for about a half hour. I had to come across the fields because it was still daylight. Land crabs and dogs. That's about the sum total."

He accelerated down the narrow highway toward the airport. The highway was obviously less used than the coastal road; cracks in the pavement were filled with sand and weed. He braked sharply and turned left onto the gravel strip near the British Petroleum sign. Slowing, he passed the deserted clapboard terminal and pulled to a stop behind the single-engine Comanche, which shone briefly in his headlights.

He switched off the lights and got out, Holly joining him. He handed her the Luger and opened the rear passenger door, dragging Heiss out feet first and then grasping him under the shoulder blades and dropping him onto the hardstand. Heiss grunted with the impact and then lay over on his side, breathing heavily. Next, Loss opened the right front passenger door and extracted Stroud. He undid the tape and leg bonds, leaving his hands tied. Leaning close to Stroud's ear Loss whispered, "We do our stuff now. Don't overdo it

246

either way." Stroud nodded, his smile momentary and almost ironic.

He tied the hands of each man to opposite sides of the front bumper of the Ford, each man sitting on the hardstand, back resting against the bumper. Loss increased the number of turns on Heiss's bonds, checking their security with a penlight he had taken from Stroud's pocket.

Loss lit a cigarette, cupping his hands carefully to shield the match. Exhaling, he sat down on the hardstand in front of the two men. Stroud looked at him intently, his face a mirror of anger. Heiss had leaned his head back against the fender, eyes closed, simply waiting.

"Gentlemen," Loss said. "It is time we began. First of all, I have to apologize to you, Stroud. I know that you were gracious enough to bring Holly up here and we repay you by stealing your aircraft. But that can't be helped. You'll get it back in time."

"Mr. Loss," Stroud said between clenched teeth. "I can only advise you to release me. From all appearances, you're in a great deal of trouble already. You don't know how to fly my aircraft, and I warn you that there's relatively little range on the petrol remaining."

"Sorry. I can't stick around. I'll make it to Haiti at least. I can get fuel there tonight before anyone knows I've gotten away. Where are the keys?"

"He keeps them under the floor mat in the baggage compartment," Holly said. "I think it's unlocked."

"Bad luck, Loss," Stroud said. "The baggage compartment is locked, and the key is back at the hotel. You should have thought of that when you came around tonight waving that Luger."

Loss stood up and walked around to the rear of the Ford. He returned, carrying his briefcase, the plastic garbage sacks, and a tire iron. Handing Holly the briefcase and tire iron, he said, "If the baggage com-

247

partment is locked, force it open with this. Get the keys out and open up the cabin door. Leave the keys in the ignition, but don't touch anything else. And scrounge around in the cabin and see whether you can find any sort of flight manual, operating instructions, maps, that sort of thing. Leave them on top of the dash. We'll be out of here in twenty minutes and sooner if anyone comes. After you get things organized, stay up on the wing of the plane and keep an eye on the approach road. You should be able to see headlights when they're still three or four miles away."

Loss crouched down again in front of them. Laying the Luger within easy reach, he carefully unfolded another plastic garbage bag. This time Heiss watched him carefully, eyes reflecting pinpoints of moonlight, mouth slightly agape.

"All right, Heiss. It's your turn." Loss pulled the bag over Heiss's head and shoulders in one quick motion. Grasping the edge of the bag, he twisted it to form a seal. At first Heiss sat motionless, breathing slowly, the bag winkling in and out with slow regularity. Loss counted the seconds mentally.

Thirty-eight, thirty-nine . . .

The bag was flexing more quickly now.

Fifty-four, fifty-five, fifty-six . . .

Heiss was beginning to struggle now, his chest heaving.

Eighty-one, eighty-two . . .

The body was frantic now, chest and lower torso rocked with spasms. Loss caught the acrid odor of urine. Heiss was losing control, his head bucking as if to throw off the bag.

Loss slowly remove the plastic shroud and sat back, listening to Heiss's gasping, lungs racking in fresh air.

"For God's sake," Stroud spat out. "God in heaven—"

Loss cut him off. "Shut up, Stroud. This bastard's name isn't Bolken—it's Heiss. He's a Russian agent

248

or close to it. And he's going to give me information before I leave, and you're going to listen to it and report it word for word to the police. And to the press if you can find anyone who will report it. So look and listen and learn, but keep your mouth shut." Loss turned to Heiss and patted him on the head.

"Very good, Heiss. You lasted nearly a minute and a half. You see, it's not that you're running out of oxygen under there. It's just that all the carbon dioxide you exhale triggers some breathing mechanism and you start to pant, producing more carbon dioxide. That's what suffocation is all about. The North Koreans used it. The record is supposed to be over three minutes. Sometimes there is moderate brain damage. You'll probably make a very nice carrot."

Heiss screamed and Loss smashed him across the face with his hand, silencing him abruptly. Blood now streamed from Heiss's nostrils in the dim moonlight.

Loss sighed and sat back on the hardstand. The moon was just a sliver of light, already setting in the west. The sky was cloudless, except for a few thin wisps of cirrus. The wind was as Campbell had reported, moderate and in the east. This thing was gruesome, and he wondered whether he could go through with it. Sighing, he talked to Heiss, almost gently, like a slightly irritated parent would to a son who had dinged the fender of the family car. "Heiss, I don't have all night. I am going to ask you some questions—some of the same questions I asked you back at your cottage. You will answer them. If I think you're lying, I will put the bag over your head again and take a short walk. I will be gone twenty seconds longer than your last exercise in the bag. I don't want to kill you. That will be, very simply, your own free choice. Now, for our English audience here, I want you to repeat who you are, what you did for Klist, and most important, whether I stole the Aztec."

Heiss glared at Loss with hate, his eyes black voids beneath the brows. He said nothing. Loss sighed and opened the bag, preparatory to placing it over his head.

"No, Loss. Don't. Look, I can give you everything I've got if you get me out of here. A Zurich account. Just drop me in Trinidad or Venezuela. I've—"

Brian sighed and dropped the bag over Heiss's head, mentally starting to count. Heiss was screaming inside the bag. Loss twisted the bag closed and stood up, brushing off his pants. He could not keep the bag on much more than the first time, but it would seem like an eternity to Heiss.

It was worse this time. No initial attempt to keep still. Heiss was in trouble within thirty seconds.

"Sixty-two, sixty-three . . ."

Heiss was bucking now, trying to stand, actually pushing the car backward, then he collapsed. His body was racked with convulsions.

Removing the bag with a jerk, Loss stood over the body, watching the chest heave, lungs sucking in the air. Heiss vomited, gagging, coughing.

Loss walked away quickly and was sick behind the trunk of the Ford. Please Christ, let this thing talk. I've got to get it out of him, he thought, the bile taste thick in his mouth.

He walked back to the front of the car, wiping the spittle from his lips, moving slowly with great calm.

He squatted down directly in front of Heiss. No preliminaries now. "What's your real name?"

"Heiss. Carl Heiss. Jesus. I can't talk. Volgel, the lawyer, will kill me. If he thinks I've talked, he or Klist will kill me."

Loss picked up the bag again, his heart pounding. He opened it, a motion that Heiss reflected in abject terror.

"Yes, Loss, yes. What else," Heiss said in a thin wail.

"Tell Mr. Stroud here why we made the flight."

Heiss was almost incoherent now, the words gush-

250

ing out between great gulps of air, as if oxygen were forever rationed. "Klist directed the flight. He was aboard. Loss only did what his employer said. He didn't steal the aircraft. Klist got away. To Cuba. By a boat. I don't know how."

"Who's Klist? I mean his real name. His nationality?"

"Petrov. He's Eastern bloc. He's setting your senator up for something. I wasn't told what. Just that I was supposed to record their conversations. Pictures."

Loss patted his cheek. "Keep going, Heiss. You're going fine. Where are these tapes and films? Did you ever listen to them?"

Heiss shook his head violently, saying nothing.

"You're lying, Heiss. I don't think you can take another session in the bag. If you made the recordings, you probably listened to some of them. Quickly, Heiss." Loss lifted the bag and slowly started to lower it over Heiss's head. Heiss was screaming again, his voice cracked and thin.

"No, Loss. Please, Loss."

Brian snatched the bag off and thrust his face into Heiss's, spitting out each word. "The tapes, you fuckin' bastard. What was on the tapes? I'm going to leave in two minutes and your answer means that you either suck your guts out on dead air or you live." Loss slapped Heiss across the face, his fingers scalding with pain from the force of the blow. "Come *on*, Heiss. I know something about it from Welsh. What . . . was . . . on . . . the . . . tapes?" He was shaking the man now by the hair, slamming Heiss's head against the fender, the frustration of the last five days boiling over, concentrated on one man. This thing.

"I—don't—know," Heiss sobbed, "only—"

"Only what?"

"Only one tape. The rest Petrov—he kept them.

251

He said he had some mark on the tape to show if they had been replayed. I didn't know!'' Heiss retched again, this time a dry heaving.

"Go on. Go on. What was on the one tape?''

"I bugged Petrov and that bitch. Just to see if I could find anything to use later. It was all in Russian. I can read it, but I don't speak the language. Just a few words. He said something about Welsh being president and about, something like *hood*. A place, I think. And the word *hussar*. Or *Huzar*. A highway robber.''

"What else?''

"Jesus God, Loss. That was all. I don't know more than that. That's everything. But take me with you. Volgel will—''

"You'll live, Heiss,'' Loss said, getting to his feet. "Just get in touch with Campbell. I think you've met. He can probably protect you.''

Loss paused, standing there in the dim moonlight and looked at the two men. "Stroud. I've got to go now. Your wrists aren't bound too tightly. You should be able to work out of them and if not, they'll find you out here tomorrow morning. There's a flight in from Nassau at eight-fifteen. It's up to you, but I would suggest that you leave Heiss tied up and let the police take care of it. If there is any press coming in on the plane, try to get to them before you talk with the cops.''

Stroud nodded. "Perhaps we'll meet again, Loss,'' he said. "I guess I can understand—everything. Why don't you wait for them yourself? I'll back your story.''

Loss shook his head. "No, Peter. I've already committed three of four more crimes they can hold me for. I'll wait until the dust settles. Adios, mother.'' He said it kindly.

Heiss and Stroud sat there, each bound to the car, watching Loss disappear into the cabin of the aircraft. In three minutes, he had fired up the engine and taxied

252

out to the western end of the runway, lights extinguished but with the blue flame of exhaust pulsing in the blackness.

They heard the growl of the engine, rising in crescendo. The noise grew; the aircraft flashed by them in the moonlight. It cleared the end of the field and climbed, glinting briefly in the moonlight as it turned to the south.

God speed, you Yankee bastard, Stroud thought, smiling thinly. Heiss struggled futilely against his bonds beside him, muttering senseless words against the blackness of night.

Chapter 17

Petrov was seething. He lit another Cuban cigarette and after inhaling once, submerged it in the remains of his coffee, now grown cold. He rose from his desk and stood over the shoulder of a sandy-haired young rating who sat at a console, headset clamped across his ears. The young man looked up questioningly. Petrov only glowered at him. The operator replied with the merest shake of his head and resumed his concentration.

Petrov walked along the rubber-matted aisle behind the consoles, checking each one in turn. Air conditioning masked the sounds of guarded conversations, the steps of other officers checking the work of their subordinates and the staccato beat of teleprinters.

Petrov regarded the situation display, which was projected on frosted glass that covered the front wall of the command post. The display covered the Caribbean Sea from the Straits of Yucatan on the west to eight hundred kilometers east into the Atlantic, the coast of Venezuela and Colombia on the south to the Gulf Coast and Florida in the north. Coastlines were projected in red with lines of latitude and longitude etched in lighter traces of white. Tracks of ships were plotted in green and identified by type of ship, nationality, speed, probable destination, and special remarks—all in abbreviated code. Aircraft tracks, which at this minute were Petrov's immediate concern, were in brilliant orange, each aircraft identified in a manner similar to the ships. He watched one track in particular, an elliptical path some one hundred kilometers long and only a few kilometers in width, like some superelongated racetrack. The major axis of this track was placed roughly north-south in the Windward Passage, the body of water that separates Cuba from the Bahamas.

The timer over the display gave a digital wink and registered 22:10 Greenwich Mean Time, or 6:10 local time. Too long a wait, he thought, the acid of his stomach burning holes in his composure. He forced a belch, trying to ease the pain. But the raw feeling of doubt remained.

Petrov walked to the desk console of the senior duty officer. The man, a lieutenant commander of the Russian fleet, Atlantic Division, rose immediately. Petrov motioned him to sit down, noting that the man was grossly overweight and that his uniform was in need of pressing. Thick glasses, a fat wife, and probably entitled to share a dacha on the Black Sea in his retirement. The name tag on his plastic security badge identified him as Lieutenant Commander Vladimirovich Alexandrovsky.

Petrov bent over the desk, splaying his fingers out over the surface. "Any further transmissions, Commander?"

The naval officer nodded. "Yes, Colonel, But just routine transmissions for our reconnaissance aircraft.

Nothing as yet from Comrade—'' he paused and looked down at his desk log, "from Comrade Volgel since he reported his position at the airstrip."

Petrov hoped that Volgel was accurate in his assessment of Loss's intentions. It would solve a lot of problems.

Petrov had landed in Cuba seven days before, completely exhausted. After much gun-waving and rough treatment, the Cuban militiamen had delivered him to a Russian interpreter. From there on in, it had been simple to establish his identity. Through the Russian Embassy in Mexico, Petrov had immediately arranged for a KGB agent in Miami to fly down to Great Inagua, equipped with a portable transmitter and a weapon. His cover was to be legal counsel for Heiss. The agent, Ernst Volgel, had done well. Heiss was to be set loose after paying a fine, and Loss was under close surveillance. Both Heiss and Loss would be eliminated, Heiss once he left the Bahamas, and Loss whenever the opportunity presented itself.

It now looked like that opportunity was presenting itself. Volgel had called in the early afternoon on his regular schedule and said emphatically that the small aircraft, a single-engine Comanche, was being prepared for flight by its owner. Petrov had no doubt now that Loss would attempt to escape the loose security of the hospital ward and make a run for it. With the authority granted him by a rapid teleprinter interchange with Moscow, Petrov had ordered a reconnaissance aircraft to maintain station in the Windward Passage. Using this aircraft as an airborne tracking station, Petrov would launch a flight of night interceptors to destroy Loss, once he was over the open sea. Things were resolving themselves nicely, he thought.

"Tell me, Commander," Petrov said, easing down onto the edge of the desk, "what is the capability of your reconnaissance aircraft?"

Commander Alexandrovsky, well aware that Petrov was KGB, answered promptly, even though their ranks were equal. "It is a Tupulov TU-18. Equipped with radar and infrared scanning. They're presently at 10,000 meters altitude. I'm sure you're familiar with the performance figures." He fished a cardboard box of Red Star cigarettes from his tunic, offering one first to Petrov before taking one for himself. Petrov accepted the brown-paper-wrapped cigarette and bent forward while Alexandrovsky flicked his Western-type Zippo. Petrov noted, in the brief illumination of the lighter, that Alexandrovsky's bald head had a sheen of perspiration.

Petrov turned away and watched the display board for some minutes, smoking the cigarette and tapping the ashes on the polished floor in obvious disregard of the ashtray centimeters from his hand. He hated cigarettes, but when he was nervous, he resorted to them for something to occupy his hands. The thing tasted like dried excrement. In disgust, he dropped it to the floor and ground it under his heel. "And how long have you been stationed here, Commander?" Petrov asked, not really interested but wanting something to ease the waiting.

Surprised that the KGB man should express interest, Alexandrovsky replied, "Our communications unit was transferred here six years ago. Before that, we were based in East Germany. I would just as soon go back."

"And how so?"

Alexandrovsky shrugged. "The weather. The food. We don't mix with the Cubans. No opportunities for, well, fun."

Petrov nodded. "And what are your duties specifically?"

"Mine personally? Well, I'm shift commander for this section. The Group, of course, monitors all movements of military shipping and air traffic in the Caribbean. We also handle all the communications for the submarine installation up at Cienfuegos on the west coast." He leaned back, relaxing, and continued,

"The submarine boys up there get first-class treatment. Fresh food flown in from Russia. New movies. Down here, we eat Cuban dog shit."

Petrov scratched at the rash on his neck. "And the reconnaissance aircraft and fighters. Are they ours or Cuban?"

Alexandrovsky shook his head. "The recons are ours. Direct support of the subs, of course, and intelligence gathering on the movement of U.S. subs, shots from Cape Kennedy. The usual thing. But the fighters are Cuban. Our noble allies." He snorted in derision.

"They're not competent pilots?" Petrov asked, stifling a yawn.

"Oh, they're good enough, but no discipline. They think these aircraft that we have given them are toys. Incidentally, speaking of the fighters, we've directed Cuban Air Command to position a flight of four MIG-19s on runway alert at the Baracoa fighter strip in Oriente Province. They can be airborne within two minutes of your orders and over Great Inagua in twelve."

Petrov stood up and stretched. "Good. Call me when anything develops. I'll be in the duty officer's day room." He turned and walked away without further comment.

Alexandrovsky watched him go. Perhaps I've been indiscreet talking about the Cubans, he thought. Petrov was a cold fish. No telling about that kind.

He reached into his desk filing cabinet and reread a copy of the deciphered message that had arrived within two hours after Petrov had first arrived with the Cuban major from Havana. It read:

CENTRAL COMMITTEE TO CMDR 288STRATCOM CUBA COMMA SECURITY LEVEL NINE STOP PERSON NAMED YOUR INQUIRY IDENTIFIED AS COLONEL ANATOLI ANTONOVICH PETROV STOP PETROV TO RECEIVE YOUR FULL-

EST AND UNQUALIFIED COOPERATION
AS PER HIS VERBAL ORDERS STOP POS-
ITIVE IDENTIFICATION OF FINGER-
PRINTS AND PHOTO BY FOLLOWING
DIGITAL SCAN TRANSMISSION STOP
TELEPRINT KGB/VICTOR IN TACTICAL
CODE NOVEMBER COMMA QUOTE SAL-
MACIS UNQUOTE STOP AUTHENTICA-
TION REPLY IS QUOTE PORT ARTHUR
UNQUOTE STOP SIGNATURE FIRST
SECRETARY STOP END MESSAGE

Alexandrovsky read and reread the message form.
This man Petrov was not to be fooled with. He returned the message form to the file and waited.

Petrov entered the day room. The occupant sat at
a desk, engrossed in the playback of a miniature cas-
sette recording, making notations occasionally and
then rewinding the tape to verify his conclusions. The
voices on the recording were those of Welsh and Klist-
Petrov.

"Do you think I'm ready for the theater, Vasili?"
Petrov asked, wearily stretching out on the rumpled
blanket that covered the iron-framed bunk.

Vasili Rametka shook his head and held his hand
up demanding silence. He rewound the tape for a second and replayed the segment.

Petrov could barely hear the converstaion, recognizing only the vaguely thick words of Senator Welsh
arguing, and himself replying in smooth, even cadence. Very persuasive.

Rametka snapped off the recorder. "Very good,
Anatoli," the older man said, unbuttoning his vest and
leaning back in the leather chair. "Very good."

"There has been no further transmission from Volgel. The situation remains static," Petrov said, his
face lined with fatigue. He bunched up the pillow and
fell back into it, his blond hair almost bleached white
by the tropic sun. Tanned. But looking very tired.

Rametka removed his steel-rimmed glasses and rubbed the bridge of his nose. The physiological traces of what, in Western circles, was referred to as "jet lag" disturbed him. Disorientation, inability to sleep, a lack of natural timekeeping sense. The flight from the Urals via Moscow to Havana on the Aeroflot Supersonic had stretched over seven hours, but in real time was half a world away. But there was no doubt—Petrov's work with Welsh had been first-class psychology. The rest was a different matter.

Rametka dropped his pen on the desk, the point nicking the worn linoleum. He loosened his tie and, as an afterthought, removed it roughly. Petrov still lay back, relaxed. *He knows,* Rametka thought. *He's young and he smells my fear of failure.*

Vasili Rametka made a notation on the pad with his gold-plated pen. "Anatoli," he said, "I don't doubt that our psychological analysis of this Senator Welsh was very exact. He reacts in the tapes as was expected. I think that there can be no question that he will use our help in political situations to further his own career. Should he ever have any doubts about his involvement, we have the photos, tapes, and his signed statement to keep him well within our control."

Petrov nodded, his eyes still closed. "But?" he said, waiting.

"But," Rametka continued, "the plane flight didn't go as we planned it. We have this present situation to contend with and—"

Petrov suddenly sat upright, anger reducing his eyes to stark blue pinpoints. He thrust his finger at Rametka. "But!" he spat out. *"But* for this and *but* for that. Yes, Dr. Vasili Rametka, Order of Lenin, *we* planned the flight. I emphasize the *we*. By utilizing Welsh's plane, Heiss and I were to fly out of the Caribbean into Mexico. The aircraft conveniently is lost at sea on its return trip, eliminating any trace of connection between Welsh and myself. Welsh simply loses his pilot and an aircraft. Another tragedy in the

Bermuda Triangle. Welsh returns to the United States to resume his role in politics, completely under our control.

"There are three folders in your files concerning the capabilities of the aircraft, the radio equipment in the aircraft, the competence of the pilot. Perfect! Perfect, Rametka, except for the imponderables of bad weather and the quixotic actions of a pilot who that very morning chose to quit working for Welsh."

Rametka leaned back in his chair. "Go on," he said, sucking the gap between his molars.

Petrov fell wearily back into the bed, disgust evident in his tone. "So this pilot Loss chooses to disregard his employer's instructions and heads for the southern coast of the Dominican Republic in order to judge his flight path and retain the option of refueling. Subsequently, he decides that we have to land to refuel."

"So you land in Great Inagua?"

Petrov looked at the scientist. Rametka was making notes with that cheap Western pen. More fuel for the report. "Yes, we land in Great Inagua. When Loss made his decision to land, I recontacted our people in Mexico. I had already planned on Great Inagua as a possible alternate because it is close to Cuba, has a minimum of officials, and has good fuel supplies. Loss agreed to this. The rest of the flight was like black dog shit. Uncontrollably violent. Nothing like I have ever seen. The rest of it you know."

Rametka sat silently at the desk, the ball point scratching on the pad. He took the glasses from his face and set them down on the scarred linoleum desk top and thought for several minutes. Finally, he looked up and said, "And what do you intend to do with the Swedish couple and their boat?"

"It will be taken to sea and the seacocks opened. The Swedes should be disposed of. Leave this to the Cubans."

"Is that what you learn in Section V, Anatoli?"

Petrov nodded wearily. "I don't like it either, Vasili. But they are otherwise a liability, even here in Cuba.''

"And this man, Volgel?" Rametka said.

"Volgel is a very competent operative. We use him a great deal in Florida.''

Rametka nodded. "How do you see the outcome tonight?"

Petrov shrugged and fell back heavily on the bed, eyes closed. "You want some sort of equation, don't you, Vasili? Plug in seventeen variables, feed it to the computer, and be assured that, within some high percentage of probability, our special situation is under control.'' He paused, thinking, and then continued, "No, there is no assurance, but to some degree, the situation is within our control. If Volgel does well, then we can go ahead. Until then, you can dream of the order that you wish to have pinned to your imitation Western suit upon retirement, and I will sleep.''

Forty-three minutes later, the infrared scanners of the TU-18 recognized the thermal signature of the small aircraft on Great Inagua as it started its engine.

Ernst Volgel chewed tentatively at a bit of cuticle on his left index finger. He was slightly nervous and pollen from the weed he lay in was making his eyes water. But his night vision was unimpaired. He watched Loss's movements in front of the sedan. The woman had already climbed up on the wing of the aircraft. Volgel checked the digits on his watch and settled back, patiently waiting, sure that it aouldn't be much longer. Indeed, he thought, Loss might do the job for him.

Volgel's shirt was damp from contact with the ground and his thin body was sore from lying on the rough terrain. It was a great deal better working in the States, he thought. Usually much less complicated. Just a name and a photograph and a date by which the party was to be terminated. Volgel was quite expert in chemically induced heart attacks and curbside hit

261

and runs. On two occasions it had been a crude mugging, but those jobs had offended Volgel's sense of professionalism.

He withdrew the Walther from his belt clip and checked that no dirt had clogged the barrel. Volgel, like any good craftsman, liked to be meticulous with his tools.

But this job had its complexities, and Volgel detested any personal involvement with his clients. Only the one job on the Puerto Rican labor leader had borne any trace or connection to Volgel. The Latino's car had not burned quickly enough and he died slowly, trying to gasp out a description of the thin man with a balding head. The police composite drawing had resembled Woody Allen more than it had Volgel and he had kept a tear-out of the drawing just for pure amusement.

Still, Volgel was relatively pleased with the way things had turned out thus far. He realized that the selection had been simply based on expediency. Of four KGB agents held in reserve for assassinations only, Volgel had been physically closest to the Bahamas. His control in Washington, D.C., had taken the unprecedented step of a direct telephone call. From there, Volgel had shifted to an outside telephone booth. The control had been blunt and direct, laying out the exact actions that Volgel was to take. It was a frightening violation of security, and the way in which it was done had underlined the necessity of immediate action.

Stripping his account of twenty thousand dollars, Volgel had been in Nassau within three hours of the call, posing as a lawyer. It took one discreet meeting with a Bahamian go-between who was known to be very well connected. Volgel had described to the man how short his life could be and how it might end if results weren't immediate. By noon on the following day, he had Heiss released into his own custody and had set up a close surveillance on Loss and the woman. But no matter how well done, Volgel knew that he was leaving a trail and he didn't like it.

Patiently, he continued to watch the figures in the dim light. Loss was taking far too long. Out of habit, Volgel hummed a hymn beneath his breath. For a man who could have no close friends or business associates, Volgel had taken to going to a small Catholic church on West Flagler Street. He had a clear, sweet voice—a wonderful tenor, the priest had told him. And he loved the majesty of the Mass, the magical bond which encompassed him and those who stood around him. Without too much involvement, he felt a part of them, a sense of belonging that he desperately needed.

In a short time, Volgel found himself drawn into the fringes of church social life, resisting it at first and then embracing it with the realization that it gave his cover normalcy. Initially, there had been his assignment to help in the collection. He had been very good, he realized. Volgel's plate always overflowed. For he would picture in his mind the image of each parishioner as the plate was passed to him—a garrot around his neck. Volgel would mentally tighten it if the offering was too meager. Then, for one summer, Volgel had taught Sunday School as a volunteer replacement. His speech became sprinkled with biblical sayings and he reveled in it, the irony of a paid assassin from a state that recognized no God, officially sanctioned to kill and to take the sacraments.

He started to shiver, both with the expectation of what he had come to do and because of the cool night wind that was beginning to cut through his thin jacket. It would be good to get back to Miami, to clean sheets and the small business which he managed well. And there was to be a fund-raising dinner next Friday and he didn't want to miss it.

The exhaust on the single-engine Comanche barked and belched blue flame, then settled into an even roar. Volgel looked up, somewhat surprised. It hadn't taken much time. So in the end, I was correct, he thought, pleased with his own perception. Loss was going to make the attempt.

He withdrew the small Sony portable and keyed the transmitter that had meticulously been fitted into the small confines of the case. He spoke softly, his breath just catching a bit in anticipation. "Songbird. Seagull here. Engine start. Stand by."

The reply came back almost instantaneously, clear but hollow, like listening down a drain pipe. "Songbird standing by." Volgel smiled and slung the radio over his shoulder by the small leather strap.

The Comanche had taxied to the eastern end of the runway, its sound swept away by the eastern trades. Volgel stood up, brushing dirt from his pants and shirt. He looked at his watch, pressing a small button. The dial glowed in digital display: 8:21.

Reaching beneath his sports jacket, Volgel extracted the 9-millimeter Walther P-38 and screwed in the gray-aluminum silencer, carefully fitting it to the barrel to prevent cross-threading.

The Comanche was now rolling and Volgel, after chambering a round, ran over the low embankment and down to the edge of the strip. He sat down heavily in the gravel, bracing the elbows of his arms on his knees, the weapon gripped easily in both hands. The moonlight glinted briefly on the aircraft's canopy. It was airborne. He waited. It passed over his head, wheels already being sucked up into the wings; it looked like a cross against the sky. The Walther coughed in his grip twice. And each time, he was sure of a hit in the cockpit area.

He stood and turned to watch the dim silhouette of the aircraft diminish into the blackness of the night. Its profile suddenly altered, banking to the south, the noise of the engine now lost. Puerto Rico? Perhaps.

He unslung the transmitter, turning up the receiver volume.

"Songbird, Seagull here. Blackbird off 8:24 to the south."

"Seagull, Songbird back. Confirm the south."

Volgel gritted his teeth. "Affirmative. The south."

A pause, with only the restless brush of static across the black sea.

"Seagull, Songbird back. Any strikes?"

Volgel pressed the transmit switch, smiling. "Two strikes," he said softly.

Another delay. Volgel began to walk toward the parked sedan, half a runway distant. He felt comfortable, loose, the weapon light in his hand, the radio to his ear. Almost lightheaded.

The receiver stuttered, "—itize area. Confirm."

Volgel spoke into the mike, "Songbird, this is Seagull. Say your last transmission again."

"Seagull, Songbird back. I say again. Sanitize area. Confirm."

Volgel broke into an easy jog. Pressing the transmit switch he said, "I confirm sanitize area."

Stroud saw him coming. The fishing line bit into his wrists as he struggled. He wished suddenly for the cold north of Canada, the wild geese honking. The foxes running free across the grass. The man beside him was now frantic, and the disease of fear is communicable.

The man stopped before him, slim and short in stature. Stroud sensed rather than saw the man as poised. Dressed well. Something over his shoulder. Something in his hand.

"Where did Loss go?"

Stroud hesitated.

"Where did Loss go?" Volgel repeated, his voice now more insistent, the timbre of his voice dropping to a hoarse whisper.

"I don't know. The south, I think," Stroud replied.

The light blossomed in front of his eyes, pink-white. There seemed to be no sound. Stroud looked up at

Volgel, the shock of pain to his chest unbelievable at first. Stroud first thought he had been kicked. His head suddenly cleared. He looked down, and watched with detached interest as his shirt darkened with wetness. There was no pain now. Not even feeling.

"Where did he go?"

Stroud slowly shook his head.

"Go in peace," the voice said graciously and the pink-white light blossomed again, going rapidly to red and black. Stroud died with a dim instant vision of a fox running free.

Heiss was making incoherent sounds, jerking against his bonds, the sedan swaying with the force of his effort.

Volgel kneeled down in front of Heiss, his movements those of a priest resting before prayer and supplication. He fished a cigarette from his pocket and lit it, then gently placed it between Heiss's lips.

Volgel spoke first, his words soft and reasonable. "You know that I have to kill you, Carl?"

Heiss nodded dumbly, the cigarette falling from his lips.

"You know as well," Volgel continued, "that I can't negotiate this. It is a matter of you telling me quickly what you told Loss." He picked up the cigarette from Heiss's lap and flung it away into the darkness.

Heiss nodded again, his eyes now closed, arching his head back against the fender, all struggling ceased. The smell of the man beside them was a stench, the fluids now released, his perforated body giving up its life.

"There is no reason to withhold the information," Volgel said. "If you do, you will simply die more slowly. We both know how this is done."

"I told him nothing because I know nothing. Let me make my own way, Volgel," Heiss said, knowing that it was useless.

266

"I have to ask you again, Carl," Volgel said, a thin edge of impatience on his voice. "Where did Loss go? How much range? What did you tell him? Please spare both of us the lies."

"Loss went south. Haiti, I think, for fuel. He had only short range. Stroud said that he had not refueled. I don't know of these things. Please, Volgel—"

Volgel shot him in the kneecap, using the weapon surgically. There would be a minimum of blood, the pain unbelievable. He had hoped for better cooperation from a man of the same cloth.

Heiss sat there, his mouth open in a silent scream, blood running from the tongue he had partially severed wih his own teeth.

Volgel leaned toward him, making the words simple and unmistakable, enunciating each syllable.

"Carl. Let me finish it cleanly. Once more, where? And what information did you give away?"

Heiss flung his head from side to side, his teeth sawing into his tongue. "South," he said. "Nothing. I said nothing."

The Walther coughed again, its breath singeing Heiss's face as it disappeared. His heels beat a tattoo, and he was still.

Volgel got up, feeling the freshness gone, the power spent. He found the gas tank and broached it with a jab of his penknife, the ground saturating with fuel. He waited in the pale moon, allowing the pool to expand, watching the stars wheel. More work now, eliminating the traces of his footsteps, returning to his hotel. The inquiries in the morning. Of course they would think that it had been Loss's actions.

The tank was dry now. Volgel walked upwind, turned, and aimed at the bumper between the two silent forms. He fired once without effect. The second shot struck a spark and the mass of steel, rubber, fuel, and flesh went up in a huge white-hot tongue of flame. Volgel scuttled back up the runway, vaguely dissat-

267

isfied with Heiss's sense of loyalty. I would have told, had it been me, he thought, scuffing at the tracks and then climbing the embankment.

"Songbird, this is Seagull, over."

A rush of static. "Go ahead."

Volgel, tired now, his bridgework irritating his gums, body sweating, keyed the transmitter. "South is confirmed. Heiss and Stroud sanitized, over."

"Seagull. This is Songbird. Out."

Volgel walked to his car over the uneven ground. The sedan was now a mass of yellow flame. He turned and entered his Morris Minor, switched on the key, and started the engine. He drove carefully to town, skirting the main street through the back alleys. In his cottage, he stripped and showered, the water blasting against his pallid frame. He brushed his bridge and set it in a cup of water. The sheets were cool and clean. He crossed himself once before falling asleep.

Chapter 18

Lieutenant Iosif Sidorov adjusted the gain on the in-frared scanner, reducing the blob-like heat source 11,000 meters below to a hard pinpoint of light. He keyed the intercom, making a notation in his log at the same time. "Commander. ECM here."

"ECM. Go ahead, Iosif," the voice tired and with a tinge of boredom.

"Sir, I have a target movement on the airstrip. It's the aircraft we've been monitoring. It's just started its engine at . . ." he referred to his log, "zero zero two one, GMT."

The aircraft commander of the TU-18 relaxed, the

vigil drawing to a close. He hated the Cubans, the Caribbean, and long-range patrol duty in particular. He turned aside to the copilot and nudged him awake, indicating that he take the controls. Then he made a notation on his knee pad. Good, he thought. He keyed the intercom. "Anything else? How about radar contact?"

The electronic-countermeasures officer had anticipated the question. "Negative, sir. The target is still obscured by ground clutter. He won't be visible on the AWA-23 until he's well above two thousand meters. But the infrared scan on him is solid." Lieutenant Sidorov drew heavily on his oxygen mask. Interesting now.

"All right, Iosif," the pilot replied. "Our instructions are to maintain contact on the target aircraft. Call Songbird and give them the information. Use the tactical code frequency that Seagull has been using. Scrambled in Mode 17. I'll start to let down a bit. It might enable you to pick him up on radar as well."

Lieutenant Sidorov keyed the mike in acknowledgment and changed to tactical frequency 249.7. He selected Scramble Mode 17 and called, "Songbird. Eagle here. Copy?"

"We copy. Go ahead."

"Blackbird engine start now."

The reply from Cuba came back immediately. "Affirmative. We have received that information already from Seagull. Give us a track after takeoff, over."

"Affirmative. Understand track heading," Sidorov replied. "Eagle standing by." Very pleased now, the Soviet lieutenant logged the calls and expanded the scale of the scanner to encompass the entire island of Great Inagua. The power plant now showed on the edge of the scope, a truncated orange return. A few other point sources of heat were defined, none of them moving. Homes. Perhaps a stationary vehicle with its engine running. Nothing more.

The frequency crackled. Sidorov anticipated the transmission, but it was between Cuba and the remote unit on the island below.

"Songbird, Seagull here. Blackbird off 8:24 to the south."

Sidorov watched the scope and confirmed that the point source of heat began to move. Good enough, he thought. Once the aircraft is airborne and over the sea, I'll be the only one capable of tracking it. He followed the transmission between Seagull below and the command post in Cuba.

The aircraft was out over the sea now, vectoring south toward Haiti. Sidorov waited until the transmissions between base and Seagull were finished. He caught the interchange between the land stations: the instructions to sanitize. Seagull signed off.

Lieutenant Iosif Sidorov settled into the job. The work was familiar. Another six months of this and back to the Mediterranean Fleet air arm. A promotion soon. Which calculated out to eighty-seven rubles more per month.

The aircraft below was climbing out now, the point source of heat strong, as it would be under maximum engine operation. He laid out the cursor over the track and punched data into the computer. The readout gave a track and ground speed of 179 degrees magnetic at 210 kilometers per hour.

"Songbird, Eagle."

The reply transmission from Cuba came back, the voice now a different operator. "Eagle, go ahead."

Iosif keyed the mike, his voice flat within the confines of the oxygen mask. "Songbird. Eagle here. Target now twelve kilometers south, tracking 179 magnetic." He started to release the mike and realized that a large heat return had blossomed on the infrared scope. The position was right. "And I have a stationary target on the runway. Stand by."

He quickly reduced the gain and contracted the scan to sweep the runway. The point source of heat was the vehicle that had been positioned near the hard-stand. There was no doubt about it. It was afire. He keyed the mike again. "Songbird. Eagle here. Target on runway stationary burning vehicle, over."

"Affirmative, Eagle. Maintain information on Blackbird track and speed. We will have four interceptors in the air for your vectors. Their flight leader call sign is Cane Cutter."

"Understand flight leader is Cane Cutter. What type?" Lieutenant Sidorov could imagine the alert klaxon screaming in some dusty fighter base in southern Cuba.

A short pause from Songbird, then, "MIG-19Gs. Do you have radar contact with the target?"

"Negative. I have a solid infrared scan. I should have radar contact when he climbs out. Presently just ground clutter." Iosif rechecked the radar PPI scope. Nothing. "Stand by, Songbird." He reset the cursor on the infrared scope and noted the still southerly course. The computer readout flickered, minor changs in raw data. He keyed the mike with the foot switch, using his deft, stubby hands to manipulate the controls of the scope.

"Songbird. Eagle here."

A rush of static, then, "Eagle. Songbird here. Go ahead."

"I have the target still tracking southerly, course one-eight-eight magnetic, speed 183 kilometers per hour. Eighteen kilometers south. Negative radar return as yet."

Petrov handed the headset back to the young controller and turned to Rametka, smiling. "He's airborne, Vasili."

Rametka nodded without comment. He watched Petrov as the man stalked back and forth along the aisle, highly charged. As if he were waiting for a duck to fly over the blind. His face was not taut, the fatigue faded from the eyes.

Petrov lit another cigarette, disregarding the one

271

smoldering in an ashtray on the edge of the console. His hair, bleached by the sun, was silver-white in the light of the operator's repeater scope. He had a brief conversation with the naval commander, Alexandrovsky, laughed, and returned to Rametka's side next to the console.

"The fighters scrambled two minutes ago, Vasili. A flight of three MIG-19Gs. The fourth fighter aborted with an overheat. They maintain their aircraft with machetes for tools and idiots for mechanics. The Chinese were better. Much better."

They stood silently now, listening to the controller work the flight of three night fighters, vectoring them south and east to intercept the lone Comanche. The controller's instructions were crisp, economical. Probable contact in eight minutes.

Rametka absorbed the tenseness of the hunt from Petrov. It seemed an electronic game, the bright return of the fighters repositioned on the controller's scope with every sweep of the antennas, the TU-18 slower in its southerly track. No plot on the Comanche, but it was there, over the horizon, below the curvature of the earth. He turned to Petrov and said in a low voice, "Volgel thought he had two hits on the aircraft, is that correct?"

Petrov nodded, more intent on the screen than on the man beside him. "Yes. Just small caliber. Perhaps in the fuel tanks. They would be hard to miss."

Rametka picked at the edge of his nostril. The skin seemed oily, even in the air-conditioned environment. "So Heiss is finished. And now Loss and his woman friend. Then the Swedes."

Petrov turned to face Rametka, his forehead furrowed, the radial wrinkles in the corners of his eyes fracturing the hard planes of his face. "Yes, Vasili. They are all finished, in one way or another. Heiss is finished. Like a burned piece of trash. That is what he was. I have no regret. The Swedes—something else." Petrov sat back against the desk behind him and fumbled in his shirt pocket for another cigarette. He found one, slightly crumpled, and lit it. The smoke was wraithlike in the reflected luminescence of the radar scope.

"No," he continued. "I don't like the loss of the Swedes. They are real people. You know, when I forced them to bring me here to Cuba, the man, Anders, attacked me with a wooden fid. An instrument to splice rope with. I had to shoot him in the leg with the shotgun." Petrov looked down at the glowing tip of the cigarette as if it would give him some answer to his unspoken question. "He lay there, his leg blown away, looking at me. Working over in his mind how he could kill me. I can admire a man like that."

The controller turned to the two men behind him, standing in the half-light of the command post.

"I have a contact. It's the target. Do you want a positive identification, Colonel?"

Petrov nodded wearily. No words. The rating turned to his scope, rapidly fingering a keyboard to the computer terminal. He spoke in terse sentences to the flight of aircraft, giving directional vectors and range.

Vasili Rametka edged back, settling on the edge of the desk next to Petrov. He could smell the stink of his own sweat. Or was it Petrov's? "So with Loss's aircraft shot down, will we go ahead?" He asked, watching the blips beginning to merge.

Petrov looked straight ahead, sight unfocused. "Yes, we will go ahead. We would have gone ahead even had Loss reached Nassau alive. He basically knows nothing. He will be blamed for the death of Heiss and Stroud."

"The timing," Rametka said. "Do you feel that it is affected?"

Petrov looked aside at Rametka, feeling marginally sympathetic for the man. From a role of inspector, tutor, and mentor, the man had lost his power. Like all old men, his actions were influenced by the thought

273

of failure. "The timing is good. The device will leave Vladivostok on a Z-Class Fleet Submarine. Three hundred twenty kilometers west of British Columbia, we will transfer it to a small trawler with Canadian markings, really one of our craft that normally fishes in the Gulf of Alaska. From there, it will be carried to the yacht."

Vasili Rametka nodded. He touched his nose again. It was bleeding slightly, the light smear of blood on his fingertip almost black in the harsh cold light of the cathode-ray tube. "The device, there will be handling problems at sea?"

Petrov shook his head curtly. "No, I don't think so. It's packed in a wooden shipping container. It will have a false top container of oceanographic research equipment for any casual inspection. The device is cushioned inside with cellular molded foam. It could be dropped on concrete from three meters without damage. Three men could handle it easily. I'll be there when it's transferred to the *Hussar*."

Rametka raised his eyebrows. "For what reason?"

"Just that I want to see it safely on board. Talk with our people that have chartered the yacht and make sure there are no last-minute problems." Petrov leaned over the back of the chair, watching the trace on the radar scope. "It's attention to small details that make something like this work, Vasili. Quite different from sitting at a desk and planning."

"How do you plan to enter the States?"

"I'll fly into Vancouver with a West German ski group. From there, I'll drive. I'll be meeting the *Hussar* sometime around the sixteenth or seventeenth of August. From there I'll move down into the target area."

"What about support?"

"Emil will have a team of six men on the charter ski flight. If I need support, they'll be available. Hopefully, there'll be no problems."

The controller seated in front of them turned and

pointed to the scope with his light pencil. "Sir. The MIGs have radar contact. The flight leader will be making an identification pass first."

Petrov nodded. "Yes. I want a positive identification first. What type of armament are the MIGs equipped with?"

The controller spoke rapidly into his headset microphone, received a reply, and said, "Cannon, sir. Twenty-millimeter rapid-firing cannon. And the flight leader says they're nearly within Haitian airspace."

Petrov turned to Rametka, eyebrows raised. "Not good." To the controller, "Have them finish the identification pass. Then force the small aircraft to turn north before they shoot it down. I don't want the Haitians to catch this on their radar."

The controller turned back to the screen, speaking rapidly in Spanish.

Petrov pointed up at the situation display of the Caribbean. The track of the TU-18 was farther south, in the Windward Passage between Cuba and Haiti, still well over ten kilometers high. The fighters, lower in altitude, were no more than fifty kilometers to the north of Haiti. "I felt sure that Loss would try to fly north," he said, almost to himself. "There is only one hundred kilometers between Great Inagua and the north end of Haiti. I can't believe that he would try to escape to the south. Stupid."

Alexandrovsky, the duty officer, scuttled toward the two men who bent over the shoulder of the radar controller.

"Colonel Petrov. The Cuban Fighter Command says we can't go farther into Haitian air space. They say—"

"Shut up," Petrov snapped. "They've got him now." The points of light on the radar scope were merged.

Chapter 19

Loss stabbed the right brake and wheeled the aircraft around on the end of the runway. The instruments, lighted by dull red illumination, indicated normal. There was no sign of any vehicle as yet. Take your time, he thought, and he carefully read through the checklist.

Pitch in fine, power run up to 1700 rpm, engine
    instruments in normal ranges
Left magneto drop 125 rpm
Right magneto drop 110 rpm
Carburetor heat application. Normal rpm drop,
    good suction pressure
Prop cycle from fine through coarse pitch back to
    fine. Sounds healthy
Gyros set, altimeter to sea level elevation
Boost pump on

Just ten degrees of flap. He looked out the window and could see the flaps cycling down through a small arc in the beam of his pocket penlight.

Leave the navigational and strobe light off. Sometimes it doesn't pay to advertise.

He looked down the runway. The strip was black on black, the asphalt blotting up the last bit of moonlight. He turned down the instrument panel lights to their lowest level. This time, there was some distinction; the grass edging the runway was a lighter shade of gray. He picked a star that was aligned with the runway, using that for a heading reference. Bellatrix? No, maybe Procyon. Anyway, something in the Canis Minor constellation. "Are you ready?" he said, glancing over at her.

She squeezed his arm lightly. "Let's go," she said.

Loss smoothly applied power, very light on the rudder pedal, trying to keep the track of the aircraft straight. The Comanche accelerated, rpms up at 2,350. The controls were growing stiffer with the pressure of the slipstream, and his eyes flicked down and glimpsed fifty knots registered on the airspeed indicator. Then sixty-five. Seconds now. She lifted off with a touch on the controls and was climbing.

He hit the gear switch, starting the retraction. Wait for the flaps just a bit longer. The Lycoming was singing a deep tenor. Bless Stroud and his maintenance, he thought briefly.

The first shot did little damage. It entered the aft section of the cockpit, creasing the fabric on the back of the left front seat. It plowed its way through the fabric liner and insulation of the cabin roof and mushroomed through the top of the fuselage. The sound was lost in the engine's bellow and the noise of the gear retracting into the wells.

Volgel's second shot was spaced one foot further aft and to the right. The nine-millimeter copper-jacketed slug tore through the belly of the Comanche, penetrated the rear seat support that housed the ten containers of fuel, and impacted in the middle container, bursting its walls.

Loss heard the shot this time, only as a muffled crump, followed by the overwhelming stench of raw fuel vapor. At first he thought a fuel line had burst, and he could only think of fire. One spark, or the red hot exhaust manifold. He started to shut down the electrical master switch and stopped in time. One spark from a relay opening as the power was shut down would blow the whole thing.

277

"Open your door," he shouted across at her. Jesus, not again, he thought.

She was trying now, pushing against the unlocked door with her small frame, pressing against the force of the slipstream that pinned the door inward. She had it open, only a crack.

"Jam it open with something, jam it open," he yelled in her ear. She shook her head, and he knew that she could not do it alone.

He fumbled with one hand on the floor of the cockpit, trying to find something to wedge the door open. Tennis shoe, he thought, and pulled off his right one. Both of them heaved against the door panel, and it opened sufficiently for her to insert the shoe in the howling gap.

The cockpit was vacuumed out of papers and loose dust. A roll of paper towels that Stroud had used to clean the windshield was sucked out through the thin crevice, towels shredding in the wind. Loss leaned back on his side and hunched against the small Plexiglas storm window, sucking at the clean, cold air. His lungs felt seared by the fumes and his mind was numb. One of the fuel cans in the back seat had ruptured from—what? They weren't interconnected, so all the banks wouldn't drain through the ruptured one. Most of the fuel would leak through the flooring and find its way back into the hollow shell of the fuselage, where it would rapidly evaporate. Cursing his own stupidity, he belatedly opened the ventilation cowls, bringing more fresh air into the cockpit.

Already, he could tell that the fumes were dissipating. The smell would be there for a long time, but if nothing blew in the next ten minutes, it would be all right. He looked over at her and saw that her face was pressed against the open crack, hair snapping out in the slipstream.

The instruments looked solid; everything in the green. The oil temperature was a little high. He realized that he had not yet reduced the power setting for best climb speed and the engine was overheating. Pulling the throttle back to twenty-three inches of manifold pressure, he slowly reduced the prop setting to 2,350 rpm and waited for the air speed to stabilize and then retrimmed the controls. His eyes were watering profusely now and he had a spasm of coughing. He looked over at her, and she was crying and shaking her head as if to clear it of the fumes. He leaned over and tapped her shoulder, giving her the thumbs-up sign. She nodded, head bowed, and closed her eyes.

Loss turned over in his mind what could have gone wrong. The pressure couldn't have done it. Nothing fitted together. Perhaps it would be better to keep the southerly heading in case there were something major wrong with the aircraft. Haiti was the closest lighted airfield, forty, maybe fifty miles to the south. At least there, he would be temporarily safe from the Bahamian authorities. Would they have any sort of extradition treaty? Maybe taking Stroud's airplane qualified as skyjacking. He decided that he would keep to the south, building up altitude and allowing the gas fumes to vent. When it was safe, he would examine the debris in back.

They climbed for another eight minutes, topping a thin cloud deck at 11,000 feet. He retrimmed and leaned the mixture for maximum range. The fuel smell was almost gone now. Before them, they could see the dark form of Haiti in the dying moonlight, and the individual lights of villages and then the blink of the marine beacon on Mole St. Nicholas, the northwestern tip of Haiti.

"How are you feeling now?" he asked.

She smiled in the dim glow of the panel lights. "Better. What happened?" She blew her nose on some paper toweling that was left in the dash compartment.

"That's what I want to find out. Take the penlight and look in the back. You'll have to unstrap your safety belt and crawl back there. I'm going to see whether I can get a bearing on Port-au-Prince. We

279

may go in there if it's anything serious." She started to crawl over the seat, and he said as an afterthought, "Check each fuel can to make sure that the remaining ones are full. I can calculate our range from that."

Loss looked out to the west. The moon was getting lower now. If they had just lost one tank, he could make it. If not, there was always the possibility of putting down somewhere in Florida, refueling and getting airborne again before anyone knew the difference.

"I think you'd better take a look, Brian," she said, playing the penlight over the aft compartment.

He engaged the autopilot, unfastened his seat belt, and turned to face aft. The ten containers were arranged in two rows in the area where the rear seat would normally be. The front middle container was burst along its welded seams. There is only one way that a metal container can be deformed like that.

"And look here," she said and stuck her finger into a hole in the roof upholstery.

"About forty-five caliber," he said, finding the entry hole in the floor and the scar in the upholstery of the back seat.

"Who would have done it?" she said. "Not Heiss. You had him trussed up like a chicken."

"Police, maybe," he replied uneasily knowing that, somehow, this was Klist's doing. He didn't want to think of Stroud.

"Well, anyway, the other nine containers are full and none of the transfer lines is broken. How does it affect our range?"

He helped her into the front seat, and they withdrew the shoe from the door and locked it.

"Cinderella?" she said handing it to him and he smiled. "Now, how about the range? Do we swim?"

He turned toward her and kissed her lightly on the nose. "No problem. We can still make it direct. If not, then we'll drop in somewhere along the east coast of the U.S. around dawn. I better swing this crate around to the north and get out of here. We're almost over Haiti. By the way, do you have any of those chocolate bars in your—'' He froze as he caught a glint of moonlight off beyond their right wingtip. His night vision was bad, both from the gas fumes and from the recently used penlight. He looked again. More definite. A plane with no wing lights.

"Holly. Look out there.'' He pointed in the direction.

"What do you see?'' she said, looking down toward the sea's surface two miles below.

"No, higher. Just level with us.''

She looked back, aft of the trailing edge of the wing. Stars. And then she saw it. An airplane. Just the dim outline in the waning moonlight—a reflection of light sliding along its canopy. And it was closing with them, flying a slightly converging heading. "It's an airplane. A jet, I think. He doesn't have any light switched on.''

Loss felt fear reaching into his chest. His mind raced. It wouldn't be Bahamian. Haiti, maybe. They had old Mirage IIIs. The paranoia over Cuba. He reached down on the panel and switched on the navigational wingtip lights and the anticollision beacon.

"He's coming in closer,'' she said, craning her neck to watch the aircraft edge in. "And he's dropping his landing gear!''

Loss handed her the flashlight. "Holly, it's a Haitian night fighter. They probably saw us on radar and sent up this guy to look us over. He's just slowing down to look us over. Take the flashlight and blink morse code for USA . . . dididah . . . dididit . . . didah. Got it?''

She nodded her head and started to flash the message. No reaction from the night fighter, which Loss could see plainly now, just a silhouette one hundred yards or less off their right rear quarter. He thought of calling Port-au-Prince approach control and trying

281

to explain. He tried to think what would look like a nonhostile thing to do. Maybe turn on the interior lights and the landing lights. Start a slow descent for Port-au-Prince. Would this guy be trigger happy? Too close for a firing pass, but then the thought struck him that the rest of his flight would be sitting back half a mile, covering their leader, ready to make a firing pass if ordered. He looked over the cowling. The north coast of Haiti was just under the nose, a thin chain of lights rimming the shore where the coastal road would be. A larger city down to the east.

The jet switched on its landing lights, the dazzle blinding. "He's looking us over. Wave at him!" and Loss realized how ludicrous it would look to the fighter pilot.

The landing lights switched ofd and the fighter grew in size as it slid in alongside them, no more than ten yards off their wingtip. Now Loss could see the shark-like profile and the conventional swept wing. The fighter's gear and flaps were down, trying to slow to the speed of the Comanche. But the shape didn't match the delta of a Mirage III.

The fighter was beginning to turn toward them, forcing Loss to turn with him to avoid a collision. The turn was very slow but deliberate. Forcing Loss toward the east, paralleling the coast of Haiti.

Loss looked more closely, the jet's features more apparent in the low luminescence of the splinter moon and starlight. An older subsonic or transsonic fighter. Speed fences on the wing. A bell was ringing in the back of his mind. The insignia of the fuselage was a dark inverted triangle with a white star.

The two aircraft kept turning, slowly, the fighter edging in closer, keeping the turn tight. Compass now rolling through northeast, away from the coast.

No missiles under the wings, he thought. Cannon or rockets housed in the wings or belly. It came to him: MIG. MIG what? Seventeen. Maybe a fifteen.

The insignia was *Cuban*. And there would be at least one other bastard sitting back there, radar locked on and firing switches armed. That's why this guy next to him was turning. They wanted him to get away from the Haitian coast, over open water. Loss turned in his seat, looking out the right window, scanning the sky. He couldn't see the other one, but he would be back there. The leader would break away and then there would be the swift firing pass. And it would be like chucking rocks into a garbage can from three feet. They couldn't miss.

The heading was north now, the jet still on their wing, racked over in the shallow turn that was forcing the Comanche to a northwesterly or westerly heading. Toward Cuba. He could hear the rolling thunder of the jet's engine at high power settings, barely above a stall, mushing along to match the Comanche's speed. The pilot in the cockpit was encased in a helmet with oxygen mask dangling from his face. He was visible in the greenish-white light of the radar scope set in the panel before him. Loss wasn't sure, but he imagined the man was smiling.

He didn't want to wait until the turn was finished. The leader would break off quickly, and that would be the end of it. He certainly couldn't outclimb or outdive them, but if there was a way of getting right down on the deck, along the coast of Haiti, he could hide in the radar clutter of the shoreline.

Jesus, he thought. One week or so ago he had been a normal human being. Life without pain, life without worry, someone to love. Good clothes to wear, and no one to bother him with the aggravations of surviving. Now it seemed that he had fallen to the lower order of those that kill and are killed. Like some mouse, running before the cat, not knowing why he was hunted but sure that the smallest mistake would lead to pain and violent death.

The fighter's rate of turn was decreasing, the wings

starting to level. So it's now, he thought. He leaned over to her.

"We're getting down to sea level fast. Just read me the altimeter setting at every thousand feet and hold on tight."

Loss pulled on the carburetor heat and then gradually reduced power. The Comanche started to slow immediately, Loss holding the nose up to stay level with the MIG as the air speed bled off. The MIG was starting to overrun him now, shifting from his wing position to slightly ahead, still banking. Loss could see the flame from his tail cone—a hard feathery blue. Airspeed still decaying rapidly, the air-speed indicator down to eighty and the controls getting mushy. He reached down and switched off the navigational lights and collision beacon. The controls were buffeting now, the Comanche right on the edge of a stall. Loss applied full back pressure on the yoke and stomped full left rudder. The aircraft shuddered for a split second and then the left wingtip dropped, initiating the spin. The pitchdown was violent but then flattening and increasing in rotational speed.

"Ten thousand," she called, her voice tight.

Loss kept the rudder in and the yoke back, watching the stars whirl across the windshield. They were falling like a greased brick now, spinning. Rate of descent well over three thousand feet per minute. But most important, the aircraft was falling in a tight spiral almost straight down. There was a bright flare of light above them, tracers arching away into the night, curving like a scythe as the fighters tried to turn after him.

"Eight thousand," her voice higher pitched now.

The rotational forces were throwing him against the outside of the cockpit, and he wished hey would put shoulder belts in these damned aircraft . Stupid, he thought. Stroud should know, should have known better. The nose was starting to tuck down now and this worried him. How much altitude to allow for recovery? She was saying something about thousand, and he saw just the flash of something sweeping across the windshield and a torrent of orange flame from phosphorous tracers licking the sky above him. He felt their passage as the MIG's shockwave buffeted the Comanche.

Three or four turns now, the lights of stars merging with the lights of Haiti. Disorientation.

"Five thousand!" Belated, he turned on the boost pump, to keep the fuel pressure up. The engine was barely ticking over now, no power and the black sea below them coming up to meet them. Pretty soon now. Very soon. He rehearsed in his mind the actions he would have to take.

"Three thousand. Brian, three thousand!" he already had his right foot on the rudder pedal, cramming it into the firewall. The rotation to the left was slowing, but not enough, and he pushed harder as if that would do any good. Come on, you bitch, stop! Stop. The Comanche went through one more lazy rotation and stopped turning. He relieved the rudder pressure and dumped the yoke forward, waiting for the controls to firm up. Air speed picking up now and he slowly applied back pressure. The lights along the shore were bright and individual now. There were cars moving along the coast road and scattered pools of brightness where clusters of houses would be. Beyond that was the shape of dark mountains blotting the southern horizon. The nose was nearly level, and he slowly added power just to check his slow descent. Everything was very quiet now, just the sound of the engine at low revs and the gentle rush of wind past the airframe as they glided for the shoreline.

"Eight hundred," she said, almost softly. He slowly added power as they descended, leveling off above the wavetops. He kept the power setting low, stabilizing the air speed in the low eighties. The coast was off their right wingtip as he flew east into the trades.

Their ground speed would barely be sixty. Let them find me here, he thought. Sometimes the mouse runs where the cat can't.

He concentrated intently, flying barely above the breaking coastal surf, the minutes ticking by. Nothing else.

She lit him a cigarette, placing it between his lips. He inhaled, and she removed the cigarette for him as he exhaled.

"They say you can die from lung cancer," he said.

Chapter 20

Five miles above the Windward Passage, the TU-18 executed a slow bank toward the west. Lieutenant Iosif Sidorov turned up his gain. The three bright infrared returns of the MIGs merged into one as they assumed close formation, streaking westward for the strip in Oriente Province. Of the small aircraft, nothing. It had disappeared in the blackness, the return from its exhaust dying as the flight of MIGs first made contact with it.

He keyed the intercom. "Commander. ECM here. Heading for Camaguey two-eight-eight magnetic. Estimated arrival at thirteen after the hour." As he spoke, he made notations in his log. The oxygen mask was beginning to irritate the bridge of his nose. He knew that they would begin letting down now. Good to suck real air again. Not bottled shit.

The aircraft commander, Major Aksyonov, rolled out on the heading and turned the controls over to his copilot, poking his thumb downwards to indicate a slow descent. The turbojet engines died in a low whine. God, he thought, these things are buckets. Gives one's ass hemorrhoids. He waited, knowing Lieutenant Sidorov would brief him. He had heard the undisciplined chatter on the fighter frequency, but all in Spanish.

"Commander, ECM here."

"Shoot."

"The fighters got the prop aircraft. They're reporting that he spun out after cannon hits. One of the flight followed him down to 1000 meters. The aircraft was single engine. He says it was out of control. It crashed in the sea just 3 kilometers off the coast."

The aircraft commander smiled. It would look good in the debriefing. In the mission report. "Can you confirm their kill?" he asked.

"Affirmative. The infrared return faded just as they closed in. It never reappeared. Just normal heat along the coast. Nothing moving fast, trucks. The power generation plant at Cap Hatier. But definitely no aircraft." His voice was tinged with smugness.

"All right, Iosif. Call Songbird and give them the information. Be sure that your mission log is complete. They'll want seven copies." He settled back in the seat, listening to the ECM officer make his report. Good phraseology. He might make a good officer yet. The commander eyed the altimeter, willing the TU-18 lower, to an altitude where he could remove the oxygen mask and drink tea from the thermos. He started to compose his own mission report mentally, the phrases falling to his mind with ease. But it would be nice, he thought, to know why so much effort had been expended in bringing down the small aircraft. "Enemy of the people" was a standard phrase. He smiled, without humor.

The controller was chattering rapidly in Spanish, writing. He turned to Colonel Petrov. "The aircraft is a confirmed kill, sir. Impacted in the sea just north of Haiti. Here are the coordinates. The flight leader of

Cane Cutter says that he positively identified the aircraft as a Comanche. Two passengers in it."

Petrov sighed. He regretted the death of Loss as one pilot regrets the death of another pilot. "And do we have confirmation from the recon aircraft?"

The young enlisted man smiled broadly, showing his fillings. The rest of his teeth were slightly crooked. "Yes, sir. Confirmed. We will have their mission report by morning."

"Have them telephone me when they land. I don't leave until morning. We will be in the fleet communications room." Without waiting for an acknowledgment from the young controller, he turned to Rametka, taking him by the arm. "Let's get the messages off, Vasili. And then a few drinks. And sleep."

The two men left the command post, Petrov leading. Rametka noted how the gait and bearing of the young colonel had changed from minutes ago. Petrov was now erect, decisive. A curt nod, perhaps with a smile to the senior duty officer, the quick, offhand scrawl of his hand in the signout register, a friendly word to the security guard in the corridor. They walked along the gray painted corridor leading through the complex to the communications room, through the fluorescent lighted hallways, past security personnel who snapped to attention as they passed.

They entered the communications room, pausing for credentials check by the fleet marine stationed at the double doors, through the massive room partitioned with low walls of acoustic material that separated each operator, and into the duty officer's alcove office. The officer, a plump woman, rose to meet them.

Petrov curtly handed her his security pass for inspection, then a folded teleprinter message. "We will need your office, Lieutenant."

She clicked her heels, a ludicrous gesture, Rametka thought.

"Of course, Colonel. My office is at your disposal. Shall I order tea?"

288

"Coffee, Lieutenant. Cuban coffee, very strong and black. With cream. And some buns."

She clicked her heels again, the motion transferring minor shockwaves through her body, causing the plump fat of her arms and bosom to jiggle. Rametka almost smiled.

Petrov settled into the officer's still warm chair, Rametka taking the small lounge. In spite of the air conditioning, the room smelled strongly of floral perfume.

They watched the main communications room beyond the officer's plate window for some minutes in silence. Petty officers patrolled the perimeter of the room, stopping to examine the logs of each individual radio operator, coding technician, and teleprinter personnel. Perhaps over twenty workers. Unattended facsimile machines recorded weather satellite transmissions, photos, and other graphic data, spewing the material into waiting hoppers for collection and dissemination.

The lieutenant returned, carrying a tray. She placed it upon her desk, collected some sheaths of message forms, and, clicking her heels again, withdrew into the main communications room.

They drank their coffee, still not speaking, their eyes meeting only as they tasted the doughy buns. Petrov discarded his into the wastebasket. "We spent four hundred and forty-eight billion rubles last year on our military budget. Yet it doesn't seem that we can afford two kopecks for a decent roll. It's stupid, Vasili." Rametka only nodded, waiting for Petrov to open the conversation for the decisions yet to be made.

Petrov lighted a cigarette and leaned back, placing his feet on the desk. He tried for two consecutive smoke rings and failed. Without preamble he said, "Do you really believe the Cuban fighters got Loss?"

Rametka shrugged. "It seemed obvious, Anatoli. Why do you ask?"

Petrov readjusted his feet, still staring at the ceiling,

watching the smoke rise gently upward, then to be sucked into the grillwork of the air conditioning exhaust. "Because I have some doubts. I have flown interceptors, as you know. A small plane is a difficult target."

Rametka removed his steel-framed glasses and wiped them on a handkerchief. He placed them in a case and slipped them into his breast pocket. Momentarily, his hands touched the small enameled badge attached to his lapel, the Order of Lenin, as if to draw reassurance. He sighed. "Does it matter?"

"Perhaps not. But I want to personally question the pilots. And the ECM operator on the TU-18."

"What about the rest? The device. And Welsh?"

"Yes, we go ahead as planned," Petrov said emphatically. "I'm going to activate the special situation as of tonight. AW-4 will handle the mechanics of routing the device via the Pacific. The Z-Class submarine should be in position in the Gulf of Alaska by August ninth. This will allow a latitude of four days for the transfer to the fishing vessel. The fishing vessel will then proceed to the north end of Vancouver Island and down into the Queen Charlotte Straits to meet the yacht off North Broughton Island on the sixteenth or seventeenth. From there, the yacht will have four days to position herself in the Hood Canal."

"How positive can we be of the sailing date of the American Trident submarine? And what if they decide to sail at night?"

Petrov momentarily ignored him, tapping on the glass to obtain the attention of the lieutenant. She approached the office. Petrov held up his cold cup of coffee and gestured for two more. She nodded. "The sailing date?" Petrov replied. "Yes. I think we can reasonably be sure of that. August twenty-second. We have people within the U.S. Navy and with the civilian subcontractors. It's just a matter of putting together leave dates of shipboard personnel, supply deliveries of perishable food for the submarine. The usual thing. As far as the submarine leaving at night is concerned, the best intelligence would seem to argue against that possibility. The U.S.S. *Ohio* is quite large, over one hundred fifty meters long. About the displacement and general size of a destroyer. It will require tugs, while on the surface. Probably up through the Hood Canal and Puget Sound. This is not the kind of operation normally carried out in darkness.'' Petrov picked a small particle of roll between his teeth and continued, "At any rate, the yacht will be positioned at night in the smaller harbor of Squamish at the north end of the Hood Canal. There is an opening bridge through which the submarine would have to pass, which is only one mile away. That would be close enough. Hopefully, the operation will take place in daylight and at a much closer distance."

Vasili Rametka nodded. "Yes," he said. "That would seem reasonable. Our computer estimates indicate that as long as the device is detonated within five hundred meters of the vessel, it will appear that the submarine itself detonated. And even if the American navy claims sabotage, who would believe them? Not the Canadians, I think. Certainly not Western Europe! But we have anticipated their reaction. As long as doubt exists, they will not retaliate, and if they do, we would be ready for them." He tapped his pen against his teeth. "Not a pleasant prospect if they do, Anatoli."

Petrov nodded slowly. "Yes," he agreed. "It would not be a pleasant prospect. This is the major element of risk involved. But the American press has been expressing an increasing concern over just such an accident. And the Canadians have been very vocal about having a nuclear sub base only eighty kilometers from their border. If Welsh performs according to cue, the reaction of the American people will be that of outrage. They would disarm overnight." He paused, watching the lieutenant approach with yet another tray of coffee and soggy rolls. "And I think we both agree that such a prize is worth the gamble."

For over thirty minutes, the Comanche kept to the north coast of Hispaniola, first along the shores of Haiti and then across the border and along the coast of the Dominican Republic. Except for the lights of a few villages and vehicles winding their way along the tortuous coastal highway, they saw nothing except the flash of white seas breaking on the ragged reefs beneath them.

Loss flew the aircraft between two hundred and five hundred feet above the sea, keeping always to the coastline, navigation lights extinguished. For the first twenty minutes of the flight along the coast, Loss waited for cannon shells to tear through the thin frame of the aircraft. Fatalistically almost expecting it.

But with increasing time and distance, Loss felt that the interceptors had given up, probably thinking that they had forced him down into the sea. The radius of action of a jet interceptor is not great, particularly at low altitude and low air speeds, where the turbojet engine is relatively inefficient. And their radar sets would be ineffective, scratching for his presence amongst the clutter of ground return along the coast.

Thirty or more miles to the east, they could see the loom of light from a larger city, probably Puerto Plata, and he decided that they would have to turn north now, away from the coast and north toward the Bahamas.

He turned to Holly. "Get the map out of the case. It will be a large one, JNC-47, for this area and the next one north of that, JN-45, I think. Take the penlight and see whether you can find Hispaniola."

She dug into the case, found the chart, and extracted it. The chart was huge when opened and she folded it and refolded it, leaving only the southern Bahamas and Hispaniola displayed.

"What now?"

He looked over briefly at the chart and turned back to concentrate on the controls. "Yes. That's it. Those blocks of lines represent one degree of latitude and longitude. Each block is about sixty miles along an edge. How many blocks are we from the eastern edge of Cuba?"

She arched her thumb and forefinger across one block and walked her fingers across the chart. "I make it to be about three blocks—one hundred eighty miles and maybe closer to two hundred if that is Puerto Plata up ahead." She paused. "Brian. The chart shows a large airfield at Puerto Plata."

He nodded. "Yes. We're not going that far east. We first came south. The fighters bounced us just north of Haiti and we turned east. But I think we've lost them by flying along the coast at low altitude. Now we turn north. I have to stay low for the first thirty miles or so, just in case there is a ground radar station at Puerto Plata." He stole a quick glance at the chart and stabbed a finger at it. "You see the islands north of here?"

She bent down to the chart, penlight shielded. "There are several of them: Grand Turk, North and South Caicos. After that, there are a long string of islands up toward the northwest."

"Grand Turk. That's the one I want. There will be a number shown in a red box next to the letters GT. Give me those numbers. That's the frequency of the radio beacon station."

"Two thirty-two."

He set the frequency into the automatic directional finder and listened for several seconds to the code identification. He heard the letters GT in code barely audible above the static. The needle on the radio compass hunted in a northerly direction, unsteady now, but he knew that as they flew north and gained altitude, it would firm up on a solid bearing.

Easing into a bank, he rolled the aircraft through a

293

shallow turn to the north. There was only the black sea before them now, the coast receding behind them. As they rolled out on the northerly heading, he could pick out Ursa Major and in line with the two stars which formed the lip of the dipper, Polaris low on the horizon—true north. The clock on the panel showed 9:51, airborne now for more than an hour. He noted the time on the back of his wrist with a ballpoint pen. There would be time later to begin to compute fuel consumption and range available, but it would be cutting it fine even with favorable winds. Leaning across the width of the panel, he scanned each instrument carefully looking for any abnormality, the smallest flicker. But they were all solidly in the green. The fuel gauges on the main tank showed slightly more than three-quarter filled and they would lie on the conservative side, he hoped.

Time now for the beginning of fuel conservation. He rummaged in the dashboard locker and found the power-setting tables, written in Stroud's precise hand. One column was outlined in red felt-tip pen, the column heading "55 percent power." He followed the vertical headings of altitude to sea level and across to throttle setting and prop speed. Slowly, he adjusted the throttle back until the manifold pressure registered just over twenty-one inches and then inched the prop speed back to 2,100 rpm. The air speed slowly stabilized at just short of one-fifty.

The moon was setting in the west now, a dim orange sickle scything into the horizon's haze. They both watched, regretting the fading light. Perhaps a millennium ago man felt the same, he thought. With the light of the moon gone, there was only blackness and the pinpricks of stars in the heavens above. But the stars were cold and distant. The moon was more personal, a pale sun.

She leaned over and put her hand to the nape of his neck, rubbing and prodding the muscles. "How's

294

that?'' she said, watching his profile in the dim illumination of the instruments.

"Not bad. Really tired. My head hurts like hell.''

"Can you put it on autopilot? If you tell me what to watch for, I can wake you up if this thing begins to act up.''

He stretched his muscles under her probing fingertips. "Nope. Not yet. As long as we're close to the water, I have to hand-fly the aircraft. I wouldn't trust the autopilot. Once we get another ten minutes north of here, I'll start to climb out. But for the present I want to stay well under any radar that they may have in Puerto Plata.''

"Are we going to have enough fuel?'' she said, looking down at the gauges.

"I think so. You're looking at the main fuel tank quantity. When I switch over to the auxiliary tanks in a few hours, we have another five hundred miles range in them and then another seven-fifty in the fuel tanks in the back seat.''

"Yes, but haven't we burned up a lot of fuel in the last hour?'' She pushed the hair out of her eyes, a gesture that had always stirred Loss.

"Not that much, I think. Maybe twelve gallons. I've kept her as slow as possible. But at any rate, we'll easily make New Jersey, New York State. Somewhere in there. And with good winds, Nova Scotia. It should be dawn tomorrow before we start to go dry.''

She sat and thought for several minutes, twirling a strand of hair around a fingertip. She turned to him pointing back to the west. "Those were Cuban aircraft back there?''

He nodded.

"And they were trying to shoot us down?''

He nodded again, edging in nose-up trim to start the shallowest of climbs. The sea was black beneath them, no visual perception of height. The altimeter read six

295

hundred forty feet, the rate of climb indicator nudging upward at fifty feet per minute.

She resumed rubbing his neck, remaining silent. The stimulation to his muscles produced a warm tingling. His forehead still ached, but less so now. If the fuel held out, if the engine held together . . . Lots of ifs. Not to think too much about it and just fly the airplane. Even if he couldn't make Canada, he would have a fair trial in the U.S. Holly would testify. Momentarily, he thought that it might be better to just set the aircraft down in the States and let justice grind away. The only trick was that he was accusing a senator of the United States of—what?

Loss eased in more power for the climb and watched the air speed settle to 143. The stars were brighter now as they climbed above the salt air. Ursa Major, the Big Bear, wheeled westward, the Pole Star by itself on the dim horizon.

Chapter 21

The sky was black but changing, slowly mutating to progressively paler shades of cream. The stars dimmed, one by one in the east, the dissolution spreading west until only Venus and Saturn were left to flicker in the vacant dome.

The dawn was only a dirty red smudge on the horizon, suppressed by a complex frontal system which smeared the eastern horizon with high cirrus, clustered thunderstorms, and rain.

Beneath them, the sea was pocked with oily green-white waves, rolling across the fetch of the Atlantic to break upon the New England coast. A massive supertanker labored southeastward, seas breaking over her superstructure, engulfing her decks with white foam. He watched the ship until she was gone from sight, the only living thing that shared the bleak void of sea and sky.

Loss eased the mixture control back fractionally, watching the cylinder-head temperature waver near the top of the red arc. The Comanche hung on its prop, mushing. But the fuel flow meter fluctuated marginally and stabilized at seven gallons per hour. He fumbled with the computer, punching in figures, time, and distance. The display gave back an answer of two hours and fourteen minutes to dry tanks, discounting the long slow descent from altitude when fuel consumed would be even less.

He rechecked the computations twice, his mind fuddled with the cumulative effects of high altitude, lack of sleep, and physical fatigue.

He looked down on the sea once more, watching the pattern of the swells from the southeast. Aloft, the wind seemed more southerly, giving the Comanche a boost of thirty miles or more for each hour flown. Or so he guessed. Three hours before, he had passed ninety miles west of Bermuda, using the VOR from Kindley Field to establish his track. The results were generally believable, the tailwind boosting him along, extending his range.

But the information was imprecise, and now, 420 miles to the north, the weather system would have changed and with it, the winds.

Holly stirred in the right seat, curled into a ball, feet drawn up beneath her. Even in sleep, her face was composed and gentle. Loss felt a surge of compassion for her, something far more than love. For three hours last night, while he slept, she had monitored the instruments, alone with her thoughts in a single-engine aircraft 15,000 feet over the black Atlantic. She had awakened him only once to point out the lights of an

297

aircraft passing high overhead to the north, bound toward the mainland. She never once questioned his actions, simply believing his articles of faith: a litany of fuel and time and instruments. Sometime after five, she woke him again and they transferred the last of the fuel from the back seat tanks. By 5:30, an hour before dawn, he ran the auxiliary tanks dry, the engine shuddering and coughing as he switched to the main tanks once more. But now she slept.

Loss selected a frequency of 113.3 on the VOR and watched the indicator for any sign of movements. The needle lay dead in its cage, but the headphones gave out the faint beat of morse code. He listened intently, trying to pick out the individual letters. The station was on the south coast of Nova Scotia, the town of Yarmouth. The Kent farm was ninety miles beyond that, on the eastern coast two miles south of the town of Lunenburg. Kent had described the airstrip as "Grass, cows, and about two thousand feet long. Near the edge of a peninsula." A fragile thing to pin your hopes on, he thought.

He switched on the low frequency ADF radio and dialed through the broadcast bands. The reception was a tumult of voices and crashing static. He found one clear station, probably in Boston. The announcer was giving hockey scores. Then an ad for Fiat electric cars. More hockey scores. Loss fumed, waiting for some means of identifying the station. Finally, a woman's voice:

"Maine, New Hampshire, and Vermont will continue to enjoy unseasonably warm weather today with highs around 15 Celsius, winds from the southeast. Some cloudiness this afternoon in northern sections of Vermont and New Hampshire with a 20 percent chance of rain by this evening. Here in Bar Harbor, skies are partly cloudy, temperature 12 degrees Celsius. Barometer ten thirteen millibars and falling. And here's Jack with some good news about saving money on your coal heating bill—"

298

Loss flipped the selector switch of the antenna to ADF and watched the radio compass needle point to the west. That would put him abeam of the station in northern Maine. The bearing wasn't that solid, but it was an indication that the tailwind had been as good as expected, perhaps better. He roughed out the bearing on the enroute low altitude chart and noted the time. Spanning the distance from the bearing to the southern coast of Nova Scotia with his fingers, he estimated 110 nautical miles. No indication yet, he thought, looking at the VOR indicator, which was tuned to Falmouth.

She stirred in the right seat, pushing hair from her face. Sitting up, she squinted out at the eastern horizon and yawned. Leaning over, she kissed him lightly. "Looks cold down there," she said, yawning again. "Where are we?"

"Ninety, maybe a hundred miles from the south coast of Nova Scotia. I think we'll squeak by."

She looked over the cowling of the Comanche. The sea three miles below them and to the north looked like a sheet of hammered lead in the spring sunlight. "Do you think anyone has seen us? On radar or whatever they do?" she asked, crossing her arms on he padded instrument cowl and resting her chin on her forearm. Watching the northern horizon.

"Bermuda did, possibly. I doubt it. I don't know about the southern coast of Nova Scotia. Falmouth might have approach control radar."

"What will they do if they see us on radar?"

He scratched at the growth of beard. His mouth felt foul. And the cut over his forehead was starting to throb. "I don't know. Possibly think we were an aircraft out of Halifax. We can fly to the east of them so we'll be on the edge of their radar range. There is a local radio station shown on the sectional map of Nova Scotia about eight miles from the Kent farm—CKBW. If we can get a positive identification, we can home in on that."

She nodded and was quiet, watching the north horizon. He withdrew two candy bars from the dash compartment, and they chewed on the chocolate in silence.

The oil temperature was creeping upward now, fractionally higher than it had been an hour ago. Loss remembered that Stroud had warned him of excessive oil consumption. He opened the engine cooling cowl, disliking the additional drag that it would develop, robbing them of a few miles per hour. Perhaps he could start the descent once the VOR at Falmouth came alive. He looked closely at the sectional, searching for the radio station. He found it, ten miles to the west of Lunenburg. Dialing in the frequency, he listened. The voice was clear, a Canadian accent, discussing the fisheries program in the Gulf of St. Lawrence. Switching to the ADF function, he watched the needle swing to the northwest, a full forty degrees to the left of his present heading. He disengaged the autopilot and turned the aircraft left until the needle was centered.

She raised her eyebrows. "What's wrong?"

"Nothing much, I hope," he lied. "We must be further out to sea than I thought. But the ADF needle is locked onto CKBW."

"Will we have enough fuel?"

"I don't know now. We probably have . . ." He hesitated and looked down at the chart. He checked the time, subtracting the fuel used since the earlier bearing from Bar Harbor. "We probably have about one hour forty minutes' worth of fuel left. That translates into about two hundred forty miles, discounting the effects of a wind. And if the engine runs dry, we have about another forty miles of playing glider."

She looked down at the sea beneath them. "How cold is the sea?" she said, her breath condensing on the perspex of the cabin window, her forehead resting against the pane.

"You'll freeze your balls off," he said, looking down on his side.

"I'm serious."

"So am I. The chart shows that the southern limit of pack ice in March is just north of here. We would last about five minutes in the water. But we're going to make it."

"Yes," she said, leaning against him. "I guess we have to. What about the Kents? It's a lot to expect of them."

Loss laughed. "Not really. Supposedly, I've only stolen two airplanes, left the Bahamas without clearance, and entered Canada illegally."

"Seriously, Brian. He's a retired RCAF officer. It would probably be very difficult for them if we're discovered."

"Holly, I think the Kents are part of a vanishing breed." Unconsciously he looked at the oil-temperature gauge. It was lower now, but still hovering in the red. More ominously, the oil pressure was down fractionally. He avoided looking at the panel, as if ignorance would keep the engine from betraying them. "The Kents will put us up for the few days that it takes to get this thing sorted out. Stroud will," he paused, thinking about Stroud, "Stroud will be able to clear the thing up in Matthew Town. If I have to, I'll go down to New York to confront Welsh. There has to be some explanation."

She sat up, stretching, working her arms against the tiredness. Looking out over the engine cowling, she scanned the horizon.

"Brian, how far can you see from this altitude?"

He hesitated, eyes scanning the instrument panel. "Oh, about fifty, sixty miles. It's fairly clear."

She pointed ahead and his eyes followed her fingertip toward a brown smear on the horizon. They both watched intently, willing it not to dissolve or change into cloud bank. The smear expanded, slowly filling the horizon. Farther to the south, a rocky headland emerged and solidified. And before them, the brown became greens and blues and whites, great forests of fir and spruce dotted with yet-frozen lakes.

Just to the north of their flight path, two great bays,

301

separated by headlands, harbored fleets of fishing vessels. Offshore, but within the protection of the bays, were hundreds of isolated islands, mostly barren except for spots of stunted spruce and birch.

As they passed over the coast, he closed the throttle and began a slow descent.

They sat next to each other, chaise longues inches and miles apart in the last illumination of the June twilight. Welsh watched as lightning bugs flickered through the grove beyond the lawn. Sometimes it seemed to him that their flickering coincided in a silent, screaming chorus.

"You have it all," she said, sipping from her glass.

"Not all," he answered. "Not all by a long shot. There are miles to go."

Judith Welsh turned her head, chin touching her shoulder, barely able to see his features in the dusk. He was like this now, uncommunicative, withdrawing into himself. She turned away, wanting to draw him out and yet afraid of the consequences of provoking him.

The children were farther down on the broad lawn, small shapes running across the manicured grounds, swirling in the gathering darkness like dust devils. Their shrieks drifted back from the open space, echoing. Judith watched the shapes collide, turn, flee from each other. Beside her, Welsh lit a cigarette, briefly etching his features in bas-relief.

"DeSilva's ecstatic," she commented, pouring more wine into her glass. "Six talk shows have offered interviews this week. Is that right?"

"Something like that," he answered.

"Your father would be proud." She said it without rancor.

"Don't be bitchy." He flung the partly finished cigarette away into the dark. But she was right. The old man would have choked with a mixture of pride and jealousy. DeSilva was beginning to tally votes, winnowing wheat from chaff, for although Welsh had en-

302

tered no primary elections, both *Time* and *Newsweek* had carried cover stories about him, and a *Washington Post* editorial had forecast is entry into the race as a dark horse.

In less than two months, he had achieved what four presidents in fourteen years had failed to accomplish: withdrawal from the Panama Canal with what was perceived as honor. He had followed that with substantive discussions with Cuban leaders on the ownership of Guantanamo Bay. The result had been a phased withdrawal of Americans in exchange for withdrawal of Cuban troops from Africa. The Administration had made noises about specific language, and the secretary of state had farted around for a few days, but the result was there and U.S. voters knew it. It was all going the way Klist had predicted.

"You're really planning to go through with it?" Judith asked. She was slurring her words a little and he would have simply put it down to the wine with tonight's dinner and the drinks after, except that her drinking had followed this pattern ever since their return from the Caribbean.

"I'll be at the convention, if that's what you mean. Beyond that, I can't say."

"You *sound* like a candidate now. How quotable."

He turned toward her. "Your drinking's getting out of hand, Judith. That thing at the fund-raising dinner last week, and then in front of the insurance adjuster."

She held the glass up against the night sky, just barely able to discern its outline. "Did he pay you?"

"The Aztec was a total loss. They didn't have any other choice."

"What about the other Loss. Did they pay you for him as well? Just enough for a little bronze marker? Maybe one for the girl as well. We could have put them side by side, down near the carriage house."

"That was Brian's own doing. Breaking out of the hospital and stealing the other plane had nothing to do with us. That subject is closed."

One of the children had switched on a flashlight and

held it under his chin, making a death's mask. The younger ones screamed in mock terror and ran past their parents toward the main house. Welsh could almost touch the palpable delight of childhood in their stumbling, windy passage.

"Look," he said, turning to her. "I've told you. The involvement with Klist is finished. There's nothing more." He could hear her swallow and then pour more wine. Silence was her worst condemnation.

"It's finished," he lied, repeating a lie.

"Three million from an account in Switzerland," she replied. "A provision in your father's will that you not be allowed to touch the money for ten years after his death. And even with taxes, over two million to fund a campaign. And these wonderful little speeches you gave in the Senate. Suddenly whisking down to the tropics for conferences in Havana and Panama." She belched politely. "And what mar-ve-lous . . ." she stretched out the word, repeating it, ". . . marvelous results." She reached over and patted his wrist with a damp hand. "Marvelous, Clifford."

She stood up slowly, overly cautious, picking up the bottle of wine. "I'll put the children to bed."

He reached out and caught her free hand. "I need you, Judith. The campaign is going to be tough—far tougher than I thought. But all the ties with Klist are broken. From here on in, I've got to go it alone." He thought briefly about the grasslands of Wyoming and the paradoxical extremes of sheep grazing and missiles waiting, and how the two images, linked together, would turn a nation of voters toward him. Klist had been right. The power was there, ready to grasp if you took the chance.

She pulled her hand away. "I've lived with you for twenty-two years, Clifford. You know and I know you're not finished with Klist. Lie to DeSilva and to the voters, but don't lie to me."

She turned and walked unsteadily across the lawn toward their home, which overlooked the muddy Hudson.

Chapter 22

Ian Campbell shaded his eyes from the hard sunlight with one hand, puffing nervously on the Dunhill with the other. The skin on his hands and his face was a bright red, for, like most men of his complexion and personal habits, he never tanned. Purplish veins, like tributaries of a river, flowed across his cheeks and nose, the testament of heavy drinking. His chest thudded dully, for even without exertion, his heart could barely maintain the flow of blood to the fat-laden arteries.

He looked across the concourse of the terminal and the service entrance, seeing thousands of people, seeing no one in particular. Grunting softly with relief, he settled himself on the battered leather two-suiter and waited.

His scalp prickled with the heat, and he removed the light woven straw hat, scrubbing the crown on his head with a handkerchief. His hair, wispy around his ears, overlong at the collar, was matted with perspiration. The light breeze felt refreshing.

He checked his watch again, irritated with the delay. Over twenty minutes late. Campbell was a punctual man, and he considered it the rudest of faults for a person to be late, even what is termed fashionably late. If a chap said 3:10, then he should *mean* 3:10. Not 3:15. Or twenty. Like stealing time from the person you were meeting. All very well to be late. Then you were assured that the person was there cooling his heels, waiting for you. Lood psychological practice. But damn rude.

He watched the tide of people flowing through the terminal entrance with some curiosity. Canadians? God, they looked *American!* Mod clothes, the ever-present American type of attaché case. Not a decent briefcase with sound leather and good stitching. Plastic things trying to look like leather.

A swept-wing aircraft thundered into the sky to the west, laying down dark tracks of smoke, straining toward the sun. The fuselage was emblazoned with stripes of red and gold and green, the logo of some Canadian airline or another. Looked like a flying stick of candy, he thought.

"Mr. Campbell?"

He turned on the luggage, craning his head toward the speaker, the sun in his eyes.

"Yes, I'm Campbell. You're Kent?"

The man who stood before Campbell nodded his head, economically. "You're alone, Mr. Campbell?"

"Of course. You specified that I was to come alone in the letter."

Edwin Kent nodded and smiled, extending his hand. "Yes, we thought that it might be better. I hope that the information that we included was of some use."

"It was," Campbell grunted, grasping the other man's hand in greeting. "But whether we can do anything with it is another thing."

The two men walked to the dusty Chrysler sedan, Kent limping. The deep, brittle blue of the Nova Scotia early summer was cloudless, vacant. Despite the smells of jet exhaust, Campbell caught the underlying scent of great tracts of spruce and a hint of the salt sea, which lay a few miles to the east.

Campbell had never been in Nova Scotia, but as with most Britons of his era, he had always pictured Halifax as the bitter end of a frayed lifeline across the Atlantic in the early years of the war. For every three ships that left the coast of Nova Scotia, two steamed past the Nab Tower into the Solent to land their cargo on the fire-blackened docks of Southampton. His son—his only son—had sailed on those convoys and had been lost in a collision off the Irish coast. Campbell tried not to think about this, ever, but he would want to see the town and the harbor and the place called Pennant Bay from which his son had sailed on the great convoys that had gathered in the winter's dusk.

Kent placed the suitcases in the rear seat and eased himself into the driver's seat, awkwardly lifting his right leg with his hands to swing it over the sill and place it on the floor.

"The war?" Campbell said, nodding toward the leg.

"One of them. The cold one. Not all that bad, this leg. Just can't do some things. They want to refit it with the newer mods. Gears and relays and solid state. That sort of thing. Doubt that I could stand all the whirring. Besides, I'm sort of fond of the old one. Keep telling Margaret, my wife, that I've fitted a rum flask into the calf. Actually found her looking for it one night after I had taken the damn thing off to go to bed." Kent laughed and started the engine.

They traveled south on the expressway, Kent graceful in his driving, handling the machine with casual ease. Campbell thought that Kent would do all things like this with economy of motion, the direct mind-machine link that is the blessing of few.

"Air marshal, weren't you?" Campbell asked, lighting another Dunhill, watching the green blur of spruce rush by.

"Yes, was," Kent replied, watching the road ahead. "Now just on pension. Golden handshake. I miss it sometimes. By the way, it's Ian, isn't it?" Campbell nodded. "Then just call me Kent. Everyone else does, except my wife. Calls me Edwin, which I suppose is a proper Christian name." He paused and then briefly glanced across at the Englishman. Campbell was no fool, he thought. Just looked like one. "Ian, I suppose that you'd like to know about Loss. We have only about thirty minutes before we're back at the farm. I think you need background."

Campbell nodded. "Yes. Everything that you can give me before I start with Loss. And I want to make something clear. For the record, I'm here on holiday. No official function. Depending on Loss and what he may or may not be willing to do, my department may come into it. But it's a very touchy thing right now."

"In what way?"

"Don't you see, Kent? Technically, we're involved in intelligence activities within a foreign 'friendly' country. Neither the RCMP nor the CIA has wind of this. For Loss's safety, I want to keep it that way as long as possible."

Kent lit his pipe, sucking on the flame. He nodded. "It sounds reasonable. But frankly, it seems to me to be a dead end. Loss is really shaken. His confidence is gone."

Campbell pursed his lips briefly. "Yes. I can understand why it would be. But carry on. Tell me about him and the woman."

Kent swung off the expressway and onto an asphalt coastal road, still heading south and west. Through little towns, with clapboard-sided salt boxes, elm-lined streets. Towns with names like Fourteen Mile House and Beechville. The New World, Campbell thought. His son must have liked it here.

"Loss." Kent squinted against the late afternoon July sun. "Yes, Loss. He came two months ago in April. In Stroud's plane. He made it in one direct flight from the Bahamas." He turned to Campbell, explaining. "You see, he had extra fuel. Had it in the back seat. Remarkable that he didn't blow himself up. At any rate, he came into a little cow-patch airstrip I have on the farm. There was still a bit of snow around. Muddy too. We had to drag the aircraft off the strip with the tractor. It's in the barn now."

"Did your aviation authorities ever detect the aircraft?"

"No, I doubt it," Kent replied. "Loss was off course, well out to sea. Came into Nova Scotia in an area where there is not too much radar coverage. Besides, this is not an area where there is much of a light-plane security problem. Most of the border smuggling takes place down toward Quebec."

"And then."

"Yes. Well, Loss explained that he had been accused of stealing his employer's aircraft and that the Bahamians were going to jail him for it. To use his words, he said that he was being 'set up.' So he used this other aircraft to escape in with the permission of the owner, this chap Stroud. On top of all this, he was jumped by three jet interceptors shortly after takeoff. The woman confirms his story. I put them up in the guest cottage without contacting the authorities until Loss could sort it out."

Campbell chain-lit another cigarette, spilling ashes across his lapels. He stubbed the fag end of the used cigarette out in the smoking tray. "I can understand why you would help them," he said. "However, it may be somewhat difficult to explain to the Royal Canadian Mounted if that time comes."

Kent nodded. "Yes, I've thought of that. Margaret, my wife, thinks that the whole thing is slightly insane. At any rate, we got word over CBC that Stroud and this person Heiss were murdered. The authorities in the Bahamas obviously concluded that Loss had done it. So consequently, he can't give himself up to the authorities without some evidence of his innocence, which seems to be severely lacking. Of course, there are also counts of drug smuggling and grand theft against him. He's very depressed about the whole thing. Blames himself for Stroud's death."

"Why doesn't he turn himself in to the American authorities? I would think that he would receive a fair trial."

"I can't reason with him on that score, Ian. He seems to be convinced that Welsh was involved in this whole thing. It would be Welsh's word against Loss's.

And as you know, Welsh is presently well thought of in the States. The Panamanian and now this Cuban Accord. Personally, I think Loss is right. Welsh was a part of it, although perhaps unwittingly."

"Loss *is* innocent," Campbell said, yawning. He stretched his arms. "At least on my findings and the conclusions that we can determine from somewhat limited cooperation on the part of the Bahamian government." He ticked off on his stubby fingers like a schoolmaster. "One. Heiss-Bolken was a Russian agent. A very unsavory person. Two. There was a third person aboard that flight as Loss claims. A man known as Klist—Petrov—take your choice. We know nothing about him. But his "wife" has been traced back to East Germany. Obviously not his wife, but very probably in Russian service. Petrov disappeared, but we think he stole a small yacht. The yacht has never been found.

"Three, and probably most important in terms of Loss's innocence, I found a couple of nine-millimeter cartridge cases quite far down the runway. They are of the same caliber as the weapon that Loss owns, but the extractor marks on the cases don't fit the design of the Luger's extractor. We feel that it was probably a Walther. I have two photographs of the ballistic marks on a bullet we recovered from Stroud. The rifling doesn't match the barrel construction of Loss's type of Luger. Again, evidence indicates that it was from a Walther P-38 type weapon."

"You presented this evidence to the Bahamian police?"

"Yes," Campbell sighed. "But I had a feeling that they didn't want to know. Or at least someone within their department, fairly high on the ladder, didn't. I was told, very politely, mind you, to go back to London."

Kent passed through a small town that seemed to be composed solely of white churches, a boatyard, and a general store. There were children skipping rope in a graveyard. They waved. Near the edge of the village, Kent swung left onto a dirt road and bumped across a cattle guard. He pulled the scdan to a stop beneath the shade of a cluster of maples. Cows, munching on long-bladed grass, raised their heads in dull curiosity and stared, still masticating.

Kent switched off the engine and turned to Campbell. "Then, what you have would help to clear Loss? With the U.S, authorities, I mean."

Campbell nodded. "Yes, in the sense of criminal justice, I think it would. But we see something much more involved than just Loss. Something, perhaps to use a grandiose phrase, of global importance. Loss is just the dog who got his tail caught in the crack of the door. We see this connection between Petrov, Heiss, and Welsh as the main crux of our interest. Very much so now, in view of Welsh's political development. What really further complicates the issue is that Welsh is selling unilateral disarmament to the American people, a view which seems to coincide with our present government's outlook. Our department is essentially nonpolitical. We have reservations about the wisdom of such a policy."

Edwin Kent looked down at his weathered hands, which were tanned and strong from working the fields. His stump hurt like hell. He turned to Campbell, eyes hard and flat gray. "So you can't help Loss? Is that what you've flown from London to tell me?"

Campbell smiled. "No, Kent. Not exactly. I said that one of the conditions was that my department's help might be somewhat limited. We can provide research, contact, surveillance, that sort of thing. But all the links between Senator Welsh and the others— Heiss, Volgel, and Petrov—are broken. We can only help Loss if he leaves his burrow and starts to run. Then we shall see who the hounds are."

Margaret Kent removed their coffee cups and withdrew from the study, closing the door behind her.

Kent sat behind a scarred desk, right leg up on a footstool. Behind him on the wall were black and white photos, framed uniformly in plain black molding. Some of the photos were faded, turning shades of sepia. Kent with squadron comrades: serious young men in leather jackets, hands stuffed in pockets, some with mustaches. A spotted dog in the foreground, held by a young man dressed in military blouse and forage cap. Others of a very young Kent sitting alone in the cockpit of a Gypsy Moth, smiling shyly.

Bookshelves lined two walls of the study, well thumbed, with dust jackets torn or bearing finger-marks. The complete set of Churchill. Jane's *Aircraft of the World*, Bertrand Russell, and surprisingly, a wide-ranging set of volumes on the history of the Canadian railways.

Campbell rose from the leather ottoman and poured three glasses of cognac neat. He placed one before Kent, handed another to Loss, and retained the third for himself. They raised their glasses in a diminutive toast and drank.

"Confusion to our enemies," Campbell said, wiping his lips with a handkerchief.

"Something like that," Loss muttered. He leaned back in the leather chair, balancing his glass on the upholstered arm. Loss had grown a full beard in the three months he had hidden in Nova Scotia. The cut on his forehead was healed, but the white puckered flesh stood out prominently against the deep tan he had acquired working in the fields. Even now, he wore the faded denims of a field worker, the smell of earth engrained within the fabric. He looked up at Campbell. "So you don't think that the ballistics test would help me?"

Campbell hunched his shoulders. "Inconclusive, Brian. It would only indicate that the weapon used on Stroud and Heiss was not a Luger. That is, assuming that the Bahamian police would accept my work. Look at it from the standpoint of a jury. You take an aircraft from Welsh. He states that you stole it. Then you escape from a hospital, abduct both Stroud and Heiss, and take them to the airport. Next, you leave them tied to Stroud's rented car and flee the country in Stroud's aircraft. Both men are found shot and burned to death." He paused for effect, lifting his shaggy eyebrows. "What would be your judgment?"

"Ian, there must be some way out of this. For God's sake—"

Campbell snorted. "Of course there is. Turn yourself in at the border. I'll give you all the help that I can muster. But remember that this is a matter that occurred within Bahamian jurisdiction. You would be extradited and tried there. Back to square one."

Edwin Kent sighed. "The other alternative, Brian, is staying here. You're welcome, you know. An entire lifetime if you choose. I'm too old to keep the farm going, and this leg isn't much help. You and Holly can simply keep the guest house and manage the farm while I sit down and write a history of the Canadian Pacific Railway."

Loss started to object and Kent interrupted. "No, Brian, hear me out. Margaret and I have talked before about this. We never could have children, and it's nice having you both around the house. Ian can fix you up with documents showing that you're Canadian citizens. Maybe we could buy that old Newfi schooner that's down in Chester. Have David Clark's firm fix her up. Do some sailing. Eventually, we would leave you the farm." Kent was smiling now. "It's a good alternative, Brian."

Loss sat a long time staring at the photographs above the study's fireplace.

"It's true," Campbell added. "Kent and I have talked it over. Regardless of your course of action, you're going to need a new identity. I have Canadian passports for you and Holly. General documents, backgrounds, the whole business." He flicked his hand as if it were nothing. "But, of course, you would

313

have to not reveal the source if you're ever picked up. Very embarrassing to my department."

Loss looked down at his scuffed boots, embarrassed. "I can hardly thank you, Kent, for your offer. Holly and I love it here. Maybe the first time in my life I've been at peace. You and Margaret have been—"

Kent pushed two matchsticks together on his blotter, keeping his face averted. "I mean it, Brian. We want you to stay."

"But you understand, don't you. I've got to find out what the hell made Welsh do this thing. And what his involvement is. If I could nail that down, the rest would begin to fall into place." He looked up at Kent. "If I can get this resolved, if I have any alternatives other than just sitting here for the rest of my life knowing that I've been screwed, then I'll take it."

Campbell refilled their glasses and them lumbered over to the window, watching the quiet countryside change to deeper umber, melting into the twilight. The wind smelled of green growing things. Kent has found his son, he thought. Lucky man. He turned toward Loss, shoving his stubby, veined hands deeply into his pockets. "You talked about an alternative. Are you sure you want one?"

"Yes. It's as I've said before. I want it cleared up. I want Welsh, particularly."

"We have very little to go on, you realize. It may be completely futile."

"What do you have, Ian?"

Campbell retrieved a sealed folder from his briefcase. Breaking the seal with the nail of his thumb, he extracted a perforated computer printout and laid it out across the desk. Line upon line of type, in the misshapen font of computer graphics, covered the sheet. "This is all we have," Campbell said.

Kent pulled the sheet around to read it. "What does it represent?"

Campbell settled back heavily into the ottoman and

lit a cigarette. He exhaled, creating a blue haze under the desk lamplight. "It represents the attempt to link the two words that Heiss revealed to Loss. Words that Heiss had heard on a tape recording that he made secretly of Petrov and the woman. Something that Heiss thought he could use later. Perhaps sell to the Americans. Unfortunately, the conversation was in Russian. Heiss picked up only two words, English proper nouns. We have tried to utilize MI-5s data banks to establish the connection between the words *hood* and *hussar*. Either one or both, of course, could be code words for an operation of some sort. But we tend to discount this since the code words originated by the Russians would most likely be Russian words. We have gone on the premise that *hood* is the name of a place. *Hussar* we feel is a *thing*, a name you give to an object. Perhaps a ship, an antique shop, a pub. Something of that sort."

Campbell looked down at the printout. "I don't think that either of you can realize the magnitude of this job. Because we didn't know what we were looking for, it was decided that it would be necessary to optically scan telephone directories, the atlas, trade magazines, etc., ad nauseum, just for the compilation of names and things that matched the key indices. From there, we attempted to obtain matches based on chronological events happening to *things* at *places*. In practice, we favor the latter theory. That is, the establishment of a thing called *hussar* in a place called *hood*.

"Do you have any results?" Loss asked.

"Three believable, all told," Campbell replied. "Some of these matches are tenuous at best. That is not to say that others don't exist."

Loss looked at the sheet. "Only these three?"

"Yes," Campbell replied, picking at a small infection on his cheek. He drew some white matter and then looked at his finger with disgust. He wiped his cheek with a stained handkerchief.

"These digits in the column under Hood are coordinates?" Loss asked, running his fingernail down the brief set of listings.

Campbell nodded. "Yes. Latitude and longitude. The other adjacent column is the *Hussar* link."

"What are they, then? They're all coded, aren't they?"

"We thought that would be wise," Campbell replied. "Most of the printout is flim-flam at any rate. But the three correlations—links if you will—are all in North America. The first is Port Hood on Cape Breton Island. No direct *hussar* link, but there is a pub called The Highwayman. You see, we included various definitions of *hussar* in the search. Most people tend to think of a hussar as a cavalryman. But the word is derived from the Serbian word *huzar*, meaning pirate, or highwayman.

"The second match is Port Hood on the Columbia River in Oregon. There is no direct link there except that we feel *Hussar* may be the name of a ship or a smaller vessel." Campbell dabbed at the red splotch on his cheek, examining the handkerchief with each dab to see whether the oozing had stopped. He scowled, somewhat irritated, but continued. "The third match is the Hood Canal in the state of Washington. This is a deep-water seaway leading down from the Strait of Juan de Fuca. Again, the link may be a ship of some sort."

Loss perched himself on the edge of the desk, looking down at the computer printout. "What about ships named *Hussar*. Is there any central registration of names?"

"Lloyd's of London," Campbell replied. "Lloyd's registers. Covers all commercial shipping. Also Bureau Veritas. Also DOT in Canada and the States. Collecting ship's names was a relatively mundane task. In all, there are sixteen *Hussars*. Some high-tonnage merchant vessels; the balance documented yachts. Of the sixteen, I think that there are only two of interest. One is a sailing yacht with registration in the state of Washington. The other candidate is a Liberian-owned freighter which plies between Seattle, Vancouver, and the Philippines. Both of these vessels might have occasion to navigate the Hood Canal."

Kent doodled on a yellow writing pad. "It all comes down to a few choices then, Ian. The Columbia River, Cape Breton Island, and the Hood Canal."

Campbell shook his head. "Possibly, although I think we can pay less attention to the first two. Port Hood on Cape Breton is not a seaport to speak of. The same holds true of Port Hood on the Columbia River. No, we feel that it is the Hood Canal. Major shipping area and all that. And the Liberian freighter would seem to be our *Hussar*. The yacht in question, even though she uses these waters, is American-owned. Just plays about on the coast. Never been offshore to speak of. Local boat."

"What's the connection between Welsh and Petrov and the ship?" Loss asked.

Campbell shook his head slowly, jowls sagging, looking down at the printout. "Not the foggiest, Brian. We can only speculate that Petrov wants to ship something or someone in or out of the States. It's my own guess that Petrov's link with the *Hussar* and his link with Welsh are two entirely different operations. Separate but perhaps supportive."

Kent leaned back in the chair, lobbing the pen into the target area of the yellow pad. He looked at the Englishman carefully, as if to detect some visible flaw in the man that would, in turn, invalidate the data. "Ian. Surely, there is some other Hood-*Hussar* link. Or at least places named Hood. It seems to be tossing all your eggs into one basket."

"True on both counts, Kent. There are many places named Hood: Mount Hood, Port Hood, Hoodsport. But note that most of them are named for the Right Honorable Lord Hood, Admiral of the Ocean Seas. Seaports all. There are only four places in North

317

America named for Hood. We have discounted the mountain and a small town in California. I don't intend to demean your thinking. Yes, there are other Hoods. And a few Hussars in the form of pubs, gift shops, and hotels. But most are ships. And ships make port. We think there is a link, and circumstances argue for North America. Agreed?"

Kent nodded. "Agreed." He bent over the desk, looking at his notes. If Campbell was truthful in his description of the complexity of the data collection there was a great deal of effort and money involved on the part of MI-5. Something more than mere desire to aid Loss. He phrased it bluntly. "What is your government's interest, Ian?"

Campbell ambled over to the fireplace, looking into the dark chasm of blackened brick. He turned and leaned his bulk against the low mantel. "My government's interest? I think you would really mean my department's interest.

"My government's interest is in dealing with the trade unions, the falling standard of living, and the bloody pound sterling. And inventing new methods of putting people on the dole. But my department's interest is in Soviet intentions. In Europe, in North America. Wherever. The fact that Petrov, who we must presume is a Soviet agent, has in some manner struck a bargain with a U.S. senator concerns us. Particularly now that your good Senator Welsh is standing in line for a go at the presidency. On what seems to be a ticket of unilateral disarmament. Very destabilizing."

Kent raised his eyebrows. "Why destabilizing?"

Campbell grunted, shaking his head. "Kent, you of all people know the answer. The nuclear balance of power has worked for thirty years plus. Not the best way to maintain peace, but workable. But once that balance is altered significantly, we feel that the Soviets would exploit any major weakness. It has been argued that were the United States and Western Europe disarmed, the Soviets would have no reason to attack. Historically, the Kremlin has proved this concept to be inaccurate.''

Loss leaned forward in his chair, mildly irritated. ''I don't know, Ian. All three of us were associated with the military for years. We see things—events and national policies—in a different perspective than most people. Too often in recent years, I think we've been wrong. The Russians have shown restraint in the Middle East, in Indo-China. It just could be that with the threat of NATO removed and the U.S. military reduced to home-defense forces, the Russians might turn inward to develop their own standards of living.''

''Good argument,'' Campbell agreed. ''And I've heard it at a thousand dull cocktail parties. But it doesn't wash. Willing to hear me out?''

Loss settled back into the chair, watching the Englishman pace erratically before the dark maw of the fireplace. A moth flickered beneath the desk lamp, senselessly beating its wings against the shade.

Kent lit his pipe and shook the match out. ''Go on, Ian.''

''We tend to equate things,'' Campbell said, ''in terms of what we understand. So we equate the motives and actions of the Russian ruling class in terms of Western thinking. But there *is* a major difference between the two forms of government that we all tend to discount. In the West, the form of national policy is derived, more or less, from the will of the people. Obviously, the people don't always know what is best for them, but it tends to produce governments that are responsive to human desires. And for this reason, there generally is no log-term national policy other than ever increasing the standard of living.

''However, in Russia, there is a national policy that has long-term continuity. Since the death of Stalin, there has been the dominant concept of rule by committee based on the precepts of ultimate world communism. Each of these men who now rule has been programmed by his education and experience to accept this idea as the only workable form of government. They are not responsible to the people, only to themselves and to one central ideal. So the faces and names change, but the ideal goes on. There are sometimes policy shifts within the Russian government that we attempt to analyze in terms of Western thinking, but these policy shifts are really still within the basic framework."

Kent nodded. "I basically agree."

"Let's take a closer look at the construction of 'rule by committee,' " Campbell continued. "In the forties, fifties, and early sixties the Russian government had more individuality. Stalin, Beria, Bulganin, Khrushchev. Each of these individuals was ultimately singled out as ruling by the so-called cult of personality. And ultimately, and in terms of the central ideal of world communism, these rulers were judged to be deviationists. And they fell from grace. Since Brezhnev, we have had a collective group of individuals who have survived all the various purges because they have simply adhered to the central ideal."

"You're saying then that the Central Committee members conduct Russian foreign policy in terms of Marxist idealism," Loss interjected.

"No," Campbell replied. "I'm saying that Russian foreign policy is conducted by a group of men who are afraid to disagree with a central ideal of an expansionistic policy that works. And that policy has been to expand slowly and surely, without direct confrontation. Sometimes there's a hitch and consequently we see the Russians taking two steps forward and one step backwards. But there's a steady net gain. In the meanwhile, the West constructs stop-gap measures to counter the Russians without ever drawing a definite line. And if there ever is a line drawn, it changes with each election of a new U.S. President."

Kent reamed out the dead ashes with a penknife. "Where does it stop?"

"It doesn't," Campbell replied. "Not until the world is under one flag, probably a red one. Do you remember the plaque that was photographed by a UPI stringer in 1974? The one in Stalin's wartime chambers. It read 'He who does not rule is ruled.' Put yourself in their place. As an individual, each man in the Central Committee continues the policy of his predecessor. The policy works. You see the vision of a world united under one flag. No more war. No bickering, lads. Meet your quotas, pay your dues, and enjoy the new era of world socialism. You see Russia as the core of a new and better world order. Divide up the wealth, the food, the industrial production, reserving, of course, a percentage for the Fatherland. Sort of a commission for keeping things on even keel." Campbell laughed. "It's not hard to visualize. England tried it, as did the Romans. And Germany. Very decent concept, really. Very humane. Except that it violates the precepts of political freedom."

"So you're saying that disarmament by the West would be the removal of the last block to Russian world domination," Loss said.

Campbell picked up a silver mug on the mantelpiece and studied the inscription. He smiled and set it back down, carefully, in its place. "No," he said. "Not quite. Because disarmament is a relative word. The United States might withdraw gradually from NATO. Reduce its nuclear strike forces. But there would be a residual force left. Interceptors, some missiles. Perhaps home-defense forces. Still a force to be dealt with. But the important thing is that the United States would no longer be able to inflict massive punitive damage on the Russians as a counter threat to a Russian first strike."

"Why would the Russians even consider a preemptive war against us if we were stripped of a strike force?" Loss asked. "It would seem that the United States would no longer be a threat."

"Three reasons, Brian," Campbell said. "One.

321

Russia wants your industrial and agricultural output, particularly the latter. Ultimately, food will become the most precious commodity on the face of this planet. The equation is simple—less land to grow foodstuffs on and more mouths to feed. The control of those foodstuffs will ensure long-term control of occupied countries. Withdrawal of food supplies will be a form of discipline.

"Two. If the United States were to retain its own freedom, it might be possible to rearm. The Russians would find it mandatory to eliminate the potential threat. Permanently.

"And three. If the Russian Presidium has a vision of the world under one flag, they don't want another flag getting in the way. Constant comparison of consumer goods, standards of living, free expression, all that sort of thing is very hard on the morale of the working classes.

"No, Brian, don't delude yourself. If the probability for success is high enough, the Russians will go for an all-out first strike. The trophy for winning is an entire world under Soviet rule. And unilateral disarmament by the United States, even to a moderate degree, reduces the risk to the Soviets to an acceptable level."

"You're leading the whole thing back to Welsh, aren't you?" Loss asked.

Campbell smiled. "Yes. Full marks. As we see it, the Russians have picked Welsh as the political key to American disarmament. The Soviets have to be supporting him in these political coups with Cuba and Panama. But even that isn't enough. His chances for the presidency are still very slim indeed. There's still a missing part to the puzzle. Something that will catapult Welsh into the White House by a landslide. We think it must be the Hood-*Hussar* link—an event that Welsh, and Welsh only, will be able to capitalize on. The Man of the Hour syndrome."

"You really believe this?" Loss asked, frowning.

Campbell picked up the bottle of cognac and refilled

322

his glass. He raised the glass and drank it down, then wiped his lips with the stained handkerchief. "Believe it? I know it! Forgive me if I sound condescending. It comes from being a cynic. But we who live in the so-called free world actually live a fantasy. The good life. And it seems to us that it will go on forever. So we tend to ignore the facts as they are presented, unless they conform to our thinking. Good God, man! For the first time in the history of man, a single nation has at its disposal the weapons to conquer the world and more important, the philosophical reason to justify that conquest. We don't see it because we choose to ignore the disagreeable." Campbell paused. "Sorry. I'm getting argumentative. Always get this way with a few tots."

Kent cleared his throat, as if to speak. He refilled his pipe and lit it, puffing deeply to draw the fire down into the bowl. "No, Ian," he said. "You're right, of course. We all stick our heads in the sand. It's all too easy. We can't get used to the continuing fight. No enthusiasm, I expect. Hard concept to sell in a democracy. Ideals and things." He puffed on the pipe but the fire was dead.

Unconsciously, Loss traced the scar on his forehead with his fingertip. "Where does that leave us?"

Campbell jammed his hands in his coat pockets. "Absolutely nowhere. We have the names Hood and *Hussar*. And their probable location."

"Why not ring in the CIA and the RCMP," Kent said.

"Too soon," Campbell replied. "And perhaps too dangerous. Either organization might be penetrated. Expose our hand to the wrong people and we might end up getting it cut off." He turned and looked out the window, across the fields. "No, not yet. I can field adequate men. Run down all the bloody Hoods and *Hussars*. But it's Loss I really need." He turned on his heel and faced Brian squarely. "Think of it. All the connections severed—Heiss, Stroud, Petrov, his

323

woman. And the Russians must assume that you're dead. And what happens if you surface, poking around, asking questions?''

"I'm dead meat.''

"Ultimately," Campbell replied without irony. "But the Russians are meticulous. They would first want to find out how much you knew, who your contacts were, and how you tracked down the Hood-*Hussar* connection. And *then, only then*, would they eliminate you. The theory is that we keep you under round-the-clock surveillance. If any attempt to contact you is made, we intercept it, attempt to track it to its source." He turned to Kent. "Nothing nice or legal. No attempt to obey conventions. We would find out any Russian intentions if it were physically possible. Chemically possible, I perhaps should say. We feel it's that important."

"And if I don't choose to play your way?" Loss asked softly.

Campbell pondered the question for a long time, walking back and forth before the gallery of photos. "I suppose that I could inform the Mounties. Hope that you get a fair trial. I would testify on your behalf, of course. But I think that you, more than I, want to resolve this thing. Or do you want to be a refugee for your entire life? Cowering in one place? I would think not." He sat down heavily in a Morris chair. "Remember that my head's on the chopping block for this one. My department chief's head as well. If we have British agents caught in the States on this operation, it will be the least of our offenses against the Crown or your Constitution."

"Then you're saying that I'm it."

Campbell refilled his glass and then walked to the window, looking out into the dusk. "Yes," he answered. "I suppose that you're it."

Chapter 23

David Fox leaned against the rigging of the *Hussar* and watched the gulls sweep the shore of Booker Lagoon in the last hints of twilight. The yacht lay at anchor close to the eastern edge of the shore in ten fathoms; bluffs of rock towered above them spotted with small stands of cedar. The anchorage was nearly still, the wind dying with the sun. The sounds of deer crashing through the brush carried clearly in the damp evening air. Fox sighed with some contentment and sipped at the coffee cup filled with rum.

In the seven weeks of charter, the *Hussar* had wandered through the San Juan Islands, up through the Strait of Georgia and into the far northern reaches of Queen Charlotte Strait. To the east of them lay the still-snow-capped mountains of British Columbia, and to the west across the Strait the hazy land mass of Vancouver Island.

The days had been a mixture of fog and sunshine, rain, and the startling blue of late summer in the high latitudes.

Fox snorted, laughing at himself. The trip had been nearly perfect. Most of the equipment was working well, and there had been ample time to keep the ship well maintained. The charter party itself was the easiest aspect of the trip, consisting of only two men, both of whom were undemanding and agreeable company. Both were of muddy U.K. citizenship. Amed had said that he was born in Lebanon to an English father and an Egyptian mother. It looked as if the mother had the more predominant genes. The other, called Trig for some forgotten boyhood reason, was the product of a white Jamaican planter family.

Both had used the charter, which had been a gift from Amed's father, as a learning experience. Most of their days were ashore, photographing Indian ruins and botanical specimens. But the experience extended to life aboard the yacht. They had adapted to the *Hussar*'s demands with alacrity, immersing themselves in shipboard routine with a will. Fox had taught them the sequences of getting underway and making sail. Amed had proved to be an exceptional helmsman, both under sail and power. Trig had learned the layout of the engine room and now insisted that he take care of the daily maintenance chores on the diesels and generator. They enjoyed it, they said, and Fox offered to let them run the ship as they cared.

Now, the *Hussar* lay in a lagoon at the southern reaches of Broughton Island, with only the Gulf of Alaska before them to the north. Fox regretted that they would shortly turn south.

Myra emerged from the forecastle hatch, pulling on an oiled wool sweater.

"A good day, wasn't it?" she said easily, slipping an arm around his waist.

"I've seen worse," he laughed. "There, you see? Deer. About five of them just beyond that cluster of rocks."

She couldn't see them in the dim light without her glasses, but she nodded happily. "Davy, you know, we could try it."

"Try what?" he said, shifting his position against the shrouds.

"The Caribbean. With the money from this charter and the other one in late September, we would have enough to get down to charter off Mexico and even on the Atlantic side." She turned back to him, looking into his face, which was tanned and had sun wrinkles in the corners of his eyes. He was thinner now and more muscled. "David. We've got to give it a try. If we stay up here through another winter, we'll rot."

He nodded and then sipped at the rum. "Yes, I've thought about the same thing. We know the *Hussar* better now. And Jane looks like she might make a first-rate cook. If I can pick up a good deckhand-engineer around Vancouver, it would lighten the load a lot. Yes," he squeezed her shoulder, "let's think about it some more, and when this charter is finished, we'll begin to make some definite plans." He turned and started aft toward the cockpit. "Come on. Let me light the cockpit lamp so they'll be able to find us."

She followed him aft into the cushioned cockpit, and he lit the oil lamp. The orange-yellow glow reflected from the polished brass fittings, and the warmth and smell of food cooking drifted up from the galley. She snuggled against him in the coolness of the evening, and they both listened as a loon swept across the water, the sound of the bird's cry ringing back from the cliffs.

"You know, Davy, it really has been perfect these last seven weeks. Trig and Amed are about as easy to please as a couple of kids. And he's so polite, Amed, I mean. They make up their bunks in the morning. It couldn't be better. I almost feel guilty taking their money."

"Don't," he laughed, pleased that it was going so well. "Amed's father is loaded. Oil broker of some sort. Works for the Arabs."

"And Trig. Where does he get the money?"

"He doesn't," Fox said, polishing off the mug of rum. "This is all gratis of Amed's father. Trig is just a former school chum. Now they both work in Europe for the French, so says Amed. Underwater acoustics, magnetohydrodynamics, all very esoteric deep sea stuff. Said that they hoped that we could get down

327

into the Hood Canal to see the first Trident sub. I don't see why not. I'd sort of like to myself."

"Incidentally, what time are they coming back? I've got to tell Jane something about the serving time."

He looked at the luminous dial of his watch and scowled in the half-light. "Should be within twenty minutes. Less, maybe. They said that they wanted to look over a Kwakiutl Indian site down past Cullen Point. Just inshore of where that big trawler anchored this afternoon. Amed said that they might drop by the trawler to see whether they could buy some pipe tobacco." He stood up and stretched. "What's on for dinner tonight?"

"Salmon. Some corn. Butter clams for an appetizer. How does that sound?"

"Tremendous, as usual." He paused in the top of the companionway. "Jane's been quite a help to you. Have you settled on any wages for her?"

Myra hunched her shoulders. "Nope. She says that she asked for the job just to get the experience. Wants to eventually buy a boat with her boyfriend and cruise the Pacific. I wouldn't worry about it. She'll probably get a good tip at any rate. But you're right; she's been a tremendous help. I'm spoiled." She handed her husband an empty glass. "If you're going down, how about fixing me a Beefeater and tonic."

He raised his hands in salute and backed down the companionway. He passed through the salon, past the gimballed table already laid out with good china and silver, past the staterooms and into the galley.

She looked up from the saucepan and smiled. Beads of perspiration had formed on her bare shoulders and in the cleft between her breasts. She hitched up the apron and wiped her hands on a towel. She smiled again, a more genuine grin. "Are they back yet?"

Fox unconsciously pulled in his stomach and stood straighter. She was attractive with her long blond hair

328

now roped up in a knot. French bun was the word, striking a chord in his memory. He laughed good-naturedly, thinking of French buns. "I'm sorry," he said, laughing harder. "It just got to me." He splashed some Mount Gay into his mug and rummaged in the locker for the Beefeater.

Holly spilled the remainder of mushrooms into the saucepan and stirred, her face set in a noncommittal smile. The whole thing was a waste, she thought, watching the slabs of butter melt. Loss was two hundred miles to the south, probing the various Hood, *Hussar* combinations that Campbell had outlined. This one, she thought, was a dead end. The Foxes were normal enough, and the two men in the charter party were shy, almost too polite. In a few more days, the yacht would start south again. She was anxious for the trip to end.

"No, Jane," Fox said, still laughing, a slightly drunken vision washing against the edges of his mind, "they're not back yet. Pretty soon." He saw the look on her face and thought he understood. "I'm sorry, Janey. I'm not laughing at you. Just that Myra and I are—well, we're having a great time. I guess the first in years." He watched her face and seeing no comprehension, changed the subject. "Lucky thing Myra met you. You've been a tremendous help. Great food. We have to pay you for the trip."

"No," she shook her head, her blond hair bobbing. "It was all my doing. I found out from your broker that you had a charter and there were only the two of you. I tracked Myra down and asked for the job. No pay, just experience. I'm happy if you are."

"Myra said you had a friend," he said, standing straighter, trying to focus his eyes.

"He's down in Seattle." She added lemon juice to the sauce, avoiding his look.

There was silence for a minute; the only sounds

were the gas stove hissing and small waves working against the hull. He nodded and left.

They came back a quarter of an hour later, rowing across the lagoon, one of them singing a tuneless song, the sound of their occasional laughter following the splash of a missed oar stroke. Fox turned on the spreader lights and stood near the boarding gate, ready to help them aboard.

A clinker-built rowboat emerged out of the darkness with three men, two rowing in tandem and the third in the stern sheets. The *Hussar*'s inflatable dinghy trailed astern of the rowboat, bobbing along like a black rubber duck. Fox quickly dropped fenders over the cap rail and leaned over to receive the painter. Amed turned his face upwards, smiling at Fox. "Yes, Captain Fox. Good evening. I am sorry that we are late." His teeth were brilliant in the light, contrasted by his deeply tanned skin and thick black hair. "We have brought a friend. For only a moment."

The rowboat came alongside, squashing the fenders slightly. There was a confusion of oars being removed from oarlocks and stowed, a laugh, and men crawling up the boarding ladder. Amed came aboard first, extending his hand as he always did, shaking Fox's. Just a quick cool touch. His handsome Arabian features were accentuated by high cheekbones, deeply set brown eyes, and powerful build. Fox could imagine him in a burnoose, bowing, hands pressed together.

Trig next: small, corpulent, and balding, with thin wisps of hair combed straight across his sunburned scalp, glasses forever sliding down the bridge of his nose. He looked up at Fox, smiling hesitantly. "Evening. Really sorry we're late. Long row back," he said, unnecessarily pointing across the black water to the west. Then more formally, "And this is Mr. Krissholm. From the trawler."

330

Krissholm swung up through the boarding gate and offered his hand. He was tall and thin, without suggestion of frailness. There were several days of blond stubble on his face. His eyes were blue ice. "I'm pleased to meet you, Captain Fox," he said formally. They shook hands and Fox gently herded them aft to the cockpit, automatically offering a drink. Myra introduced herself and went below with drink orders, agitated that supper would be delayed.

David Fox offered each of them cigarettes. Only Krissholm accepted. Fox was vaguely uneasy for no reason that he could specify. He lit Krissholm's, then his own.

"You're from the trawler, then?"

Krissholm nodded. "Yes. *The Franklin Gaines III*. Rather a long name for an old fishboat. I'm just with them for a short while. Really with B.C. Fisheries."

Fox rubbed the side of his nose, unconsciously irritated. He tapped the ashes into a cockpit drain. "You mean, like our Fish and Game people?"

Krissholm nodded. "Yes. About the same. I really invited myself over to see your vessel. And to get away from the smell of fish for a while." He laughed.

Fox couldn't detect the smell of fish, but it wasn't important. "So how is the fishing?" he said for lack of anything else to say.

"Not too good, I think. But I really work on the measurement of mercury poisoning. A lot of that up here with our pulp mills. Worse than in the States, I suppose. Keeps me busy at any rate." He looked around the cockpit, noting the radar scope, fathometer, and engine controls. "Very well equipped."

Fox nodded. "Thanks." Myra appeared in the companionway with a tray of drinks. She put a dish of crackers and a plate of cheese on the cockpit table and disappeared below. She's pissed, Fox thought.

"Can you stay for supper?" Fox said, half-heartedly.

"No, thank you. I really came over just to meet you and ask you a favor."

Amed brushed his hair back and leaned forward on his elbows. "Mr. Krissholm has asked *us* a favor, and I suggested that he speak to you."

"Yes, Captain Fox," Krissholm interjected. "I hope that it won't be too much to ask, but I have a box of Nansen bottles that our department has been collecting for the University of Washington's Oceanographic Department. Normally, we would ship these down by the next ferry going south from Alert Bay. But that's ten days from now. It would help greatly to get them down to Port Townsend or Anacortes directly. Amed here has offered to have them forwarded by United Parcel. If you can just carry them as deck cargo . . ." Krissholm smiled deprecatingly, tapping the cigarette ash into his cupped palm.

"Where is the box and how much does it weigh?" Fox said, relieved at the lessened chance of one more for dinner. He wanted to make it an early night.

"About one hundred and fifty pounds. And it's in my boat. Boxed and labeled. If you can carry it on the foredeck, it shouldn't present much of a problem. I brought two bottles of good Canadian whiskey as well. Sort of a bribe." He laughed.

Fox sighed and then smiled. "Yes. That's fine. We'll take care of it. Amed, you know where it goes?"

Amed nodded. "Yes. It already has the labels for shipping. It is no problem for us."

Expansive now, a drink in his hand, Fox smiled. "I think it should be OK. Let's get it aboard now, and then we can have another drink." He finished his, not noticing the others had hardly touched theirs.

They went forward, Krissholm and Amed crawling down the boarding ladder into the rowboat. They passed up a pine box, insisting that Trig help Fox. The box measured less than three-feet square, was well constructed, and padlocked. Four of them moved it along the teak deck by the rope handles and then secured it with a line that Krissholm provided just aft of the forecastle hatch to ringbolts in the deck.

Krissholm stood up and dusted his hands. "I think that should hold it." He grasped Fox's hand and shook it. "We like to cooperate with the Americans as much as possible. Thanks again, Captain Fox. I mean it. You've been a great help to us."

Fox nodded. "It's my pleasure. Really, would you like to stay for dinner?" The alcohol was heavy on his tongue.

Krissholm squeezed Fox's arm and then walked to the rail. "No. This is quite enough. Many thanks." He shook hands again with Trig, Amed, and Fox. Myra came forward after switching on the spreader lights. He shook her hand formally and stood, momentarily, looking aloft at the rigging and mainmast. "It's a fine yacht you have," he said and then clambered down the boarding ladder. They watched him row off into the blackness.

Holly Stone watched from the starboard galley porthole. Watched the man lift his hand in farewell as he rowed off into the blackness. She returned to the galley and stirred the burning carrots, turning off the gas. Petrov, she thought, stunned.

Loss paused in the rain outside the arcade, scanning the tarnished brass nameplates that lined the stone façade. He found the one he wanted, wrinkled the corner of his mouth, and entered the shabby foyer. The light in the tiled hallway beyond was dim and he paused, allowing his eyes to adjust to the light. In the reflection of a tarnished mirror, he examined his face. His hair, now long, was artfully cut, falling over his forehead to conceal much of the scar. His beard was full but equally well trimmed. He bared his teeth, wishing he had brushed them. They tasted sour and gritty.

Near the elevator, he found the directory and under "W" a single entry: Western Pacific Shipping, oom 212. The "R" was missing.

The single elevator registered that it was still poised at floor seven. Loss took the staircase at the back of the musty hallway. At the first landing, he paused to look out through the mottled window and rusted grill, down on the wet Seattle street. The traffic was getting heavier in the late August afternoon, parking lights coming on in the misty rain. A woman scurried across the street, umbrella held like a shield against the oncoming traffic. Loss smiled. I know how you feel, he said, lips barely moving.

The offices of Western Pacific Shipping consisted of one door of pebbled glass in an otherwise deserted hallway. Loss could hear the sound of a lone typewriter, pecking out the truth. He opened the door and entered.

She stopped typing and looked up at him expectantly. "Yes?"

"I'm trying to get some freight schedules on the shipment of some crates from Manila. About three tons. General furniture."

She tapped a type eraser against her teeth, looking at him more closely. Her hair fell straight and black, her eyes almond. Quite beautiful, thought Loss.

"We have two schedules. One on the *Lancer* and one on the *Hussar*. Which ship and who is the consignee?" She started to rummage in a drawer, swore under her breath, and retreated to a filing cabinet.

"*Hussar* and consignee is Golden West Imports," he called across the office. Golden West sounded big enough.

She returned with a dog-eared mimeographed sheet. "Hussar, ah, September twenty-eighth Seattle, October fourth Vancouver. And we don't have any loading manifest as yet. Generally don't get it until a couple days after they sail from Manila." She looked at him and grinned.

Loss frowned. "I thought she was due in earlier. Something like about September sixth."

"Boilers. New fire brick or something," she said. A shrug. "Anything else?" She smiled again, displaying several teeth smudged with lipstick.

"I guess not. I'll come in to see the cargo manifest when you get it, which would be about—?"

"About September tenth. We notify all the consignees then. Was it Golden West?" And she made a note that Loss knew would find its way to the trash basket once he cleared the office.

"Correct."

"See ya," and she turned to her ancient IBM.

He left the arcade, walking back down the rain-slick street toward the parking lot. The buildings were grimy turn-of-the-century structures, fronted with mom-and-pop stores, windows barred with grillwork, selling used clothing, dusty stamps, and soggy pizza.

Stopping often in the entranceways, he watched for subtle alterations in the flow of pedestrians. But there were few people on the street; mainly secretaries on errands or the occasional wino. It was not a part of the city that attracted those shopping for pleasure.

In three weeks Loss had not caught even a faint hint of a tail. He had followed Campbell's instructions, keeping visible and yet alert to possible surveillance. But if Petrov had him covered, it was by someone so expert that he was invisible.

Shit, he thought. He felt like a kid on a make-work errand. Campbell must have been wrong. Hailing a cab, he rode the three blocks to the parking lot. As far as he could see, no one followed. On the way back to the motel he stopped for gasoline. As he paid the kid and peeled off ration tickets, Loss noticed an Oldsmobile pulled over to the curb, engine idling. He had seen it before: dark green with a crease in the left rear fender. The driver was a man, bulky in a plaid lumber jacket, and as Loss watched he unfolded a street map and scanned it. Loss got in Kent's old Chrysler and started the engine. Pulling out into the street, he accelerated slowly, watching the rearview mirror, but the Olds didn't move. Loss waited three blocks beyond in the parking lot of a liquor store, but the green Olds didn't appear. Thinking back, he realized that the Olds in his motel's parking lot had probably been black. Or maybe dark maroon. It had been foggy that evening.

After locking the car, Loss popped his head into the motel office. The night manager, his face eroded by heavy drinking, was propped up on a recliner chair, eating a sandwich and watching a game show. A piece of lettuce was attached to the corner of his mouth with mayonnaise and he stared, fascinated, at the tube. He shook his head without taking his eyes from the screen.

"No messages, Mr. Lange. Nothing. Hey, watch this!" He stabbed his finger at the set, his mouth agape. "It's for twelve thousand bucks. Name three baseball players who hit over . . ."

Loss shut the door on him and ducked under the skimpy eaves, edging his way down to the room. The strip of cardboard in the crack of his door was undisturbed and the hair on his briefcase had not been moved. He sighed and sat down heavily on the hard bed in the stale room and looked at his fingernails. It was as if no one cared that he existed. Campbell's plan was a bust.

On impulse, he dialed out direct and placed a call with the Vancouver operator. The phone answered immediately, as if someone was nesting on it.

"Thurston residence."

"Let me talk to Campbell," Loss said.

"I'm sorry. There's no one here by that name." The voice was male and fruity.

"This is Loss. I'm calling Campbell. Stop playing dumb games and put him on."

A long delay, then, "I'll try. I'm putting you on hold." No smile behind the voice this time.

He lit a cigarette, impatiently tapping the ashless tip against a tray. The line clicked twice.

"Mr. Lange?" Campbell's voice was a thick mutter.

"Let's quit playing secret agent, Campbell. There's nothing going on down here. The ship doesn't arrive until September twenty-eight. And I've been down to Port Hood on the Columbia River. Also up and down the Hood Canal. I've done everything except crap on the Russian consulate's front porch. The whole thing has been a big waste of time."

"Where are you calling from?"

"My room. Someone ripped the handset out of the telephone in the parking lot. It doesn't matter. Nobody's following me."

Campbell coughed and cleared his throat, long distance. It sounded like an empty ashcan rolling down an alleyway. "You realize that you were only to call in an emergency and only from an outside booth? If your phone is tapped, we're all blown."

"I'm telling you, Ian. It doesn't matter a damn bit. No one is hanging around. It's as if I didn't exist."

"Not entirely true, Loss. I have two people covering you." Some papers rustled in the background. "I'm told that you had fried clams, salad, and two beers last night. Saw a movie and were in bed by eleven. We've got you under protective surveillance twenty-four hours a day."

"And they haven't seen anything either, have they?" Loss challenged.

"Not yet. We don't expect results overnight."

"Bullshit," Loss exploded. "It's been three weeks now. We're on the wrong track."

"That's my end of the business," Campbell snapped. "You just stick to your schedule." He paused for a second, coughing. "So as you'd know, there's been a bit of a problem up here. Nothing serious. But your lady friend was supposed to get a look at the yacht, find out what the characters were like and find out where they were going."

"And . . . ?" Loss said, quietly, gripping the receiver.

"And instead she somehow got aboard as a cook. Tracked the yacht to a place called Britannia Beach, a little town just north of Vancouver. Met the yacht owner's wife in a supermarket and somehow got hired on the spot."

"Where are they, Campbell? You shouldn't have let her . . ."

"I didn't let her do *anything!* She took it upon herself. As best as we can determine, the yacht is up in the northern reaches of Queen Charlotte Strait. I've got one man on it. He's been keeping track of the yacht's movements by chartered seaplane. Damned expensive."

Loss pulled the Rand-McNally folder from its place on the bedside table, flipping through the pages to British Columbia. He picked up the locations of the small islands of Queen Charlotte Strait between mainland British Columbia and Vancouver Island.

Campbell was saying something. Loss pushed the map folder aside. "Sorry, I was occupied with something."

Campbell cleared his throat. "I was saying that the yacht was anchored at a place called Broughton Island yesterday. Everything looks normal. They seem to be making normal passages, anchoring each night. My man reports that there is no special activity on board."

"What about the charter party. Anything on them?"

"We've checked with the charter broker. Two men in their early thirties. Seems one of them comes from a very wealthy family. The trip is something of a gift from one of their fathers."

"Has Holly called in?"

"Just once, about a week ago. She said they were

338

quite normal and that the owners are an older couple. She thinks it's a dead lead. They'll be back down here in about a week."

Loss leaned back on the pillow, catching the scent of disinfectant. The sheets had a plastic underlay, as if they expected him to wet the bed. "I'm going up to Vancouver," he said finally.

There was a long silence, and then static, as if the connection had been severed. Two clicks. Campbell came on again, hacking directly into the mouthpiece. "Bronchitis—sorry." He cleared his throat. "You're to stay there. She's all right. I'm sure that something is more likely to occur down there. Just give it time and, for God's sake, don't use an open line again. If you must, call from a public phone." There was a pause. Loss heard a voice in the background. Campbell came on again. "One other thing, Brian. Your friend from New York is on TV tonight at seven. A panel show called 'Meet the Media.' Touted as something of a major policy speech, so I understand."

"Where does he stand in the polls?"

Campbell didn't reply immediately, then came back on. "I'm informed that thirty-one percent indicate him as their choice, and it's rising."

"Jesus," Loss swore. "And that in just three months from nothing."

"Exactly," Campbell replied. "Three months from a cold start and he hasn't participated in one single primary election. It's been the Canal and Cuba accords. Something else now, I expect, in his speech tonight."

The line was empty, each waiting for the other to speak.

Loss broke the impasse. "Ian, something's bothering me. Who do you have down here covering me?"

There was a hesitancy in his voice. "Something I don't want to discuss over the phone, Brian. I wanted at least four people, but my department is cooling off

339

on the importance of this. You're correct in the sense that we've had no response from the opposition. But I assure you that both people I have are top . . ."

"Is either one of them a heavy-set man—mid-forties—in an Oldsmobile?"

Campbell sucked in his breath. "Loss—call me on an outside line." The connection broke, followed by a dial tone.

Loss chambered a shell in the Luger ano tucked the automatic in his belt. Pulling on a raincoat, he left the room and walked quickly through the parking lot and down two blocks, then paused in a used car lot, watching the motel entrance. Nothing. He waited, shivering, the rain seeping down around his collar. Traffic was heavy now, cars moving almost bumper to bumper in the evening rush hour. Loss waited a while longer, unsure, and then turned down a side street, through a residential area and then doubled back, one block farther north on the main artery. Still nothing.

He found a phone in a bar and grill called the Oyster Shack.

Campbell replied almost immediately, accepting the charges. "Where are you?"

"A bar. I checked. No one followed."

Campbell exhaled heavily. "I have two people on you—a woman in her thirties. She's booked into a room two doors down from yours. Keeps tabs on your room during the daytime and evenings. The other's a man. Early fifties, thin. He drives a van marked Associated Electronics Repair."

"I haven't noticed either. The guy I'm talking about—I'm not sure. I saw him today and I think once before in the motel parking lot. He's driving a dark green Oldsmobile coupe with a sunroof. Washington plates."

"Is that all you can remember?"

Loss looked out the window at the passing traffic. The rain was pelting down almost vertically, creating showers of steel nails in the headlights of passing cars. "I'm sorry," he finally said. "That's all I noticed. Ah, he was wearing a plaid lumber jacket." It sounded pathetically amateurish in retrospect.

"I'll check," Campbell said. "Call me back in an hour. This may be what we're looking for." He hung up.

Loss had an order of fish sticks and fries, washed down with beer. He sat at the far end of the darkened barroom, watching the door. Two men came in and then left after quickly downing shot glasses of bourbon. Other than that, Loss had the place to himself. The bartender finally drifted down to his end of the bar, polishing a glass. Loss noticed that an electric clock next to the cash register indicated 7:03.

"Anything else?" The bartender removed the plate and mopped the bar with a greasy rag.

"Another glass of draft. That thing work?" Loss nodded toward a TV set slung in chains over the Coors sign. Like vines, silver tinsel was wound around the chains and two broken Christmas tree ornaments dangled from the bottom of the set.

The man flicked the set on. "Anything special? 'Gettin' It On' is pretty good." He rummaged through the channels.

" 'Meet the Media,' " Loss said. "This guy Welsh is interesting."

"Fuckin' creep if you ask me." The bartender switched to channel seven and walked away, talking to himself. Loss decided to double his tip.

He had just caught the opening minutes of the show. Welsh sat there in a dove-gray suit, face carefully made up so that no lines showed. He was composed: two-dimensional but impressive. The moderator, Louis Rickter of UPI, introduced the panel: Harris from Associated Press, McKennin from the *Manchester Guardian,* and DeRouche of Reuters. The screen dissolved into a commercial on life insurance and Loss

341

sipped his beer. The bartender was at the other end, chatting up a middle-aged woman with a beehive hairdo. Her giggle carried the length of the room.

The screen showed an insurance agent in shining armor, impaling a dragon marked *Old Age Insecurity* with a lance, and the tube dissolved to the studio. The camera panned to the moderator.

RICKTER: It gives me great pleasure to present the United States senator from New York who has so recently caused far-reaching innovations in American foreign policy. Senator Welsh, welcome to "Meet the Media."

WELSH: Thank you, Lou. It's entirely my pleasure.

RICKTER: First of all, Senator, there has been a great deal of speculation in the media concerning whether you are a candidate for your party's nomination next month. Would you care to comment on this?

WELSH (lowering his eyes, slightly embarrassed but with a smile): As you know, I didn't participate in any of the primaries. I understand that there's been some unofficial grassroots support for my candidacy, which I am most honored by. But to answer your question, I'm not a candidate at this time. I do plan to go to the convention as (a very broad smile) an observer.

General laughter on the panel. Jesus, Loss thought, he's too precious for words. The gestures, the phrasing. Like it was a script.

RICKTER: Yes, we understand, Senator. But our viewers are interested to know whether you would actually accept your party's nomination if it were tendered? The polls show you running a close second to the president in popularity.

WELSH: I believe that I would have to evaluate

342

that situation if and when it occurred. I do feel strongly about contributing to the platform committee on foreign affairs. I've had (modest smile) some experience in that area within the past few months. Of course, I'll support whomever our party puts forward in nomination.

HARRIS: Along that same line of thought, Senator, it's been reported from inside sources close to the president that your name is being considered as a possible replacement running mate for the vice-presidential ticket. What are your feelings about accepting such an offer?

WELSH: I don't believe that I could accept the nomination for the vice-presidency. In all fairness, I don't believe that my viewpoint is well-enough aligned with the present Administration to assist the party in that manner. And in addition, there are still pressing obligations I must consider in terms of my constituency and my seat in the Senate. But as I've already indicated, this sort of discussion is speculative and I would have to evaluate each circumstance if and when it arose.

DEROUCHE (removing his glasses and giving the camera a nice profile): Mr. Senator, those of us in Europe have witnessed, within the last three months, some hope for a new understanding in international affairs—a resurgence, if you will, of hope that the United States is seeking, admittedly through your initiatives, meaningful accommodations with the world. Your negotiations with the People's Republic of Panama and, more recently, with the People's Democratic Republic of Cuba, have awakened belief that progress can be made through concessions rather than confrontation. Would you care to comment on this?

WELSH: Concessions? Some of my conservative colleagues on the floor of the Senate have used that term. (He smiled, coolly) I think a better word is "accommodations." It has always been my belief that the concept of "dealing from strength" as the present Administration likes to term its heavy-handed policy, is a debased form of power politics. To put it another way, it essentially can be equated as to how much the Administration can shove down some other country's throat.

Eyebrows of the panelists raised. Welsh was throwing down an obvious challenge to the leadership of his own party. Loss watched, fascinated.

WELSH (continuing): I believe that in this constantly evolving relationship of nations, those that have the power are in the best position to share that power—to make accommodations where need be. (Arching his fingertips together) I feel that there can be a new spirit in American foreign policy, a new era of understanding. Any position of national leadership that I may ever attain (he said this very carefully, emphasizing each word) will carry with it my pledge to work for a lasting world peace. We are a strong nation, a generous nation, and it is we who can take the first steps toward such a peace.

HARRIS: Yes, Senator, but this sort of idea has been put forth before. In all fairness to your most recent accomplishments, how do you account for your startling degree of success?

WELSH: I think that we all too easily forget that foreign powers are still groups of men. And all men respond to an open-handed approach, particularly when the stronger of the two parties is unilaterally willing to make accommodations. My speeches on the floor of the Senate have tried to suggest preconditions which would establish an atmosphere of trust and goodwill in our foreign dealings. With my suggestion that the United

States withdraw its territorial claims on both Panama and Cuba, the leadership of those two countries responded in kind with gestures of peace and friendship. We now can see the remarkable fruits which generosity bears.

Loss almost gagged. He watched Welsh's face fade as the station broke for a commercial. Welsh's new poise, for a person who knew him intimately, was incredible. Gone were the hesitations of speech, the odd ducking movement of his head when he was asked a question. The words came smoothly, the voice carefully modulated. And yet he hadn't said a goddamn thing. It sounded grand unless you listened carefully.

The sixty-second commercial terminated, showing an elderly couple tap-dancing along a rainbow plastered with insurance policies. The camera framed McKennin and zoomed in.

McKennin: Senator Welsh. You disclosed in a press conference yesterday morning that you felt that there were, and I quote you, "Major new avenues of peace to be explored." Can you expand on this statement and tell our viewers what new initiatives you have in mind?

Welsh (stroking the bridge of his nose, as if in consideration of what he was about to say): What I suggest concerns the Strategic Arms Limitations Talks, specifically the forthcoming SALT III. We are entering the fourth decade of a cold war with the Soviet Union. In that period of time, both our countries have built up massive and dangerous arsenals of nuclear weapons. But during this entire time, not once has either country seriously considered going to war with the other. Both countries are now wealthy, powerful, and uncontested, yet both of us are locked into a useless series of meetings, debating the quotas of yet even more terrifying weapons that we may each add to our armories.

I feel, and I know every sensible American will agree, that we must do something to reduce and ultimately eliminate this deadly threat. As I have already pointed out, I feel that we are strong enough to initiate the first steps.

McKENNIN: Are you saying, Senator Welsh, that we should begin to unilaterally disarm?

WELSH: I think that we must give immediate and serious consideration to the idea. Not only to lessen tensions but also to avoid the accidental holocaust which we, ourselves, invite. There are no less than six thousand nuclear warheads stored in this country and at least half as many in Europe. One single accident in handling, a defective mechanism, could trigger a catastropic accident involving millions of people. Many of these weapons storage facilities are near major cities. I sometimes think that we have more to fear from our own folly than we do from the Soviets.

RICKTER: You're saying then that the Administration should shelve the SALT III talks and proceed unilaterally in disarming?

WELSH (laughing): I'm afraid you're putting words in my mouth. No, that's a determination which can only be made by the Administration. There may be reasons why the president feels he must pursue SALT III. But remember, these negotiations are basically conducted by the military and the Department of Defense. It is against their basic philosophy to eliminate one single rifle from our inventory. And there are powerful lobbies in Washington which represent the defense industry.

I feel that if we, as a people, take the initiative in starting disarmament, bypassing so-called military considerations, we may find that the Soviets will respond in kind. And a major reduction in arms on our part would prove our good faith.

He's done it, Loss thought; Welsh was coming out of the closet for unilateral disarmament. There was a bombardment of questions from the interviewers and Loss reached up and turned the volume down, catching only scattered words. Welsh was expanding his view and Loss caught the words "eliminate NATO." The West Germans will love that, he thought. Shades of Munich in reverse. There was no doubt in Loss's mind now that the Russians would soon issue a statement praising Welsh and hinting at the possibility of similar reductions in armaments.

He watched Welsh manipulate the panel for another five minutes. Seasoned, hard veteran newscasters all, they fed Welsh questions that he smoothly fielded, turning the interview into a political statement.

Something in the interview nagged at Loss. Something that Welsh had said or implied. Unilateral disarmament wasn't that new. He had talked in that vein over five months ago. It sounded good in theory but the hard core of the voting public distrusted Russian intentions. Welsh wouldn't be able to muster enough votes by milking that particular philosophy.

Something else. Accidental detonation of one of our own nuclear weapons? The thought solidified. If Welsh was warning of this danger and it actually happened—happened before the convention, then Welsh would be stampeded into the nomination by an electorate demanding disarmament.

The idea became more and more concrete in Loss's mind. Petrov, somehow, would be the cause of the accident, an accident involving the Hood-*Hussar* link of Campbell's computer projections. And to be effective, it would have to take place prior to the convention, which would eliminate the rescheduled freighter. Which left the *Hussar*. Loss felt a tremor of panic. Ten, twelve days left at the most, probably less.

He dropped a bill on the counter and then called Campbell's number, collect. The line was busy. Screw it, he thought. Regardless what Campbell thought, it

347

had to be the yacht and she was still aboard it. And the yacht was still up north in Canada. He could leave at dawn and be in Vancouver by nine.

He walked back to the motel, keeping to the back streets and then cutting across a high school baseball field to approach the motel's parking lot from the rear. The cardboard strip was still undisturbed. He let himself in quickly, locking the door and chaining it.

Campbell's number was not busy this time. The operator let it ring ten times but no one answered. He had her redial and it rang again and again without answer.

Something was wrong, perhaps very wrong. He thought of the woman agent that Campbell had mentioned. She might know how to contact Campbell by some other means. Campbell had mentioned that she was "two doors down." But on what side of the passage way and in which direction—toward the street or the rear of the building?

He dialed the front office.

"Yeah?" There was a sound of canned TV laughter in the background.

"This is room seventeen. There's a woman staying a couple of rooms down from me. I lost her telephone number."

The man gave a snort. "I figured," he said.

"What do you mean?"

"Look, Mr. Lange. You're in deep shit. Her husband knows."

"I don't know what the hell you're talking about!"

The desk clerk gave a cynical laugh. "Look, friend. You're talking to a guy who's been tending this office at night for five years. Half the business we get is from people comin' in here to shack up. And a lot of them are wives lookin' for more talent than their husband's got in his pants. This guy came in about half an hour ago. Said he was paying off his wife's bill and checking her out of the room. I saw them leave together in his

348

car about five minutes later. She was all bent over in the right front seat. I bet he belted the hell outta her."

"Was it a dark green Olds? Big beefy guy in a plaid jacket?"

"You got the picture." There was a hestitation and then he added, "One more thing, Mr. Lange . . ."

"What?"

"He told me not to say anything but I figure I oughta warn you. And I don't want cops crawling all over the place."

"Warn me about what?"

"Like I said, I don't want any trouble. But before he left, he asked me when I thought you'd be back. And about ten minutes ago his car pulled up across the street. He's waiting for ya, buddy."

Loss felt a sudden tightening in his chest. "OK," he finally said. "I get the picture, Swanson." He hesitated, thinking. "Look, I'm paid up through the rest of the week. I'll be leaving about five A.M. Use my credit to pay off any telephone charges and keep the rest for yourself."

"Thanks," the man answered. "All part of the service." He laughed. "Just remember in the future that hookers are cheaper in the long run." He hung up.

Call the police? Loss wondered. And what in hell would I charge the guy with. And if he were Petrov's man, what would ensure that he could provide any information on the Petrov operation? Get up into Canada and contact Campbell was the only answer. And get her off that damned boat. The Englishman would have the contacts and resources.

He laid the Luger out on the bed within easy reach and quickly packed his bags. Leaving the bedroom lights on and the drapes closed, Loss moved his bag into the bathroom, shutting the door behind him. The window was small, placed high on the wall above the toilet. Using his Swiss army knife, he unscrewed the cranking mechanism and then gently removed the win-

349

dow, lowering it carefully into the shower stall. He switched off the light and waited for his night vision to adapt.

The window overlooked an unkempt lawn, littered with papers and bordered by a wooden fence. Low clouds reflected lights of downtown Seattle to the south, and the air smelled of wet earth and autumn.

Through the scrubby trees bordering the street Loss could see the occasional car moving over the wet pavement. He watched, carefully, until a vehicle with its high beams on passed, sweeping the cars parked on the opposite side of the street. He couldn't be sure, but one of them was a dark color. The scrawny pines shielded him but also partially obscured his vision.

Taking a deep breath, he tossed his bag out first and then worked his way through the narrow opening and dropped to the ground. Keeping to the side of the building, using the shadows, he worked his way to the front of the motel. Then lowering himself onto the soggy ground, he crawled under the low-hanging branches of the pines closest to the street.

It was the Olds. The darkness prevented him from verifying that there was anyone in it. And then a truck passed. In one brief instant, headlights swept the Olds. A man sat in the driver's seat, slumped low as if he were napping.

He drew the Luger from his waistband and snicked off the safety. He could try it, but then again, what was there to gain?

Swanson, the night clerk, would probably be watching, alert for any hassle. Even if I could take over Plaid Shirt, Loss reasoned, I might find myself in a police lockup on a charge of murder. Plus everything else a computer search with the FBI would turn up. It wouldn't solve anything.

It suddenly occurred to him that his phone had been tapped. Probably just the outside line, unless Swanson was part of it, which he doubted. But his call to Campbell . . . ? That was how they had identified the woman

350

as Campbell's agent. And now they would be expecting him to run, probably planning either to bag him in the hotel room later that night or follow him if he left in Kent's car. As Campbell had suggested, they would probably want him alive to learn what he knew. What followed that was something he didn't want to visualize. He briefly remembered the newspaper accounts of Heiss's and Stroud's deaths, then rejected them. Not really something good to contemplate.

Retracing his route, he scuttled along the side of the building, pausing only long enough to pick up his bag.

The back of the building was in deep shadow, only a few cars parked in the gravel lot. Plaid Jacket won't have a clear view of the lot unless, he thought, I turn on the Chyrsler's headlights.

Then, realizing that the interior light would snap on when he opened the door, Loss raised the hood and, working patiently and by feel, slowly twisted the cable terminal off the battery post. Unlocking the door, he jammed a matchstick into the courtesy light's microswitch in the doorjamb and then replaced the battery terminal. Let there be no light, he thought as he hammered the terminal down. And there was none.

Beyond the driveway, across the street, the Olds remained dormant. Momentarily, Loss caught the glow of a cigarette from the Oldsmobile's interior.

The rain had saturated his hair, leaking in rivulets down his neck. He felt cold, tired beyond reason, and it was just beginning. Lowering the hood, he pressed it closed as gently as he could. The latch clicked into place with the sound of a truck colliding with a brick wall. The sound seemed to echo from the walls of the motel. He froze, watching the Olds, but there was no reaction.

With the Chrysler in neutral, he pushed it into the shadow of the building and then started the engine.

Leaving by the driveway was out. With the headlights off, Loss put the gear selector into low and drove carefully across the vacant field adjacent to the back of the parking lot, bottoming the suspension heavily in weed-choked ditches. Once on the baseball diamond, he took second base, cutting third, and accelerated past home plate.

Weaving through two blocks of back streets, he swung onto Route 99 and headed north toward the Canadian border.

He watched the rearview mirror intently, keeping his speed up, but no headlights tracked him.

Chapter 24

He came to the border at 1:05, slowing the Chrysler under the mercury floodlamps, stopping opposite the booth. A short man with longish gray sideburns accentuating a bony face stooped to his open window. He wore the brown twill and badge of Canadian Customs and his breath smelled of mouthwash.

"Wha' do ya have to declare?" The accent merged with mainstream Canadian but still showed a trace of the highlands.

Loss looked at him in the harsh chrome-yellow light, his beard accentuating his tiredness. "Nothing. Just personal effects. A few packs of cigarettes."

"An' you're from wheer?" Very conversational. His glasses were bifocals, magnifying and dissecting the brown irises of his eyes. He wore a clear plastic mac over the twill.

"Nova Scotia." Loss thought of Kent and the sandy hills spilling down to the sea. "From near Chester, on Mahone Bay."

"Do ya have some identity, Mr. —?"

"Passport, if that's enough. And my name is Lange. Brian Lange." Loss turned and fumbled for the briefcase in the back seat.

A larger man was walking toward him now, dressed in an orange rain slicker, his campaign hat dripping from the rim with sparkling pinpoints of rain, each drop luminous in the cast of the mercury light. He stopped on the passenger side and briskly rapped his knuckles on the glass. Loss leaned over, rolling down the window.

"RCMP." Just a flat statement. Christ, Loss thought, Sergeant Renfrew of the Mounties. He turned on the interior light and saw the officer was in his early twenties, his face unlined, with the shadow of a mustache growing like a sick weed on his upper lip. "Please pull your vehicle over to the inspection booth." He pointed with a gloved hand toward a turnoff, his eyes steady on Loss.

Loss turned back to the Customs inspector. Another officer had joined the transplanted Scot, standing behind him, clipboard in hand. Loss almost giggled with the idiocy of it, caught at the border because of a routine inspection on a dull, wet night when he would just as soon be sitting in a pub, drinking beer with these men.

"Take booth number one, Mr. Lange," the Scotsman said, noting down his license plate number and passing the slip to the man who stood before him.

Loss dropped the shift selector into low and the car drifted forward toward the covered bay. An overhead light snapped on, floodlighting the area. His mind was racing now. The passport would stand up, as would the other identity papers and the credit cards. The Luger, holstered under the front seat, would not. Campbell had warned him of taking it, as had Kent, but he wouldn't part with it. Too old a habit. The decision made, he pounded the pedal to the floor, swerving back into the main lane and streaking for the

353

barrier. He took it at eye level, and it shattered the right windshield into a starry glaze of crystalline pebbles. The Chrysler, like a startled horse from a gate, rushed out of the lights into the blackness. Loss heard the shriek of a police siren and caught the blue flash in his rearview mirror. The old Chrysler would never last three miles in a chase. The road swung gently to the left, blanking out the view behind him. Loss slowed, swung into the left lane and then spun the wheel over to the right, leaping the curb and plowing through bordering shrubs and undergrowth. The bellypan scraped on rock, and the sedan tumbled down a shallow embankment, rolling once as if in slow motion. More glass shattered and his briefcase arced from its place on the back seat into the dashboard, grazing his head in its flight. The car came to rest, making the last roll in microtime, tottering slowly over to fall heavily back on its wheels. He sat there stunned, thinking that all this had happened before in time. The engine was still running and he switched it off.

The shriek of the siren passed; blue-light flashes touched the tops of the firs, and then the sound died into the night.

The rain was slanting into the car's interior through the fractured windshield. Loss leaned against the steering wheel letting the wetness saturate his hair, feeling the trickles run down his collar. His ribs ached. He sat like this for what seemed hours, listening to the sound of the wind and the rain and of time unwinding. Slowly, his head cleared. There was no smell of gasoline, and he lit a cigarette, taking time to think. The Mountie might estimate that the bare two-minutes lead time would be enough for Loss to make the turnoff to the coast toward Langley. Three possible routes. They wouldn't set up roadblocks, but the Chrysler with its Nova Scotia plates would be on an all-points bulletin. And they knew his name, at least the name Lange. It was unlikely that they would discover the car's track through the shoulder tonight. Screw it, he thought, and unbuckled his seat belt and climbed into the back seat, opening the sleeping bag and spreading it over himself. He drifted off into fitful sleep.

He awoke at dawn, the first cracks of light penetrating the cloud bank receding to the east. The sky overhead was clear, the air cool and dry. He climbed to the top of the embankment, slipping occasionally on the wet grass.

The Chrysler had left no marks. What tire tracks there might have been were erased by the rain. The resilient shrubbery looked undisturbed despite the Chrysler's passage.

The car itself was another matter. A black pool of oil spread across the dirt beneath the engine, soaking into the earth. He checked the dipstick and found it dry.

Loss sat on the fender and thought. Running the border would probably be considered serious. Undoubtedly the Customs people would think it was drug-related, and they might call in choppers as soon as it was light to search the fields bordering the highway.

The engine started without difficulty. He drove it into a grove of fir trees a quarter mile farther back from the highway and stacked branches over the top. The Chrysler would be virtually undetectable from the air and only a ground search would be likely to run it up.

Unpacking his shaving gear and using water from the radiator, he shaved off his beard and moustache. Surprisingly enough, the shaving part was easy, but the razor kept clogging with hairs and he had to change blades three times, each time throwing the spent cartridge into the bushes. It would be helpful if they thought him still fully bearded.

His watch showed a little after five. He changed

355

into old corduroy pants and a leather jacket, then consolidated most of his gear into a duffel bag, leaving only a few shirts and the sleeping bag behind.

He tried stripping the plates from the car but the nuts were frozen tight. Thinking about it, he guessed it didn't matter. Engine serial numbers would be checked as well and eventually Kent would have some explaining to do. As a last thought, he wiped the steering wheel and door handles, attempting to remove any fingerprints.

He paused for a minute before leaving, looking at the shattered windshield and dented body. Add running a border station to the tally of charges, he thought, and smiled. And suddenly he realized that he didn't give a good goddamn. Campbell has been dead right in using me as bait, he thought. The edge of Petrov's operation had been exposed by Plaid Jacket's involvement. And if there was an edge there would be a center, with Petrov at the core. Loss realized that he had to contact Campbell as soon as possible.

Breaking into a jog, he ran along the gully and then across a field, intersecting the highway a further half mile to the north. Ten minutes later he caught a ride from a bakery truck headed north.

The two of them sat together in the cab, the driver singing under his breath. The smell of fresh bread was overpowering, yeasty and moist. His stomach rumbled.

"Smells terrific," he said, nodding his head toward the back of the truck.

"Yeah," the driver snorted. "I drive around with a hard-on half the time. Smells like a woman just after you've screwed her." He grinned, turning toward Loss. He was a big, florid-faced man with an easy smile, red hair running down into jaw-length mutton chops. He stuck out a huge hand, matted with red hair. "Name's Corrigan. Michael Corrigan, but they call me Muff. You American?"

"Not likely. From Nova Scotia. I came out here to

keep from freezing my balls off. I'm looking for work."

Corrigan fitted on a pair of sunglasses against the glare. "Thought you might be a Yank, being so close to the border. Can't stand the bastards."

"I know what you mean. They're all over Nova Scotia in the summer with their campers. Complain about the weather and the food and don't spend a dime."

Corrigan nodded. "Same here. Burns my ass, it does. They truck moose and deer outta here in the fall like they was trying to feed all of California. Makes me sick." He glanced sideways at Loss. "You look like you got banged up recently."

"Automobile accident. Nothing serious." Loss dug down in his pants and came up with a bill. "Any chance of buying a couple of doughnuts?"

Corrigan smiled. "Perks," he said. "All I can eat. Reach behind me, in the carton."

There were cinnamon buns, and a thermos stacked in a box, along with styrofoam cups. "It's got milk and sugar. Help yourself and pour me a half cup. Too much of the stuff and the caffeine eats holes in my stomach." Corrigan paused, overtaking a VW. "I didn't get your name."

"Lange. Brian Lange."

"What's your trade?"

Loss hesitated. "Farmer, I guess. Pipefitter. Whatever I can get." He chewed on a bun and washed it down with the tepid coffee. On the opposite side of the road an RCMP cruiser passed, heading south, moving slowly with the traffic toward the border. Loss realized that Corrigan had noticed his reaction.

"You in trouble, Lange?"

Loss shrugged. "Nothing much. Got into a hassle with a guy in Seattle." He guessed quickly at what kind of a story Corrigan would buy. "He played a lousy game of poker. Said I was cheating. We had a punch-up."

"You win?"

"I guess so. I left him with daylight showing between his teeth."

Corrigan laughed. "Good for you, mate. But you better get some suntan on your face where you shaved your beard off." He pulled a long cheroot from his breast pocket and lit it, igniting the wooden match with his thumbnail. "Relax, Lange—I don't give a damn what you've been up to. I tend my own business."

Loss turned toward him. "Thanks." Corrigan grinned back, the skin wrinkling up around his eyes. The irises were smoky gray, hard. Loss guessed he would be good in a fight.

The roadway was still damp from the night's rain and vapor was rising from the pavement as the morning sun washed over it.

"Great day," Corrigan said. He scruffed at his sideburns, scratching as a dog will do, just for pleasure.

"Not half bad," Loss admitted. Just as he was speaking, Corrigan swerved suddenly to the right, the truck swaying dangerously on its suspension. A green Cadillac sped past them and then swung in ahead of the truck, barely missing the left front fender.

Corrigan laid on his horn and cursed the rapidly accelerating car, spitting out a string of curses. A woman looked back through the Cadillac's rear window, smiled sweetly and gave Corrigan the finger. The car had California plates and a luggage carrier lashed to the roof.

"Fuckin' bastards," Corrigan spat. "Think they own us. Take our gas and oil and timber for nothin' and then come up here and run us off the road. Sell us junk made in the U.S. of fuckin' A. with labels on it so you'd think it was made in Canada."

He ranted on, getting it out of his system, puffing heavily on his cigar, reducing the cab's interior to instrument-approach conditions.

Loss leaned back, relaxing, glad that Corrigan had

358

his mind on something else, injecting grunts and "yeahs" to keep the conversation going. The suburbs of Vancouver were starting to materialize from the vacant green fields. Buildings rose on the skyline with mountains backing them to the north. They passed another RCMP patrol car, pulled over to the side, flashers turned off. The Mountie was leaning against his door, watching the vehicles pass. Loss slumped down marginally as they passed, feeling the man's eyes bore through the truck. He sweated, waiting for the shriek of a siren.

". . . and the fuckin' Yank pigboats," Corrigan was saying. "Probably blow Vancouver into eastern Alberta. Stuck the base right on our border. Parliament bitched about it but the goddamn White House jerks said they could care less. So all our weenies in Ottawa tell us voting people that 'what's good for Washington is good for Canada.' Pure fuckin' gall, I say."

Loss sat up, listening to Corrigan. "I didn't catch that."

Corrigan flipped his smoldering butt out the vent window. He rubbed his forearm across his mouth, glaring out at the bright hardness of the August sun. "Yeah. I was saying that the Americans stuck that missile sub base down just south of the border. Bangor, Washington—just thirty miles south of here. A-bomb rockets stacked up all over the place like cordwood. One accident and poof." Corrigan made a fist and then splayed his fingers out in an explosive gesture.

"You mean the navy base at Bremerton?"

"Shit, no! They built a completely new base, just for the new atomic submarines. Carries twenty-four rockets, all of 'em with A-bomb warheads. Base the damn things down in Las Vegas for all I care, but not on the Canadian border." The fact that Las Vegas was five hundred miles from the sea was obviously lost on Corrigan.

Loss felt a shiver in the small of his back. "I never

359

heard about it." Christ, he thought. How could I be so dumb?

Corrigan, with Loss as a captive audience, warmed to the subject. He lit another cigar, offering one to Loss. "Cuban cigars. Damn good, eh? Yeah, like I was saying. They built this secret base down there near Seattle. Plan to do all of the maintenance on the subs right there. The crews live on base and rotate patrols. Every six months each sub is supposed to come back, get stuffed full of ice cream and a fresh crew, and then drive up the Hood Canal and fuck off into the Pacific to God knows where. Right out the Strait of Juan de Fuca on *our* border. If one of them ever collides with a freighter, Vancouver would turn into an ash heap." He tapped the cigar against the vent. "Saw this show on CBC about a month ago. First sub is scheduled to leave about a week from now."

Loss felt his heart hammering. "Where did you say this base is?"

"Bangor. Little town down on the Hood Canal," Corrigan repeated, pulling out into the left lane and overtaking a school bus. The kids waved at them as they edged past. Bright faces, big bread-eaters. Corrigan waved back, grinning with a massive collection of teeth.

"I've been down there," Loss said. "I never heard anything about it. Nothing." The thing had been right under his nose.

"Doesn't surprise me," Corrigan said to the windshield, blaring his horn at a slow driver in front of them. "They keep it quiet. After all those layoffs at the Boeing plant, the politicos don't bitch about anything that provides jobs. So there the base sits, a pile of A-bombs big enough to blow western Canada right into the Pacific." He shifted easily to a monologue on atomic power plants and how they were messing up the weather and then ranted about Canadian Indians who were sucking the government's tit for welfare. Loss stared blankly at the road ahead, thinking.

The truck entered the suburbs, passing the old fair grounds. Stopping at a light, Loss dropped off the truck, pausing in the doorway to thank Corrigan. They gripped hands and Corrigan squeezed, grinning. "Take care, Lange. Stay outta fights and get some sun on your face. We're all working stiffs, eh?" He banged the door closed and drove off, singing.

The small shopping plaza wasn't open yet, but Loss found a British Petroleum station with a phone. He dialed Campbell's number. It answered on the second ring.

"Thurston residence."

"This is Lange. I want to talk with . . ." He hesitated. "Put the old man on." The voice wasn't the one that Loss had talked to yesterday. There was the slightest inflection to the voice, an almost-unnoticeable accent. "You'll have to hold on. He's in a conference. Give me your number and I'll have him call you back."

"I can't wait," Loss answered. "I'm at an outside booth. I'll call again after I get a room."

"Where are you?"

Loss dropped the handset on the hook. He wanted desperately to get off the streets. But he had to call Kent. Punching in a quarter, he dialed the Kents' farm, reversing the charges. Margaret answered. Trans-Canada clicks, the operator's voice spelling out Lange in a bored nasal voice.

"It's me," Loss said, watching the attendant pump gas into a small Morris. The boy kept glancing toward Loss.

"Yes," she answered. "Edwin and I thought you might call. They've been checking about the car. Edwin told them that he sold you the car for your summer vacation. There's no real problem here."

"I had to leave it in a ditch. It's a write-off."

361

"Oh, don't fuss so. It's too old anyway. We've got insurance, and I've been pestering Edwin to get an MG sedan. But he thinks they're too flimsy."

Loss fumed with impatience. "Look," he injected. "You don't understand. I crashed a border station. They're out looking for me."

"Oh, dear." She paused, then said, "Here's Edwin."

"Hi," Loss said, weakly.

"Brian, listen carefully. The local constable called up last night. I told him that you had borrowed the car and that it was all right. Probably that you just panicked at the custom station because you didn't have any ownership papers. I think they believed me." His voice echoed, as if the conversation were being relayed by satellite.

"It's wrecked. I probably left some prints on it."

"I wouldn't worry about it," Kent replied. "This sort of thing probably happens a lot. If they do check, they might only search through Canadian sources for prints. I doubt that they'd go much further. I'll do what I can on this end. I have a few friends that I can lean on."

"Thanks, Kent. Sorry to put you in this position."

"Not to worry, Brian. It's the least I can do. How goes it on your end of things. Anything yet?"

"Yes. I'm in Vancouver now. Someone started to tail me in Seattle. Campbell thinks this might be it. I'm going to see Campbell today, but I'm convinced that it's big. Something really big. I'm going to write to you today, laying it all out, just in case anything happens to me." He paused, glancing toward the service station office. The attendant was talking with an older man in mechanic's overalls. They were both looking at Loss.

"Look, Kent. I'v got to go. Thanks for everything."

"God bless, Brian. Take care of that girl. We've

362

got a place here for you when you come back. Remember that." He hung up.

He found a cheap motel three blocks from the gas station. Looking uneasily at his rough appearance, the woman asked for cash in advance, handed him a bar of soap and a towel and retreated into a living room beyond the office, locking the door.

Loss dialed Campbell's number immediately. This time it took only one ring.

"Thurston's . . ."

"It's me again. Put him on."

"He's still in conference. Give me your number and location. He'll meet you this evening . . ."

Loss felt a sense of uneasiness. "I'll save that until I can talk to him in person."

There was a click on the line. "Where are you—a motel?"

"Something like that. Look, tell Campbell that the guy in the Olds *is* the opposition. I think he got the woman."

"You're screwed up," the voice said. "He was just a replacement. The woman got food poisoning. Now quit playing around and give me your—"

Loss hung up on him. He felt skittish, unsure of anyone or anything. He would wait, settling for nothing less than Campbell.

He lay down on the bed, eyes closed, trying to reconstruct what had happened. What Corrigan had said about the sub base fell into place, the missing piece in the jigsaw. In a way, Welsh's speech confirmed it. And the *Hussar* had to be part of it. He drifted off, exhausted, dreaming in confused sequences, parts of the old nightmare mixed with images of Welsh and Petrov jogging, and a car with people in it, shouting his name as they passed him. In one reoccurring part Loss struggled, trying to swim upward into the air, flailing his arms, unable to overtake a figure that was always at the edge of his vision. He awoke in the late

363

afternoon, his body tangled in the twisted sheets, body saturated with sweat.

He called Campbell's number immediately.

This time another voice. Crisp and efficient, with a midwestern flatlands tang to it. "Thurston . . ."

"I fell asleep by accident. Put him on. He's expecting my call."

"Listen carefully, Loss. Campbell is talking with some people in the government. Very important. He'll meet you at nine tonight." There was a long pause. Loss could hear the man breathing.

"You tell him that *I'll* call. I want to talk to him before anything else happens. *Him personally!* You got that?"

The man sounded irritated. "That's not possible, Loss. Canadian Internal Security has picked up Petrov. Campbell's been interrogating him for five hours now. This thing could last half the nigtt."

"Petrov!" The shock floored him. *"When?"*

"This morning. Picked him up coming off a plane from Japan. They'll want to question you as well, but Campbell says that there's nothing to worry about. No charge will be lodged against you."

"What about the *Hussar?* Where is she?"

"I don't have any idea. That's something you'll have to check out with Campbell. You have a car?"

"No, it's wrecked."

"Okay. You'll have to get a cab. Have the driver take you to the south entrance of the Royal Canadian Mounted Headquarters on Market Street. Ask the desk sergeant for Lieutenant Fletcher of Internal Security. You got all that?"

"You said this guy's name was Fletcher?"

The voice spelled it out. "One other thing, Loss . . ."

"What's that?"

"Campbell said to wear your best bib and tucker. Some lady you know is coming in this evening. Campbell sent one of our people to Vancouver Island to

364

pick her up. They should be back, ah, say by midnight."

"Holly?"

"I think that was the name. Listen—be at the Market Street entrance by nine P.M. And Loss . . ."

"What else?"

"Don't forget to wear clean underwear." The man laughed and hung up.

Loss sat down heavily on the edge of the bed, stunned. In one swift turn of events everything was resolved. He felt suddenly lightheaded, as if the accumulated weight of the last four months had been lifted from his back. But something gnawed at the edge of his euphoria. Distrust, once learned, is a difficult lesson to forget. He picked up the telephone directory and leafed through the pages until he found the heading for Royal Canadian Mounted Police. The fifth sublisting was Internal Security.

He punched in the seven digits, listening to Canadian Bell beep a random cadenza.

"Internal Security, Mrs. Weller speaking."

"I'd like to speak to Lieutenant Fletcher."

"He's not in at the present time. May I ask who's calling?"

"My name is Loss. I'm a friend of Mr. Campbell."

She paused. "Umm, I see. Is there any message?"

He thought. "No—only that I'll be there at nine."

"I'll see that he gets it. Do you have a number where he can reach you?"

Loss tapped his lighter against the bedside table, thinking. "No," he finally answered. "Just see that he gets the message."

Now confident, Loss quickly scribbled a note to the Kents, outlining the events. He thought about the last paragraph for a long time and then wrote:

If the invitation is still open when all of this mess

365

is cleared up, I'd like to bring a bride back with me and visit for a while.

Showering, Loss laughed aloud, recognizing that Campbell's man had been unknowingly perceptive. His clothes were filthy. Taking one hundred dollars of his dwindling reserve of cash, he checked with the motel's manager, the pinch-faced woman, and then walked eight blocks to a shopping center. Saving only the leather jacket, he trashed the corduroy pants and shirt and then spent a leisurely hour eating steak and salad, often glancing at the fake marble wall to admire his reflection. In tapered slacks and a preppy sweater, he looked like a normal human being. Perhaps happier.

He got back to the motel by seven forty-five. Anxious now, he packed his bag and as an afterthought, carefully cleaned the bathroom. As he mopped, he sang about the cowboy from down in Col-o-rado. The leaves would be turning golden in Vermont, he thought. And it would be a fine, cozy winter.

At eight, he looked up taxi service in the yellow pages and chose Veteran's Cab Company just in remembrance of Kitzner. A woman who seemed to be snapping gum promised him that they would have a cab there by eight-thirty.

He brushed his teeth for a third time and then packed his shaving gear. He thought briefly about leaving the Luger behind but decided to take it. If the Mounties didn't like it, Campbell would get him off the hook.

The letter to the Kents was propped up on the dresser, as yet unstamped. He took it and left the room, leaving the door unlocked, and went to the office. The woman came out, in a housecoat and stirring a mug of cocoa.

"I need some stamps and the charges on my telephone calls. I'll be checking out tonight."

He saw, in her expression, the acknowledgment that

366

he was not a member of the working class. The clothes proved it, as did a shave and clean nails. She smiled, a smile she probably reserved for favorite nephews and American Express Card holders.

"Why certainly, Mr. Lange." She flustered around, getting the stamps, pulling the lapels of her housecoat closed. "We enjoyed your stay. Have a pleasant evening."

He dropped a bill on the counter, overtipping her, but feeling marvelous. The mailbox was two blocks and he whistled all the way.

Returning to the motel, he cut across somebody's yard, stumbling over a plastic tricycle. A dog yapped. He picked his way over an empty lot, walking carefully to avoid broken bottles and then squeezed between two cars parked in the motel's graveled lot. Pausing, he looked toward his room in the monotonous ranks of brown-birch paneled doors. A man stood before his door, plaid jacket the color of Madeira wine in the stingy lighting. He was not knocking, just listening, ear pressed against the door's panel. A newspaper hung over his right hand, folds draped over his wrist like a waiter's napkin. Even in the poor light, Loss recognized him.

Plaid Jacket tested the knob, turning it slowly. He paused nervously glancing back and forth along the phalanx of doors.

Loss stooped down, groping along the edge of the asphalt for one of the whitewashed stones that marked off the flower beds. It came loose easily and he was conscious of the noise as it broke away. He stepped out of his loafers, footsteps now muted as he stalked across the gravel. Closer now, he could see the muzzle of a pistol protruding from under the paper over Plaid Jacket's arm.

"Veteran's Cab," Plaid Jacket said softly, raising the weapon to chest level. He tapped the fingertips of his left hand lightly on the door.

Loss raised the stone, the size of a grapefruit and

tombstone-cool in his hand. In two more steps, he
could crush the man's shoulder. His foot crunched on
the gravel.

The man wheeled and fired, two quick shots in
succession, both missing low and to the right. The
muzzle was coming up, the shape of a silencer elon-
gating the barrel. Loss heaved the stone and fell flat
to the gravel. Another round spanged off, glass shattering somewhere, the muffled sound of the weapon
a light *crump*.

The weapon clattered to the ground, the man making a gasping sound. Loss looked up to see the man
reeling away in the dim light, his face a mask of blood,
features flattened and unrecognizable. The pistol lay
there, a Colt Lightweight. Loss scrambled to his feet,
scooping the .38 up in his left hand and then stumbled
into the darkness after the man. Plaid Jacket was
twenty yards ahead of him, running blindly, ricochet-
ing off the edge of the building near the service entrance, then across the decking of the poolside. There
was the clatter of an overturned pool chair and then
a tremendous splash. Loss pulled up short of the tiled
edging and looked down into the water. Wavelets still
lapped over the edge, soaking his socks. The man lay
face down in the pool, arms grasping his head, legs
jerking. A hemorrhage of bubbles burst through the
surface and the body began to sink, spreading a dark
stain in the floodlights.

"Oh, shit," Loss breathed, in a kind of prayer. He
threw the .38 into the pool after the sinking body.

A door was opening behind him, preceded by the
rattle of a safety chain and the snick of a latch. He ran
past the opening door, face down, spitting words at
the startled face.

"Police. Close your goddamn door!" He heard it
slam behind him, shutting off a jumble of voices.

He swept through his room, picking up the bag and
unholstering the Luger. Leaving the lights on with the
TV blaring, he snapped out the entrance light and

slammed the door behind him, running low for the parked cars. Picking up his loafers, he looked back once and then toward the street. There was a light in the office now, the woman moving behind the venetian blind. She had a telephone in her hand. But no one was on the street.

Plaid Jacket hadn't walked here. He headed in the opposite direction from the mailbox, keeping in the shadows of trees, away from the street lights. He found the Olds, one block down. It was unlocked and he climbed into the driver's seat, brushing aside a bag of cookies. The passenger seat was littered with the remains of take-out containers for hamburgers and a crushed milkshake carton. He found the key in two minutes, hidden under the right seat floor mat.

He drove west through the suburbs for fifteen minutes, his ribs pounding and his mind a blank. Munching on the remains of Plaid Jacket's cookies, he watched cars slide past his windshield. Nice middle-class neighborhoods, the occasional bar. A movie theater advertised a rerun of *2001: A Space Odyssey,* a flick, he thought, that he had always wanted to see.

The blur of the last half hour was something he could still reject from his mind. Barber, he remembered, had said in one of his more lucid moments that "adrenaline had anaesthetic properties." There were images now, but he pushed them back. The Olds was smooth, bucket seats almost sensual. Holly would condemn it and love it, in one breath. It even had a sun roof. He opened it and sucked in the night air. But he was feeling just a little sick.

Suddenly and uncontrollably he felt his stomach heave, and he swerved into a parking lot next to an unlighted store. He vomited over the right front seat, unable to roll down the window in time. His hands and legs were shaking now, vibrating, dead, wooden things. Like a vase rattling on a table as the train passed. He gagged again, felt the alien shock of fluid filling his mouth, and unable to contain it, spewed it

369

out on the drive shaft tunnel and gear selector. The stink of vomit filled the car, and he gagged again, this time convulsing on an empty stomach, heaving in spasms, spittle drooling from his lips.

The convulsions subsided and he lay back, his neck cushioned against the headrest, blankly looking at the night sky between the low buildings. Hazy, he thought, but with pinpricks of stars, yellowed by the smog. The air tasted like tin and leaves and milk turned sour.

How far I've come, he thought. I killed a man with a rock. Like you'd kill a rodent, with anything handy. The man's face had been like raw meat, and it would have been better if he had screamed, but he had just made sucking noises. Where pain was so intense that it transcended the ability to shriek. And running, careening off things, like a rabid animal in his last minutes, crazed enough to eat his own intestines. And I ate his cookies, he thought irrationally. All of them.

Somehow Petrov had done it. Without being able to analyze it, he knew that Campbell was finished and that he was alone.

He lay down in his own vomit and cursed and wept and then finally slept. Dew gathered on his windshield, blanking out the darkness and then the light.

He awoke after seven the next morning by the clock on the dashboard, feeling used and sick, his stomach aching. He started the car and used the wipers to clear the windshield. He rejected thinking about last night, only knowing that he had passed the edge. He looked into the rearview mirror, turning it to see his reflection. A normal set of eyes stared back at him. The chin looked all right but pale without its beard and with just a small growth of blue stubble darkening it. His nose was still lopsided. All normal. Really . . . except the eyes.

He chose a McDonald's, changing first into faded blue cotton slacks and a sweat shirt, crouched in front of the fender like a kid in the bushes before swimming in the river. The vomit was still moist and the smell

370

putrid. He pulled the floor mats from the car, folded them over carefully, and stuffed them into a white trash barrel. Ninety-seven dollars worth of new slacks and a preppy shirt and sweater combination followed. But he felt better, part of the working class. With work to do. He smiled briefly, realizing that there was probably no union.

He ordered something called McMuffins, informed by the container that he was the thirty-millionth plus customer to make that selection. But the coffee was pure ambrosia, and he bought another cup, the girl smiling as she took his change. Indian, with subdued features and high cheekbones, hair black as soot, and slender fingers. Corrigan would have been glad to know that his characterization of the Indians was not entirely accurate, he thought. Where was Corrigan now? Pushing his truck up Route 99 singing? Coffee and crullers. Spitting and black Cuban cigars. He would like to have Corrigan with him now.

He slowly finished the coffee, eying the public phone. Rehearsing the conversation, he realized, was a trivial effort. He didn't know what to expect, but he retained the idea in the back of his mind, knowing that he alone was the only one left to stop Petrov.

It rang four times and then there was an electronic thump, followed by ringing, this time with a different tone, more like a PBX. The same voice as yesterday, clean and shaven and awake, answered. "What number are you calling?"

"This is Loss. Put him on." There was a long pause, nearly two minutes. Loss finished the styrofoam cup of coffee, waiting.

A voice, antiseptic, "Loss, this is Klist. Where are you?"

"We've been through all that before. Where's Campbell?"

Petrov sighed into the phone. "That's a very long story."

Loss heard the snap of a lighter and Petrov exhaling.

"You always seem to leave a big mess behind you, Loss. The police are out looking for you."

"No doubt." It sounded like a weak opening move but he tried it. "I think it's time I gave myself up."

"To our famous Lieutenant Fletcher? He's never heard of you or Campbell. He's on a murder up in Prince Rupert. And besides, I doubt that Holly would benefit."

Loss hesitated long enough to let Petrov know he had won. "Where is she?" he finally asked.

"Safe," he replied. "Let's not drag this conversation out. I'll meet you, person to person, no guns. We discuss your silence for the return of the woman. It's that simple and there are no alternatives to discuss. Make up your mind."

"Where?"

There was a long pause as if Petrov was thinking, but the line had a dead quality to it as if a hand were over the mouthpiece. "A good place, Loss. Something very public without being crowded. There's a breakwater with a two-lane road on it leading out from the mainland to a ferry terminal in Tsawwassen. It's over a mile in length. Meet me midway at noon. No weapons and by yourself. I'll be alone. We can chat then."

"Noon," Loss said. "I'll be there."

"One other thing, Loss. You'll undoubtedly check. This phone is now listed as a disconnected number. The wires melted when the house burned down the night before last."

"I'll be there," Loss whispered.

"I thought you might want to," Petrov said and hung up.

He drove west and then south, toward Tsawwassen, following the ferry signs. The day was a late autumn showcase, trees in full flush, sky brilliant. Kids played with garden hoses, shrieking at each other as they ran across well-tended lawns.

Campbell was gone. He had to accept that. Petrov

372

would try to capture or kill. There would not be any Alice in Wonderland deals.

A clock over the entrance of a branch of the Royal Bank of Canada winked 9:21, temperature 27°C. Two and a half hours to save the Western world, he thought without amusement. Lions seven, Christians zero.

He found a library on South Twelfth Street and parked the Olds in back. A young woman with a limp was returning books to the shelves. She sniffed delicately, and showed him the shelf. Walking gamely away, her left ankle dragging, he caught her looking back, face set in a professional mask. He returned the look, smiling weakly.

He found the *Cruising Guide to Puget Sound and British Columbia* and Xeroxed the map showing the passage down from Queen Charlotte Strait to the Hood Canal. Under periodicals he found a current schedule for the British Columbia ferry and, running short of change, pocketed it. Next, he studied both *Small Arms of the World* and *The Luger and Variations*. He Xeroxed two pages from the latter. And for the remaining half hour, Loss sat back in a deeply cushioned leather chair, planning what there was to plan, guessing at what he might have to improvise. At best, he could describe it as open-ended.

Petrov would either attempt to kill him or to abduct him. With at least two other men at the Russian's disposal, Loss realized that his only chance was to take Petrov prisoner and use him as a shield. What he would do later would be played by ear.

He finally stood up and left, smiling. Barber in one of his fractured idioms had summarized Loss's course of action: *Screw unto others as they would screw unto you!*

There was a shopping complex across the street. He bought rubber bands and wrapping twine in an office supply store. From a hardware store, he purchased a coil of clothesline and a penknife, to be left in the car in case he had a chance to tie Petrov up.

373

By eleven he had refueled the Olds, and then went into the men's room at the filling station to change. Locking the door, he stripped and, using a towel and the washroom soap, sponged off the smell of vomit. He pulled his jeans back on and then sat down on the toilet to reread the Xeroxed pages. As he read, he retrieved the Luger from his bag, and following the schematic, disassembled it, removing the grip and trigger mechanism. What remained was only the barrel and receiver mechanism, roughly eight inches in length and less than an inch square.

Experimentally, he cocked the toggle and then depressed the sear mechanism with his fingertip, listening to the firing pin snap into the empty chamber. Satisfied, he cautiously chambered a cartridge and closed the toggle, then bound it to the receiver with ten of the heavy rubber bands. Now, by depressing the sear he would have a single shot zip gun, the rubber bands keeping the toggle from recoiling. He bound the barrel loosely to his forearm with twine, repositioning it twice so that the weapon could be shaken down with a flick of the wrist. He put on a loose-fitting blue shirt with long sleeves, leaving the cuffs down but unbuttoned.

After three or four attempts he found that he could flick the weapon down into his hand in under a second. As he turned to go he grinned at the mirror and the reflected image leered back, looking no more menacing than a tired commuter. It's all I've got, he thought, leaving the tiled room.

The station owner said he couldn't spare a man but that he knew a kid. Within fifteen minutes, a lanky boy pumped into the station on a ten-speed, slewing onto the gravel as he stopped.

Loss took him by the arm and led him under the shade tree bordering the side street. He produced two ten-dollar bills.

"This one," he said, "is for driving me to the Tsawwassen causeway. I want you to drop me about halfway out. Park the Olds on the ferry and leave the keys in the bottom of the ashtray.''

''What's the other ten for?''

''If I don't show up, take it across and leave it on the other side.''

''Is it legal?''

Loss humped his shoulders. ''For you it is.''

The kid smiled. ''Throw in another twenty to cover expenses and my fare back and you got a deal.''

Loss nodded, handing over the money, and it disappeared into the kid's pocket.

They left the station fifteen minutes before twelve. The boy talked endlessly about soccer, rattling off names of teams and players that Loss hadn't even heard of. He listened dimly to the boy, watching the streets and traffic.

The causeway was a thin strip of concrete, two-laned with sidewalks on either side, supported by riprap. Loss had the boy slow down, taking his time. Near the end two men were sitting on wooden crates, fishing. They were both Orientals, less interested in fishing than in arguing. They didn't even turn as Loss passed. Beyond, in the distance, Loss could see a lone figure leaning against the rail.

The kid dropped him off at the midpoint of the causeway a hundred yards farther out from the shore than Petrov.

The Russian had on expensive slacks and a short-sleeved sports shirt. He turned as Loss approached him, sticking out his hand. Loss ignored it.

''Sorry that you feel that way,'' Petrov said. His hair was shorter now, and bleached white. His face was tanned and his eyes, like chips of glass, picked up the blue of the surrounding sea.

''How did you get my address?'' Loss leaned against the railing, his left hand casually clasped over his right forearm. He could feel the sear under his finger through the thin material.

Petrov carefully extracted a cigarette from his shirt

pocket and lit it. "We had your motel in Seattle tapped. Once you called Campbell, we knew his number. It took only two hours to trace it. Campbell, of course, identified where the woman was."

"I mean the motel in Vancouver."

Petrov leaned back against the railing, relaxed. "You were obviously suspicious, Loss. So ask yourself who you would most trust in a meeting and where the safest place might be."

"A cop at a police station."

Petrov nodded. "So rather than trying to dig a telephone number out of you, we let you give it to us."

"You had someone in the cab company?"

Petrov frowned disapprovingly. "You'd never make a spy, Loss. Not devious enough. No, we knew that you would call in sometime between seven-thirty and eight. There are these marvelous little devices called radio receivers. So you can listen to the police and the firemen . . ."

". . . And cab companies."

"Better. Once they gave your address and destination as the RCMP on Market Street, we telephoned them and canceled the cab. And substituted one of our own people."

"Fletcher?"

Petrov shrugged. "Fletcher is Fletcher. Secretaries are universal in two aspects. They always take messages and they never tell where their boss is. Fletcher has been away for four days now. Your message, whatever it was, will be meaningless to him and, I would guess, about two days too old to do you any good."

"Where's Campbell?"

Petrov shook his head and turned to lean on the railing, looking down into the water. "Campbell was an old man. Second rate. He hadn't run a field operation in years. And when he did, he forgot some of the basic rules."

"And you killed him."

Petrov threw the cigarette away, then turned to Loss. "Remember this, Brian. This is a business that one doesn't make mistakes in. You can't write off your losses on a tax form. Campbell regarded this project as pulling a plum out of a pie. Something nice to retire with: perhaps Queen's Honors List. And then found out too late that he was undermanned, under-financed, and without his department's full support. We watched him from the time he returned from England. When he sent two operatives to Seattle we simply followed them and they led us to you."

"What's the point of all this?"

"I think that would be too time consuming, Loss."

"It's the *Hussar,* isn't it? And getting Welsh elected?"

Petrov smiled. "You're playing with yourself, Loss. Heiss knew nothing. And the very fact that you came to Seattle indicates that neither you nor Campbell knew anything. Now Campbell is gone. And all of his merry little men. And you're the last." He shrugged. "In a way, I was hoping you wouldn't come."

"When does the big, black limousine arrive?"

Petrov broke into a grin. "You mean 'the big snatch'? It doesn't. You're going to be shot."

Loss stepped away from the rail, moving back, but Petrov ignored him, speaking in a conversational tone. "Don't worry, I'm not armed. But you're covered by a very competent man with a telescopically sighted magnum rifle from up there on the bluff. And the other end is covered as well as a precaution. It's your mistake, I'm afraid."

Loss looked up at the bluff less than half a mile away. A thousand yards and very little wind. Not a difficult shot. "So what do you want to do now, Petrov?" He watched Petrov's shirt for the beat of his heart; a spot five inches below and to the left of the alligator symbol, where he would want the bullet to enter.

"Nothing in particular. I thought we'd chat for a

few more minutes and then I have to go. You'll be free to leave when you please. As long as you can outrun a speeding bullet." He backed away a step. "I'm sorry that the girl can't be permitted to live. You'll have to believe me. But no one will touch her."

"Bastard!" Loss said explosively. He felt his muscles contracting, the sudden surge of anger pumping adrenaline into his bloodstream.

"Don't even move!" Petrov warned, his voice still calm. "It only takes a half a second for the bullet to travel from the bluff. The man is an expert. Besides, Loss, you only have yourself to blame. You were the one who involved her in this and you, not me, are the one who bears the guilt."

Loss could see the ferry quite close to the shore, the distinctive upper deck making it look more like a floating cake than a ship. He estimated that it would dock in two or three minutes.

"How did you know Holly was aboard, Petrov?"

Petrov glanced down at his watch, impatient. "I didn't. Not until Campbell told me. He had a very weak heart, you know. We had to be very careful questioning him. But like the Kents, smoking in bed was fatal. I doubt that the police will even be able to identify him."

"The Kents?" He didn't want to believe Petrov.

"Yes. There's no point in elaborating." He looked down the causeway. "The ferry is in, Loss. They'll be offloading cars rather soon. I think it's time I left." He started to turn.

Loss flicked his forearm down, sliding the Luger's barrel into his right hand, his left grasping the sear. He kept both hands below the level of the iron railing, removed from the direct sight of the sniper.

"Keep your hands down, Petrov. This is a one-shot Luger. Don't make any movements except slow, natural ones. You'll die if I die."

Petrov started to move his hand toward his pocket. "Rather good. I saw some sort of a shape under your sleeve but I thought it was a knife. I must be—''.

Loss cut into his words. "Put your hands on the railing. Just as you did before. Very casually. I don't want any sudden motions.'' His heart was pumping heavily—a staccato. He moved in carefully toward the Russian, keeping the barrel clear of Petrov's elbows. "Last and only chance, Petrov. You do exactly as I say or you lose your spine. We're going to back away from here, across the roadway. You'll be in front of me. I doubt that you can stop a slug from your man on the hill but you can certainly slow it down.''

Petrov was breathing heavily. Loss saw him tense his forearm muscles, and then the Russian started to wheel, right elbow coming up.

Loss jammed the barrel of the Luger brutally into Petrov's kidney and grabbed his belt to keep him from falling, pinning him against the railing with his body weight. The Russian gasped, air sucking into his lungs in prelude to a scream. There was the snap of a miniature shockwave as the bullet whined past his face, spanging off the concrete behind them. He pulled Petrov closer, forming a shield between him and the bluff.

Cars from the ferry, a whole line of them, were getting closer. Loss flicked a glance at them, their images distorted by refraction, wobbling in the wave of heat rising from the causeway pavement.

"*Now!*" He rammed the barrel in again, dragging Petrov backward by the belt into the roadway. Petrov was coughing violently, dragging down onto the pavement. Another shot whined by, close enough for Loss to feel the breath of its passage. Concrete chips splattered up against Loss's shins. The sound of the shot was a distant popping.

Loss grabbed Petrov by the shirt collar, dragging him into the far lane opposite the approaching cars. "With me, Petrov. You're coming with me or I'll kill you.'' The Russian was half stumbling, half crawling.

They cleared the first one, a small Fiat. Loss caught

a brief glimpse of the driver, a white-faced woman, too startled to reach for the horn. Behind her was a solid stream of cars, imposing a barrier between him and the sniper. He bent low, dragging Petrov, running for the ferry terminal half a mile farther out from the shore. Petrov gagged and then stumbled and Loss turned to drag him to his feet.

A horn blared behind him. Loss glanced over his shoulder to see an old Mustang pulling out across the solid yellow line and accelerating in an attempt to pass the few vehicles in front of it. Loss dove for the sidewalk, feeling the cinders dig into the skin of his hand, the car missing him by inches. The Mustang was in a panic stop, brakes locked, slewing sideways. Metal exploded against metal, a shrieking, tearing sound; the Mustang ricocheted between the curb and the Fiat.

Loss had a brief glimpse of Petrov up and running, holding one shoulder with the other hand. Loss tried for a shot and the Mustang was back against the curb, blocking his aim. He caught a flash of Petrov's body as he vaulted the railing and dove for the shallow water.

There was another whine, and this time Loss felt the passage of the bullet as it plucked at the fabric of his shirt. He bent low and ran back into the right lane, keeping within feet of the passing traffic. The first half of the distance to the terminal took less than two minutes, but his lungs were searing, sucking hot exhaust-laden air. There were no more snaps of high-velocity slugs that he could hear, but his senses were remote and dull; he felt now only the ache of his legs beating against the pavement and the triphammer of his heart pounding against the walls of his chest.

Loss looked over his shoulder, slowing to a jog. The shoreward stream of vehicles was stopped, a large crowd gathering around the wrecked Mustang. And as he watched, a rust-red open-bed pickup truck wheeled through a U-turn and came back out the causeway, heading for him. It had Alberta plates, two faces perched in the high cab. He waved them down, standing in the roadway.

Loss ran to the driver's window and rapped on the glass. The man, complexion ruddy with sunburn, the face of a farmer, was wearing a flowered sports shirt. The woman's face was pale. The man pulled the ball cap back on his head. "What's the problem?"

Panting, Loss pointed toward the ferry and terminal building.

"That guy—" He swallowed for breath. "Got to get an ambulance." He panted, the explanation incomplete.

"Get in the bed of the truck. There's a phone back at the dock."

Loss nodded, still panting and pulled himself up over the tailgate. He felt exposed, the bluff in clear view. He slumped down in the bed of the truck, picking up what protection he could from the side panels.

They stopped at the ticket gate briefly and then were waved through, Loss low in the bed of the truck, undetected. The truck squealed to a stop near a maintenance building, and the driver yelled back at Loss something about a tow truck and loped off toward the building's door, fat moving in waves beneath his bulging shirt.

The Luger barrel was still in his hand, its form a black extension of his fingers. He slid it back up beneath the sleeve, using two loops of the twine to secure it, and crawled out of the bed of the truck. The grating for the ramp was only twenty yards further from the building, and he walked calmly onto the *Queen of Victoria*, capacity forty-eight cars and two thousand tons, eight dollars round trip Tsawwassen-Vancouver Island and back.

He passed a deckhand in an orange vest, who was chaining the gates. "Guy injured back there in traffic," Loss said. The man nodded, not looking up.

The passenger deck above him was crowded with a mass of people looking down at the causeway. Several were taking pictures, proof of their touch with death. No one was looking down at him.

He passed from the sunlight into the tunnel gloom of the starboard side, amongst the parked vehicles. There were only fifteen or so on this side and he couldn't see the Olds. He stood next to a camper, letting his eyes adjust to the darkness. Petrov had said that both ends of the causeway were covered. Loss had no doubt. They obviously would know the Olds's registration, but did they know he was using it?

When his eyes were better adjusted and he was breathing evenly, he walked through the midship passageway, checking the port side. The Olds was last in line, the second lane outboard. He watched the lines of cars and his own for over a minute, suddenly feeling very tired. The deck plates were vibrating under his feet now as the ferry went astern. Three long blasts on the ship's siren. There was no movement on the car deck. Only the sounds of the engine thrashing beneath his feet and bulkhead doors slamming. He headed for the Olds, walking softly on the balls of his feet.

The car was empty, the passenger side locked. He walked around the rear of the car, looking back across the empty loading deck to watch the shore recede. A crewman in jeans and a denim shirt walked across the loading platform and swung through a bulkhead door, pulling it shut after him. The shore was more distant now, green and white roiled seas foaming under the stern. Gulls were following the ship.

Loss moved down the left side of the car and tried the driver's door. It was open and he dropped into the thick upholstered seat. The keys were not in the ignition, but he found them in the ashtray, buried in burned-out ends of cigarettes. Good kid, he thought.

He caught the first movement, a flash of yellow in

the rearview mirror. A man running toward him. Loss cursed, wishing he had used the time to reassemble the Luger. He was fumbling for the barrel lashed to his forearm when a movement to his left startled him. He raised his hand defensively, diminishing the impact as a tubular object smashed into his forehead. Loss clearly read the speedometer as he fell to the cushions. It told him that he was going nowhere.

Chapter 25

He awoke to the sound of chain roaring through an iron pipe. It diminished slowly, then ceased. There was movement beneath him, as if he were slewing sideways. All his senses were responding now, confused messages back from the perimter of his consciousness. A feeling of dampness and smells of mustiness. Loss opened his eyes to watch a fly traverse a painted wooden beam within an arm's span above his head. He tried to move his arm and couldn't. No movement possible in his leg either, but his foot could flex.

He shut his eyes again and just rested, absorbing sounds. His mind was reeling as if he had too much to drink too quickly. There was a vague, unpleasant acid taste in his mouth; his tongue felt spongy and dry.

A door opened, rasping on the sill as if poorly fitted. He opened his eyes and craned his neck up from the prone position.

A woman stood there, hands thrust into cardigan pockets, peering at him, expressionless. Loss thought she might be in her late thirties and then decided she was older; her straight black hair, which was clipped severely at shoulder level, had traces of silver. The skin of her face was without crease or furrow. No smiles, no frowns. No emotion. Her high cheekbones and the hint of almond in her eye structure suggested she might be Oriental. But not a face to remember.

"Do you wish more air, Loss?" Her voice was that of a child's: high and thin but soft. "You may not talk loudly." She pushed the door fully open and entered, moving to a porthole and opening it. He felt the breath of fog.

"Where am I? What's happened?" He listened to his own voice and found it hoarse. "I want some water."

"In a short time," she said and closed the door behind her.

He had no means of telling time, since his arms were restrained by some sort of strap secured to the bunk he lay on. The light through the small brass porthole was the washed-out white of thick fog. It could be morning or evening. Or in between.

The room he lay in was triangular in shape; the apex was formed by a wedge-shaped bunk he lay on and the deckhead above him had beams of oak with teak planking. The rest of the room at the foot of the bunk had limited standing room under a raised coach roof. The only light was from the two portholes. By its shape and general construction, he guessed that he was confined in the forecastle of a small power cruiser. An iron pipe of about four-inch diameter ran from the center of the compartment through the deckhead. Spurling pipe? The source of the noise that woke him? It guided the chain up from the locker beneath the cabin sole through the deckhead and over the windlass. So they were anchored in the fog—where?

He heard a muttered conversation aft, beyond the door, and then the starting cough of a small generator that settled to a low hum, more vibration than sound.

He lay back on the bunk and rested, his left temple a dull throb. He slept again.

Loss awoke minutes or hours later. There had been no apparent passage of time. The porthole still was muzzled in the gray light of thick fog. A man bent over him, shaking him gently by the shoulder. "Do you feel like some food now, Mr. Loss?"

He felt the chest straps being released. The man bent down to undo the bindings on his legs and Loss caught a glimpse of a slightly balding figure as he stooped.

"Who are you?" Loss said, easing himself up onto his elbows.

"Call me James. Come out into the main cabin. We have some food prepared, but I warn you that I want no violence or noise. Otherwise you will be sedated." The man turned and left the cabin, a thin figure in blue corduroys and a thick navy pea jacket. Loss followed him, stretching his tendons, reeling slightly from dizziness. James indicated a position at the gimballed mahogany table where a setting of utensils and a napkin had been laid. Loss slumped down onto the settee and leaned on the table, head between his hands. The woman set a plate covered with fried eggs and hash-browned potatoes before him. She added to this two slices of toast and then a large enameled mug of black coffee next to his elbow.

"Eat now," she said and walked aft down a passageway toward what Loss supposed were the sleeping cabins.

Loss ate alowly at first, ignoring his surroundings and the man who sat opposite him. He ate with total concentration, the food delicious, almost separable into individual flavors of salt and bitter, sweet and sour. As if each individual taste bud responded in a separate totality. He closed his eyes, chewing on the toast. Each kernel of wheat, each molecule of yeast, each salted trace of butter seemed to leap to his senses. The coffee was incredible, unbelievably good. He

385

mopped the plate with the last crust and leaned back. James offered him a cigarette and a package of wooden kitchen matches. Loss's hand shook as he lit the match and inhaled. "She cooks well," he commented, extinguishing the match, exhaling. God, he thought, I've never tasted food before. Not food like that.

"It's a side effect of the medication," James offered, opening a notebook which lay closed beside him on the settee.

Loss carefully studied the man opposite him. Like the woman, he had light Asian features, and he was balding with straight black hair cut very short by contemporary standards. His eyes, encased behind yellow-tinted glasses, were birdlike: bright and black and unwinking. The rest of his face was unremarkable except for the fine, hard line that his lips formed. Loss resisted the compulsion to say "Ah, so!"

"You find this situation funny?" he said, staring at Loss.

"No," he replied, "not funny. Just that I'm washed out."

James nodded. "I suppose so. Again, part of the side effects." He made a notation in the notebook and snapped it shut. He started without preamble. "Brian Loss, born thirty-nine years ago, U.S. citizen. Former service in the U.S. Air Force. Pilot to Clifford Welsh. And there's much more here."

"Where am I?"

James looked down at his watch. "You've been unconscious for, for, ah, fifty-two hours. The vessel is the *Sunflower*. And presently we are anchored in Squamish Harbor on the Olympic Peninsula of Washington."

"On the Hood Canal."

James nodded. "Yes, on the Hood Canal."

"And you are . . . ?"

"James. As I said before, you can call me James. I think that you would have to say that I am with the government. A division of external security."

386

"What division? CIA?"

James nodded. "Something like that. We cooperate with the CIA on situations such as this." He paused, looking down at his fine-boned hands. "There is a very large segment of Chinese- and Japanese-Americans on the West Coast. As with blacks and chicanos, Caucasians do not readily notice us." He hesitated, stroking his forehead with a delicate fingertip. "Do you dislike Orientals, Mr. Loss?"

Brian shrugged. "I've never thought of it much. Like or dislike, I mean. I have unpleasant memories of Vietnam. People tried to kill me on occasion." Surprisingly, Loss found that he wanted to cry. His hand was shaking again, and he hid it beneath the table.

"Don't be concerned with your reactions, Mr. Loss. Your nervous system has been heavily strained. One night of normal sleep and you'll be fine. More coffee?"

Loss nodded, leaning back against the cushions, his eyes closed. James left the compartment and returned in a few minutes with the cup refilled. "There is sugar and dried cream in the locker behind you." He ruffled through several pages of his notebook.

"You mentioned medication. What kind of drugs?"

James raised his eyebrows. "Drugs that I'm sure you wouldn't be familiar with. But we had no time for half-truths or opinions. We wanted everything you knew and very quickly. I suppose that you would term them truth drugs, but that would not be quite accurate."

A wave of nausea and disorientation hit Loss. He gagged, trying to keep the bile down.

"Put your head between your knees," James said curtly, removing the cigarette from Loss's hand. "It will pass. I would suggest that you refrain from smoking for a few hours." Loss kept his head tucked down, and with his eyes closed he felt motion as if he were tumbling in space and then, just as quickly, his mind cleared.

387

Slowly he sat up and looked at James. "Jesus, you bastards don't fool around. Whatever you gave me is crap. And fuck-all unnecessary. I would have gladly told you everything that I knew."

James studied Loss for a moment before replying. "I doubt that, Mr. Loss. You would have told us what you *thought* you knew or what you wanted us to know. In this manner we were able to extract, as you would say in industry, raw data. I'm sorry that we, ah, violated your civil liberties. You can take that up with the proper authorities if you care to when the time comes. But I might point out that without our group, you would be dead."

"For Christ's sake, James, stop the Charlie Chan act. You're here to tell me something or ask me something. Otherwise you'd have me stuffed away in a cell or a padded room. Isn't that what you guys usually do? Get to the fuckin' point."

James stood up and turned his back to Loss, obviously angered. His hands were slowly clenching and unclenching as he fought down a retort. Finally he turned to face Loss, his face utterly expressionless, his eyes calm. His voice was even as he spoke. "Mr. Loss. I would like you to refrain from vulgarity. I find it offensive. Your present reaction is that of confusion and fear. I am here to inform. Nothing else. From the information you gave us, I feel that you will be prepared to do one final task in this affair." He sat down on the settee and opened the notebook. "Do I make myself clear?"

Loss nodded, without speaking, looking down at his bare feet. James was right, of course. It was the fear and the tension of the last five days that produced the anger. "All right, James. Go ahead. What happened at the ferry?"

"Much better, Mr. Loss. And please try to absorb as much of this as possible. It may be to your benefit. Concerning the ferry, one of Petrov's men was aboard, apparently covering that end of the causeway. As a

388

precaution, we had assigned one of our people to cover him. When you arrived Petrov's man was in position behind a camper one row over. It was he that struck you on the forehead. He was about to use this on you when our agent, the woman, who incidentally prepared your breakfast, intervened." James produced a small plastic atomizer with the label of a nasal decongestant. He set it on the table before Loss. "Prussic acid. A very near thing, Mr. Loss."

Brian examined the plastic container as he would a dead rat, probing it with a spoon. "I'll take your word for it. And then?"

"Then she simply moved Petrov's man into the vehicle with you, injected you both with a sedative, and strapped the pair of you upright in the front seat with the shoulder harness. It would seem to any passerby that you were both sleeping."

"No one on the ferry noticed this, this whole thing?"

James shook his head. "As far as we can tell, no. The trip over to Vancouver Island takes roughly two hours. Most of the car passengers make use of the upper deck or the snack bar, rather than remaining in their vehicles." James touched the edge of his glasses, a curiously delicate gesture. "From there, she brought you both to a rendezvous with this vessel in Nanaimo where the *Hussar* was then located. Unfortunately, Petrov's man knew nothing beyond the immediate operation. We're holding him in a private psychiatric clinic under heavy sedation."

"Suppose you go back to the beginning, Mr. James, or is it just James? How did you find out about the Welsh-Petrov thing. Campbell?"

"As I said before, just call me James. The beginning? We didn't know about Welsh or Petrov. Our knowledge of the affair started in Russia. Through sources there, we knew that the Russians had produced three nuclear weapons at the Zhignask installation, and that one of these had been tested underground. There were several curious things about this weapon. First, it was produced in only a quantity of three, an unusually low number for what presumedly will be a production weapon. More important, from our analysis of intelligence and from limited sampling of some of the alloys that were used in the production of the cases, we found that there was a remarkable resemblance with a weapon presently being manufactured in the United States for use in the Poseidon C-4 warhead. That made it something surely worth watching.

"We traced the movement of one of the warheads to Vladivostok where it was placed aboard one of the older Z-Class Fleet submarines. From there, we tracked it across the Pacific with one of our own nuclear submarines. The device was transferred to a Russian trawler with Canadian Fish and Game markings off the coast of British Columbia and then onto the *Hussar* at Broughton Island. Petrov either accompanied the weapon all the way from Russia or was on the trawler. We don't know this for sure. We do know that he had the device placed aboard the *Hussar*, which two men working for the Russians had chartered."

"He saw Holly then?"

"No, it doesn't seem that way. He was only on board for a few minutes, seeing to the transfer of the weapon. Your woman friend must have been below deck because I feel that Petrov would surely have recognized her. The other two men apparently didn't know her identity and thought she was a normal part of the crew."

"So she was still aboard the *Hussar*?"

James nodded. "Yes, we saw her on the yacht in Nanaimo. Everything seemed to be quite normal. The device is on the foredeck of the yacht, lashed down with rope. It appears to be marked with an address, as if it were a parcel of cargo. We can't tell as yet."

"You mean that you haven't stopped the whole op-

eration yet? Jesus Christ! What are you waiting for?"
Loss stood up, infuriated, immediately feeling a wave
of dizziness sweep his consciousness.

The woman came immediately into the cabin and
pushed Loss back down onto the settee, gently but
with an undisguised trace of distaste. She handed him
a tablet and indicated that he should wash it down
with the remaining coffee. James was mute during this,
placidly thumbing through his notes and checking the
weather through the opened porthole. When Loss was
quiet, slumping back against the settee, James continued. "You see, Mr. Loss, your heart has been heavily
strained over the last few days. The drugs unfortunately account for this. One good night's sleep and
you will be normal, but you must remain calm."

The woman looked at James for any further instructions. He replied by a fractional shake of his head.
She left the room, closing the door softly behind her.
James removed his glasses and, laying them aside,
massaged the bridge of his nose. "No, Mr. Loss.
What you don't seem to realize is that the Russians
cannot simply be arrested. To do that would expose
a situation that would be recognized as an attempt by
Russia to detonate a nuclear device within the confines of the United States. The only response for the
United States would be to accuse Russia and possibly
precipitate a total war." He paused to think and then
said, "I believe all that would be counterproductive.
The way that this must be handled is to neutralize the
weapon and simply eliminate all the people connected
with Petrov. The result will be a warning to the Russians, a hardening of United States policy, and perhaps some degree of rearmament by the United States
to reachieve a parity in military power. The public
should not be informed of this. Welsh, of course, must
be removed permanently."

Loss heard the deep moan of a foghorn in the distance. It was so muffled and distorted that it seemed
like the moan of some animal. He looked down at his

hands. There were still occasional tremors, but his feeling of disorientation was subsiding. "How did you find out about me?"

James made a scratching noise in his throat. "Through Petrov. After he placed the weapon aboard the yacht, he returned to the trawler. We thought that he would put to sea, but instead, the trawler took him down to Alert Bay and landed him there. The following morning he flew to Vancouver. From there on in we followed his movements, which eventually led to your meeting on the causeway at Tsawwassen. Through you, we've been able to put all the unknowns in place. His plan is quite evident now."

"And that is?" Loss interjected.

"That the Soviets have subverted an American presidential hopeful by arranging situations within their control. The Cuban reaction to Guantanamo was stage-managed by the Russians, as was the Panamanian accord. As you had noticed, Mr. Loss, in Welsh's last television interview he made a statement about the proliferation of nuclear weapons and the dangerous practice of having so many within U.S. borders. It would seem that they planned to transport the device to the Hood Canal in time to detonate it as close as possible to the first Trident submarine leaving on patrol with fully loaded and armed missiles. The detonation would appear to have originated with the submarine, thus fulfilling Welsh's predictions of playing with fire. His election would have nearly been assured. All in all, a very clever scenario."

"Petrov might be dead!"

"We don't think so. Our men on the shore side of the causeway saw him dive clear of the railing. He seemed to be swimming strongly for a point of land north of the causeway. It would appear that he wasn't as disabled as you thought. At any rate, his death probably wouldn't have any effect on the situation. The weapon is in place and I doubt that the men on board the *Hussar* have any idea that there is anything wrong. Typical Russian compartmentation of espionage. Each element works independently of the other."

"How many men?" Loss said.

James stood up and walked over to the navigation table. He returned with a pile of black-and-white photographs and lay them in front of Loss. "Only these two. Do you recognize either one of them?"

Loss leafed through the stack. All were obviously taken with a telephoto lens, with characteristic foreshortening of the background. One of them was a man with Arabic features, almost handsome. The other, nondescript, a typical anyman. Loss shook his head.

"No, I thought not," James said half to himself. "The Caucasian one," he tapped the first photo, "is English. We can find nothing concerning him except that he had a fellowship at Cambridge in physics. Also a good linguist. The other one, the Arab, we know much more about. Amed Menkar. A young Libyan naval officer, something of an expert in electronics with an advanced degree in terrorism gained from work with the PLO. Attended the University of Leningrad in the late sixties. Now a Russian citizen. A strange pair to select for what would seem a suicide mission."

"Do you think that's the idea?" Loss rubbed his forehead, feeling slightly sick. "I mean, that it's a suicide thing?"

"Not very likely," James replied. "They are probably there for the purpose of assembling and then activating the weapon. Their backgrounds would indicate that such is the case. They have probably been instructed to place the yacht in a position as close to the submarine as possible. There might be a switch that they activate to start the firing sequence. On the other hand, their role might be passive as far as the device is concerned. It could be activated by an outside source such as a transmitter or even, in some way, the presence of the submarine itself. This is our assessment."

"Look, James. All this is very nice. I'm truly impressed. The drugs I don't mind. I admit that you probably got more out of me than I would have freely given. But there is only one essential thing that has to be done. Stop those two guys on the *Hussar*. And get the crew off safely. There are only two men. Surely, you can contrive some situation where they both will be on deck at one time. Knock them off with automatic weapons."

The muscles in James's cheeks tightened, giving his face a hard, angular tone. "Loss, we don't know how that weapon is to be triggered. It could be by some switching device on the storage box, but it could also be by radio impulse. Eliminating those two men doesn't guarantee that we stop the device from detonating. Besides the people living in this area, Seattle is less than twenty miles to the east of here, directly downwind."

Loss hammered his fist down on the table, upsetting the coffee mug. "For Christ's sake, James, what in hell do you expect to do? Do you have to have an act of Congress to move your ass?" He started to rise and then sat down suddenly; the sensation of his senses tumbling flooded him in a wave of nausea.

James reached over and felt Loss's pulse. "Not good," he said softly. "Keep your emotions under control, Mr. Loss." He stood up and walked over to the porthole, looking at the fuzzy forms of boats anchored in the bay. It seemed to be thinning out. He turned back to Loss and sat down, exhaling heavily. "I have already made preparations for taking the *Hussar*. I am only waiting on approval from people further up in the government."

"What are you planning?" He tried to watch James's face, but he had trouble keeping it in focus.

"The *Hussar* is anchored on the other side of the bay. The U.S.S. *Ohio* is scheduled to put to sea tomorrow morning at five in company with four tugs. We doubt that the *Hussar* will move before dawn.

Consequently, we plan to destroy the nuclear device tonight."

"Destroy it how? Don't you run the risk of detonating it?"

"Unlikely," James replied. "The heart of the weapon is basically an atomic bomb, a fission weapon. This is first triggered to create the intense heat necessary for a hydrogen fusion reaction. This atomic 'trigger' is a ball of plutonium encased with a special type of high explosive that must be detonated by electrical impulses in a highly complex sequence. If we fracture that high explosive, the trigger mechanism is destroyed. The result at worst would be an explosion of perhaps twelve kilos of high explosive. The core material would be shattered and there would be some radioactive contamination of the local area. But no nuclear detonation."

"How do you know that it will happen this way?"

"We don't exactly," James replied, looking down at his notebook. "But this is the best estimate that our technicians can provide. If we are fortunate, there will not even be any high explosive yield."

"How about the crew?" Loss asked.

"There are no guarantees. Destruction of the nuclear weapon comes first. If there is no high explosive yield, we will attempt to get them off the *Hussar*."

"Oh, my God!" Loss buried his face in his hands.

"Yes, I know. I'm sorry. But with the time remaining, there is no other way. We will take the *Sunflower* very close alongside the *Hussar,* as if we were reanchoring closer to shore. We must be close enough that the first rocket from the anti-tank missile launcher cannot miss. We cannot chance having to fire a second time."

"James, you can't—"

"There is no alternative to this plan, Mr. Loss. We will follow the missile with satchel charges if there is no detonation. We must be positive that the device is destroyed."

Loss looked up, tears of anger spilling down his face. "You cold-blooded prick! And who pulls the trigger? There are five people on that yacht. And you're the bastard that gets a medal for defending flag and country!"

James looked small and fragile in the pale light. He rubbed the back of his neck reflectively, looking up at the overhead. "For flag and country? That's an odd expression." He paused, thinking. "I suppose so, Mr. Loss. Ultimately, it is for flag and country. More to the point, because we are ordered to do it." He smiled at Loss, his lips compressed. "We will have to be no more than fifteen meters from the device when we launch our attack. I will be one of the men firing the missile."

"Jesus Christ," Loss shouted. He staggered to his feet, reeling. "What kind of a bullshit organization is this? Some CIA Kamikaze team?" He suddenly faltered, feeling sick, tears flooding his eyes. He sat down on the cabin sole, trying to neither giggle nor cry.

There were muttered voices in the background, and he felt the needle sliding into his arm before he could protest. His last image of James was a pair of tennis shoes attached to legs rising to a body beyond his contracting vision.

Chapter 26

He came awake slowly, the persistent pressure on his arm an annoyance. His senses, he felt, were dead and he wanted to return to the depths where he had been.

"It's time," the voice said. Then, "Shield your eyes." A light snapped on, flickering yellow with the pulse of the generator. The bulb was dim, but it felt as if a strobe had been fired. He blinked, tried to focus.

"Get up," the voice said. The woman. She undid his straps and he experimentally flexed his arms. Squinting, shielding his eyes, he looked up at her. She had backed into the doorway, a small automatic held in her hands.

"What time?" Out of habit, he looked down at his wrist but the watch was gone. Automatically, he glanced toward the porthole, but there was no external light.

"One A.M. Get up slowly. Stand first for a while before you walk. I have food for you and then we will leave." She backed away, into the saloon. A dark blue pea jacket was thrown over her shoulders and she had changed into black corduroy pants.

He eased off the berth, testing his reactions. His limbs were numb, but only from the straps and inactivity. Surprisingly enough, he felt good, rested. And hungry. He caught himself, about to tell her. Instead, he steadied himself in the doorway, leaning against the jamb, shielding his eyes.

"You have slept seven hours, Mr. Loss. With food, you will feel better." She made a brusque motion with the automatic toward the table, as if she was an usher seating him halfway through a performance. "Sit down. Keep your hands above the table. And no sudden movements. I have your food ready."

Loss glanced aft along the corridor, looking for any trace of James. A woman with a Saturday Night Special didn't seem to be much of a barrier to escape—as long as she was the only one he had to handle. Except, he realized, he would have to play down his feelings of renewed strength.

"I don't feel much like food," he said hesitantly. Squinting, he moved his eyes from one object to another, as if he was disoriented. No indication of James. The pea jacket James had worn was not hanging from any of the hooks in the companionway. Like a drunk, he shuffled into the saloon and dropped heavily onto the settee. Wiping his nose with the back of his hand, Loss inhaled sharply, shaking his head as if to clear it.

"I will not argue," the woman said, watching his face, "but don't take me for a fool." She set a plate down before him. "Eat if you wish."

He looked up a little and found a plate mounded with rice and small strips of meat. It steamed, giving off the smell of saffron. She dropped a spoon onto the table. "There's more if you want. I'd advise that you take something. It's cold on the water and we have a long passage."

He spooned the food in mechanically, eating in silence, absorbing the sounds of the vessel. The generator was running, its vibration felt through the table. She had seated herself on the opposite side of the saloon, legs crossed, body relaxed, drinking from a cup with one hand, the automatic held easily in the other. Loss finally gave her a weak attempt at a smile between mouthfuls. She didn't return it but nodded. Halfway finished, he heard the voice of a man on deck, a sort of singing in a monotonous, nasal voice. It was repetitious; a chant or even perhaps a prayer. But it didn't sound like the thin, reedy voice of James.

"Where is James?" he asked, mopping at the remains of the sauce with a wedge of bread.

"Li Po?" she asked, raising her eyebrows. "I thought he had told you."

"James Li Po?" Loss asked. He stopped chewing the bread.

"Li Po Ching," she said carefully. "Not 'James'. That's simply a name he uses in the English-speaking countries." She said it all, very steadily, watching his eyes. "He is from the same province as our chairman—Hunan."

"Hunan—mainland China?" In the silence that followed he could hear the ticking of the ship's clock, the sound of the refrigerator's steady hum.

It seemed that she waited minutes before answering. "There is only one China, Mr. Loss. A civilization of four thousand years. And a small island of dog-sucking merchants does not make a separate China." Her eyes were brittle and cold. She sipped at her mug, watching him.

He slowly pushed away the plate, almost mechanically. At first he thought she was joking, then realized she was not. "For God's sake, why . . . ?"

"Because it is in our national interest." She set the mug down, wiping a drop of tea from her lip with a delicate movement of finger. "Or should I say for both our countries' mutual interest. It was *we* who had penetrated Zhignask and determined the unusual nature of the weapon, and it was *we* who tracked it to Vladivostok and hence across the Pacific. Had there been time we would have drawn the U.S. intelligence organizations into it, but the pattern was incomplete until you linked the Soviet operation with Welsh. And now it is too late. We must act alone."

"That doesn't answer anything!"

A brief flicker of impatience and distaste crossed her features. "It doesn't, Mr. Loss?" She withdrew a package of cigarettes from her coat pocket and tossed it on the table, together with a pack of matches.

"Perhaps not to your way of thinking. But we have over fifty-five divisions of Soviets along our border, panting like dogs to be set free. Were your country to pose no counterthreat to them, they would not hesitate for the span of a heartbeat."

Loss lit a cigarette, sucking in the smoke, exhaling. He was watching her face, her hands. And most of all, her eyes. There was a metallic quality to the eyes, no longer gentle gray but a flame-hardened black. "So it's the U.S. that plays guard dog for China?" he said.

She visibly relaxed, as if she had found it necessary to ease the tension. And smiled. "If that is how you choose to describe it. Perhaps it is necessary for us to pick a flea from your coat on occasion." She shifted in her seat, impatient to be going. "But you must understand, Mr. Loss. that both our nations require time to adequately arm against the Soviets. Given a more pragmatic leadership in your country, we think you will rearm. There must be no more thought of détente in the sense that it us used by your administration. It is a new reality that you face. And China stands ready to face it with you. Between our nations, we can keep the Soviets at bay until we are strong."

He ground out the cigarette. "And what of a new, strong China?" He realized that he didn't even know her name.

She shrugged a little. "That question will not be answered for fifteen years," she answered. "Or even perhaps in our lifetimes. But like all strong nations, Mr. Loss, we will be a force to be dealt with in our own day."

There was a silence between them. Loss slumped back in the settee. "James is a part of this?" he said finally.

"Ching is our commander. He is ashore telephoning for final approval for the attack. The radio would be unsafe. Arrangements are to be made by my embassy for us to meet U.S. intelligence representatives in Everett, Washington, just after dawn. From there . . . ?" She left it as an unanswered question.

"CIA?"

She nodded. "Both you and I are essential. If there are no survivors from the attack, then you and I will be the only ones left to verify what has happened. You understand the importance of this?"

Loss lit another cigarette, wanting to stretch out the time, seeking an opening. He caught a glimpse of the ship's clock; one-fifteen. Then looking up at her, he shurgged. "I understand what you're saying in the broad sense. Someone has to be left to tell what happened and to stop Welsh. But that doesn't help save the *Hussar*'s crew. When does Ching attack?"

"After five A.M. But before six." She paused, studying him. "I understand your personal feelings. Ching will try to save the crew, but that's secondary to the destruction of the device. He wanted you to understand that he would do everything he could. But it is more important that you realize that your information on Welsh, Heiss, and Petrov is needed for verification. Alone, I am only parroting what you said under the influence of drugs. That, and the fact that I am an illegal alien and the agent of the People's Republic of China. Not a combination to inspire confidence in your CIA, Mr. Loss." She set the mug down and swallowed, as if the tea had left a bad taste. "He wanted your word that you understood the importance of your part in this."

"Understood," he answered. But understanding and doing were two different things, he thought. He motioned his head toward the opened hatch. "What's his job?"

She stood up, keeping the automatic leveled toward him. "He will swim to the *Hussar* with satchel charges and place them on deck, if possible, in case Ching misses with the antitank missile. It is a French design and not always entirely reliable."

"And he was praying?"

She gave him a look of scorn. "We no longer find that necessary, Mr. Loss. He was asking his ancestors for the necessary courage." Her face softened and

401

then she added, "Yes, it is a form of prayer." She tossed him a foul-weather jacket. "Wear this," she said. "The trip is over four hours and it will be cold."

"Where's the *Hussar?*"

She motioned him to the porthole, standing back. "The single light. They lit the anchor light at dusk but there has been no movement on the deck since then. There was just one man visible—the Arab, we think."

He looked across the black water of the anchorage, inshore. There were some shore lights, but in the intermediate distance he saw the loom of a vessel, sparse—dark form against the sky. Five hundred feet, he thought. Maybe less. As his eyes accommodated to the blackness he thought he saw the dim flicker of a light forward. The anchor light, raised halfway up the forestay, described ellipses of orange against the sky as the *Hussar* rolled in a slight swell. And there were some stars. The sky was clearing.

"Now," she said. "We have a distance to go."

He moved up the companionway, the woman following. In the darkened deckhouse, he saw the form of the man. She spoke to him in Chinese and the man returned a grunt. Then, preceding both Loss and the woman, the man moved out onto the deck, leading them forward. A small launch was tied up alongside with a boarding ladder hung from the rail.

The woman descended the ladder first, the man holding Loss by the elbow and pressing the muzzle of a gun into the small of his back. The woman moved aft in the launch and, after two pulls, started an outboard, small enough in size that it made almost no noise.

"Down," the man said. Loss got the impression of a very young man, compact and wiry. In the half-light, Loss saw that he wore thick-lensed glasses and a wet suit. Loss shuffled forward, his feet feeling for the rail. The man steadied him and spoke softly in accentless English, "You will be careful, Mr. Loss. You will not trip and dive overboard. You will do as she tells you."

His grip tightened on Loss's arm, viselike. "Understood?" The voice was conversational. "She has instruction to deliver you—alive if she can, but if need be, dead."

The woman gave a low hissing sound. The man nodded and guided Loss down the ladder, then cast off the launch's painter as she applied throttle, accelerating the launch away from the *Sunflower*. Loss had the impression of the man standing there in the darkness, very erect. She called something softly to him as they drew away, and the man replied.

"What was that about?" Loss asked.

"We wished each other luck." She gestured with the automatic. "Sit down on the floorboards, facing away from me. I will change positions with you after an hour. And I want no more talk."

Loss had thought it over, weighing one plan against the other. It had been too risky on the *Sunflower* with two of them, both armed. But with her alone it might be different. To starboard he could see the outline of the *Hussar* receding in the distance. It was too far away to swim with the woman in control of the launch. And James would be back—when? He cursed himself for not asking her. He chanced a glance back over his shoulder. She sat aft in the sternsheets, the steering arm of the outboard held in her left hand and the automatic in the right.

"I told you down, Mr. Loss," she whispered. "Down on the floorboards." He nodded and settled between the bow section and athwart, watching the bow wash, luminescent, rolling away from the side of the launch in the darkness. Lights along the shore were scattered points of yellow, with clusters in areas marking small settlements. A glow lighted the east where he knew Seattle would be, some twenty miles away. Above him he made out stars through the breaking overcast. From the position of Cassiopeia he knew that they were headed north and east.

The cold was starting to penetrate his jacket and

flecks of salt spray wet his face. Swimming was out of the question. He had to get possession of the launch. Underneath his fingertips, he felt the floorboards. But they were firm, well screwed in, nothing to use as a weapon. The oars would probably be further aft. His right hand inched forward, exploring, and found the wet coil of line that was the bow painter. Ten, maybe fifteen feet of half-inch nylon. Carefully, now using both hands, he started to coil it, ensuring that it would run free without snarling. Another minute, perhaps two, passed. Give it three more minutes, he thought. The launch was doing about six knots and over a period of ten minutes would travel one mile. But the calculation seemed wrong and he worked it out again. Mind still muddled, he thought. With the coils smooth and carefully held in his left hand he decided that he would turn to the right, diverting her attention, then drop the coils to his left, just over the bow. Mentally, he started a count. One-thousand one, one-thousand two, one-thousand three. Mechanically, he ticked three minutes off.

He half turned to his right, drawing his legs up under him. "I feel sick," he whispered and then, using his right hand to cover his mouth, shoved his index finger down his throat.

As the gorge rose in this throat he dropped the painter from his left hand, feeling it run smoothly, dragged aft by the wake. Against the skyline he saw her, half rising, already reducing the throttle setting. The automatic was still in her right hand. Suddenly the engine died, the line of the painter fouling the prop in a rat's nest of nylon, and the launch abruptly slowed, then rose stern first as the wake rolled forward, overtaking the hull. The woman was caught off balance and teetered forward, not quite falling. Loss sprang from the floorboards, realizing in a sickening moment that his reactions were too slow, that she would fire before he reached her. A blow to the side of his head, blurring his vision into points of light, and then they were grappling in the bilge, tearing at each other in desperate silence. He retched again, spewing vomit across her chest, and she hissed back, clawing to free her hands from the jumble of their interlocking bodies. He realized that she had hit him with the barrel of the automatic and that she was raising it again, club-like, trying to free her arm for a downward stroke. In the closeness he could smell her breath above the stench of puke and feel her spittle flecking his face as she hissed a stream of invectives, all of it in sibilant Chinese. The blow came but it missed his head, hammering down on the tendons of his neck. But this time he pinned her arms across the thwart, bearing down on them with his right arm and chest, using the other to try to wrestle the automatic from her fist. Their faces were inches from each other, both immobilized in the press of his weight, both straining for the advantage.

"Fool!" she spat.

The gritty strength behind her founded features and formless body had surprised him. It kept running through his mind that she was a woman, that somehow, she should be easy to take. But she was hard, well muscled, desperately unwilling to accept defeat. His grasp on the barrel was slipping, her leverage better. The barrel inched inward toward his chest. Seconds now. Teeth clenched, he brought his head down and forward, smashing against her face, crushing her nose. With a sucking intake of breath, a scream, she toppled backward, the gun clattering to the floorboards, and it was over.

She lay, head back against the stern thwart, weeping in sharp intakes of breath, hands held to her face.

He felt for the automatic, retrieving it from the ice-cold water slopping in the rolling bilge. It was a double-action, something like a small Browning. He thumbed back the hammer and, holding it, squeezed the trigger. The safety was on. He lowered the hammer and eased the safety off. She had never intended to fire, he realized.

"Get up," he said.

She nodded, her hands still covering her face, then crawled forward blindly like a wounded animal. He kept the gun wide of her, still wary that she might fling an arm out, try again. But it was truly over. She hunched down, her head between her knees, slowly shaking her head, the sounds muffled by her hands.

He was shaking, not from cold, but with the reaction of combat and expected death. He couldn't keep the automatic still.

"Frigging cold," he told himself but he knew that it was a lie, that he had touched the edge of death. A few more seconds and she might have won.

"Would you have fired?" he asked. She didn't answer, impervious to all but her pain.

It took him more than ten minutes to free the line, feeling blindly with one hand for the snarled prop while keeping his eyes forward, watching her. The nylon, freed, was badly chafed by the edges of the prop, but still whole. He used it to tie her feet, leaving her hands free. He squatted beside her, holding one shoulder.

"Use some water on your face. It's cold." In the starlight and reflected glow of Seattle, he saw that blood had seeped from her nostrils and smeared across her flattened cheeks where her hands had cupped. Tears formed in the corners of her eyes, clenched shut against the pain.

Her voice, nasal, almost unrecognizable, was still strong. "You are a fool, Loss. You can do nothing by yourself. Think—"

"I've thought. I'll do it my way." He felt a ridiculous need to explain it to her. to try to ease the pain she felt in defeat. She's right, he thought. But I have to try. He moved aft toward the stern thwart. The outboard started with the fifth pull.

Chapter 27

It seemed as though it had taken a long time, but without a watch he had no way of knowing. He had turned south, retracing the route, back down the Hood Canal. He skirted the anchorage by a good quarter of a mile, yet still able to see the outlines of the two yachts and a hodgepodge of vessels tied to floats farther inshore. A Gulf sign glowed over the marina fueling dock like a smog-dulled sun, and a few lights still farther inshore defined the main street of the small town.

It seemed lighter but he realized that it was only because the mist had dissipated and that there were stars. Well south of the anchorage he steered closer to the shore, watching for summer homes or boathouses which were unoccupied. Some he rejected because they were too hidden by trees to determine whether they were inhabited; others he avoided because of the glint of starlight on the hood of a car or the dim form of a cabin cruiser tied to a finger pier. He tried to estimate distance traveled, but it was nearly impossible in the dark and without a watch.

Finally, skirting a small inlet, he found two cabins, close to each other, the waterfront overgrown with grass. Two small boats were drawn up on the beach and overturned. He guided the launch into the dock, cut the engine, and listened. Besides the humming of mosquitos and his own breathing, the place was silent.

"Do you intend to kill me?" she said, her voice distorted but even. Although whispered, it seemed very loud.

"No," he countered impatiently. "Keep quiet. I'm going to check the house out. If it's vacant, I'll leave you here." He eased out of the launch onto the dock, trying to make as little noise as possible. "But if you make a racket, I'll have no choice but to use this." He held up the automatic so that she could see it in outline. He felt foolish. She had sunk down onto the floorboards, working at keeping the pain quiet, not moving more than was necessary. As an afterthought, he took the oars and the gas line from the fuel tank.

It was a small cabin with a matching shed. Loss carefully worked around the fringing trees, warmed by the protection from the night wind. The cabin was silent and grass had overgrown the driveway. The shed was nothing more than that, partially finished but with one side open. Beneath the roof he found a cement mixer and stacks of bagged cement. Some lumber was stacked haphazardly under the eaves, smelling of mold and slippery with moss.

He moved around to the rear of the cabin. Looking up, he could see no silhouette of power lines or phone cable. He tried a window at the side, then the door. Both were locked. He tried knocking, first softly and then louder, more insistent. No reply. He waited a minute and tried again. Nothing.

Scraping up some mud from around the downspout, he packed it against the front window next to the doorway, then, using a log from a stack of cordwood, broke the window. It shattered, the sound loud enough to echo across the small inlet. He stood, breathing hard, waiting for a shout or some sign of alarm, but the echo died and the inlet returned to silence except for the sound of small wavelets chuckling along the base of the seawall.

The lock worked smoothly and he let himself in and stood, absorbing the sounds and smells of the cabin. With his hands outstretched, he moved forward in the blackness, nudging the edge of a chair, then a card table. His hands found the wall and he moved crab-wise, edging along the chinked logs until he met stone. There was a damp smell of ashes doused with water. He felt for and found the chimney, then the mantel-piece. There were two burned-down candles in a dish, then his fingers touched a box. He picked it up, fumbling it open and struck a match.

The cabin was disused, filthy, with mattresses spread at random across the floor. In the center of the single room there was a deal table and a couple of chairs. A closed door sealed off the end of the room. He lit one of the candles and explored. In an alcove there was a small sink, rusted red under the spout of a hand pump. A blackened wood stove hunkered in the corner, top cracked and laced with streaks of burned food. At the other end the closed door opened to a windowless bunk room. A mouse scurried before Loss's footsteps and disappeared into the shadows. Good enough, he thought.

She hadn't moved. He untied her feet and without saying anything, she moved up onto the dock. He tried to guide her but she rejected his arm, pushing ahead toward the cabin. Inside, she sat down heavily on the mattress.

"Into the back room," he said. "There's a bunk and a couple of blankets."

"Do you understand what you're doing?" she asked, head bent. "If you try to board the *Hussar* you are endangering not only the woman, the crew, but a million people. Your countrymen," she added, "not mine." She looked up at him, her face caked with dried blood, features flattened, the area beneath her eyes swelling. ". . . and if the weapon detonates, the Soviets will have won. There will not be one person left . . . you, me, anyone . . . to tell what is known."

"I have as much chance as Ching. Better. And if it doesn't work . . ." He thought of it. Somewhere he had read that the ignition temperature of a nuclear weapon was in the millions of degrees. That there would be no knowledge on his part if he didn't succeed. "You'll survive," he finally said.

The guttering candle flame made shadows, moving as if of their own will across the wall. "Nothing will survive within a ten-mile radius, Mr. Loss. Nothing."

His body felt old, used up. He motioned with the automatic. "Get into the bunk room. There are blankets. I'll tell the police where you are when this thing is sorted out."

She didn't move, just looked at him. "You are a fool, Loss. An absolute fool. If it was in my power, I would have you shot. Not as an enemy of my country but as a traitor to your own." She paused, moving a hand across her face, probing gently at the swelling. She shook her head. "Leave it to Ching. He at least knows that he may need to give his life. You think like a movie spy. Boom-boom, and you save the girl and walk away. That easy, Mr. Loss?"

Loss shrugged. "I've got to go. Tell me what you know that'll be of use. Ching—James, whatever, said the goddamn thing was laced down on the forward deck. What else?"

She shook her head. "Nothing else. We know only that the weapon is housed in a wooden crate." She shook her head again. "Except that if you survive, you must call the Greentree Motel in Everett. By that time, your intelligence people will know something of this. You must contact them there. Or call my embassy. Ask for Lee Sun Kwow. Ching has been in contact with him."

He guided her into the bunk room. There were two soiled blankets on a rack and he tucked one around her. She lay back, looking at him, her face now swollen almost beyond recognition. Holding the candle up and inspecting the room, he could see no way for her to escape. The wall carried up to the rafters and, although of crude construction, was strong. "I'll take the candle," he said, backing toward the door.

410

She answered him in Chinese, the words running together in soft accord with one another. And she gave an attempt at a smile. It was more of a death's head grimace.

He paused in the doorway. "What was it that you said?"

"Just that 'Even fools sometimes go with the gods.' "

"I thought that you said you didn't believe in that stuff."

Her face was in darkness now. "We don't, Mr. Loss. It is just an expression."

He closed the door on her, then used an andiron from the fireplace to jam the catch. Retrieving the oars and gasoline feed line, he padded across the damp grass, got into the dinghy and headed north, toward the *Hussar*.

The *Hussar* was a black hulk silhouetted against the distant skyline. The intricacy of her rigging was just a blur, sometimes picking up reflections from the silver moon in brief slurs of light as she rolled. As he drifted closer, the masts, foreshortened, loomed impossibly high above him, and the details began to emerge.

He had motored back, north along the canal, keeping more to the middle, trying to formulate some plan. But it seemed impossible. Intricate plans were always a bust. He had the pistol and the element of surprise. Placing himself in the position of the two men, he imagined that one would be asleep and the other on watch, waiting for the dawn and the appearance of the Trident sub with four tugs. Stopping twice to test the wind, he maneuvered the launch dead up wind and, at what he estimated to be one hundred yards, cut the engine. With the wind to his back and one oar, he drifted down slowly, watching for a movement on deck. But the *Hussar* remained dark, silent.

He backpaddled to within ten yards of the hull, moving toward the bow section. Incredibly, he could hear a weak but distinct strain of music—something vaguely symphonic or with the structure of disciplined progressive jazz. A machine was working within the hull as well, the softer undertone of a motor running at slow speed.

With the hull looming over him, he half-crouched, using his fingertips to keep the launch from thumping into the hull. Then, thrusting aft gently, he moved the launch farther forward, out from beneath the bow, under the bowsprit.

A thick rigging wire ran from the hull's waterline over a projecting strut and terminated at the outboard end of the bowsprit. Loss smiled briefly, remembering Kitzner had been a stickler for accuracy in identifying nautical equipment. He tested the bobstay's rigidity. It was at least three-quarter-inch-diameter wire rope, tightened by turnbuckles to a humming tension. The bobstay strut had been served in position with wire, preventing any possible movement. Loss had often used the same method to board the *Surprise* after swimming.

He bent down and sloughed off both shoes and eased himself up onto the bobstay, holding the launch's painter between his teeth. Drifting with the wind, the launch lay back against the *Hussar*'s hull but the canvas-covered fenders which protected its sides made no more than a light scuffing sound.

He waited, minutes he calculated, but there was no movement on the deck or below—just the thin sound of music from within the hull. Satisfied, he eased himself up onto the bowsprit, then dragged one leg and then the other over the rail. He waited again, listening. The motor's sound was louder and he felt the lightest of vibrations from its motion.

His night vision was excellent now, the adrenaline flowing, heart beating heavily. He craved movement, the chemistry of his body anticipating the demand. "Better than Ching could pull off," he thought. But his stomach was tightly knotted and he noticed that

412

his hand shook from the tension. He breathed more deeply, trying to slow his respiration. The name of the game, he reminded himself, was to get her off without trouble. Let the Chinese take care of the rest of it.

He started, a halyard slatting against the mast. He felt a light tremor run through the deck. But there was no noise from within the hull. He waited another few minutes to be sure, then secured the painter to a cleat with a half-hitch, slack enough so that it would come loose with no more than a hard tug. Bending over, he could see the dim outline of the launch, lying in the shadows alongside the *Hussar*, moving a bit in the slight swell but not enough to create a sound that would be transmitted through the hull plating.

Loss crouched, feet on a grating just aft on the bowsprit, trying to pick out details on deck. The anchor light directly above him had a base of some sort, so that the light—he guessed it was an oil lamp—did not play directly on him. But it did provide enough flickering illumination to give form to the lower sections of the masts and the deckhouse.

Looking aft, he could see the anchor winch just feet from where he crouched against the furled forestay sail. It was in this area that Ching said that the device was lashed down on deck. But all Loss could discern in the weak light was a clean expanse of teak deck. Checking more carefully, he was sure of it. The crate had been moved.

Farther aft, the center section of the deck rose in a low coach roof, broken occasionally by metal wind scoops. They glinted in the weak light, reflecting multiple images of the anchor light aloft. The cowls were rotated forward and he realized that they would scoop the wing and direct it below. And if they directed wind, they would direct sound. Something to remember. Farther aft, a windshield slanted upward and was topped by a low roof. This would be the deckhouse. Beyond that, his view was blocked. Somewhere aft, the deckhouse would probably terminate and the lower

413

level of the coach roof would continue, covering the aft cabins. Conventional motor sailer, he thought.

The enormity of what he was doing suddenly swamped his mind. There was a nuclear device on board; something hundreds of times as destructive as the Hiroshima thing. And he had no way of knowing how it would be triggered. Perhaps a weak radio pulse, the contacts of a timer closing or the flick of a finger on a switch. Something that would detonate with the heat of the sun, fusing to molten glass everything within miles. Loss remembered the expression *ground zero*. That was where he now stood.

He looked back out to the east, trying to pick up the outline of the *Sunflower*. But she was gone or, more probably, blacked-out. Ching would be back by now, thinking the woman had pulled out, taking Loss with her as instructed. She had said that the attack would come "after five A.M., before six." So somewhere out on the black waters of the canal, men were preparing an assault with no real thought of taking the *Hussar*—just of destroying her. Except the wooden chest had been moved. Loss resolved to act quickly.

Thinking ahead, he tried to push aside the possibilities of what might occur. If Holly was still alive, and he didn't want to examine the grim alternative, he would have to have her clear of the *Hussar* by five. Much, much sooner, if possible. He realized that he had no idea when dawn would come in these latitudes and at this time of autumn. Two, or was it three, days ago on the Canadian border he had awakened with the sun. Then it had been sometime after five, but the exact time had seemed unimportant. He knew with certainty that Corrigan's truck had picked him up about five-thirty and the sun had been hard on the horizon, a ball of red gilding the spires of Vancouver's skyscrapers. So, he thought, I've got until dawn. No later. He glanced to the east, but there was no lighter cast on the horizon—just the silver moon, sickled upward, predecessor of the sun.

He pulled the automatic from his waistband and re-checked the safety. It was a pathetic thing, a woman's purse weapon, not much larger than a .22. Hardly big enough to stop a man. He eased away from the sail, moving aft past the anchor winch. His toe grated against a fitting on deck and he bent down, feeling it with his hand. It was a ring bolt; another matching one was secured four feet away. From Ching's description, it seemed obvious that this was where the chest had been secured. He had to get Holly the hell out of here and fast.

He could still hear the music, faint, but almost surely Bartok. It seemed almost incredible to him that the agent of a foreign power, nursing a nuclear weapon in its last hours, would amuse himself with classical music. *Concerto for Ground Zero,* he thought. The thought suddenly struck him that there might be no one left on the ship. Like a huge mechanical toy, the vessel was still alive, systems functioning as long as the batteries lasted.

If I move much farther aft, he thought, I'll be within the cast of illumination from the anchor light. Not clearly illuminated, but plainly visible to anyone keeping watch from within the deckhouse. He toyed with the idea of a direct assault, running ten-fifteen strides down the deck and into the deckhouse. But he would be the target, coming from dim light into darkness, backlighted by the anchor light, not knowing where his opponent would be. He sunk down to the deck. If any of the crew were alive, they would be locked in cabins, out of the way. Amidship, where the cockpit was, were the radios, engine controls, steering. So it was likely that the crew would be confined either in the forecastle, directly beneath where he stood, or in the aft cabin, an area far less accessible.

He felt his way along the deck, moving from the port side to the starboard, past the anchor winch. Unlike the *Surprise* or the *Mintar,* the *Hussar* lacked any sort of raised forecastle hatch. But some opening in the deck would be required to pass headsails below for stowing. He probed the deck with his fingers, moving aft from the winch, and found a cold strip of metal. He traced the outlines. Rectangular, about three feet on each side. His fingers found the hinges, set flush into the deck on the after side. Tracing further around, he touched a recessed ring, also set flush, no more than five inches from where his knee rested.

The ring lifted easily. He tugged upward and felt the hatch lift a fraction, then stop. He lowered it gently, aware that the noise of the hatch's movement would be amplified below. It didn't make sense. It would be probable that the hatch could be secured from within the ship's interior, but it also seemed logical that some locking device would be required topside, to ensure that seas sweeping the deck would not suck the hatch open. He probed around the perimeter of the hatch. Nothing. He lifted the ring again, moving it experimentally. The ring turned. His mouth dry, heart pounding, he twisted it through 180 degrees and pulled. The hatch lifted smoothly on well-oiled hinges.

The sound of the music was stronger now, but it sounded farther aft, in a cabin or the saloon. Supporting the hatch with one hand, he groped with the other and found a ladder set into a bulkhead, leading down. He tucked the automatic into his waistband and eased himself down, dropping the hatch gently into place over his head.

It was a corridor, dead black with thick carpeting under his feet and the smell of oiled wood around him. He reached out experimentally. On either side the paneling was smooth, waxy to the touch. Aft, a door blocked the corridor. He tested the handle and found that it would turn easily, the door opening a fraction unexpectedly. He pulled it closed and eased the handle shut. Near the bottom of the door he noticed a crack of light and, lowering himself to the carpet, found a frame of louvers. He could not see through them but could hear the music more distinctly and feel a draft of air.

Turning through 180 degrees and moving forward cautiously, he felt the cabin sole slant slightly upward. He took two cautious steps and found the corridor blocked by another door. He gripped the handle, moving it in increments, and found it locked. His hands searched for the lock and touched a keyhole. It was empty, the key missing.

"Stay out of here." Her voice was muffled, anxious. It jolted him. He pulled the automatic free, thumbing back the hammer, wheeling toward the aft door. Nothing. Just the thin flow of music. He waited for the footsteps but none came.

Putting his lips to the door he whispered, "Holly. It's me, Loss." He searched his mind, looking for a point of contact.

Silence. Then a movement from behind the door. A floorboard creaked. Her voice was clear now, whispering. "Down here, the louvers."

He dropped, fingers tracing down the door's inset panel and found the same arrangement for ventilation as he had on the aft corridor door. Her voice, strained, was inches from his face. "Good God, Brian. They'll kill you!" She paused and he could hear the rustling of her clothes. "It is you . . . ?" Her voice sounded as if she was on the edge of panic.

"Yes. Dammit—keep your voice down," he whispered. "Carriacou, Whistler Mountain . . . ah shit . . . you know that place in Montana I met you." He couldn't think of it and then did. "Missoula. Where we had enchiladas."

Her breath expelled. "Oh, thank God," she breathed.

"Where's the key to this door?"

"Amed. He's on watch now. They keep it with them." He could feel her breath against his face, even smell a hint of the soap she used. He paused, listening. The music had stopped. He heard a footstep in the corridor beyond the aft door, the sound of a pump cycling.

"He's in the galley," she whispered. The pump

417

cycled again and then the footsteps retreated. The music was replaced by an announcer. Loss caught the words, "Vienna Symphony Orchestra," another phrase less distinct and then the opening strains of something vaguely baroque. He could feel sweat saturating his back.

"When does he unlock you?"

"He doesn't. I mean, I always wait for the other one to be on watch, the Englishman. He doesn't bother me." There was a catch in her throat. "Amed—Amed's an animal. He keeps telling me that he's going to—to have me."

Loss gritted his teeth. "Where's the Englishman now?"

"Sleeping, I think. They take turns. No regular pattern. Just that when the one on watch gets tired, he wakes up the other."

"Sleeping where?"

"I . . . don't . . . know!" She drew the words out, frustrated.

He shifted his legs, a cramp beginning to pull in his thigh.

"Brian . . ." she whispered. "Both of them have guns. With those tubes—silencers."

He had expected no less. "The rest of the crew, the couple. Where are they?"

She was silent. He could hear her breathing. "Where?" he repeated.

"A day ago. Captain Fox found out about the chest. He was paranoid about dope. Something like that. There was a big argument and then Amed killed them."

Loss closed his eyes. Jesus, he thought. The tiny automatic seemed no more than a toy.

He bent down again, his lips to the louvers. "Holly, how can you get Amed to come up here without too much noise? Without waking up the Englishman?"

There was a pause. "I can call him." She moved

a finger between the louvers, a tip of it touching his face. It smelled of her. "Brian . . . just leave. Get help."

He didn't want to take the time to tell her that there was no help, that the *Hussar* was ground-zero for a nuclear fireball. "I'll get you out," he finally said. "What other way to get Amed up here?"

He listened to her breathing, the short intake of air. "The faucet!" she said almost aloud. Then more quietly, "The faucet. There's a hand basin in here. It runs off an electric pump. After you turn on the water, the pump starts and runs as long as you have the tap open. Captain Fox always used to warn me about using too much water."

"What makes you think Amed would do anything about it?"

"Just that we're low. Almost out of water. And Amed told me not to use it except to drink."

"OK," he whispered. "We'll give it a try. Turn the faucet on and then stand back from the door. If he comes, tell him that you're—you're washing yourself. Give me thirty seconds before you turn it on."

She was silent for a second, then whispered, "Brian. Take care." A pause. "I love you."

He moved rapidly up the ladder, pushing open the hatch, counting. Eleven—twelve. He cursed himself for failing to tell her to turn on a light in her cabin, something that would look normal, something that would divert attention from the open hatch. Eighteen, nineteen, twenty. He had the hatch open, propped back against the forward break in the coach roof. He pulled himself up through the hatch and turned, belly down on the deck, his hands free. He reversed his grip on the automatic, holding the barrel as if it were a hammer and checked his swing into the opening below. The corridor had a low deck head, no more than would accommodate a man of slightly more than average height. Say, six-two . . .

A light snapped on in her cabin; parallel bars of light spilled through the louver and lay across the corridor's rug. Twenty-eight, twenty-nine . . .

The pump cycled. Once. Twice. Then settled down into a stuttering series of cycles. He could hear water splashing. Incredibly, she was humming.

He wished for something heavier. If Amed came forward, he would have to pause, fitting the key in the lock. It would give Loss two seconds. And if he looked up . . . He made sure that the safety was off. Loss knew that he would kill the Arab if he had to.

The pump cycled again and again, and then suddenly stopped. He strained to hear any sound but it was as if the ship had died. The music was gone, the cycling of the pump, the splashing of water. Loss held his breath, his heart going up to a triphammer's pace. Nothing, he thought. Goddamn nothing.

The after door slammed open, the knob crashing into the paneling. Below him a penlight probed the darkness of the corridor, washing over the knob and keyhole. There was a movement below him, the light now steady. Loss could see the slotted tube of a silencer, then the weapon, then the foreshortened shape of the man.

"I told you about the water," he rasped, his voice heavily accented. She didn't reply. The hand of the man, fist reversed, rapped on the door. "You understand? I cut the circuit breaker." The voice was impatient now. Loss tensed for the strike, just as the man bent down, his eye to the keyhole. And Loss heard a sharp intake of breath.

Her voice came back level, agitated, muffled. "Amed?"

The man didn't answer. He laid down the pistol, then using the penlight, took a key from his pocket and centered the beam on the keyhole. He slipped the key into the lock, then twisting. Loss could hear the metallic click of tumblers moving.

"Amed?" she cried. "Stay . . ."

The Arab had pushed the door open and paused,

looking. She stood just feet beyond, naked, a towel pulled up around her body. Her face and throat were glistening wet, her cheeks flushed, eyes wide.

"Ins'Allah," Loss whispered. It was the only word he knew in Arabic.

Amed wheeled in surprise, looking aft. Loss brought the butt of the automatic down just as the Arab looked up, putting everything into the stroke. His face was laid open to the bone, blood welling up from his hairline down to his jaw. The scream caught in his throat and he hacked, spitting out teeth. Dropping to all fours, he scrambled blindly for the weapon, shouting now in Russian, trying to clear the blood away from his face with his free hand. His hand was on the grip just as Loss pumped four rounds into him. Loss could see the bullets hit, the Arab's chest heaving with each strike. The final shot took him in the neck and he collapsed, falling as a rag doll falls, downward and folding inward on himself. One leg twitched spasmodically and then he was still. Loss felt like gagging, and then did, not able to control his stomach.

Somewhere within the vessel a door slammed open. Loss held his breath, looking back down the hatch. Holly was immobilized, blood drained from her face, staring at the heap sprawled on the rug. Loss wanted to tell her to turn the light out, but his lips wouldn't form the words.

There was a metallic cough. The partially opened door to her cabin splintered, the bullet whining off steel in the ricochet. She still stood transfixed.

"Stand where you are, Holly." The voice was forced, thin and almost effeminate. She looked up, toward the corridor which led aft.

"Your hands, Holly. Get them up. Walk toward me." She dropped the towel, placing her hands above her head and passed beneath Loss, moving aft.

"You, on deck." The man's voice was under control. "Drop whatever weapons you have down the hatch. Then climb down."

She was beyond his vision, gone. His stomach was

knotted, his senses dead. He thought about the launch. It was a leap to the rail, a dive into the waters of the Hood Canal. He looked over his shoulder and saw the eastern horizon was a pale shade of opal. Not dawn but close to it.

She screamed, the shriek drawn out.

"He'll probably break her arm," a voice said from behind him. Not the same voice. "Move and you're dead."

Loss drew in a deep breath, then expelled it. He tossed the gun down through the open hatch.

"Very slowly, Loss," the voice said behind him. "Come aft along the deck. Hands behind your neck."

Petrov was crouched on the coach roof, half-hidden by the mast, a gun held in his hands. His face was illuminated by the anchor light, eyes in shadow, but the features unmistakable. "Good morning," he said conversationally, waving Loss aft with the gun. "Mind your step. Into the cockpit."

Loss stepped over the cockpit coaming, onto seat cushions and down to the cockpit flooring. It was a large, semienclosed cockpit with thwarts running fore and aft and a steering station placed amidships.

"Move over to the companionway where I can see you. Hands laced behind your neck. Trig is below, covering you, so if you want a bullet, you have a choice of front or back." Loss heard Petrov jump down lightly behind him. "All right, Loss. Down below. Keep your movements slow."

He moved down four steps into a carpeted saloon. It was a wide, luxurious area, carpeted thickly in a bronze-colored rug, inset shelves filled with books, a spacious dining table. On the port side, there was a leather settee, a stereo center, and a navigational desk. A weak light glowed under a gooseneck lamp over the chart table. The Englishman stood hunched down in a stairwell at the forward end of the saloon. The stairwell, Loss realized, would lead forward to Holly's cabin.

"Where is she?" he demanded. He heard Petrov behind him, sliding closed a hatch.

"Just sit down, Loss," Petrov said. Loss felt himself propelled roughly forward toward the settee. He stumbled in his stocking feet, catching one foot with the other, falling forward onto the leather surface. "What did you do with her?" Petrov said aside.

"In the starboard guest cabin," the Englishman replied. "I've locked it. Nice little tart," he added. "Lovely tits."

Loss glared at him. He could see the Englishman better now. Short, no more than five foot six. Heavy, but with no fat except a fullness in the cheeks. His hair was thin and sun-bleached, like rye grass bent back by the wind.

"Go forward and check how badly injured Amed is," Petrov said. The Englishman bobbed his head and disappeared down the companionway. "Drink?" the Russian asked in a bland tone. He slid down behind the dining table, the automatic laid down carefully as if he did not wish to scratch the varnish. With his eyes on Loss, he reached over, fumbling for a switch and then turned the table lamp on.

"How long have you been here, Petrov?"

"No ice, I'm afraid." He lifted a small recessed lid in the table and drew out a bottle. "Clever things, these yachts, aren't they. Good utilization of space. You don't mind a paper cup?" Without waiting for an answer, he reached behind him, eyes still on Loss, and drew two paper cups from a stack on the ledge. "How long . . . ?" He poured two measures into the cups and pushed one in Loss's direction. "Slowly, Brian. I'm offering you a drink, not an invitation."

Trig rushed up the companionway. "He's dead." He looked toward Loss.

Petrov raised his eyebrows. He lifted his cup and drank from it. "Can you handle it yourself, Trig? The setup? Running the transmission verification and the timer setting?"

The Englishman took off his glasses, pocketing them. "I'll have no problem. We were both trained. What about him?"

"That's my area," Petrov replied. "He has a few questions to answer." He tilted the cup, looking at the amber whiskey as if making a decision. "Start up the generator, Trig. I want the batteries well charged. And leave us alone for a while. I'll call you."

"How about Amed?" The Englishman was backing down the companionway, still watching Petrov, then flicking side glances toward Loss.

Petrov gave an almost imperceptible shrug. "Move him. One of the empty cabins. Secure the hatch and pick up the weapons. I want them up here." The Englishman grunted something and disappeared down the corridor.

"A mess, isn't it," the Russian said, leaning back. He pulled both hands, palms flat, back over his hair, down along his neck. There was a blond stubble on his cheeks. He picked up the whiskey and took another sip, pursing his lips as he rolled it around in his mouth, then swallowed. "A real mess, Loss."

"How long have you been here?"

"For two hours." He looked down at his wrist watch. "What time were the Chinese planning to attack?"

The question was like an explosion in Loss's mind. "What the hell do you mean?" But he knew his voice betrayed him.

Petrov smiled. "And the Chinese woman. Where is she?"

Loss averted his eyes, saying nothing. From down below and forward, he could hear Trig moving about. He wanted a cigarette badly.

"What did she tell you?" Petrov waited for a moment and then exhaled, impatiently. "It doesn't matter particularly," he finally said. "We've known about the *Sunflower* for two days. Since our little . . .

424

meeting in Tsawwassen. We had a second man on the ferry. He watched the whole process and then followed the woman when she took you and our other man. From there on in, it was just a matter of surveillance."

Loss looked up at him.

Petrov poured another round into the small cups, then lit a cigarette and passed the pack to Loss. "Help yourself," he said. He shoved a disposable lighter across the table. "Two of them left the *Sunflower* at midnight. They landed at the marina, then took a car which was waiting for them. By the time they returned, I had four men positioned. It was a very brief meeting. From there we rowed out to the *Sunflower*. The one on board didn't die gracefully." Petrov took a long drag on the cigarette and then exhaled. ". . . But he didn't tell us where the woman had taken you." He smiled briefly. "But here we are again, reunited."

"Where's the *Sunflower?*"

Petrov stuffed the cigarette out. "The *Sunflower?* I would say that she is probably in the Strait of Juan de Fuca by now. I would guess that she'll probably be on the bottom in some convenient bay on the Canadian side by mid-afternoon." He picked up the automatic. "Come on, Brian," he said. "I have very little time. Where did you go with the woman?"

"What woman?"

Petrov stood up and moved carefully from behind the table, toward the companionway, never taking his eyes from Loss. The silenced automatic remained boresighted on Loss's midsection.

"Trig!" Petrov called. There was an affirmative answer. "Activate the weapon's battery." Trig appeared at the bottom of the companionway, his face beaded with perspiration. "Should I set the backup timer?"

Petrov shook his head. "Not yet. Not until I have the final radio contact with Emil. Just do as I say." Petrov turned to Loss and studied his face, then

425

glanced down at his watch. "Very little time left, Brian. I think that you can understand that you and the girl will die."

Reflexively, Loss tensed. The pit of his stomach contracted, fear biting into his nervous system. Petrov raised the weapon rapidly in a warning gesture. "But not yet, Brian. Not yet. And how you and the girl die is up to you. Either very cleanly or with a great deal of pain." Petrov eased back, relaxing marginally, the automatic still unwavering, its black mouth aimed at Loss's stomach.

"So we won't waste any more time," Petrov continued. "I want you to tell me several things. I know the answers to some of the questions, but not all of them. The Chinese on the *Sunflower*, toward the last few minutes of his life, tended to slur his answers a bit. Let's see whether you can do better."

"I have nothing to tell you, Petrov. Nothing that you don't probably already know."

"Perhaps," the Russian replied. "Perhaps. But I think that I'll have to be the judge of that." He gave Loss a bland smile. "I know what you're thinking. Where there's life there's hope. Correct? But consider this. That device which now sits in the engine room, when detonated, will create a fireball nearly two kilometers in diameter. Where you are now sitting will reach, very briefly, the temperature of the sun. And nothing, Loss—nothing for a distance of ten kilometers will be anything more than radioactive dust, carried on a fire storm which will consume much of Seattle by nightfall."

Loss's face was ashen. "Jesus—you're insane!"

Petrov shrugged. "Insane. You mean the mad bolshevik bomb thrower?" He laughed a little at the mental image, and then his face hardened. "The decision to carry out this project was not mine. I have no personal desire to see millions of people die—even Americans. But the decision was made by sane men, in the same way and for the same reasons that your own

426

President Truman made the decision to use nuclear weapons on the two Japanese cities. Out of military and political necessity." He lifted his free hand, turning the palm up. "No, not insane. This is simply the beginning of a final resolution of power between Russia and the West. The first strike, you might say." He dropped his hand back into his lap. "What I am saying, Loss, is that once we activate the device, nothing can stop it from detonating. The Chinese might have succeeded, but their effort was a last-minute one—ill prepared and undermanned and, as you know, that attack will not come. The device will detonate as the U.S.S. *Ohio* moves past this anchorage on her way to the Pacific."

"How does it detonate?"

Petrov raised his eyebrows. "Very good, Brian. You've answered one of my most troublesome questions. What you're saying is that the Chinese didn't know how it would detonate?"

Loss thought about it. There didn't seem to be any reason not to tell Petrov. Like past history, it wouldn't affect the outcome. "No," he answered. "They didn't seem to know."

"It wouldn't have mattered if they had known, or mattered very little, because there are two firing sequences. The primary one is triggered by a pulsed radio signal. But just in case of jamming, the bomb also has a timer. Either one is sufficient." Beneath their feet there was the cough of a generator starting. It picked up speed and then settled into a steady hum. Loss heard a steel door slamming, cutting the noise of the generator to a dim whisper. Trig, shirt wet with perspiration, appeared in the companionway.

"The generator's on," he said. "The weapon's battery is activated and showing full voltage. I've got three amber lights on the confidence circuit. It's ready to go." He went aft and pulled a beer from a small refrigerator set under the library shelves.

Petrov nodded. "Warm up the radio. We'll give

427

Emil a call in a few minutes. It's almost five-fifteen."
He turned back to Loss. "A few questions . . . how
did the Chinese plan to blow up the *Hussar?*"

Loss looked at Petrov and then to the pulled drapes
beyond the Russian's back. He could see nothing
through them but there was an orange cast backlight-
ing the drapes, the rising sun. "I don't know," Loss
replied.

The Russian stood up, impatience furrowing his
mouth. "I've spent precious time with you, Loss.
Chatting in a friendly manner, giving you whiskey. I
thought you understood the alternatives." Aside to
Trig, Petrov snapped, "Bring the girl up. And the
torch."

"She doesn't know anything!" Loss rocked forward
to the edge of the settee.

Petrov thumbed back the hammer, holding the
weapon in a two-handed combat stance. "One move
more and I'll fire. At your stomach. It's a very painful
way to die."

Trig passed behind Petrov and disappeared forward.
There was the sound of a door opening, her voice and
then Trig's, arguing. Both of them appeared in the
companionway moments later, Holly dressed in an
oversized man's bathrobe, Trig following closely behind, the automatic in one hand, a butane blowtorch
in the other. He set the torch on the chart table, lit it,
and adjusted the flame to a hard, blue feather.

"Lie down," Petrov commanded. Her face swollen,
a dark bruise welling up across one cheek, she looked
at Loss, tears forming in the corners of her eyes.

"Down, little girl," Trig echoed, pushing her shoulders forward and tripping her. Unbalanced, she teetered forward and fell to her knees. "On your back,"
he snapped and picking up the torch, stepped forward,
straddling her chest and pinning her arms with his feet.
He looked up to Petrov, waiting for the command.

"Pain is relative, Loss," Petrov said quietly. "You
can choose to make it a microsecond for her, or minutes of agony." He nodded to Trig and before Loss

428

could react, the torch had been passed rapidly across her hair. She screamed, more in shock than pain. A black mass of burned hair fused, filling the saloon with a sickening stench.

She was sobbing now, terror stricken. "You see," Petrov said. "Is withholding information that important to you?"

Loss was wild-eyed, his teeth set. Without taking his eyes from Holly he whispered, "Good God, Petrov. Get that—that fucking animal *off* her! I'll tell you whatever you want."

The Russian relaxed. "All right. No lies, no hesitation. What did the Chinese intend to use to blow up the *Hussar?*"

"Explosives. They told me satchel charges. I never saw them."

"Excellent. I *did* see them. And the woman. Where did she take you?"

"She didn't—I mean she was going to. To Everett, Washington. To meet CIA types. She wanted me there to verify the story."

"And . . . ?"

"I . . . And I got the gun away from her. We had a fight."

"You killed her?"

Loss shook his head. "No, I took her south along the Hood Canal. Left her locked up in a deserted cabin. She knew the whole thing—the bomb, the Welsh end of it. I planned to go back and pick her up after I got Holly off."

Petrov laughed. "You mean you thought that you'd be able to overcome two armed men, destroy the device, and get the girl out?"

Petrov was right. It sounded insane. "No," Loss answered. "Not quite. I thought I could get her off before the Chinese made the assault, something like that." He looked down at her. Her eyes were shut, hands gripped in small fists.

Petrov brushed back a drape. Beyond him Loss could see a pale apricot sky, cloudless. Petrov's features were lit by the diffused light of the dawn reflecting off the water. He dropped the drape and turned, facing Loss.

"Describe the cabin. What side of the canal. Anything to identify it."

He thought about the woman. Just a woman. Forties, fifties perhaps. The full, soft features of an Oriental, the precise voice. The toughness, and yet the way that she had wished him luck.

"I don't know," he said finally. But he knew the delay had been a betrayal. Petrov looked at him.

"Try harder. More details." Trig looked up at Loss and then down at the girl. He adjusted the blue feather, turning the valve up, so that the flame extended in a hard yellow jet of intense light. The sound of the burner was deceptive, a fluttering hiss.

He said it in a rush, stumbling over the words. "It was a cabin, two cabins, but one was just a shed. Rundown place. Log construction. A dock. With two boats, canoes, I think, overturned and up on the lawn. And it was on the west side of the canal. About a mile and a half, maybe two miles south of here."

"Anything else?"

Loss thought, trying to pluck details from his memory. "No, just that it was probably a hunter's cabin. Dirty. There was a name painted on the door—*Sans Souci*."

"Without care," Petrov translated. "Very cute. That leaves me without care. Two-miles radius from the ground zero." He motioned to Trig. "Let her up. I'll call Emil now." He waved the automatic at Holly. "Next to your boyfriend."

Trig handed Petrov a small, transistorized radio. Petrov snapped it on and keyed a mike button. "Truck Number Three, this is Warehouse. Do you read?"

A burst of random noise and then, "—arehouse. This is Number Three. I've been trying to contact you for half an hour. Over."

Petrov thumbed his mike. "All OK. We had some troubles with the union. What's your position?"

430

"Forty miles south. The cargo you're lookin' for has already been shipped. Over."

Petrov turned to Trig, his face contorted. "The *Ohio* has left dock!" He glanced at his watch.

"Warehouse, you read? I say again, the cargo has already been shipped. Over."

There was the edge of panic in his voice. "What's the estimated time of arrival here? Over."

"Warehouse . . ." There was a delay, the empty hiss punctuated by bursts of static. "Warehouse, this is Number Three. Our calculations show about forty-six minutes from now. Five fifty-one. You copy that, Warehouse? Over."

Petrov turned aside to Trig. The Englishman's face had broken out with beads of sweat. His face was vacant of expression, like a man who is in shock. "We have time," Petrov rasped. "We can be gone in three minutes. Four to get inshore. We can be thirty miles to the south by the time the device fires." He turned back to the small transceiver and thumbed the mike.

"Number Three Truck, this is Warehouse. I copy you all OK. We don't have much time on this end. Stand by to give us a transmission on the other frequency. We need a minute to set things up. Do you copy?"

The reply came back almost laconic. "Number Three standing by."

Petrov wheeled on Trig. "Get down to the engine room. Set up the device for the confidence check of the trigger tone. Then set the timer!"

The Englishman was pleading with his eyes. In disgust, Petrov was at the companionway stairs in two strides. "Never mind. You keep Loss and the girl covered. I'll do this myself." Almost as an afterthought he shouted up the stairs, "If they move, shoot." A steel door banged open. From below, Petrov's voice, muffled, shouted, "Tell Emil to transmit the trigger tone!"

Trig visibly collected himself. He was sweating profusely, his shirt saturated. He spoke into the mike,

431

"Number Three, this is Warehouse. Go ahead with your transmission on the other frequency."

The voice came back. "Transmitting . . . NOW!"

Loss watched Trig, measuring the distance. He couldn't bring himself to move, delaying, trying to zero in on some means of distracting the man. Loss started to inch closer to the edge of the settee, shifting his weight forward onto the balls of his feet, sliding his hands behind him as an added means of thrusting himself forward. It would be seconds now before Petrov returned.

The voice shouted up from the engine room. "Tell him transmission received. I have a green light on the trigger tone circuit. And I'm setting the backup timer to forty-four minutes."

"Number Three, this is Warehouse. Your transmission received. Our inventory is ready to go. I repeat, our inventory is ready to go."

Number Three came back instantly. "Understood. I figure forty-three minutes to run. See you up north. Get moving, man."

"Timer set to forty-four minutes and running. All confidence lights green," Petrov shouted.

Trig keyed the mike. "Warehouse is in good shape. Everything checks out. We're ready to handle the cargo. Warehouse over and out."

Loss launched himself, using his hands against the back of the settee, his legs bunched and then uncoiling against the paneling beneath the settee. He went low, diving flat for the Englishman. A sledgehammer blow ruptured his left arm, and it all seemed suspended in time: the look on Trig's face, the muzzle coming around, the feel of burning gases blowing past his face, the shock, not feel, of part of his body blown away. But he had the momentum. He collided with Trig, his arms flailing, trying to keep the muzzle away. He absorbed everything like a man apart, a spectator of Trig's panting and of the pressures of muscles stressed beyond limits, of the stench of sweat, both from effort and fear. The automatic, cumbersome because of the silencer, was in Trig's right hand, arcing around. From the corner of his eye, Loss saw a blur. The blue steel bottle of the butane torch smashed into Trig's head, opening a flap of. flesh across his neck. Then Holly was on him, battering Trig from behind as Loss wrestled the gun from his grasp. Loss turned in time to see Petrov, face upturned, climbing the stairwell. Loss fired.

High. The paneling above Petrov splintered with the impact of the bullet. He fired again, but the Russian was gone.

Two shots snapped out of the darkness of the corridor, both missing and plowing furrows in the insulation of the overhead. Loss grabbed Holly, pulling her down to the carpet. Trig was still upright, reeling away, smashing against the furniture. A bright weal of blood flowing from his neck.

There was a moment of silence. Loss listened above the hammering of his pounding heart, the roughness of his breath, gripping the automatic. Small bits of dust from the insulation drifted down through the half-light. He could hear a sound in the corridor forward, the movement of a door swinging on hinges, of a latch turning. The shock of the wound was beginning to set in. He felt down along his left arm with his right hand. He had no feeling below the elbow, the left hand useless, unable to flex. Blood welled up through the sleeve, saturating the cloth. Loss realized that he was light-headed, afraid of passing out.

The hatch rattled behind him. He half turned, afraid to take his eyes from the companionway.

"Trig's getting away," she cried. She started to rise; Loss jerked her down. The gun in the corridor below coughed, the bullet shattering the glass window a foot above their heads. He didn't know whether Petrov had aimed for Trig or himself. Footsteps pounded down the deck. Seconds later, a large outboard engine started, over revved, and then dropped in note as the engine's clutch bit in. The revs picked up, whining, the sound diminishing into the distance. Then silence; just the sound of labored breathing, the small random sounds a vessel makes, the underlying vibration of the generator.

"Petrov, you hear me?" Loss steadied the automatic, aiming for the head of the companionway. He squeezed gently, taking up the slack in the trigger.

The voice was startling in its nearness. "I hear."

"Your friend took the speedboat."

Petrov sighed. "So I gather. Trig is what they call a survivor."

Loss rolled his head to one side, speaking to her in a hushed whisper. "Crawl out of the line of fire. Off to one side. And watch the forward hatch."

"I could hear that," Petrov said. "You needn't bother."

His arm was an agony, the shock wearing off. Loss tried to collect his thoughts but the pain kept overriding his concentration. Blood, saturating his sleeve, was staining the carpet. Irrationally Loss caught himself worrying that the stain would ruin the fibers.

"You understand what has happened, Loss? That regardless of whether you kill me or not, the device goes off?"

"You can disarm it." Loss said it as a command.

Petrov snorted. "Not even the designer could. The firing circuits are armed and running. There is no so-called fail-safe switch. The device will fire on either the recept of Emil's trigger tone or when the timer runs out." His voice paused. "Therefore, you win but you lose, Brian."

"The Chinese said it could be disarmed by blowing it up."

"Possibly. Very possibly. I assume that you have three or four kilos of high explosives lying around. Assuming, of course, that I let you."

"You want to die!"

434

There was a long silence. Finally Petrov replied in a tired voice, "No. I have no desire to die. But even if we left the *Hussar* now, we would still be within the killing radius when the device detonates." He paused and then said, "Thirty-nine minutes to go, Loss."

Loss suddenly realized the impact of what Petrov was saying, that they were the walking dead. Even if they were to reach the launch, its speed wasn't much over six knots. Three miles in half an hour. But she might have a chance on shore. His mind cleared, started to function with greater clarity. He motioned to Holly, making a scribbling motion, pointing toward the navigational table. She frowned and then, understanding, nodded. Reaching over, she grabbed a pencil and the chart and then pushed it across the carpet toward him.

His left hand was useless. Risking it, he laid the gun down and then scrawled,

. . . launch tied up forward on bowsprit. Get to shore. Get car, go south. NOW!

He underlined the *NOW* and pushed the chart toward her.

She read it, shaking her head and made short, choppy strokes with the pencil, pushing it back.

I LOVE YOU. NO!

He looked across at her. Blond hair disheveled and tangled, face swelling, eyes red, she smiled at him, a smile that was partly a communication of love and partly a statement of independence. She wrinkled her nose and then stuck her tongue out at him.

"Loss, you're too quiet."

"I was thinking." He was. The marine radiotelephone was recessed into the forward bulkhead, out of

435

Petrov's line of fire, but on the opposite side of the saloon. She could crawl behind me, he thought, while I cover the head of the companionway. He scribbled on the chart,

If you can operate radio, crawl behind me, keep low and then call MAYDAY on distress freq. Bomb on board. Clear area!!!

She nodded and started to move behind him.

"Loss, what are you up to?"

"Nothing. What's the time?" He said it loudly, trying to cover the sound of her movements, trying to distract.

"Thirty-seven minutes."

She snapped on the transmitter, then moved the channel selector. The saloon was filled with a rush of sound, snatches of conversation as she changed through the different channels. From below, a steel door clanged; there was a shuffle of movement and the door slammed shut. Loss fired into the corridor but it was empty.

"Mayday, Mayday, the yacht *Hussar* . . ." The light on the chart table died, the transmit light winked out. From below, he could hear the snapping sound of switches being thrown.

She dropped the mike. "He's thrown all the circuit breakers," she whispered. "He's in the engine room."

As she said it, the sound of the generator altered, dying. In seconds, it rumbled to a stop. The vessel was silent.

"Loss," the muffled voice yelled.

"It's your dime!"

"That's the last of your stupid mistakes. I'm in the engine room and the door's bolted. There's one thing I didn't tell you about the device."

"We're going now," Loss said to her in a whisper.

"Loss—you listening to me?"

"I'm listening, Petrov."

"The timer can't be stopped and it can't be set back.

436

But I can turn it forward. You or the woman move and I'll reset it to detonate right now. I want to hear your voices all the time from now on!"

He looked at her. But she was standing, looking forward through the windshield of the *Hussar,* her face expressionless. He stood up slowly, the pain of his arm surging with each beat of his heart. Beyond the anchorage, very far down the canal, the morning light glinted off the black hull of a submarine. Its size dwarfed the tugs that rode on its flanks. He estimated that it was three miles away.

"Loss, you understand?"

"Yes. I understand." He sat down heavily in a chair. "How long?"

"Thirty-five—thirty-four minutes now."

Loss remembered that Petrov had called it "the back-up timer," but that there was a signal transmitted as well. "What causes your man in the truck to send the signal?"

He could hear Petrov laugh. "The 'truck' as you call it is a fishing boat, the one that I was going to take a very pleasant cruise on to a Red Banner Fleet submarine in Canadian waters. He transmits the signal based on a very secret electronic surveillance device called a television set."

"What do you mean, 'television set'?"

"A portable television set, Loss. Two local Seattle television stations are broadcasting it live. It will be our luck to go up in the middle of a soap commercial."

Loss pushed himself up. She was sitting on the settee, her face buried in her hands.

"How do I get into the engine room? There's got to be some other way."

"No," she whispered. "It's only got one door, a steel one. Captain Fox called it a collision bulkhead. We always had to keep it locked at sea. There's just a tiny plate-glass window so you can look in. Four or five inches in diameter."

"How about vents?"

"Yes—two of them. But they're on deck. They go

down through some ducting to blowers to vent the bilge. Fox always started them five minutes before he started the engine.''

"Why? Because of the heat?''

She nodded her head. "Partly that, but the blowers suck out any gasoline or cooking-gas fumes before the engines are started.''

"Gasoline? There must be some on board?''

She shook her head. "No, they always kept it in the speedboat. And the cooking gas won't work. He'd smell it right away. They put the smell of garlic in it, just in case of a leak in the gas line. He'd reset the timer right away.''

"What are you doing up there?'' Petrov called.

"Having a cigarette. You want one?''

The Russian laughed, the sound of his voice strained. "No, thanks. But I'd take a whiskey. Should have brought the bottle with me. But be my guest.''

He looked down the canal. Before it had just been a shape, but now he could see the bone of white water under the tug's bows. He looked away, not wanting to watch it. He turned to her, drawing her to him. "It's a mess, Holly. I'm sorry.'' There seemed nothing more to say. She hugged him back, her face buried in his neck.

"Twenty-nine minutes now, Loss. You really think there is a God?'' His voice was cracked now, either from shouting or from nervous strain. Loss could imagine the Russian sitting among the machinery in the dark guts of the ship, smelling oil and bilge water, waiting for the minutes to run out. Loss flicked his eyes down the canal. He guessed it would be less than a quarter of an hour. If he could just get a shot at Petrov and then fire the few remaining shells at the device, it might be enough.

"Holly, what else goes into the engine room? Pipes, wires, cables? Something large enough to get the barrel of a gun through?''

She was unresponsive, her head still buried in his

438

neck. She finally lifted her face to his, tear stained. "Nothing," she whispered. "It's all behind wood paneling. Very tightly fitted."

"There must be something—tubes or pipes running into the engine room. Come on, think!"

She shook her head. "I don't know. I didn't go in there much. A lot of plumbing, I suppose. For the fresh water system. Bundles of wires, cable to the cockpit engine controls, the fire extinguisher pipes—"

He cut her off in midsentence. "What kind—the fire extinguisher? Water?"

Her eyes widened. "No, gas. Carbon dioxide. There are two huge green bottles in a locker in the aft cabin. If there's a fire in the engine room, some sort of a gadget down there melts and both bottles flood the engine room." She inhaled sharply. "Brian . . ." she gripped his arm, ". . . there's a manual release in the cockpit. In case there's a fire, the helmsman can also release the gas. It's a red handle housed in a red metal box just under the engine controls in the cockpit."

"Pull it! I'll cover the engine-room door in case he tries to get out."

She sucked in her breath. "Brian, he'll die. He'll suffocate!"

"Dammit, don't think about it. Pull the handle when you hear me talking to Petrov. Not before."

Loss tucked the automatic under his left armpit, his left hand useless. With his freed right hand, he scooped up the bottle of Scotch and moved cautiously down the companionway. On the port side, he found the door to the engine room. It was steel with a heavy latching handle. A small glass window was set into the upper part of the door. He tapped with his fingertips, lightly.

"You still there, Petrov?" He heard a movement from within, the hollow, metallic sound of a heel scraping on a grating.

"Probably here until I die, Loss." The voice was only inches away, on the other side of the door. He could hear Petrov move again.

"I brought down the Scotch."

"Thoughtful. Where's the girl?"

"In the saloon. She—doesn't feel well."

There was a long pause. Loss listened, waiting for her to pull the handle. He had to keep Petrov away from the device, far enough away so that the Russian couldn't reach the timer.

"Who keeps the keys to the Kingdom?" Petrov said. He hadn't moved.

"Peter—St. Peter."

A pause. "I'm not sure that I'd want to go to my Maker with alcohol on my breath." Petrov laughed, but it was a bitter laugh. "Tell me, Brian . . ."

"Shoot."

"That's the point. We don't have enough time left to go firing nine-millimeter bullets at each other." He paused. "Twenty minutes left. I trust you, you trust me. If either of us shoots through this little window, the glass would be thick enough to deflect the bullet. Leaving the other man a clear shot. I have a proposition."

Loss listened, but he could not hear Holly. Nothing. He swore bitterly under his breath. "I'm listening, Petrov."

"I'd like to have a cigarette and a glass of whiskey with you. The thing is beyond us now. I'll turn on the engine-room circuit breaker. So you can see me. I'll drop my automatic in the bilge. Then I turn on the galley circuit breaker. I'll be able to see you through the window. You drop yours in the galley sink. I open the door. We have a drink together. Agreed?"

"Why, Petrov?"

"Why not?" the Russian replied. "We've both made mistakes. Now we pay for them. You know that anyone who lives up to what he believes in, takes risks. It's the price for not leading a dull life."

440

"OK. We get rid of the guns," Loss said.

A light snapped on, flooding the engine room with a harsh white light. Loss backed away from the door, cautious of the window. He saw a movement—the Russian looking back at him and then dropping his weapon between the frames of the bilge.

Petrov, hunched over beneath the low overhead, approached the door. "Now you," he called. The galley light, fluorescent, flickered on.

Loss backed away, his eyes on the door. The Russian was watching, his face to the window.

The sound of the carbon dioxide firing was an explosion; a torrent of sound, as if a steam hose was running at full pressure. The light in the engine room dimmed to an opaque mist. The handle started to turn, Loss rushed forward, slamming his weight against the door, forcing it back. He dropped the locking bar into place. Through the window he saw the outline of Petrov throwing himself against the door, battering it in a frenzy of desperation. Then the battering stopped. Loss saw Petrov's face for one brief instant, teeth bared, his mouth distinctly forming the word "bastard." And then he fell to the floor, dragging his fingers down the glass.

He met her in the saloon, running in from the cockpit, her hair blowing in the stiff wind. She was frantic, pointing. He looked beyond her, across the anchorage. The U.S.S. *Ohio*, sleek and black like a great whale, slid through the water, white waves piling up over her bow sections. The escorting tugs worried at her side like pilot fish. Loss could see dozens of men in the sail, white hats brilliant in the sun, and on the decks stood ranks of men, drawn up in formation. They were less than a mile away. Minutes, he thought.

He took her by the arm with his good hand, squeezing so that her face reflected the hurt. "Listen hard. Do exactly as I say. Something you said before. What kind of fuel did you use for cooking?"

441

"Gas. Bottled gas."

"It's explosive?"

She nodded. "Very. I always had to be in the galley when I was cooking. There's a master valve . . ."

"OK. And the pumps in the bilge. What makes them go on?"

"A switch. In the cockpit—but there's an automatic pump. One that starts up if there's even only a couple of inches of water in the bilge. It shuts on and off automatically."

"You're sure?" He was tearing the words off, spittle flecking her face, the pressure of his grip sinking into her flesh.

"Yes—yes. I'm positive!"

He turned away from her, then paused in the companionway. "When I yell, turn on the bottled-gas master valve and then turn on everything—oven, burners—everything."

Loss unbarred the door and stepped aside, letting the gas escape. The engine-room door remained open, swinging through small arcs as the *Hussar* rolled in the light swell. Loss pushed the door wide open and entered. Petrov lay face down on the grating, his hair coated with frost. The entire engine room had a white patina; frost had formed as the carbon dioxide hit the humid air, freezing it. The fog of the frozen moisture was slowly clearing, settling. Then Loss saw it. In the far corner on a workbench was a wooden chest, three green lights glowing within the deeply recessed cavity.

He found the circuit breaker panel, tracing down with his finger until the label "auto bilge pump" was opposite, then clicked it on.

The saltwater intakes to the big Mercedes were obvious. Loss traced them down to where the metal pipes connected to rubber hoses, held with clamps. Beneath that the hoses snaked into a fitting against the skin of the hull. The workbench yielded a large screwdriver. In thirty seconds he had loosened the clamps, but the hoses were encrusted with salt, refusing to

442

move even when he pried at them with the screw-driver.

Frantic, he flung the screwdriver across the engine room in disgust, then grabbed a broad-bladed wood chisel. Hacking at the hose, he tore the rubber away in chunks. Trickles formed, followed by a thin high-pressure stream, and then a flood of water as the hose tore away.

"Turn on the gas!" he screamed. Moving past the bench, he looked for a fraction of a second at the device. Glowing digital numbers, running in reverse sequence briefly blinked and then registered 2:16. It flicked again but he was running, stumbling over Petrov, slamming against the door as it swung inward.

It took less than a minute. Stumbling, pain jagging at his arm as if it were impaled on a molten blade, running along the deck, Holly before him, the outsized robe flapping in the wind. The outboard started. He savagely slammed it into forward and the engine stuttered once and then picked up, rpms climbing into a scream. Behind them, the *Hussar* was shrinking, white hull growing distant, spars bright and reflecting back the morning sun. And ahead of them, the black hull of the *Ohio*—still distant but growing, the flag at her masthead snapping in the morning wind.

The *Hussar* was dying. Seawater flowed into her guts, slowly rising past the lowest frame, then touching the bellies of the engine oil pans, still rising, scum black, oil slicked, swirling in the turbulence of the incoming sea.

And gas flowed. Heavier than air, it sought the lowest point, displacing the air, filling the bilges, the floors, rising like an invisible liquid above the corridor, drifting in fragmented gusts across the floor of the saloon.

But the man and the pump were still alive. One breathing, the other, senseless, waiting. And the water rose.

A diaphragm closed against the pressure of the rising water. Contacts touched. The pump started sucking air at first and then chattered down into a steady rhythm, disgorging water overboard. The pump was not designed to cope with the massive inflow but it worked on, laboring against the load. As the pump ran the encased sides of the motor, sealed against both water and the atmosphere, guaranteed by its manufacturer to be both sparkproof and waterproof, slowly submerged in the oil-slicked water.

The man moved next, not quite dead, not really alive. The gas, freezing the moisture in the air, had seared his lungs. His eyes were filmed, the corneas glazed by the roaring inlet of carbon dioxide. Part of his brain had died, for he had breathed too long the toxic gas which filled the room. But his body responded on some lower level as the water lapped against his face, saturating his clothes, wetting his stiffened hair. He looked up but the light was dim and the forms around him were vague. A figure moved in the doorway and, from something distant in his memory, he knew it was his enemy.

His hand found the screwdriver, rolling across the grating near his fingertips. He half rose. A name imbedded in his memory reached his lips.

"Loss," he rasped, and flung the tool.

The blade of tempered steel hit the door, striking a single spark before the screwdriver clattered to the deck. A pinpoint of light, intense yellow, grew into a roaring sun. His last brief thought was that he had won.

Chapter 28

It was one of those remote, little-known shipyards on the banks of the Sacramento River, edged with mud flats and littered with the carrion of rotting hulks. The maroon van, thick with dust and bearing Washington plates, paused at the turnoff and then accelerated down the rutted driveway, swaying heavily on its suspension.

The yard was nothing more than a parking lot and a large galvanized shed with a marine railway linking it to the brackish water. Leaning against the shed was a one-story wooden office, the product of a builder of indifferent talent. It was hard to guess which building supported the other.

The van stopped, momentarily blanketed by the cloud of dust raised by its passage, and swept down from the rutted driveway by the offshore wind. It had not rained in the Bay area in over two weeks and the weeds and grass of the yard were coated with a patina of fine grit.

The man got out awkwardly, favoring his left arm, which was supported by a sling. He walked into the shed.

The interior was cool and dark. The skeleton of a partially planked sloop rested in a cradle with staging set up on either side of it. He could hear the whine of an electric drill in the bowels of the hull.

He rapped heavily on a frame. "Mr. Bedameyer? Hello!"

The whine died. Heavily booted feet moved within the hull and a man coughed, hacking up phlegm. A face appeared along the railing. It was creased with sun and weather, gaunt under the shadow of a peaked painter's cap. "Bedameyer. That's me. What's yer pleasure?"

The younger man climbed the staging ladder awkwardly, his right hand moving up the support railing between each step. He came level with the older man. "I'm Lund. I've come down to inspect the schooner for the man that called this morning."

Bedameyer nodded, putting the electric drill down on the staging. He fished into the deep pockets of his fatigues and pulled out a plug of tobacco. Tearing off a piece with his teeth, he pocketed the foil-wrapped plug. "Can't smoke in a boat shed," he said, shifting the wad into his cheek. "Yeah—some guy called. You a buyer or a tire-kicker?"

"He's serious if the price is right. What's her history?"

Bedameyer eased down on his haunches, wiping sweat from his forehead. He removed his cap and slapped it vigorously against his thigh, creating a fine cloud of sawdust. There was a strong smell of resinous pine about him.

"Old thing," he started. "Been up and down the West Coast for donkey's years—Christ knows how many owners. I remember back in forty-eight replacing three planks under the icebox where she went rotten." He squinted, looking out toward the finger pier where the schooner lay. "But she's in good shape basically. Someone's put a lot of money into her in the last few years. Originally built in San Diego in the late thirties. Alden design and bronze fastened, mind you. Not galvanized crap."

"I mean her recent history."

"Couple of kids. Stole her off her moorings in L.A. and made it this far. Put in here with a busted spreader. Some local yachty recognized her and called the cops. State police picked them up. At least they paid their bill before they got busted."

"I mean before she was stolen."

The man scratched his balding scalp. "Don't know, not much anyway. Guy down in L.A. named Kitzner owned her. Hit by a car when he was crossing a street. They said he was blind in one eye—never seen the car coming. So it was up for sale by the estate, but she's been run down. Paint looks bad. The kids didn't do a lick of work on her." He wiped his nose. "I figure a week with a paint brush and she'd be ready to go anywhere."

"You have the papers to her?"

"Yep. Power of attorney and the documents. The estate's lawyer said that I wasn't to put another cent of work into her. Thirty-three thousand firm, take it or leave it. Plus eighty bucks for dockage."

"I'll look her over," Loss said. "She might be just what the buyer's looking for." He worked his way down the ladder and then walked out onto the finger pier. A girl was waiting for him, sitting on the weathered planks of the dock, watching the highway beyond the drive.

Bedameyer squinted out of the office window, watching the schooner. Gulls wheeled, screaming under a dirty linen sky. The sun shone briefly through tears in the clouds, allowing dazzling shafts of light to sweep the river. A wind was getting up and Bedameyer reckoned there would be more rain before it cleared.

As he watched, the schooner's auxiliary diesel engine coughed black smoke and then settled down into a steady rhythm. The gulls, startled, pivoted around an invisible pylon and tracked downriver toward more peaceful feeding grounds.

Bedameyer pulled a hand down his weathered face, wiping his skin. Lund or whatever his name was had been working fourteen-hour days for a week now. Man on the run, he thought. All the signs of a husband skippin' out on his wife. Bullshit about buyin' the boat for some other man. Paid crew didn't work that hard.

And the girl was a gamey young thing, somethin' a man in his forties, tired of paying bills and getting pushed around by life, would take along. Nice tits too, he thought, cracking a knuckle.

He sorted through a stack of bills, most of them paid in cash. Lund was loading the schooner for sea, no doubt about that. But not with the usual yacht-shit. No chrome doo-dads or fancy gear that would break down in the first blow. Lund was methodically laying on oversized commercial gear, stuff that would work. The man knew ships, was for sure. Not like them people who bought boats, hung pots of ivy from the boom gallows, plugged into a marina and called themselves sailors. No, Lund and the girl were different. And as long as Lund paid, Bedameyer wasn't asking questions.

Surprise didn't look any different to the unskilled eye than she had a week ago, but Bedameyer could see the transformation. Lund had riven new line for all the halyards, replaced galvanized turnbuckles with bronze, and sent the sails out for cleaning and restitching. Bedameyer fished a lukewarm beer out of the cooler and checked the invoices. Wind-vane steering gear, an inflatable dinghy, spare engine and generator parts out the kazoo. Totaled over nine thousand, paid on demand.

As he looked up, a young man, a Jap, Bedameyer figured, wheeled a load of supplies down the creaking dock. Canned goods, it looked like. That had been going on for five days now and the schooner was four or five inches down on her marks. Most likely over a ton of food.

Yeah, skippin' out on the wife, Bedameyer concluded. Happened to a lot of them the first time they couldn't get it up with the old lady. They tried handball and losin' weight, but it was fresh pussy that generally did it. He heaved himself up out of the swivel chair and hefted the sealed roll of charts that had come in this morning. Addressed to Master, Schooner *Sur-*

prise with Bedameyer's address. By its weight, he figured that it covered the entire Pacific.

Loss looked up as Bedameyer approached. The wind-vane steering gear was nearly fitted and he was fishing the steering lines through deck sheaves to a drum on the wheel. In the trade winds, *Surprise* would steer herself. Kitzner and he had worked it all out, down to the last nut and bolt.

"Looks like you're fittin' out for serious sailing." Bedameyer had paused on the dock, one clapped-out tennis shoe with a toe peeking out posed on a dock cleat. He fished out a cigarette and lit it. "You fixin' to go to the Pacific?"

"Coast of Mexico," Loss lied. "Maybe through the Canal up to the West Indies next year. We'll play it by ear."

Bedameyer hawked and spat, ranging in on a waterlogged milk carton. A thought suddenly occurred to him. "You're not one of them crazies in the Peace Fleet?"

Loss raised an eyebrow, annoyed. The flesh wound in his arm was barely healed and the stiffness bothered him, slowing his work. There was a lot more to do in the next seven days, more than he could possibly do. Chitchat with Bedameyer he didn't need. "Peace Fleet? I hadn't heard anything about that. We don't get the news."

Bedameyer pulled his billed cap lower over his eyes as if he were going to make a pronouncement. "Fleet of boats; fishermen and yachties. Claim they're going to blockade the Narrows in the Hood Canal to keep the U.S.S. *Ohio* from comin' back in to the sub base at Bangor, Washington. That and keep the other three subs from using the base once they're launched. Christ—they claim there are traces of radioactivity all the way up into the Strait of Juan de Fuca. Tide carried it out."

Loss frowned against the glare of sudden sunlight. The river had a hard quality because of the light, deepening the greens, giving the browns a blackish luster. "I hadn't heard much about the accident. Didn't some yacht blow up near the sub?"

"Yeah, but nothin' to do with the radioactivity, so the Navy says." Bedamayer sucked down on the cigarette, pulling the ash to the filter, and then flicked it away. "They say it was a drum of radioactive chemicals that was lost off a barge in a collision two years ago. Said it just naturally broke open from corrosion."

"You buy that?"

"Shit no, I don't buy it. Some guy on Channel Seven the other night. Pee-Aitch-Dees out to here. You know the kind; some bald-headed bastard who makes more money in ten minutes than I make in a year. He said that the yacht probably blew up from a cooking gas explosion and that the shock waves were amplified by the shallow bottom and that broke some reactor cooling line." Bedameyer sounded as if he had memorized the explanation.

Bedameyer shifted feet. The other tennis shoe was in better shape and Loss realized that it belonged to a pair he had thrown away. "Then the sub was damaged?" Loss asked.

"Who knows? The damn thing just kept on goin'. Probably sealed off a compartment. Look pretty damn stupid for the military if a little shock wave could put an eight-billion-dollar toy out of action." He pushed the roll of charts across the cap rail onto *Surprise*'s deck. "Count on the government to cover somethin' like this up and then spread bullshit all over the place, blamin' it on someone else."

"So what do you think?" Loss asked.

"Who the shit would care what I think," Bedameyer responded. He turned away, toward the office. "Just as long as they don't crap uranium in my backyard. I've got to make a livin'."

He handed her a cup of tea. The Chinese woman looked up, giving him a fragile smile. A strip of flesh-

450

colored tape spanned her nose, but the discoloration beneath her eye was hidden by large-framed sunglasses. "You're leaving tonight, then?" she said.

Loss nodded, sliding into the settee. "We're fully provisioned and most of the work is finished. The man who owns the yard says we'll have to leave tonight. It's the highest of the spring tides and his entrance is silted up; if we don't go now we'll have to wait another month or hire a dredger. I don't think we can afford either."

"If there's anything else you need . . ."

He shook his head. "Nothing. Chou brought the last of the provisions this evening. Eggs and fresh meat." He leafed through the pile of documents she had brought, finally turning over the salmon-colored ship's papers. "This documentation—it gives the owner's name as Howard Long. Who's he?"

"You are," she replied. She skidded a plastic-wrapped packet across the table. "Canadian passports, driver's licenses, savings passbooks. We've given Miss Stone's identity as your wife."

Loss smiled briefly. "I haven't asked her yet."

"And the answer is No!" She had come down the passageway behind him, pulling on her oilskins. "At least until you properly romance me, Loss. Full moon, a bottle of champagne, and a decent interval of time to blush and stammer." She bent down next to his ear and whispered, "And that's what I always wanted, from the first day I met you, Loss."

He looked up at her, partially amused, until he saw her eyes and knew that she was serious.

"I had to do it my own way," she whispered. "To know that I could carry my own weight. You understand?"

"Yes," he answered, not knowing if he did, but knowing that he would in time. There would be a lot of time, he hoped.

Embarrassed, the Chinese woman had turned her head. Holly brushed his forehead with her lips and

451

then stood up, working the zipper of the jacket up to her throat. She walked over and then took the woman's hands between her own.

"There's not much I can say. Thank you for all your help. Getting us out of Seattle, the *Surprise*, and then all the equipment we needed. Chou has gotten us everything we've asked for. Thank him, too." She couldn't think of anything else adequate to say.

The woman set down the empty cup. "Your thanks are appreciated but unnecessary. But I owe you an explanation. Your taking the risk of coming back to the cabin for me was something I didn't expect. I don't think I could have gotten out by myself." A volley of raindrops splattered across the hatch. She looked up, distracted or perhaps just phrasing in her own mind what she was about to say. "The truth is that you and Mr. Loss are an embarrassment to the People's Republic of China."

Loss jerked upright. "Why, for Christ's sake? After all the shit we've been through. You said that eventually you'd make contact with the CIA."

She raised a hand, gesturing him to sit down. ". . . Which we had intended to do. But the Russians have turned the situation to their advantage. Remember that Petrov, Campbell, the Kents, and James are all dead. The three of us are the only living witnesses. The Soviets have planted evidence that the entire operation was of Chinese origin—an attempt by my government to throw suspicion on the Russians and strengthen U.S. military ties with China. Our sources indicate that the CIA knows there was a nuclear weapon aboard the *Hussar*, and that Navy frogmen have salvaged part of the weapon's casing and some parts of the firing mechanism. So who is your government to believe?"

"Interrogate Welsh!" Loss injected.

"You don't know?" she sighed. "Welsh died two days ago."

His lips formed Welsh's name, making no sound.

She nodded. "And there is one overriding factor. Because of the radioactive contamination there is a public clamor for an end to nuclear stockpiles and the signing of SALT III, regardless of the consequences. In the name of *rapprochement*, a term your President now chooses to use as a euphemism for détente, the People's Republic of China could easily become the scapegoat if it were known that we had any connection with the incident. That is something China cannot risk. Therefore, officially neither James nor I played any part in this affair, nor can we support your story. My government can do nothing else." She looked down at her hands and then back at Loss. "As you see, in some ways Petrov won."

Loss gazed at her, unseeing. The woman stood up and formally shook Holly's hand. "I wish you luck," she said. "All the luck in the world. Please—if you don't mind, I must talk to Mr. Loss alone. It is not to your benefit to know more."

Holly withdrew her hand. "I have to fill the water tanks and I'll leave you two alone—but there's something I want to know. If we were to give ourselves up and tell the whole story, who would we have to fear?"

The woman seemed reluctant to speak.

"Who?" Holly demanded.

"The intelligence services of all three superpowers." She said it flatly, without expression.

"All of them?"

A nod. "Yes, all of them. I am sorry, but that includes my country and yours. And the Russians."

Holly turned and pulled a sou'wester over her head. She paused in the companionway. "Thanks anyway," she said and disappeared through the hatch.

"You're sure about Welsh?" he finally asked.

She nodded. "It was professionally done, as if he had lost control of the car. Very little remained after the fire, but the skid marks were authentic. It was

453

classifed as 'an accidental death resulting from loss of control due to intoxication.' "

"Why, for God's sake? Welsh was exactly where they wanted him."

"Except he wasn't," she answered. "The day after the explosion he withdrew from the race. He must have realized that the Russians were using him."

"But why would they assassinate him?"

She shrugged. "He knew too much." She stood up and glanced out a porthole, then looked at her watch. "Is there anything more we can do for you? Do you have enough money? You understand that we have very limited funds?"

"We have enough," he answered. "It'll see us through at least a year." He looked up at her. "This was your idea, wasn't it?"

She nodded. "Yes," she said. "I felt we owed you a debt. There are some who argue that you and the woman should be—eliminated. I'm glad you're leaving tonight. My influence is diminishing."

She buttoned up her plastic raincoat and climbed the companionway stairs. Loss followed her on deck; the last of the twilight was gone and the rain was a fine mist.

Holly had singled up the lines. The engine was ticking over, the exhaust cooling water splashing in a rhythmic cadence beneath the transom. As he watched, she ducked into the companionway, flicking on the running lights.

"All ready to go," she said, walking past him. He saw her silhouette forward, ready to cast off the bow line.

He and the woman shook hands formally on the dock, the rain falling now in heavy drops, like silver pellets in the dock lights.

"This finishes it, then," he said. The rain was starting to soak through his shirt and the wind had a cold bite.

The Chinese woman raised her umbrella. "Perhaps
454

not," she said. "Disarmament under SALT III will still be a slow process and many in your government will oppose it. But the Russians have a policy of pressing the advantage when they perceive they are winning. Our intelligence operative in Zhignask reported that three weapons were assembled. Only two have been detonated."

The rain became a downpour, pounding the surface of the anchorage into hammered lead.

"We wonder how they will use the remaining one." She turned and walked steadily toward the waiting van. Its windshield wipers flicked nervously and its exhaust rose like a white plume under the yard floodlights, like a tail. It reminded Loss of a crouching animal, unable to decide whether to fight or flee.

He gave a hand signal to Holly and then cast off the stern line, letting the north wind push the schooner away from the dock. Glancing back, he could see the dim taillights of the van disappearing up the access road. Away from the shelter of the dock the wind was more intense, setting up a steady hum in the rigging. Snicking the gear lever forward he slowly advanced the throttle, moving out of the anchorage. Abreast of the marker buoy he put the helm down, turning *Surprise* into the main channel. Before him on either side of the channel, flashing buoys marked the fairway leading to the bay and then to the sea beyond. From up forward, he could hear her voice singing faintly but very clearly,

Blow you old blue northern,
Blow my love to me
He's drivin' in tonight from Cal-if-ornia . . .
He loves his damned old rod-e-o
As much as he loves me.
Some day soon, goin' with him
Some day soon.